The Intruder You Know

by

William Holms

Copyright Material

Copyright © 2023 by William Holms.

OTHER BOOKS BY WILLIAM HOLMS

The Killing of Faith (2020) *Faith looks back on her life and describes a mysterious - but seemingly hopeless – situation. This mystery will draw you in, as you are given clues to solving the puzzle of Faith's whereabouts, the events leading up to her current nightmare, and how a woman's simple lies plunge her into a living nightmare beyond anything you can imagine.*

The Beginning of Hope (2021) *Faith is forgotten by everyone until Hope, her youngest daughter, sets out to find her mother. She will uncover the dark truths of love, family, betrayal, and the haunting question - Who can someone really trust? Her search for the truth will put her life in danger and may destroy the Brunick family forever.*

The Fall of Grace (2022) *takes you on another twisting, turning, suspense-filled journey as it continues the unforgettable story of Ryan and Faith Brunick. With both their mother and their father gone, Hope and Grace must learn to live without them as Grace's life unravels. These beloved characters make decisions that will surprise and shock you as they navigate the challenges of life, love, and loss.*

The Rise & Fall of Ryan (2022) *takes you back to the beginning of Ryan Brunick's life and that fateful day when he met his future wife, Faith. Ryan must come face-to-face with his past as he works to get Hannah out of prison for murder. Will Ryan be able to pull out another miracle or will he lose his first case. The series concludes with even more twists and turns and another unforgettable conclusion.*

The Intruder You Know (2023) *Paige Childers, a young college student left for college ready to start all over. But leaving your past behind is seldom clean and never easy. An intruder outside her home will change her life forever, the lives of everyone around her, and leave Paige in a fight for her life.*

– PROLOGUE –

When I was eighteen years old, and I'd just graduated from high school, I packed everything I owned into my car and moved to San Marcos to attend college. I didn't even tell my mom goodbye.

San Marcos is this quaint, family town, full of friendly people that sits thirty miles southwest of Austin and fifty miles northeast of San Antonio. It's known for its college, and it's surrounded by the beautiful hill country, a vast network of underground caves, a giant water park called Schlitterbahn, and the Guadalupe River. The river is fed by natural springs that keep the temperature sixty-two degrees all year round.

People come from all over the state to hike, bike, camp, and float down the river. For the most part, it's a slow, easy ride, but at times the river picks up and pours into several mini-waterfalls. Most days of the week, you'll find rows and rows of tents on each side of the river with campfires, people laughing and cutting up, and music blaring all through the night.

But, I didn't come to San Marcos because of the river. No, I came to start all over in a new town and make new friends. Texas State wasn't a terribly difficult college to get into and it was known as a "party school." I thought it'd be fun—go to school in a laid-back city, float down the river every now and then, hike the trails, head down to Austin's Sixth Street on the weekends, and get my degree. But, mostly, I wanted to leave my past behind and never look back.

And I *did* start a new life. I got enough financial aid to pay my tuition; took a part-time job as a waitress; and after a rough first semester, I got serious about school and kept my grades up. I met my husband, graduated from college, got married, had three kids, and took care of the kind of home most people can only dream about. Sounds perfect, right? Maybe for some women, but not for me.

Back in college, I asked one of my girlfriends where she wanted to work after she graduated. "Work," she said, almost laughing. "I'm not going to work. I'm here to get my MRS degree, find a rich guy, and stay at home."

This wasn't the first time I'd hear this. To me, it seemed like a big waste of time and money. I shook my head and said, "I think I'd go crazy if I had to stay at home every day."

Now, waiting for my psychiatrist to come in, I realize just how true that was. After all my work to get my degree, I gave up my job and ended up being a stay-at-home mom. This wasn't what I wanted. I loved my job and always wanted to go back.

So, here I am. I've never seen a psychiatrist before–I've never been to any therapist, although I should have gone long ago. I don't really want to be here. I've spent the last fifteen years married to one of the most famous psychologists in Texas. He knows just about every psychiatrist and psychologist in town—hell in the country. I don't trust any of them. Part of me wonders if they're all working against me.

My psychiatrist comes in, extends his hand, and with a soft smile, he says, "Paige Warren, I'm Dr. Welby."

I'm afraid to shake his hand. After the last few months, I'm pretty much paranoid of everyone. I glance nervously up at him.

He sits down on the chair across from me and asks, "So, how are you doing today?"

I hesitate for moment before I answer. Looking at the floor, I say, "Not so good."

"Well," he says with a sigh, "I'm sure this isn't easy for you. No one wants to be here. Most of my patients don't come here voluntarily, but I'm glad you agreed to see me."

I sit here without responding.

Maybe sensing my distrust, he asks, "Are you okay, Paige?"

I look up and ask, "Do you know my husband, Alton Warren?"

"I know him," he says.

"You know him?"

He sits back and says, "I know him…most people in my profession know him. But I've never worked with him. I saw him at a conference once, but I've never even talked to him."

I look up just a little and ask, "Can I trust you?"

He sounds very professional. Leaning forward, with his elbow on his knees, he explains, "You don't have to worry. Everything you tell me is strictly confidential. I'm here for you…and only you. You can trust me."

This doesn't really alleviate my concerns, but I have nowhere else to turn. I look up, fake a smile and look back down.

Then he asks, "Do you want to talk about things?"

I take a deep breath, nod my head, and say, "I guess that's why I'm here. I suppose you want to talk about that night?"

"That night?" he asks.

I struggle to get the words out. "Yeah, that night when everything happened."

With another smile, he says, "Why don't we take a step back. I'd like to get to know you first. Why don't you tell me about your family?"

This figures. They always want to know about your family. You see, leaving your past behind is seldom clean and never easy. Your past is never as eager to let go of you as you are to let go of it.

For the next two hours, mostly looking down, I tell him about myself, my family, and my hobbies and interests. I answer his questions about my mom and growing up the way I did.

I guess he got what he was looking for, because he asks, "Paige, why don't we talk about the reason you're here today?"

I pause for a second, then ask, "Where do I even begin?'

With a thoughtful nod, he asks, "Where do you think it all started?"

I pause a second to consider his question. I know the answer. Every time I think about the trouble I'm in now, I go back to that day. "Where did it start?" I repeat. "It all started when I met my husband."

"Then why don't we start there?"

"Okay," I say. "Let's start there."

He sits back, and for another two more hours I tell him how I got into this mess. I begin with that day, so long ago, that would ruin my life and cost me everything.

PART ONE

LOVE?

"To love is to burn, to be on fire."

—Jane Austin

"You can close your eyes to things you don't want to see, but you can't close your heart to things you don't want to feel."

– Johnny Depp

– CHAPTER 1 –

It's another hot August evening, and I'm in the middle of my second shift at a popular restaurant and bar located right off the river. I have three hours to go, and I'm already exhausted. The place is packed with girls in teeny bathing suits (with or without coverups) and guys in swim trunks and t-shirts. I mostly serve high school and college kids, but there are always families scattered around the restaurant. I like the families the most because they're less rowdy and tip a lot better.

I actually like my job. The money is good, and I usually wind up with more tips at the end of the night than anyone else. It's not that I'm the cutest waitress in the place—Lord knows I wish I looked like another girl who works here. She's a terrible waitress who usually forgets more orders than she remembers, but when you look like her, customers rarely complain. I have to make my tips the old fashioned way—being a good waitress with a winning personality. I'm friendly with everyone I meet.

Yeah, I may not be model beautiful, but I do okay. I have sandy blonde hair, usually tied up in a ponytail, golden brown eyes, an athletic figure, and muscular legs from all my high school years playing volleyball and softball. Everyone says my smile is my best quality, and I take it as a compliment. I have breasts that look bigger inside my slightly padded bra, so I've never had to remind guys to look up. I've been told I have a nice legs and a cute butt, and I usually get more stares when I'm walking away.

I'd probably be sexier if I wore more makeup, but that's not the kind of look I'm going for. I'd rather read a good book than a beauty magazine that only makes me feel ugly. I'm a hang out by the river kind of girl who loves to play sand volleyball, ultimate frisbee, and drink cold beer in front of a warm campfire. I can paddleboard down the river for hours.

I usually wear shorts or a skirt to work that looks a lot like my term papers—-long enough to cover the subject but short enough to keep it interesting.

Today I have on blue jean shorts and a tee-shirt that says "Well Behaved Women Rarely Make History." I have this crazy idea that one day I might make history.

I just dropped off the ticket at another table when the hostess sits three guys in my section. They all have on wet swim trunks, baggy t-shirts, and windblown hair. They obviously just got off the river. It's pretty par for the course around here.

"Hey guys," I say with a smile. "Y'all been out on the river?"

The guy closest to me grabs the menu I hand him and says, "I guess the sunburn gives it away?"

"You know," I say with a wink, "they make sunblock for that."

The guy sitting across the table takes the other menu and says, "I told you."

While they're skimming over the menu, I ask, "So, what can I get y'all to drink?"

"You have Dos Equis on tap?" Mr. Sunburn asks.

"Sure do."

"Then three Dos Equis with salt and lime."

I never need to write anything down for tables of less than five. "Absolutely!" I say with my signature smile and walk off. I can feel their stares at my backside as I head to the kitchen and then to the bar.

I return five minutes later with three beers, salt piled along the rim, and two limes hanging on the side of each mug. I put them in the center of the table, brushing against Mr. Sunburn, who makes no effort to give me a little more room to squeeze by. I stand back up and say, "Three Dos Equis, fully dressed."

"Fully dressed?" Mr. Sunburn asks.

With a smile, I nod my head and say, "Yep, fully dressed…just the way you like 'em."

He ignores the beer sitting in front of him and stares at me standing here ready to take their order. "Very witty," he says with a smile. "I love your personality."

"I think he loves your ass," his friend interjects.

Another girl might be offended by this remark, but you can't be too sensitive working here. This is central Texas, we're out by the river, and most of the guys who come in here are pretty drunk. I take it as a compliment.

Defending my honor, Mr. Sunburn turns to his friend, and says, "Keith, show a little respect." He offers me his hand and says, "My name is Alton. You'll have to excuse my friend. He's had a little too much to drink."

"No worries," I say, shaking his hand briefly. "I'm Paige."

"Nice to meet you, Paige."

The third guy breaks in and says, "We all love your…uh… personality."

I blush a little and ask, "Okay, guys…see anything you like?"

Setting his menu on the table, Alton looks up, gives me a quick wink, and says, "Absolutely."

His advance isn't lost on anyone. I put my hand on my hip, shake my head with a grin, and say, "I was talking about the menu."

"Ohhh," Alton says, looking back at the menu. "Are the hamburgers good here?"

Still grinning, I say, "Absolutely. The hamburgers are what we're known for. No one's asked for their money back."

"Then I'll take a hamburger with fries," Alton says, with a smile. The other guys say the same.

"Then three hamburgers and fries," I say, gathering up two of the menus.

When I reach for his menu, he holds it tight and asks, "What about you?"

"Me?" I say, understanding what he's asking. I tug the menu loose, and say, "No one's ever asked for their money back."

All three guys high five each other as I turn away.

Fifteen minutes later, I return with the hamburgers and fries. Seeing two empty beer mugs, I ask if anyone wants another. Looking at his buddies, who both give him a nod, Alton says, "Three more."

"Absolutely," I smile.

Before I get two steps away, Alton catches my attention. "Oh…Paige."

I return to the table and ask, "Yeah?"

"You forgot something."

I look across the table and see nothing missing. "I'm sorry," I say, a little confused. "What'd I forget?"

Looking completely serious, Alton says, "You forgot your phone number."

This isn't the first time I've been flirted with. My personality can sometimes be mistaken for flirting. Some guys leave their numbers and some ask for my number. Other guys actually ask me out right there at the table. But, three months ago I ended a long-distance relationship. We left for college and grew tired of traveling back and forth. Not sure what I want to do, I roll my eyes, and say, "I'll be right back with your beers."

Back at the bar, I lean close to my friend who's also waiting for drinks, and say, "See that guy at the end of the table?" When she looks over at him a little too long, I laugh, "God…don't stare." She turns back to me and I say, "He asked for my number."

"He's cute," she says. "Why not?"

Closing my eyes for a second and shaking my head, I say, "I don't know."

My friend takes another glance at the table and this time catches Alton's attention. They exchange a smile. "Why not?" she says with a shrug. "It's been three months now. You need to get back out there."

I return with the beers and Alton and I exchange another friendly smile. We both smile again when I walk by a little later. After the hamburgers are gone and the beer mugs are empty, I return to the table and ask if they need anything else.

Looking like I must have rejected his earlier request for my number, he says, "A check would be good."

Already prepared with the check, I place it right into Alton's waiting hand with another smile. I watch as he turns the check over to see a smiley face in the top right corner and my phone number underneath.

Over the next week, we text a couple of times and finally agree to meet at a local pub near the college. He shows up in khaki shorts and a silk shirt that looks pretty expensive. I have on a cute sundress, I'm wearing a little make-up, and my hair is loose behind my back. We order a pepperoni pizza and he asks, "Want some wine or anything?"

"How about a beer?" I ask.

We grab two beers and sit at a booth near the window.

"So tell me more about you." I ask after we settle in. "Are you in college?"

"I am," Alton answers. "I graduated with a psychology degree and now I'm in grad school." He takes a sip of his beer and says, "Just one year left. What about you?"

From his answer, I get a good idea how old he is. "Yeah," I say, also taking a drink. "I'm a junior…education."

"So, you want to be a teacher?"

"I guess so. I wasn't sure what to do, and I eventually had to declare a major. I like kids, so I thought, *what the heck, I'll teach school.*"

"What do you want to teach?"

"Well, when I found out that a second-grade teacher makes the same amount of money as a high school physics teacher, I said, "Hello, second grade!"

"Here's to second grade," Alton says, and clinks his beer mug to mine.

After a couple bites of pizza, he gives me a smile and says, "Tell me about yourself. What kind of things do you enjoy doing?"

"Enjoy doing?" I repeat. "I'm up for just about anything—especially if it's outdoors. I played volleyball in high school and now I play on an intermural team. I spend a lot of time out on the river. Do you like camping?" I ask.

"Like in a tent?"

"Yeah, a tent, a campfire…the whole thing."

"We never went camping growing up," he says.

"Well, what do you like doing?"

"I like sailing," he answers. "Have you ever gone sailing?"

I shake my head and say, "No, but it looks like fun."

"Well….let's see," he continues. "I enjoy the theater."

With a smile, I say, "I was in *Fiddler on the* Roof in high school. What else?"

His face brightens up when he says, "I was president of the chess club in high school. I made it to the national finals in Washington D.C. my senior year."

"Wow!" I say.

"I guess I read a lot on my free time," he says. "But, like you, I'm up for anything."

Halfway through the pizza, Alton asks, "So, why's a beautiful girl like you still single? You must get hit on all the time at your work."

"Yeah, I get that," I say, taking a napkin from the dispenser and wiping my mouth. "But I never give out my number."

"So, I'm the lucky guy?" he asks.

"You're the lucky guy," I say, now clinking my mug to his. "Actually, I was in a relationship until a few months ago."

"Not too bright a guy," Alton says, complimenting me.

I look down and start peeling the label off my beer. It's a nervous habit I picked up in high school. I squint a little and say, "Nah, it wasn't like that. You know…high school sweethearts. I went to Texas State, and he went to A&M. It was just too hard being apart all the time. So…."

"Let me guess," Alton says. "High school cheerleader?"

"Nope…volleyball and two years of softball."

"And star football player?"

"Baseball," I smile.

Maybe afraid he might be a rebound, Alton asks, "How long has it been?"

"Four months now."

"Do y'all still talk?"

"We did at first, but we haven't spoken in a while now. I got the feeling he started seeing someone else."

Alton motions the waitress over and says, "Well, I think another beer is just what the doctor ordered."

While Alton is ordering two more beers, I watch as he addresses the waitress. He seems smart, well-educated, and soft spoken. It's very different from what I'm used to. He isn't the cocky jock who flirts with every girl who walks by and who broke my heart again and again. No, he's polite, mild-mannered, and easy-going. He's just what you'd imagine when you think about a psychologist.

When the waitress leaves, I ask, "What about you?"

"No five-year high school sweetheart. I've dated a few girls here and there but nothing serious."

"No one has broken your heart?"

"Nope, my heart's still intact," he says, knocking on the table.

We finish our beers and walk out of the restaurant to my car. We spend thirty minutes in idle chit-chat. Alton looks right at me and says, "When we met at the restaurant, I loved the way you say absolutely. People don't say that often."

"Yeah, I saw a movie once and the girl said that a lot. I thought, *you know what, I'm going to start saying that*."

"Well, it sounds so endearing the way *you* say it—like you're thrilled to bring our beers out."

"I *am* thrilled to bring out beers," I say. "Why not? The people are nice, the money is good, and I have fun. It's a great place to work."

Alton looks around to make sure no one is watching, leans forward, and touches his lips to mine. It's a sweet kiss that only lasts a second or two. He pulls away and says, "It's been nice."

"It was nice," I agree.

Sounding unsure how I might answer, he asks, "Would you like to get together again?"

I don't feel the chemistry you'd want with someone you think about dating. Instead of simply saying no, I finally say, "I'm pretty busy…but sure…we can get together again."

"I'll call you," Alton says and walks to his car.

I'm not really interested in seeing Alton again. He's a little stiff for my taste. I really don't have the time to date, anyway. We're both studying for finals, so we mostly talk on the phone over the next three weeks. He's easy to talk to and is great at keeping the conversation going long after I'm ready to hang up. Three weeks after eating pizza together, we meet at the library and go for dinner afterwards at a little Italian place. It has pictures of Italian people on the wall and red and white checkerboard tables just like I'd imagine in Italy.

Waiting for our food, he turns to me and says, "Tell me more about yourself. Where you from?"

"Fort Worth—at least that's where I graduated from."

"Where'd you grow up?" he asks.

I don't really talk about this often. Without meeting his eyes, I say, "All over. We moved around a lot."

"What about your parents?"

I wait a moment to consider just how deep I want to go. Something about him makes me feel safe enough to talk about it. Maybe it's all his training to be a therapist.

"I was born in LaJunta," I begin. "It's a little town in Colorado. My dad took off when he found out my mom was pregnant, so I've never known him. My mom married this guy when I was two and we moved to

Texas. That was her first marriage—it lasted three years. After him, we moved from one place to another—usually with some new guy."

Alton squints his eyes and asks, "You said it was her first marriage. How many times has she been married?"

"Four….the last I checked. That doesn't include all of her boyfriends I've lived with."

Shaking his head, he asks, "How'd you do it?"

I think about it for a second and say, "I don't know. It was tough growing up. Just when we got settled in somewhere and I'd make friends, we'd move again—Amarillo, Dallas, Fort Worth, back to LaJunta, then back to Fort Worth. Every guy had their own rules and their own ideas about how I should be raised. It was rough most the time. One day I'm an only child, then I have a brother and sister, then I have three different brothers and sisters, then I'm an only child again. Mostly, I felt like a nuisance."

I really don't know why I'm telling him these things. I think it's been bottled up inside me for too long. It's hard to hold it in. I've been told I should see someone about it, but I never have.

Looking out the window beside our table, I say, "There was this one guy who I really liked. We moved into this house in a nice neighborhood. It was white with a big front porch and a picket fence." With a smile, I say, "Just like you see in the movies. He didn't have any kids, so I actually had my own bedroom."

He gives me a smile like he can picture the house.

"I was really happy when they got married. I actually thought we'd be a normal family."

"Very nice," he says.

"Yeah…but it didn't last. They were married three or four years when I woke up one morning and he was yelling at my mom—something about her cheating on him. It went on and on all day long with my mom threatening to leave. I stayed in my room praying they'd work things out. Of course, they didn't. Two days later, he moved out." Before I know it, this is all coming out so easily. "I actually went with him, but the police came a few weeks later to take me home. He told them all about the things I'd been through, but they didn't care. They didn't even talk to me. I was fourteen at the time and didn't really have a say in the matter. His name was Dean. They actually threatened to arrest him. Then they put me in their police car and took me back to my mom. She was furious. As soon as they drove off she slapped me."

"She slapped you?" he asks.

"It wasn't the first time…or the last."

Alton probably sees my full eyes. "I'm so sorry," he says, putting his hand on my arm."

Regretting how personal I just got, I shake my head, and say, "What are you gonna do? Eventually, I got my driver's license. Dean's actually the one who bought the car I'm driving. Then I got a job and started taking care of myself. I tried to stay gone as much as possible. When things got too bad, I'd stay with Dean for a day or two."

"Jesus," he says with a sigh.

"You know, I still talk to him. I'd visit him from time to time when I was still in Fort Worth. He got married and has two kids. He came here with his family a few months back."

"Do you still see your mom?" Alton asks.

"Hmmm, every now and then. She's with this guy who's made it clear how much he doesn't want me around. We got into a big argument a couple of years ago when I came home from school and found my mom pretty beat up. He told me I was seventeen and old enough to move out. My mom took his side, of course. She said it was probably best for everyone. So, I spent my senior year living at my best friend's house. They were right…it was for the best. I actually felt like I was part of a normal family."

He gives me a sympathetic smile.

"As for my mom? What can I say…she's still my mom. I go over there every now and then when he's not around, but it's usually not pleasant—too many years of drinking and whatever else she does."

This whole story seems a bit much for Alton. I take a sip of my beer and try to get the subject off of me. "I'm sorry. I didn't mean to unload all this on you."

Alton pats my arm and says, "Don't be sorry. I like learning more about you."

I look up, give him a smile, and say, "What about you? What's your story?"

With a little shrug, he says, "I don't have a story—at least not like yours. My mom and dad have been married for twenty-eight years. I have one brother. We grew up in a pretty good neighborhood. Both my parents worked a lot, so we were kinda raised by a nanny. My life was pretty easy. I guess I was lucky."

I give him a nod and say, "It sounds nice."

With a shrug, he says, "It was pretty nice. Do you have any brothers and sisters?"

"Yeah, I have a little brother, but I have no idea where he is. I barely knew him. His dad left when he was two and took him with him. I tried to look him up, but I don't even remember his last name. I asked my mom once, but she went ballistic."

The waitress brings our food and we stop all this serious talk. I've been embarrassed of my past and always avoided the subject altogether. Now he knows more about me than anyone other than my ex-boyfriend—and he usually threw it in my face. It was like he thought he could somehow lift himself up by tearing me down. He had a giant ego and was always trying to make me feel lucky to be with him. That's probably the reason why I keep dating Alton. I feel safe talking to him, and he never belittles me.

– CHAPTER 2 –

As we continue to date, I'm a little torn. We don't really run in the same circles. I like being around people, love the outdoors, and enjoy playing different sports. He enjoys his alone time and would rather relax with a good book. So, we spend a lot of time doing our own thing. Honestly, I'm not sure I want another relationship where we're together 24/7.

We obviously come from different sides of the track. He was born with the whole silver spoon thing and I was born with no spoon at all. He keeps suggesting I meet his parents, but I do my best to avoid this for fear that he'll want to meet mine…or at least my mother.

I may not have strong feelings for him, but I also have no reason to break up with him. He's a nice guy, easy to talk to, and we never argue. He's safe and makes staying together so easy.

I actually broke up with him once. I told him I wasn't ready for a serious relationship and maybe we should date other people. I went out with a guy from one of my classes and we started hanging out. Then Alton called a couple of times, and we started talking again. We went to dinner a couple of times—just as friends. He kept telling me how much he missed me. Before I knew it, he was introducing me as his girlfriend again.

That's how it's always been with Alton. Things seem to move forward like the relationship has a life of its own. He makes it so easy to be agreeable. One day he's asking, *Would you like to get together again?* Instead of simply saying no, I say, *Sure…we can get together again.* When I finally get the courage up to say, *We should date other people*, before I know it he's calling me his girlfriend and I'm beside him smiling in agreement.

After dating five months, we're lying in bed, and Alton whispers, "I love you." It takes me by surprise. *Love?* I've been in love. When you love someone, you want to be with them, and call them, and text them—all the time. Love twists your stomach into knots every time your phone rings or you receive a text, hoping it's him on the other end. You want the person you love—all of them—all the time, and will do just about anything you can to please them. No, this doesn't feel like love at all.

Sometimes, I wonder if I'm just out of the love business altogether. Love has a dark side that isn't written on those cute little Valentine's Day cards. The same love that lifts you up to heaven also leaves you crying for three nights in a row, afraid the relationship is over and your whole world is about to fall apart. One night you're screaming at him to get the hell out, and a week later you're begging him to stay. Love can be so toxic you don't dare tell a soul. You lie to your friends, you lie to your parents, and eventually you lie to yourself. Your heart wants you to forgive…and stay…while your better judgment is telling you to leave.

Alton is calm and logical. He doesn't seem like the kind of guy who'd ever be jealous—which suits me just fine. I learned the hard way that the jealous ones, the ones who accuse you of cheating, are usually the ones doing all the cheating—especially when they're hours away at a different college. Alton would never ask me to watch porn (or by now I should say turn me on to porn) or tie me to the bed. He'd never suggest a threesome or force me to have sex after another explosive night arguing about something so stupid I eventually can't remember what the argument is all about.

So, what is love, anyway? Who knows? I guess, in the end, love is different for different people. At this time in my life, Alton is what I need. Is this something that will last forever? I don't really think so, but one thing for sure, getting out of a relationship is a lot harder than getting in it.

So, here we go again. Lying in his arms, I close my eyes, give him a subtle smile, and whisper, "I love you, too."

– CHAPTER 3 –

W here did all the time go? Next thing I know, he's graduating from college and I'm sitting at a restaurant listening to him explain, with all the logic in the world, why it makes so much sense for us to move in together.

"It's a year until you graduate," he says. "You work so many hours that you barely have time to concentrate on school."

Taking in everything he just said, I look down at my dessert, and say, "I know…but I like my job."

"Sure," he says, as agreeable as he always is. "But you're working so hard to put yourself through school. All I'm saying is, it might be easier if you cut back a day or two a week. With my new job, I'll be able to pay all the bills."

With a father who left when I was two and a mother who can barely support herself, I've spent the last three years living on financial aid, student loans, and working four or five days a week. Dean sent me some money each time I didn't have enough money to cover my tuition. It's been pretty tough, and at times I've thought about taking a semester off to save up for the next semester. Financially, it all makes sense.

I reach out, put my hand on his arm and do my best to soften the blow. "I don't know. It just seems like moving in together is a giant step."

He lays his hands on mine and says, "The truth is, it's not all about the money. I love you, and I enjoy spending time with you. Between work and school, we barely see each other."

He's right. We don't spend a lot of time together. I don't really have anything to say in return. Throughout high school, my ex-boyfriend and I spent all our free time together. I put friends, family, and everything else on the back burner. My friends said he was too possessive. If so, then I was just as possessive. Maybe it was young love. Maybe we just loved being together. But now, after spending two years in a long distance relationship, I found my independence. I work at a popular hang-out where people my age are always coming and going. Every month, I get invited to more parties than I can go to in a year. I have lots and lots of friends.

I've also discovered so many things I enjoy doing by myself. Most of all, I enjoy hanging out with people at my work or friends from school. We float down the river, play volleyball, drink beer, eat barbecue, and often end up staying out overnight in a tent singing songs by a campfire. You might say I found myself, and I'm not about to lose that girl again. So there are lots of times that Alton wants to hang out, but I have other plans.

I don't want to hurt Alton, but I don't love him the way he loves me. It wasn't really a lie when I told him I loved him. On some level, I do love him…or maybe I love the person he is. But am I *in* love with him? I'd have to say no. It's kind of ironic. I was in love with my high school boyfriend, but I didn't like the person he was. I really like Alton as a person, but I'm not in love with him.

"I like spending time with you, too." I say, ignoring the *I love you* part. I look over just in time to catch the disappointment on his face just like the other times I've broken the first commandment of relationships— every time he says *I love you,* you must say, *I love you too.*

Then, I give his hand a little squeeze. With a smile, I say, "I love you too."

"I'm not trying to pressure you," he says, waiting for my response.

The truth is, I'm sure he'd never pressure me into anything. No longer having to worry about bills and being able to buy all my text books for a change also sounds wonderful. I put down my fork, lean closer to him with a smile on my face, and say, "Okay, let's do it."

It's obvious from the look on his face that I just made his day…or his year. "You make me so happy," he beams, reaching over and taking my hand.

I fall right in line when I say, "You make me happy too."

Two weeks later, I'm clearing my stuff out of my small dorm room and moving into one of the best apartment complexes in town. It has two bedrooms, a beautiful kitchen, and a pool that looks like a resort pool. I have a designated parking space for my twelve-year-old Honda Civic.

I've never actually lived with a guy. I had the same dormmate all through college who's now my best friend. Alton carries in all the heavy things—mostly boxes because I don't have any furniture—and I bring in my clothes. He insists I take the bigger side of the closet. He obviously has no strong feelings about how our place looks. Every time Alton and I go to the store to pick up the things we need, my preference magically becomes his preference. I pretty much set up the apartment however I want.

Over the next few months, we jump right over that part where most couples spend a year or two arguing over the most stupid things while they learn to live together without killing each other. We never really fight at all.

Alton loves to cook. I grew up in a meat and potatoes kind of family, but he cooks pastas, Thai, lots of curries, and other dishes from all over the world. I've never been much of a cook living in a dorm and eating dorm food, but the few times I try to cook it doesn't matter if it's burnt, raw, or burnt on one side and raw on the other. Alton never complains.

Our lovemaking is just that—nice and sweet. It always seems more about the destination than the journey. It's fine, but not so thrilling that it leaves me breathless. I actually reach my destination every once in a while.

I cut back one day a week at work, but that's it. I refuse to be one of those women who lose their identity every time they start a new relationship. I still meet up with friends, still volunteer a few hours a week at the animal shelter, and still go out to the river. I sometimes come home pretty late, but I no longer spend the night in a tent until early morning. Alton might be the most understanding guy I've ever met, but I don't want to push it.

We've been living together for two months when Alton's mom and dad come to visit. It's plain to see where he gets his mild disposition. His dad is a patent attorney and his mom is a pediatrician. They look and act so much like June and Ward Cleaver. We take their new Lexus into Austin and eat at a beautiful steakhouse.

"I'm glad we were able to get in here," his dad says after the waiter leaves to get a bottle of wine for our table. "They say you have to make reservations months in advance, but they had a last-minute cancellation."

His mom, wearing the biggest diamond wedding ring I've ever seen, turns to me. "So, Paige, it's so nice to finally meet you. Alton has told us so much about you. I feel like I already know you."

Finally? We've only been living together for two months. When I last talked to my mom three months ago, she asked if I was dating anyone, and after seven months together, I said, "I don't know. I've gone out with a guy a few times. He's nice, but nothing serious."

I reach over, put my hand on Alton's, and say, "I've heard so much about you too, Mrs. Warren." Alton lets his hand linger under mine a few seconds before subtly moving his hand away to grab his water glass.

His dad gives me a smile and says, "So, I hear you want to be a teacher?"

"That's the plan," I respond.

"Elementary school?"

I nod my head and say, "I think so. I really like working with children."

"I think that's so sweet," his mom says.

His dad takes a drink of wine and asks, "Tell us about your parents."

Doing my best not to embarrass myself, I say, "I never really knew my father. My mom lives in Ft. Worth."

"What does she do?" he presses.

Trying to rescue me, Alton interjects. "She's a stay at home mom."

"Oh, that's great" his mom says with a smile. "So you grew up with your mom at home?"

I smile back and give her a nod.

We finish eating the most unbelievable dinner, at the most unbelievable restaurant, and drive back to our apartment.

"I love your place," his mom says, doing her best to sound sincere. "Who was your decorator?"

"Actually, Paige did it all," Alton says.

"Well, it's lovely," she says, looking the place up and down.

After two hours of chit-chat, mostly about Alton's new job, his dad slaps his knees, and says, "Look at the time. I didn't realize how late it is."

I look up at the clock on the wall and see it's 9:15. "Where are you staying?" I ask.

"Oh, we got a place at the Omni," his dad answers.

We have a two-bedroom apartment and the second bedroom is set up as a guest room. "You don't have to stay at a hotel," I say. "Why don't you stay here?"

With a wave of her hand, his mom says, "Oh, heaven's no. We wouldn't think of imposing on you."

His dad stands up from the couch and says, "Well, Paige, it was wonderful to finally meet you."

"Very nice to meet you too, Mr. Warren."

His mom takes a step closer, leans closer, and kisses the air beside my face. She gives me a smile, and says, "You two have to come to Houston for a visit."

"Of course," I say, not sure if I'm supposed to kiss the air as well. "Thanks for the invite."

"Well, of course," she says like I'm being silly. "You're practically family now."

I look over at Alton and wonder what he's told her.

That night, we slip into bed and Alton says, "I know my family can be a bit much."

"Nay," I say with a yawn. "I thought they were nice."

We kiss each other goodnight and fall asleep.

Over the next year, Alton and I stay pretty busy. He's working at his job, and I'm still at the restaurant and finishing up my last semester at school. We've been living together over a year, when we're eating at a nice restaurant, and he proposes in front of four waitstaff and a family sitting next to us looking on.

Here we go again. One day we're lying in bed and he's saying, "I love you." What else are you supposed to say when the man you're lying next to says such a thing? "Ah…that's sweet?" Then he says, "We should move in together." Before I know it, I'm saying "sure" when I want to say *not so fast.* Now, I'm sitting at this fancy restaurant with everyone looking on while he's reaching for my finger asking, "Will you marry me?"

I give him my hand, watch as he slips the ring on my finger, and slowly nod my head.

"Is that a yes?" he asks.

This whole thing has caught me off-guard. We briefly talked about marriage once a couple of weeks ago and I tried to change the subject. *Now….engaged? What would I look like—and how would he feel—if I embarrass him in front of all these people? But, it's just an engagement, right? It doesn't mean we'll actually get married.*

I look down at the beautiful diamond on my hand, look back up at him standing in front of me, and say, "Yes, I'll marry you."

Several times over the next few months, I thought about calling this whole thing off—or at least slowing things down—but he gave me no reason. He's never hit me, or pushed me, or even yelled at me. He remembers my birthday, cleans the apartment until it shines, and pays most of the bills without complaining. I know he doesn't like it, but he doesn't even say much when I come home from the river reeking of pot. He's the kind of guy who'd be home every night, be a good husband and father, a good provider, and a good protector. I tell myself that's what's important in life.

CHAPTER 4

A month after graduating from college, the president of our high school class put together an informal five-year class reunion. It's been almost two years since I've been back home, so I'm looking forward to getting together with my old friends. Alton asks about going, but I tell him it's no big deal—mostly just a bunch of friends connecting again. He takes the hint pretty well.

We all meet at the Fort Worth Stockyards. It's one of the most popular spots in Fort Worth that made the city famous. This isn't just any stockyard. Some say it's where the West begins. Cowboys once herded millions of cattle up from South Texas, towards San Antonio, and straight north into The Fort Worth Stockyards. It was the last stop to rest and get supplies before crossing the Red River into Indian territory. More than four million head of cattle moved on those cattle drives. Meat-packing plants later popped up all around the stockyards.

Today, you can walk along the cobblestone streets and catch a real cattle drive that leaves once in the morning and once in the evening. There are lassoing and shooting demonstrations, fiddling contests, and gun-fights just like in the Old West. You can watch the Championship Rodeo every Friday and Saturday night. Want to country dance? There's a number of country dance halls, including Billy Bob's Texas.

I went to a high school that was small enough that just about everyone knew everyone. We all gather right inside the main entrance to the stockyards. I'm so excited to see three of my closest high school girlfriends as the group increases to about forty people. I haven't seen most of my old friends since we graduated.

When it looks like everyone is here, my attention moves away from my friends as I scan the crowd for the one person I'm hoping will make it. It's the real reason I wanted to come alone.

It's all pretty silly. I'm not even sure what I'm looking for. Not a day goes by that I don't feel the pain of losing him—or losing the love I felt for him. I wonder sometimes if I've simply romanticized our past together and the feelings I still have are nothing but an old crush that will eventually go away. I often wonder if these feelings are the reason I can't move on with Alton. Seeing him again might answer those questions.

We haven't spoken in over two years. For all I know he'll walk right past me in his old blue jeans, cowboy boots and cowboy hat, with some new girlfriend at his side—or worse, with his new wife. I scan the crowd one last time and realize he didn't come. In this moment, as I feel the disappointment deep inside me, I realize just how far I still have to go.

"Good," I whispered to myself. *I didn't want to see him, anyway.*

We all walk through the old stockyards to the one place that reminds me that I'm back in Fort Worth—the Lonesome Dove Bistro. It's a true Texas steakhouse with an upscale vibe. I always wanted to eat here, but the menu was way outside of our teenage paychecks. My boyfriend was about as poor as I was.

After we arrive at our table and order food and drinks, more people wander in. *Still no Brad.* We spend the next hour catching up on old times. The guys mostly talk about the state championship we lost, and the girls talk about who's now with who and whatever happened to what's her face. Finally, two more guys come in and sit down. *Nope—no Brad.*

After another hour, the table is cleared and the checks are dealt around the table. Some guy at the other end of the table yells, "Let's go to Billy-Bob's!"

I figured this is where things would wind up. Billy-Bob's Texas is the world's largest honky-tonk. Throughout high school, it was the place we'd come to watch some of the top country singers and dance to both old and new country music. It allowed in minors, but not before writing a giant X on the back of our hands with a big black marker that couldn't be missed by all the guys who were over twenty-one.

For my friends, this was a great place to pick up guys. For me, it was a great place to dance the night away with the boy I thought was the love of my life. We saw Ronnie Millsap, George Strait, Garth Brooks, Tim McGraw, and Rascal Flatts here.

For the first time ever, I walk through the front doors, flash my driver's license, pay fifteen dollars, head to the first bar, and order a cold beer. The guys walk right up to the mechanical bull that had bucked off my boyfriend and most of his buddies every Saturday night. They also have armadillo racing. You have to wear these big, leather gloves to make sure you don't get leprosy from the armadillos.

Once everyone has their beers, we fill all the tables along the right side of the dance floor. I can't remember the last time I've gone country dancing. Just like I did in the old days, I have on the same blue jeans I wore in high school, the dancing boots I worked for three months to buy, a western belt with a fake rodeo belt-buckle, and a red spaghetti strap, cotton top.

This may be the last place in America where guys actually come up and ask the girls to dance. As my single girlfriends head out on the dance floor with the guys they just met, I politely tell all the guys who come up and ask me to dance, "Thank you…but I can't.

Watching all the couples sliding and twirling in front of me brings back all the old memories. *Brad was such a great dancer.* This is the place where he taught me how to two-step, waltz, polka, and jitterbug. It didn't take long before we were great dancers together.

As I look to the left at people dancing by, I catch a glimpse of the men's restroom. The smile that filled my face a second ago, morphs into a dark frown. I rest my elbows on the table, lace my fingers together, and lower my forehead to my clinched fists as a memory from my past comes back again. The pain has never gone away.

Wow…how could I forget? I loved and hated this place at the same time. I loved it because I spent so many Friday and Saturday nights sliding across this dance floor, wondering how I ever got so lucky. I hated it because it's the place where I came back from the restroom one Saturday night to find Brad on the dance floor in the arms of another girl. Unable to look away, even for a second, I watched as he held her tight and moved in from time to time to whisper god-knows-what into her ear.

When they'd danced not just one, but two songs, he finally returned to my stool. Seeing the hurt and shock on my face, he looked at me with this puzzled look, and asked, "What?" like he couldn't understand why in the world I'd be so upset seeing him in the arms of another girl.

Without saying a word, I grabbed my purse, got up from my chair, and walked right out of Billy-Bob's. I was boiling with anger—not the kind where it's time to add the pasta but the boil that pours over the pot and onto the stove. I walked across the parking lot with this jackass following close behind me, insisting that I was being silly because it was no big deal.

Unable to believe the crap that was coming out of his mouth, I kept marching forward. As he quickly closed the gap between us, I looked over my shoulder, and yelled, "Get away!" Then I turned around and screamed, "Just get away from me!"

Suddenly, he stopped in his tracks and screamed, "Fine…just go then!"

Ignoring my better judgement to keep on walking without giving him the satisfaction of apologizing, I swung around, now beginning to tear up, and yelled, "What if I did it?" I wipe my tears away with my palms. "What if you went to the bathroom and came back to find me out on the dance floor whispering in some guy's ear?"

He took a deep breath and put his hand on his forehead like this was some kind of huge revelation. He exhaled slowly, and sounding a little apologetic, said, "You're right. I get it. I get it now. I didn't think of it like that."

I put up both hands and say, "You know how many guys ask me to dance every time you leave? I would never…*ever*…do that to you."

He reached forward, put his hand on my arm, and said, "I understand. I see why you're angry."

The truth is, I wish it was anger—or pure hate. At least then I'd have known I had an ounce of pride pulsing through my pathetic heart. Instead, I was crushed, what showed.

Another tear dropped down my cheek. I wiped it away and said, "I love you."

He took a step forward and opened his arms like the father waiting to embrace his prodigal son, who ran away and was finally back home. A wiser, stronger, version of me would see him standing there waiting for me to come forward and tell him to f-off. But those were the days when I was young, and in love, and my forgiveness came way too easy—again and again. I took a step forward, threw my arms around his neck, and cried on his shoulder. He never actually apologized.

Why does the mind play such evil tricks on us? When we were together, all I could think about were the bad times—and there were plenty. Now that we're apart from each other, I mostly remember the good times. It took this little trip down memory lane to bring me back to reality.

I raise my eyes and slowly shake my head, wondering why I stayed with him as long as I did. "Thank God," I whisper. In this moment, Alton looks a whole lot better. He never so much as looks at another woman. Why would I ever want to go back to that crap again?

Seeing me sitting here looking sad, Kristi puts her hand on my back. "What's wrong?" she asks.

I turn to her, fake a smile, and say, "Nothing…nothing at all."

Right then, another cute guy in a cowboy hat walks up beside me and says, "Hey, beautiful. Would you like to dance?"

Now, wanting even more to be true to Alton, I shake my head, show him the diamond on my finger, and say, "Thanks for asking, but I'm engaged."

The songs I love keep playing through the speakers overhead as people dance all around me. Right as I finish off the last of my beer, my girlfriend looks over my shoulder with wide eyes and says, "Oh….my….God!"

I turn my head, look over my shoulder, and my heart stops beating. I feel like I just got punched in the gut and do my best to simply breathe. Brad is standing right behind me.

"Paige!," he says, practically glowing, as he puts his hand right on my shoulder.

My hands are shaking, my lips are quivering, and I'm struggling to find something to say. I finally get it together, and doing my best to hide my emotions, get out, "Hey, Brad."

If his stomach is in knots like mine, you'd never know it. He comes around, slides up on the stool next to me, looks across the table, and says, "Hello, Kristi."

Kristi knows everything about me, Alton, and Brad—the whole sordid affair. Unable to believe this is happening, she shakes her head. Without hiding her disdain, she says, "Hey, Brad." She looks over my way to see if I'm okay. I'm not.

"I'm gonna get a beer," Brad says, lifting my empty beer mug off the table. "It looks like you can use one, too."

Afraid that one beer might lead to two, and then all my hard work getting over him will have to start over again, I say, "I'm fine." Unfortunately, I don't sound fine at all.

"Come on," he says, standing up with my beer mug in his hand and nodding towards the bar. "It's just a beer."

"She said she's fine!" Kristi jumps in.

As if the same force that once controlled my very soul is pulling me forward, I get up from my stool and walk with him to the bar.

"P-a-i-g-e," Kristi draws out, reaching for my arm a second too late. I ignore her effort to save me from my own stupidity and walk to the bar with Brad at my side. We look like we're starting all over again right back in high school.

Waiting for another couple in front of us to get their drinks, he puts his hand on my back, and says, "You look great."

Usually I'd tell him how great he looks, but not today.

After the couple in front of us walks off, he steps up to the bar and says, "Give us a Bud Light and a Blue Moon."

"I don't really drink Blue Moon anymore," I say, telling a half-truth. I still drink Blue Moon, but I mostly want to show him that things have changed since we broke up. I lean towards the bartender so he can hear me over the Dixie Chicks singing *Wide Open Spaces,* and say, "I'll take a Jack and Coke."

He looks at me with a big smile, like he can see right through my little charade. The bartender puts both drinks on the bar. Brad grabs the beer, hands me the glass, and throws a twenty-dollar bill down on the bar.

"I can get mine," I say, tossing down a ten-dollar bill.

I know I should head straight back to the safety of my friends. Instead, I follow behind him as he walks towards the dance floor and stops at the railing. He leans on his elbow, gives me a smile, and says, "So, it's been a while."

It has been a while. I want to give him a piece of my mind. I want to tell him what a fool he is, and that he has a lot of nerve showing up here ruining my night. Instead, I lean over the bar like I didn't hear him and watch as couples dance by.

He leans over the rail beside me, waits until I glance his way, and asks, "How you been?"

Here it is. The entire drive here, this very question played out again and again in my head. I thought of all the things I'd say when he asks this question. My answers were all over the map:

"I'm alright;"

"I'm doing great…never better;"

"I'm so much better off without you;"

"Go to hell;"

"Get away from me."

Now here we are, and I'm unable to breathe, much less talk. But, I fake a smile, and say, "You know, I've been *really* good."

The look on his face makes me think he's figured out by now this isn't going to be as easy as he hoped. "Sooo…," he says with a pause. "I hear you're getting married."

Wow! I have no idea how he found out. With another nod, I say, "Yep…I'm getting married."

He reaches down, takes my left hand in his, and raises my ring to his eyes. "Can I see it?" he asks.

I'm sure he did this just to hold my hand again. I wouldn't have thought his hand on mine would have the effect on me that it does. I'm not sure how, in a split second, things can change so quickly. It brings back the intimacy we once shared. My hands are all sweaty, my mouth is dry, and my heart is pounding in my chest.

He looks down at my ring, back up at my face, and says, "It's really beautiful."

"Thanks," I say, also looking at the diamond.

"So, he's a psychiatrist, huh?"

So someone's been filling him in? "A psychologist," I correct him, wanting to rub it in a little.

"Big bucks?" he asks, raising his eyebrows.

"Uh…I guess," I respond, turning my attention back to the dance floor. Then I ask, "So, how did you find out I was getting married?"

"Your mom told me."

I shake my head and say, "I haven't told my mom."

"Okay," he laughs. "Maybe I asked around."

"So, you've been checking up on me?"

He looks up and says, "Maybe just a little."

I take another sip of my drink and let this sink in. Out of the corner of my eyes, I watch him standing there like he's thinking of something clever to say. After a few minutes, he pats my leg and says, "My sister got married a couple months ago."

I loved his sister. She was like the sister I never had. He knows this will cause a chink in my armor. "Good for her," I say, still looking away.

Both of us stand here and people watch as the song comes to an end. Then, half the couples leave the dance floor and another group of dancers take their place.

As much as I want to, I don't do anything to continue the conversation. As he stands beside me nodding his head and tapping his boots to the music, I take a couple sips of my drink.

"How's school?" he asks, trying to enter the house from the side door.

"I just graduated."

"Congrats!" he says, patting my leg again and leaving his hand there a few seconds.

Then, before I realize what I'm about to do, I give him exactly what he's wanting. "What happened to your cowboy hat?" I ask.

With a little laugh, he says, "I haven't worn that in years. I mostly wear ball caps now."

"And how's baseball?"

With a shrug like it's no big deal, he says, "Didn't work out."

"No?"

"It's a long story. I guess my dad was right."

His dad was always too hard on him. He was a plumber and had dreams that his son would become some kind of professional one day. When he got a scholarship to play baseball, his dad spent thirty minutes explaining how few college players actually make it to the pros.

"Now I play ball for a JUCO in Waco. It's fun, you know?"

"That's all that really matters," I say.

"I changed my major and that backed me up. I hope to graduate next year. You still waiting tables at that place off the river?"

"Yeah," I say, taking another sip.

"You know, I came by there a few weeks back with a couple buddies. They said it was your day off."

For the last two years, I've wondered if he thinks about me half as much as I think about him. I figured he'd moved on to all those women he always flirted with without giving me a second thought. Sounds like I was wrong.

"Yeah," I say with a nod. "I cut back a little to concentrate on school."

Suddenly, he perks up a bit. "Oh…I saw your mom last Thanksgiving. I was in Wal-Mart and she was with some guy. Is she dating someone new?"

I shrug a little, and say, "You know my mom."

"Yeah, he looked like another winner."

"I haven't seen my mom in a while. I'm gonna go by there tomorrow."

Then, I'm left dumbfounded when *I Could Not Ask For More* by Sarah Evans begins playing over the speakers. Brushing his hair back with his hand, he lets out a big laugh and says, "Holy shit!"

"I can't believe this," I say, shaking my head and rolling my eyes.

"Come on," he says, reaching out for my hand.

"No way!" I say, pulling back a little.

"It's our song," he says, like he actually needs to remind me of the obvious.

"It *was* our song."

"One song," he begs, putting his hands together like he's praying for just one dance.

That chink in my armor is now a gaping hole. Sounding like I might break at any moment, I shake my head. "I can't. I'm getting married."

"It doesn't mean anything," he promises. "One song…for old times."

"I can't," I get out before he takes my hand in his and pulls me off my bar stool. He leads me to the nearest opening to the dance floor. In front of all our old friends, he turns me to him, puts his arm around my waist, and pulls me close.

"I can't believe this is happening," I whisper, putting my hand on his shoulder to keep six inches between us like you might do at a Catholic school dance. "Okay," I say holding up one finger. "Just *one* dance."

Ignoring my attempt to keep distance between us, he pulls me close and we start sliding forward. As we make a half-turn, I put my arm around his neck for support. He twirls me around and pulls me even closer when we come back together again. Next thing, I'm singing under my breath.

"These are the moments…I thank God that I'm alive;"
"These are the moments…I'll remember all my life;"
"I've found all I've waited for…and I could not ask for more."
Hearing me singing, he asks, "Remember the first time we danced to this song?"

Do I remember? I was sixteen-years-old when I went to a house party with two of my girlfriends. I was sitting on a lawn chair out by the pool, I was punch drunk from cheap beer and the two puffs of pot I took right after we arrived. When this song started playing, he came up, introduced himself, and asked me to dance. I knew him from school. I think everyone at school knew him. I knew nothing about country dancing, but he promised me I had nothing to fear. He took my hand, pulled me up from my chair, and we pushed between the other couples dancing by the pool. We simply swayed back and forth for a while, holding each other close. I couldn't believe this was happening.

"One more dance?" he asked when the song was over. One dance turned into another and another. For the next forty-five minutes, as he taught me how to two-step. This song would always be special for us.

I pull back, shake my head, and say, "Can we just finish this one dance?"

We continue across the dance floor turning and twisting together. When we get to the other side, he asks, "Does your husband—"

"My fiancé."

"Does your fiancé like to dance?"

I almost laugh, but hold it in. I close my eyes, shake my head, and say, "Can we not talk about my fiancé?"

"Sorry…sorry," he says, pretending to lock his lips shut.

I knew I missed country dancing, but back out here again, I realize how very much it means to me. We twist, and turn, and spin just like we once did.

As we turn the corner, he puts his hand on my upper breast. We had this one signature move that we created together. It dazzled all onlookers. Many couples came up afterwards and asked us to show them how to do it. This was his cue to get ready. I want to say *no*, but I know this is the very last time I'll ever be able to country dance again. He gracefully pushes me forward, moves me to his right, gives me a half-turn to the left, and spins me around. I duck down just in time to miss his open arm swinging over my head. He lifts me off of my feet above him before slowly lowering me, only inches in front of his face, back down to the floor. He quickly spins me three times, and I fall backwards into his arms. He puts his hand back on my chest where it started—this time a little lower. He would always kiss me at this point. When he moves closer, I shake my head, hold up my pointer finger, and mouth a big, "No!"

I cannot believe this. He goes straight to our best, most seductive move right in front of our high school friends. I'm sure it was no accident. While I'm still in his arms, everyone claps and whistles.

"I can't believe you did that," I say.

"We did that," he corrects me as we continue across the dance floor.

As the song winds down, I hear the final words we swore we'd play one day at our wedding:

I could not ask for more than this love you gave me;
'Cause it's all I've waited for;
And I could not ask for more."

When the song ends, I lean forward and put my face against his chest. He probably thinks I'm trying to get close to him, but I'm not. I'm wiping away the tear I don't want him to see that's about to roll down my cheek. The second I press against him, I pull back away.

While we're standing in the middle of the dance floor, *You'll Always Be Loved By Me,* by Brooks and Dunn, blasts out. With his arms still around my waist, he starts moving again. I stop firm, and say, "*One* dance. That's what we said."

"Just one more," he begs.

"We're not in high school anymore," I say. "That was it."

He points at me with a silly grin and says, "You know you liked it."

"I love dancing," I say. "But that doesn't make it right."

"Just one more dance," he repeats, reaching for my free hand. "I promise."

As much as my resistance is crumbling inside, I reach back, pull his arm out from around my waist, and say, "I can't," and head back to my table.

He follows right behind me as I hop up on my stool. The other bar stool he was sitting in earlier is now taken by one of my friends. He stands there for a minute, like he's waiting for someone to invite him to sit down or something. When no one does, he puts his hand on my shoulder and says, "I'm gonna go to the restroom."

As I watch him enter the men's room, a part of me wants to grab some random guy and drag him out on the dance floor so he sees me dancing when he returns. When I turn my attention back to the table, Kristi looks at me with wide eyes and says, "Paige…what the hell are you doing?"

Grabbing a napkin to wipe my forehead, I say, "It was *one* dance."

My other girlfriend, who knows nothing about the past two years, is unable to hold back a laugh. "You two need to get a room," she teases. "You looked like you were making love out there."

"Stop it," I laugh, patting my face with the napkin.

She shakes her head and says, "You two have been together forever. I don't know how y'all do it."

Kristi and I look at each other without correcting her.

When Brad returns, he stands right next to me like we still belong together. I know him well. I'm sure he'll spend the rest of the night asking me for another dance until I finally give in. The feelings I spent months and months trying to put behind me are now back, and I don't want this to continue. I grab my purse, turn to my girlfriends, and say, "I've got to be going. Meet you in the morning for breakfast…right?"

All of us hug goodbye. Kristi and I exchange a kiss before I head for the front doors without telling Brad goodbye.

As I walk out the club, I take one last look at the dance floor—and then the men's restroom—before walking out the front door. I can't believe what just happened and I'm disappointed in myself for not being stronger.

Just as I put my key in the driver's door, someone comes running up from behind and startles me. I turn around and see Brad standing there breathing heavily.

"Can we talk a second?" he asks, out of breath.

I spread my arms in amazement and ask, "About what? What do we have to talk about?"

"It's not what you think," he says, leaning over with his hands on his knees. "Just give me a minute."

"So, now a second has become a minute?" I ask.

"Listen Paige," he says, pausing to catch his breath. "I just want to say, 'I'm sorry.'"

I'm sorry...two words I didn't think he knew.

"Fine," I say, throwing up one hand. "You're sorry."

He puts his hands on his hips and says, "Paige," before pausing for a second while looking down. He looks back up and says, "I was stupid."

I raise my hand to stop him. Showing more anger than hurt, I say, "Brad, it doesn't really matter now."

"Please let me say this," he says, taking hold of my arm to keep me in place. He lets me go and says, "You gave me so much. I loved you...I really did. But...I don't know...I was stupid. I made so many mistakes." He looks up at the sky for a few seconds, looks back at me, and says, "You know, I don't want to minimize it. I made so many bad decisions. You were my first...you were all I knew. I didn't realize what I had until you were gone. But these last couple years have been horrible."

Hearing him say these things actually gives me a little satisfaction—but it doesn't change anything. Softening a little, I ask, "Why are you saying all this?"

He puts his hand on his forehead, brushes his hair back, and says, "I guess I just want you to know I'm sorry...and I love you. The worst thing is that I know I'll always love you." When I don't respond, his lips begin to quiver as he continues. "I know it's crazy, but I thought we might get back together someday."

He must think he's still standing in front of that teenage girl who would take him back again and again. All he had to do was flash his baby blues, explain how it was me who was wrong, and I was back in his arms. Instead, I shake my head and say, "Well, that's not going to happen."

Then he leans back against the car beside mine and his eyes tear up. He looks down at my hand and says, "Seeing you with that ring on your finger breaks my heart"

Seeing him this emotional for the first time ever, my eyes begin to tear up as well. When I wipe them away, a tear drops down his cheek and he says, "What we had was the best thing around."

Now choked up, I say, "It was great at times."

He looks at me sideways, squints his eyes, and asks, "Only at times?"

I lean against my car, bend over, and cover my face with my hands to hide my tears. I wipe my eyes and speak from my heart. "You had me. I loved you so much. You were my whole world. I didn't know how I'd ever go on without you."

"I know," he says with teary eyes. "I feel the same way."

I stand up straight, raise my hand to cut him off, and say, "Then you broke my heart again…and again…and again" Now beginning to cry, I say, "You treated my love like it was worthless. You treated *me* like I was worthless. A person's heart can only break so many times before *they* break….and I broke."

Then, another tear falls down Brad's cheek. He nods, presses his lips together, and says, "So, does this guy treat you good?"

With my voice cracking a little, I say, "He treats me *really* good."

"Well, that's good," he says. "I'm happy for you." Like he's afraid to hear the answer, he asks, "Do you love him?"

This is the one question I don't want to answer. "Yeah, I love him. But it's different…you know?"

"Different?"

Feeling all the old hurt come back, I wipe my eyes, and say, "I don't know. I'm not really sure what love is anymore. Do I love him the way I loved you? I don't think I'll ever love anyone the way I loved you. I never want to love anyone like that again. It hurts too much."

A tear falls down his other cheek. He steps forward, takes me in his arms, and holds me. I hear him sniffle and feel him wipe the tears from his eyes. It makes me cry. How much I wish this moment could make all the hurt go away, but I know it won't.

I finally pull back, wipe my nose, and say, "Brad…thank you. I didn't want to go here, but you gave me the one thing I really needed. You ask me to forgive you? I don't hate you and I don't want you to hate yourself. I forgive you. Please forgive yourself."

He nods his head, wipes his eyes, and says, "I know you're getting married, but I'd like to still be friends."

"I can't," I say, shaking my head.

"Maybe with a little time?"

Doing my best to fight back my tears, I say, "Do you know how hard it was to leave you out there on that dance floor? I…I somehow hoped…I somehow hoped I was over you…but I'm not…and I'll never get over you as long as you're around."

He puts his hand under my chin and lifts my face to his. "It's not too late," he says. "I really believe that. Losing you has changed me. I'm not the same person anymore. Can't we just give it one more shot?"

I can't believe my ears. I move my head back, so his hand slides off my chin. With full eyes, I shake my head and say, "I can't."

Closing his eyes, which cause another tear to drop down his face, he says, "I really believe we would have been great if we ever got married."

I wipe away his tear with my thumb and say, "I can't go there."

"So this is it?" he asks with his eyes now shut so tight like it might change my answer.

I don't want to say it. Instead, I wait until he's looking right at me and nod my head in agreement.

"Can I kiss you goodbye?" he asks.

Every month that goes by, Alton and I kiss a little less—and with less passion. For the last two years, I've thought day and night about Brad's kiss. There was a moment on the dance floor I thought, maybe even hoped, he was about to kiss me.

When I look up at him without saying no, he slowly leans down until his lips are touching mine. I open my mouth and feel his tongue press against mine, and a wave of love and desire explodes inside me. I lift myself up onto my toes, and he slides his tongue deeper inside my mouth. *It feels so good to kiss like this again.* As we continue to kiss, he untucks the back of my shirt and puts his warm hands on my back. He pulls me against him until I feel every inch of my body against his. His hands are warm and tender as he moves them up and down my back.

As we continue to kiss, he cups my breast in his hand, and I begin breathing harder. I want him. I want to be with him one last time.

When I moan just a little, he reaches down with his free hand and pops open my belt buckle. He fumbles with the button on my jeans until it releases. He slides his hand inside my jeans, and then my panties, and I moan a little louder. Then the image of this man in the arms of another woman—and all those other women—stops me. I pull back and grab his wrists. Still breathing heavy, I say, "Stop….stop…I can't do this."

He tries to push his hand deeper and whispers, "It's okay."

I pull his hand out, button my jeans, buckle my belt, and tuck my shirt back into my jeans. I take a deep breath to steady myself. I turn around, open my car door, look back at him one last time, and say, "Take care of yourself…okay?"

He closes his eyes, nods his head, and says, "You too."

The next morning, I meet my friends for breakfast and go by my mom's house for a visit. I told her I was coming, but she's either not here or not answering the door. I get back in my car and head back home.

Back home, I walk in the front door, and Alton has a beautiful dinner waiting on the kitchen counter. It's pasta covered in salmon, shrimp, scallops and clams. There's a bright green Caesar salad in a bowl and garlic bread still wrapped in aluminum foil. Two wine glasses are sitting on the table filled with white wine, and there's a little candle flickering in the middle of the table.

"What's all this?" I ask.

"Dinner, sweetie." He hands me one of the glasses of wine and says, "You've had a long drive…sit down and relax." He returns to the kitchen, fills my plate with pasta, and places it in front of me. He kisses my cheek and heads back to the kitchen to get the salad and garlic bread.

"I really missed you," he says.

"I missed you too," I say with a smile.

He puts some salad in my bowl and asks, "How was the reunion?"

"It was nice. It was good to see my old friends again."

"Tell me about it. What'd y'all do?"

I tell him what I can. "We walked around the stockyard a little bit, ate dinner, and then went to the same dance hall we used to go to."

"Just like old times," he smiles.

"Something like that."

He sits in the chair beside me, takes a bite of pasta, and asks, "Was he there?"

I know who he's talking about. I take a sip of wine to delay my answer. I take another sip, then say, "He showed up late."

"How's he doing?"

"I guess he's doing okay."

"Did y'all talk?"

 I take a bigger sip and say, "We talked a little."

"Did y'all dance?" he asks.

I told him once that dancing was our thing and he knows how much I love to dance, I've never been one to lie, and I won't start now. I shrug my shoulders like it was no big deal and say, "Everyone was dancing. We danced *one* dance."

This is the closest I've ever seen him to being jealous. Part of me wants him to be jealous—at least a little. Lord knows, Brad would have completely lost his shit. He would have broken up with me and called the wedding off. But Alton is…well, he's Alton. He clears his throat and says, "It's okay, Paige. I'm not jealous. I'm sure you still have feelings for him and that's natural. But I trust you. I know you'd never do anything to hurt me. I hope you got some closure."

It's been two weeks since we've had sex. Tonight, we slip under the covers and make love. When we're finished, we lay side-by-side, spooning. I'm lying in front of him with my head resting on his arm.

"Love you," he says, kissing the back of my head.

"Love you too," I whisper, and spend the next two hours before I finally fall asleep thinking about what might have been.

After my night with Brad, I call Dean to let him know I've decided to marry Alton. We've already talked about Alton a few times and he has a general idea how I feel. The last time we spoke, I told him I wasn't sure what to do.

"Hey Paige," he says, when he answers the phone.

"Hi, Dean."

"How you been?"

"I've been good. What about you?"

"Good," he says. "I'm sorry I haven't been up to see you lately. I've been really busy with work and kids. We need to come up and see you soon."

"I'd like that," I say.

"Everything okay? Do you need money? It sounds like you have something on your mind."

"Well," I draw out. "I've got some news. I've decided to marry Alton."

"*Really*," he says, sounding a little surprised.

"I don't know. Maybe it's not about being madly in love. He's a good man and he'll give me a family and a stable life. That's what I've always wanted."

"I know," he agrees. "There's a lot to be said for that."

"I do love him," I continue.

Giving me the same fatherly advice that he always gives, he says, "As long as you're happy. Feelings come and go, but being with a solid person who loves you counts for a lot." He pauses a second and asks, "Will your mom be there?"

With a little laugh, I say, "I sure hope so."

With concern in his voice, he says, "It's been a long time. Do you think it's a good idea if I come?"

I'm a little surprised he'd ask this question, but I understand his concern. "That's why I'm calling you," I say. "I was wondering if you'd be willing to walk me down the aisle?"

I didn't realize this would have the effect on him that it does. Obviously choked up, he says, "I…I can't believe you…you'd ask me. I'd be proud to walk you down the aisle."

Hearing him practically crying makes my heart explode. Pretty emotional, I say, "Listen Dean, I've got to go to work. I just pulled into the parking lot. Thank you so much. It means the world to me."

Clearing his throat, he says, "It means the world to me, too."

"Have a great day."

"Hey Paige," he says, like he's catching me before I hang up."

"Yeah?"

"I love you so much."

With a big smile, I say, "I love you too."

– CHAPTER 5 –

Five months later, I'm sitting at a dressing table touching up my makeup one last time. A hairdresser is standing behind me, putting on the third layer of hair spray, so not a single strand is out of place.

Kristi is standing beside me to be supportive on my big day. I guess she's here to be my getaway driver in case I decide to bolt. My cousin comes in and I ask, "Is my mom here?"

She closes her eyes, presses her lips together, and shakes her head.

"It figures," I say, looking down and shaking my head. Then I look up, raise my eyebrows, and say, "She's probably too drunk to make it." After the fourth pass of hairspray, I laugh, "Okay, okay, I don't think my hair is going anywhere."

She stops spraying, and says, "You look beautiful."

"You gonna be alright?" Kristi asks.

Will I be alright? I've considered this question almost every day since Alton slid that ring on my finger. Does it matter now if I'll be alright? How do you change your mind after sending out six hundred and fifty wedding invitations? How do you tell all these people to get up and go home…there'll be no wedding? How do you return all those gifts?

What I really wonder is who I'll become if I walk out? My mom? Drinking a twelve pack a day with my new boyfriend after my fourth divorce—arguing until early in the morning over why I came home thirty minutes late or who forgot to close the chip bag?

Who will I become if I stay? Alton's mom who I've never once seen kiss her husband or even hold his hand—living a life most people can only dream about but never laughing—and rarely smiling?

There has to be a happy middle out there, right? But that choice isn't in front of me right now. I've never really dated much. I was with Brad and went straight to Alton. The only question before me right now is do I marry Alton or return to the dating cesspool that my friends tell me all about.

I nod my head, and with a smile, I say, "I'm gonna be alright."

I move to the church vestibule and Dean is waiting for me. With wide eyes and a big smile, he kisses my cheek, and says, "You are so beautiful."

I wrap my arms around his neck and say, "Thank you for being here."

Then the organ begins to play the processional. "You ready," he asks.

I give him an uncertain nod.

When the doors open in front of me, a giant crowd of people turn in their seats and stare right at me. The place is full of more flowers than I've ever seen in my life. Yellow and white…those are the colors I chose. Alton's brother and four buddies are on the left and his family fills most of the church. Kristi is on the right, followed by my other best friend from work, my cousin, and two other close friends.

When *Here Comes the Bride* plays, what goes through my mind is: *This is it. This is how it all begins.* During the rehearsal, I walked down the aisle just like you see in the movies; but, it's so different now with everyone in the world looking on. I'm frozen in place. I feel like I did when I played Chaba in Fiddler on the Roof in high school. I sat in the wings, unable to move onto the stage.

Just when I think I can't do it, Dean squeezes my hand. I look at him and nod my head. I take one step, and then another, and another, until I'm at the front of the church, walking up the steps.

With all these people looking on, I listen as the preacher informs everyone why we're here, talks all about marriage, and reads some words from the Bible about love.

"First Corinthians says: Love is patient, love is kind. It does not envy, it does not boast, it is not proud. It does not dishonor others, it is not self-seeking, it is not easily angered, it keeps no record of wrongs. Love does not delight in evil but rejoices with the truth. It always protects, always trusts, always hopes, always perseveres."

I'm not big on the whole God and Bible thing. The last time I prayed was right before the police came and returned me to my mom. But Alton and I have what the preacher describes to a tee. He didn't say anything about love giving you butterflies or love being a hot fire that consumes your soul and makes you feel like you might die if you can't be with the other person. The way the Bible describes it, Alton and I must have love, so it must be right.

The preacher then looks at the crowd and asks, "Is there anyone present who knows any reason why these two people should not be legally wed?"

I've had a dream for the last three nights that Brad pops up from the crowd at this point, causes everyone in the church to turn to him, and says, "Stop everything! This can't happen. We love each other. We'll always love each other." In my dream, I'm standing at the front of the church in total shock and embarrassment, unsure what to do. Brad pushes through the row he's sitting in until he's standing in the center aisle. He reaches his hands out to me, and says, "Paige, please come with me."

I always wake up at this point so I never find out what I do next.

Whatever might have happened in my dreams, I now look out at everyone sitting in the pews and Brad is nowhere in sight. Everyone remains quiet. I sigh in relief.

Now that we have that out of the way, the preacher turns to Alton, and says, "Do you, Alton Douglas Warren, take Paige Childers to be your lawfully wedded wife, to have and to hold from this day forward, for better or worse, for richer or poorer, in sickness and in health, to love, and cherish, pledging to her your faithfulness, till death do you part?"

Alton takes my hands in his and looks at me like he's the luckiest man ever born. Loud and clear, he says, "I do."

"And do you, Paige Elizabeth Childers, take Alton Warren to be your lawfully wedded husband, to have and to hold from this day forward, for better or worse, for richer or poorer, in sickness and in health, to love, cherish, and obey, pledging to him your faithfulness, till death do you part."

What? How did that whole obey thing get slipped in there? Did Alton just promise to obey me? Not prepared to debate the Bible in front of all these people, I simply say, "I do."

That's it! I did it. We're pronounced husband and wife to the standing ovation of almost five-hundred people. Any doubts I might have had in the past don't matter a hill of beans anymore.

I take a deep breath and kiss my new husband. Then I look at him and get this peaceful feeling inside me. I know I have nothing to worry about. I'm married to Alton. He'll keep me warm, and safe, and dry. I'm sure everything's going to be fine. How can it not?

PART TWO

HOME SWEET HOME

"Love is a fire. But whether it is going to warm your heart or burn down your house, you can never tell."

—Joan Crawford

"Love lies in those unsent drafts in your mailbox. Sometimes you wonder whether things would have been different if you'd clicked 'Send'.

Faraaz Kazi

– CHAPTER 6 –

Dr. Warren sits here writing on his pad like this whole story isn't boring him half to death. Every now and then, he nods or asks me a question, but for the most part, I just keep talking like this stuff has been bottled up inside me for way too long.

In the middle of me talking, he clears his throat like he's ready to quit for the day. Instead, he puts his pen down and asks, "So why do you think you married him?"

I let out a deep breath, and say, "I don't know. I've asked myself that same question over and over again."

With a nod, he says, "So, how did it all work out?"

I had no idea we'd be here this long. "Can I get some water?" I ask.

He knocks on the door and asks, "Can we get Mrs. Warren some water, please?"

With shaky hands, I drink half the water down. Exhausted from talking about all this stuff, but not wanting to quit, I try to explain.

As the years passed by, Alton never changed—and neither did I—at least not at first. My fear that he would become his father played out like it was written on stone tablets on the day he was born. They look alike, have the same personalities, eat the same foods, believe in structure, plan vacations a year in advance, and don't ever kiss or even hold hands in public. I tried the kiss in public thing enough times to know it was a lost cause. Whenever we'd cross paths with some crazy couple making out in a park or anywhere else, Alton would explain how inappropriate it was. I didn't bother telling him what I was really thinking about it.

The closest we ever get to showing affection in public is holding hands every once in a while at a restaurant, and a quick kiss *one time* in the middle of the movie theater. Brad and I would often decide which movie to watch by how many people were in the theater. We'd sometimes jump over to the empty theater next to ours for a little while and pick a seat in the back corner. We'd often miss the entire plot of our movie, and we once got kicked out of the theater.

When it comes to arguing, they say it takes two to tango, which isn't necessarily true. One person can cause an argument all by himself. But it's definitely true when it comes to sex. You can lead a horse to water but you….well, you get the idea.

Alton got a job at a psychologist office. His main task was to administer psychological and IQ tests to prisoners waiting for trial or waiting to be sentenced by the court. He hated it. After working there for three years, he quit his job to open his own office. It didn't take long before his office was booked solid. His solution? He worked more hours and hired another therapist to handle the overflow. Five years later, he wrote a psychology book that got published but went nowhere. Then he wrote his second book called, *When Therapy Fails*. It was hugely successful. Within a few years, it was taught in many of the best universities and he gave talks at seminars and professional education courses across the country. He followed it up with two more books.

I took a job at a local elementary school teaching kindergarteners. I couldn't have picked a better profession. My third year I was voted teacher of the year at our school and was featured in the local newspaper. Teaching gave me so much purpose and fulfillment. I loved how these beautiful little children learned how to sit in their chairs and listen to their teacher; identify their colors; count, add, and subtract small sums; recite the alphabet; begin to read; and tell time. Every year I fell in love with twenty-five kids and watched as they moved on through fifth grade.

I always thought I'd want to have a baby, but it was kind of strange. Over the first years of our marriage, Alton never once brought up the idea of having a child, and I never brought it up either. After four years, I was starting to wonder if I'd be okay never having kids. The thought about not having a baby sometimes got me down. Brad and I talked about having a baby all the time.

Then Alton finally asked, "What do you think about having a baby?"

I wasn't sure what I thought about it. I closed my eyes and said, "I don't know."

I don't think that was what he was expecting. He got a puzzled look on his face and asked, "You don't want a baby?"

With a shrug, I say, "I don't know?"

"Don't you think these past years have been great?"

"Sure," I answer.

"Then, what? I know you love kids. Are you afraid we can't afford it? Things at my office are going great."

"I'm not saying I don't want a baby. We just haven't really talked about it."

"We love each other, right?"

"Sure."

"Well…all we're lacking is a baby."

His last words opened my eyes. *He's right.* A baby might be exactly what I'm lacking. I can raise our child any way I want. I'll make sure he or she is fun, full of life, and affectionate. All the love that's been bottled up inside me can spring forward to our child, like a jack-in-the-box that's been sitting in the attic of an old house for way too many years.

With a smile, I said, "Sure…let's have a baby."

I gave birth to our first daughter, Rebekah. It was Alton's mom's bright idea to name her after some lady in the Bible. I agreed on Rebekah after refusing to name her Mary. She was planned, of course. Everything with Alton is planned.

We barely got Bekah (that's what we call her) home before Alton brought up the idea of me staying home to raise her. This never occurred to me. I love my job way too much. Sure, I wanted kids, but I didn't see myself as a stay-at-home mom. The idea of spending all my time at home would drive me crazy. I think I'd get claustrophobic. I made it very clear that I didn't want to give up my job and returned to teach six weeks later.

After Bekah was born, I was done having kids. It's not that I want to leave Alton or anything. I just didn't want to dig my hole any deeper. Two years later, Alton wanted to try one more time for a son and I told him I wasn't ready. After eight months of "just checking back in to see if you're ready," I finally agreed. It was one of those moments in our marriage that I was actually happy—plus, one more child isn't that big of a deal.

Nine months later, we had another girl, Elizabeth, named after some other woman in the Bible. I call her Beth.

With two kids, Alton was a little more adamant that I stay home and raise our kids. His mom added her two cents one night at dinner, and his dad also thought it was a good idea. I mostly sat there and nodded now and then. Six weeks later, after plenty of back and forth, I was back in my classroom doing what I enjoy most.

Two years after our second child, we were both done having kids. For me, two kids at home and twenty-five kids in a classroom were plenty. Then came the start of the new school year and I forgot to take my birth control pills. It was easy to forget since we only had sex once every month or so. Two nights after we had sex again, it clicked in my mind that the last time I took my birth control pills was a week ago. I took two pills in a row for three days, but it was too late. I was pregnant again.

Telling my husband I was pregnant was something I couldn't bring myself to do. It's not that he'd be angry, because he wanted a son. But I knew what this meant. The thought of having an abortion crossed my mind. Alton would never know, but I knew I could never live with myself if I did it.

I told Alton, and he took the news really well. This time, we had a son and we named him Jacob. I didn't even realize this was another Bible name until he was two years old.

What about this going back to work thing? It was easy to stand firm after our first child. After our second child, I had to battle everyone, but held my ground. It was one of those few times we got into a real argument.

"Why do *I* have to make all the sacrifices because *you* want another child?" I asked. This tipped the scales in my favor and I was back in my classroom after six weeks.

But this time, Alton wasn't asking for another child and I only myself to blame. If I'd realized I'd forgotten to take those damn pills, I could have let him know and waited another month to have sex. Instead, that train had left the station—or entered the station—by the time I remembered.

After four weeks, we were at a stalemate. It's not that he was being unreasonable. He just didn't want his kids—especially three kids—raised in a daycare. The cost alone gobbled up most of my paycheck. But I didn't care about the money. I just loved teaching. "Why don't you quit *your* job and stay at home?" I asked.

Already knowing the answer, he said, "What would we live on? A teacher's salary?"

We stood there in silence, waiting for the other person to crack. I already knew that someone would have to be me. I was down to working out the details.

"How long?" I asked.

Realizing that I just agreed to sacrifice what I loved for our family, he came over, knelt down in front of me, and put his hand on mine. "It's not forever," he promised. "Just until they get a little older."

"What's a little older?"

He thought about it for a second and said, "I guess until they start high school."

Defeated and a little pouty, I said, "That's *thirteen* years."

"All right…all right. Until they start junior high."

And that's how I became a stay-at-home mom.

-61-

– CHAPTER 7 –

Now, seven years later, I'm still a stay-at-home mom. The good news? The fear that I might become Alton's mother never happened. I still wear blue jeans, eat at nice restaurants using the wrong spoon, and sometimes laugh out loud or say the wrong thing in a crowd. I drink beer instead of wine or martinis.

I never get used to staying at home. At the same time, I now live for my kids. Bekah is just like her dad. She keeps a day planner in her bookbag and has her whole week, her whole month, planned out. She's so logical and can intelligently discuss any topic like she's an adult. Her room is always clean without being told. She over-studies for every exam, always has her projects done days or weeks before they're due, is the president of her school's student counsel, and plays flute in the school band. She swears she'll be the first female president of the United States.

Beth is my creative one. She loves to draw and paint. She helps me in the kitchen and from time to time cooks the entire meal for the family. Just like me, she acts in her school plays and plays volleyball.

Jacob is still my little boy, and I wish he could stay that way. As soon as he learned to walk, he'd come in our bedroom and lay on my side of the bed. Even after Alton tried to put a stop to it, he'd sneak into our room every once in a while. Wherever I go, he's usually one step behind me.

As the years pass by, Alton's practice grows. As we go from one child to three, our houses grow as well. We move from San Marcos to Austin and buy a lovely four-bedroom home in a popular, trendy neighborhood. Then last week we moved from Austin to an incredible home on Lake Travis. It has five bedrooms, so each of our kids have their own bedroom and bathroom, Alton has an office, and there's another bedroom for guests. We have a dock overlooking the lake where the kids can swim. There's also a boathouse. I never would have never imagined I'd be living like this.

When the moving truck backs out of the driveway, I'm busy unpacking boxes, arranging furniture, hanging up pictures, and making the house a home. The front door is cracked open just a bit when someone opens it further and peeks inside.

"Helloooo," a woman says with a smile.

"Hey!" I say, motioning her inside. "Come on in"

She steps inside, and bobs up and down as we walk to the living room. "I saw y'all moved in. I know I should have called first, but I don't know your number."

"No worries!" I say, extending my hand. "I'm Paige. I'm not a call first kind of girl."

"Thank God," she says, taking my hand. "I'm Trish. We need more women like you around here. I live two houses down. I see you have a daughter."

"Two daughters and a son."

"I saw the pretty girl with dark hair. Looks like she's about fourteen."

"You saw right...she *is* fourteen."

"My daughter's fourteen, too," she smiles. "We've got to get them together."

"Definitely," I agree. "You want to sit down for a minute?"

"Oh, I see you're busy," she says, sounding like she wants to stay but doesn't want to intrude.

"Nonsense," I say. "I can use the break."

I walk into the kitchen and she follows behind me. "You want a cup of coffee or anything?" I ask.

She looks at her watch and says, "Coffee at two-thirty? Got anything a little stronger?"

"Cold beer?" I ask.

"I like you already," she says with a smile. "I thought you might offer me wine."

"Blue Moon?" I ask, as I grab two beer mugs out of the cabinet.

She waves them away and says, "I don't need no glass. I like it right out of the bottle."

"I like you already, too," I say, popping the tops off each bottle and handing her one.

She takes more than a sip from her beer and says, "You have a gorgeous place here. I would have loved to have a place on the water. Do you have a boat?"

"Not yet," I answer. "But it's at the top of Alton's list. My husband's name is Alton."

"What a unique name," she says. "Sounds like royalty or something."

"Yeah, something like that."

"So, how'd you wind up way out here?"

I take another drink and say, "I don't know. We had a nice place in Westlake and one day we were coming back from visiting someone and Alton said something about how nice it would be to live out here. Next thing I know, he found this house for sale."

"Just like that?" she asks.

"Pretty much. What about you?"

"Oh, we could never afford a place out here. It was Cliff's…that's my husband…parent's house. His dad passed away five years ago, and he got the house. It's nothing like this."

"I know how you feel," I say. "Sometimes I wonder what I'm doing here. I just know someone's going to come one day and tell me I got to get out." We both laugh and take another drink. Her beer is finished before mine, so I ask, "Want another?"

"Two beers in the middle of the day," she says. "What will you think of me?"

I grab two more beers from the fridge and say, "I think we should sit out by the water." We walk out the back door and down to the dock. We don't have any lawn chairs yet, so we sit side-by-side with our legs crossed.

It's a sunny day, and the heat is reaching a hundred degrees. She takes her beer, lays back, and soaks up the sun. "You've got it made," she says, fanning herself.

"It's nice," I agree, propping myself up with my arms behind me.

Shading her eyes with her hand, she looks at me and asks. "So, how old are you?"

"Thirty-eight."

"Thirty-eight? I thought you were younger than me," she says.

"How old are you?" I ask.

"Thirty-four."

"I wish I was thirty-four," I laugh. "Hell, I wish I was twenty-four."

Then I lay back so we're side-by-side. I look over and ask, "So, do you have many friends here?"

"Nah," she says, shaking her head. "All my friends are back home. Everyone is so busy nowadays. We wave at each other coming and going, but it's not like we socialize or anything. I saw you moving in across the street and wanted to jump right in before you got too busy."

I turn my head towards her and say, "I'm really glad you did."

"Do you work?" she asks.

I hate this question. I give the same answer I always give. "I'm a teacher. I took some time off to raise the kids but I hope to go back soon."

"Not me," she says, raising her eyebrows. "Me and work never seen eye-to-eye. I'm purty happy right here raising the kiddos."

She's cute, with a slim figure, dark black hair, and a strong accent. I can't put my finger on it. The way she talks, her hand gestures, and her facial expressions seem a little mysterious. "I like your accent," I say. "Where you from?"

"Louisiana," she answers. "I'm a creole coon-ass…born and raised."

"How'd you meet your husband?"

"Who…Cliff? He's my second husband. We met at a bar shootin' pool one night. A couple drinks later, and we were out on the dance floor with his hands all over me. I thought he might take me right there. Six months later, we were tyin' the knot."

I'm already loving this girl. Wanting to pry just a little, I say, "Wow…what a story. So, how's things going?"

"Five years and going strong," she says. "We got our problems, but who don't? Makes the make-up sex so much hotter. Know what I mean?"

I give her a smile and say, "Sure."

"What about y'all?" she asks.

"We met at college. I was working at a restaurant and he came in with some buddies. We dated almost two years before we got married."

"Yeah, it takes some guys a spell to know what they want. Did you wind up pregnant?"

I smile a little and shake my head, no.

"Good for you," she says. "Tried that with number one. Didn't go so good."

"So, your child is from your first marriage?" I ask.

"We got mine, yours, and ours. I got two, he got one, and we got one together."

"Do you still dance?" I ask.

"All the time," she says, like she's happy I brought it up. "You dance? We'd love to have another couple to go out dancing with."

I lean forward, pick at the label on my beer, and say, "Nah…we don't really dance."

"Come on out," she says with her same twang. "We'll teach ya'."

"I know how to dance," I say, continuing to peel the label off. "I used to love dancing. Alton doesn't really dance."

"Bummer," she says with a frown. "Maybe we can work on that."

I give a quick laugh and say, "It will take a lot of work. Country music isn't his thing—neither is going to bars. I don't think dancing is in the cards."

Right then, she jumps up and says, "Oh, shit. I got to go. I forgot all about it. I'm supposed to meet with my son's teacher. He's been actin' up again."

We both get up and head back inside. When we get to the front door, she says, "So nice meetin' ya'. Can we do this again?"

"Absolutely," I say with a big smile. "I'm so glad you came by."

"No problem," she says, and jogs across the street to her house.

That evening, Alton comes home, looks around the house, and says, "Wow! You really got a lot done today."

"I think I made a new friend," I say. "The girl from across the street came over. We had a beer out on the dock and got to know each other."

"A beer in the middle of the day?" he asks.

"Yeah, I asked what she wanted, and she said a beer."

"Tell me about her."

"Her name is Trish. I don't know…she seems nice. They moved here from Louisiana. Her husband inherited the place across the street. She has a strong accent."

"That's wonderful," he says. "I'm glad you're making friends."

He opens the back door and we both step outside. He looks over at the boathouse and says, "I found a boat today that I'm interested in."

"Great. You said you wanted a boat."

"I put down a deposit."

I like the idea of having a boat. "When are we getting it?"

"I have someone coming out to look at the boathouse and make sure it's okay. He'll be here day after tomorrow. They'll deliver the boat when he's finished."

He turns around to go back inside and asks, "Are we ready to eat? I'm famished."

We always eat at six thirty on the dot. I walk out and pick up the two beer bottles we left on the dock. Smiling to myself, I go back inside and call all the kids for dinner.

– CHAPTER 8 –

Two weeks later, a white pickup truck pulls up in the driveway and a man knocks on the door. He has on cowboy boots and a metal paper holder in his hands. When I open the front door, he extends his hand, and says, "Hello, ma'am. I'm Trevor Evans."

"Paige," I say, taking his hand.

"I'm here to look at the boathouse."

"Oh, yes," I say, inviting him in. "Right this way."

We walk through the house and out the back door. He unclips a tape measure from his waist, and says, "Let's take a look."

I turn around and say, "I'll be inside."

He stays out there for about an hour. Every now and then I look out the kitchen window and see him measuring boards and pushing on the posts with his boot. A little later he's up on the roof. Another time, he's kneeling on the dock, looking down into the water underneath.

He's a very nice-looking man about six foot three, with blonde hair, a strong, slender build, and skin that's well-tanned from years out in the sun.

When he's done outside, he knocks on the back door and says, "Ma'am."

I open the door and ask, "Do you want to come in?"

He shakes his head and says, "No, ma'am. I'm pretty wet and muddy. I don't want to mess up your floors."

I walk outside and ask, "So, how is it?"

He shakes his head and says, "It's in pretty bad shape. Most of the posts underwater are completely rotten. The roof has to be replaced and the far wall is sagging pretty bad. I'm surprised it hasn't collapsed already."

I nod my head and say, "That's why I don't go in there. It doesn't look too stable."

"I can't really repair it…you know liability and all. I don't want to be responsible if it falls down on someone. I recommend you rebuild it."

"The whole thing?" I ask.

"Yes ma'am—from top to bottom."

"How much will that cost?" I ask.

"It depends what you want. You want me to replace it just like it is or fancy it up…modernize it?"

"I don't know," I say with my hands on my hips. "You're going to have to talk to my husband about that. You have his number?"

He looks down at his binder and calls out Alton's number, digit by digit.

"That's it," I say.

"I'll give him a call," he says. "Nice to meet you, ma'am."

"Nice to meet you too."

He walks around the house to his truck.

That evening, once everyone is in place and we start eating dinner, I turn to Alton and say, "The man came today to look at the boathouse."

"Yeah," he says, before taking a bite. "He called me…said we need to replace the whole thing."

"Yeah, that's what he said."

"He's going to start next week."

"How much will it cost?"

"Over a hundred thousand. I already talked to the bank about a home equity loan."

"Wow!" I say, a little surprised. "How long will it take?"

"He says we have to pull permits first. The whole thing will take a couple of months."

Just as we finish, while I'm gathering up plates to bring to the kitchen, a call comes in on Alton's phone in his pocket. He pulls it out, looks down, then gets up from the table and heads to his office with his phone to his ear.

I'm in the kitchen when he comes in thirty minutes later to get a glass of water. I wipe my hands on the dishtowel, toss it on the counter, and ask, "Who was on the phone?"

Very dismissive, he says, "Just one of my patients,"

I give him a curious look and say, "I thought you stopped giving your cell number to your clients?"

"I did…for the most part. But sometimes a patient is on the edge—a danger to themselves or others. They can't wait a week to talk."

"Who was it?" I ask.

"Why?"

With a scowl, I say, "I just want to know."

Sounding exhausted, he says, "Can we please not start this again?"

"Who was it?" I ask again.

"Her name is Traci. She's having a really hard time right now." He starts to walk out but pauses at the edge of the door and says, "She's going through a rough divorce and her mom just passed away. She's expressed thoughts of killing herself so I sent her to a doctor for medications. I told her to call if she has a problem."

"Uh-huh," I say, nodding my head.

"What else was I supposed to do? I'm her therapist."

"Okay," I say, throwing up my hands as I walk by him. "I hope she gets better."

– CHAPTER 9 –

Trish comes over once or twice a week. Sometimes we eat lunch, sometimes we lay out with a cold beer, and every now and then we smoke a little pot. After a couple of weeks, I go over to her place. It's not a bad looking house, but it's kind of old and looks like it's never been remodeled. If you didn't know any better, you might think someone just moved in…or is moving out. The place looks well lived in with clutter everywhere.

The more we're together, the more I like her. She graduated from high school eight months pregnant and got married the first time way too young and for all the wrong reasons. That marriage lasted four years, and she spent five years as a single mom working as a bartender at a couple of bars right outside of "Nawlins." She took a chance on her second husband who she calls her "sweet-ass man."

In many ways, we're completely different, but in other ways we're so much alike. I think it's mostly because we come from very similar backgrounds. Her father ran off when she was ten and she was raised by her mother and whoever might have been her mom's husband or boyfriend at the time. Just like one of my stepfathers, her mom's second husband couldn't get it through his thick head that he married the mom…not the daughter. Just like me, she reported it to her mom, except her mom called the police. He was arrested and sentenced to ten years in prison.

I can see why she might have a hard time finding friends on a street like this. The people living around here aren't the kind of folks who want to "keep Austin weird." She looks kind of like a hippie. She's not pretentious and doesn't try to be someone she isn't. Her Louisiana accent and Cajun slang might turn some people off, but I love it. She makes me wonder what I might sound like if I hadn't gotten a good education.

Today she comes walking across the street in a tiny two-piece bathing suit covered only by a t-shirt cut above her waist that reads, "Classy, Sassy, and a Bit Smart-Assy." When she pulls it over her head, she reveals her thin stomach, tan legs, and breasts that barely fill the cups of her tiny bathing suit. She has one tattoo above her ankle of a dove with an olive branch in its beak. There's another tattoo on her back, just below her shoulder, that has stars, the sun, and the moon.

I'm wearing the kind of bathing suit you might expect from a thirty-eight-year-old mom with three kids. It's two piece but does a lot better job of covering all my private parts. I also have on a t-shirt and shorts. I once had a slender figure like hers, but I gained a little weight after our son was born. No longer going to work every day and in the middle of a marriage where we have sex every couple of months, I lost the motivation to slim down.

A little after we lie back in the sun, we hear Trevor banging away at the boathouse, like he's tearing it apart.

"What's going on?" she asks.

"We're building a new boathouse."

She sits up when Trevor comes out from around the side of the boathouse wearing blue jeans and no shirt. He has several boards swung over his shoulder. His strong biceps, broad shoulders, ripped stomach, and tan back, looks like he just came from the gym. He throws the boards into a pile and heads back in.

"Shit!" she says, lifting her sun glasses for a better look.

I nod my head with a smile and say, "That's Trevor."

Her eyes stay fixed on him as he comes back with another stack of boards and throws them on the pile.

"Fuuuck," she says, drawing out the words before lying back down. She pulls her hair back, and I see two purple marks on her neck. I don't say anything as we drink our beers, but they're too obvious to simply ignore.

They're not covered in make-up, and she's making no effort to hide the bruises. I wonder if she wants me to see them. I figure she doesn't have anyone else to talk to.

Lying on the dock, I turn towards her, prop my head up on my elbow, and ask, "You mind if I ask you something?"

"Fire away," she says.

"You have two bruises on your neck."

Still laying on her back, she puts her hand over the bruises, looks up, and laughs, "This is so embarrassing."

"Everything okay?"

She looks at me, turns her head to give me a clear view of her neck, and says, "They're hickeys."

I bust out laughing, now realizing they do look like hickeys.

She sits up, and says, "Did you think—"

I shrug my shoulders and say, "You never know."

"Fuck, no!" she says leaning back. "He might be crazy but he ain't that crazy. I got six brothers. They'd give him a good country ass-whoopin' if he ever tried that."

I brush her hair to the side to get a better look and tease, "Really…a hickey?"

She gives them a rub and says, "Sometimes Cliff gets going and can't stop. I don't complain cause it turns me on. Know what I'm sayin'?"

I sit for a second, maybe feeling just a tinge of jealousy. "Aren't you afraid your kids will see?"

"Nah," she says with a smile. "They know how we are. They've heard us in the bedroom going at it. I can be a little noisy sometimes. It turns Cliff on."

They know how we are? Thinking about her remark, makes me wonder if our kids know how *we* are. I'm not sure when I got so quiet. Maybe it was the babies lying in bed with us or the children sleeping right down the hall. Whatever the reason, the times we do have sex no one would ever know, even if they were standing right outside our bedroom with their ear pressed to the door.

"You know men," she says with a laugh. "It's just like my mamma always told me—remember the three F's."

Oh, Lord. Should I ask? Then I go for it. "And what's the three F's?"

"Fuck 'em, feed em' and shut the fuck up. Well, I don't cook and can't shut my mouth to save my life."

We both laugh again and I ask, "Your mom would talk like that?"

"Talk like that? She had something to say about everything. Where do you think I learnt it from? She's a psychic. She reads people's palms and does hoodoo magic. You know hoodoo?"

"Hoodoo?"

"The slaves from Africa brought it over. It's like voodoo but you use it to get people back when they done you wrong."

I think about it for a second and say, "Hoodoo, huh?"

She nods her head and says, "That shit works. I had this boyfriend who did me wrong once—really wrong. My mom did a little hoodoo spell and two days later he was walking through Walmart without a care in the world. Then, out of nowhere, a fan fell off the top shelf and hit him square on the head. He ain't talked right since."

"What?"

"But you gotta' be careful with hoodoo. It's about rights and wrongs…you know, justice. You never know what will happen when you ask for justice. It's like a roulette wheel. Everyone stands around waiting for it to drop, but no one knows where. You might get what you want and then some you don't want."

This all sounds pretty hard to believe. I'm sure things fall on people all the time. I shake this off with a little grin and say, "You believe that stuff?"

Her eyes grow wide. "You bet your ass I believe it."

Some people might be turned off by how frank, or crude, she can be, but she says these things with such animation that it's pretty comical. Wanting to change the subject, I say, "The three F's huh? Well, at least I've learned how to cook."

Squinting her eyes, she looks at me sideways, and says, "A hot firecracker like you? I thought y'all would be going at it like a couple drunk monkeys."

I laugh out loud before looking out over the lake in thought. I know a lot of women do, but I've never been a wife who discusses the problems in my marriage. I've known Trish for two months and she always pops up with some crazy new story that usually winds its way back to sex. Usually I stay quiet because she can carry on a conversation for hours with no more than a simple nod every now and then. I've never said anything about Alton and me, but for the first time, I open up a little.

I squint my eyes and say, "Sex isn't what it used to be between us…not that it used to be so hot. I had this boyfriend in high school…I was so in love. We had sex all the time. Then after we left for college we'd have sex every night he'd come home from College Station. I just figured I was young, and that kinda thing fizzles out after you get married and have children."

With a little laugh, Trish says, "Girl, I don't know who you been talkin' to, but somebody lied to you."

Getting even more intimate, I take a sip of my beer and ask, "Do you mind if I ask you something personal? You don't have to answer if you don't want to."

Laying back in the sun with her eyes closed, she gives me a slow motion of her hand, and says, "I think we done passed personal a few miles back. Come out with it?"

"How often do you—" I say, and can't get the rest out.

"Have sex?" she asks, finishing my thought.

I raise my eyebrows.

"It depends how much he works. Sometimes we only have sex a couple times a week. Other times, once or twice a day." I sit here with wide eyes. She sees my surprise and asks, "How often do you have sex?"

Well, I got this started. I should have known I'd get the same question back. I give her an embarrassing look and say, "I don't even know. Every few months."

"Every few months!" she laughs. "When's the last time y'all did it?"

I don't have to give it any thought. "On his birthday."

"And when's his birthday?"

"Last November."

"That's three months ago!" she says with eyes as big as quarters.

I hadn't even realized it's been that long. "Yeah…I guess it is," I say with a shrug.

"The three B's?" she asks with a naughty smile.

I'm already laughing, just trying to imagine what's about to come out of her mouth next. Then I get out, "The three B's?"

"Oh, come on girl," she laughs. "You know…birthday…backrub… blowjob. They like it a whole lot better than some new shirt."

"God," I say, laughing again. "I can't even remember the last time I've done that. I'm not sure he even wants it."

"Don't want it?" she repeats with a chuckle. "There ain't a man alive who don't want it. Don't he ask?"

I shake my head and say, "I don't think he'd ever do that."

She cocks her head back and says, "Good Lord…if I had a nickel every time my husband asked for a blowjob, I'd be living in your house." When we stop laughing, she asks, "What do ya' do when he comes home from work after a long day ornerier than an old crocodile?"

"I don't know," I say, tossing one hand in the air. "He comes home every day at the same time and we eat dinner."

"Eat dinner?" she laughs. "You know how many arguments I've avoided with a good blowjob? It's a whole lot easier than saying I'm sorry."

This girl has me rolling. I shake my head, and say, "We don't really argue."

"Never?"

"Not really."

She looks up with a huff and says, "Well, there goes the good make-up sex. I think Cliff wants me more when we're yelling back and forth than he does at any other time. Plus, he tries a lot harder when he just fucked up royally." She nods down between my legs and asks, "Does he…."

"Never," I say, shaking my head.

"Never? Stop…stop," she says, waving her hands at me. "You're 'bout to make me cry. That's the best part."

I bite my lower lip, pause a second, and say, "Maybe that's why I don't do it to him. I know I'm a big part of the problem, but I wasn't always like this. The guy I dated all through high school and college—" I shake my head a little and say, "Something about him always made me so hot. I *always* wanted to do that."

"Do what?" she asks.

Starting to blush, I say, "You know…don't make me say it."

With a grin, she says, "It's not so hard. You can say it."

"You know…the three B's."

"Which one?"

She won't let this go. "Blowjob…okay!" I shout with a laugh. Then I look out at the lake and say, "You know, it's not just sex. We hardly kiss or hold hands."

"Ever?"

"Well…sure we kiss hello and goodbye, but we haven't French kissed in years."

She lets out a deep breath and draws out the word, "Shiiiit."

I lean back in my chair and tell her the secret I've been holding inside all these years.

"I saw him," I say.

"Who?"

"My boyfriend. It was right before we got married. I went to our class reunion, and he was there. We'd been broken up for almost two years. He told me he wanted to see my ring and held my hand. That's all it took and all those old feelings came right back. We danced *one* dance and all I could think about was being with him. We kissed goodbye, and I thought I might explode. He put his hands on my breasts…it was over my bra…but it drove me crazy. I wanted him to go further."

"Did he?" she asks.

"God!" I say. "You gotta know everything?"

"So, did he?" she repeats.

"He put his hand down there."

"Down where?"

"On my privates, okay?"

"What's a private?" she asks.

"I'm not saying *that*!" I insist. "But I stopped him and drove off."

After drinking the last of her beer, she asks, "Why'd y'all break up

"He liked sex alright. Just not always with me."

She shakes her head and says, "Ain't that how it is? That's why I fuck Cliff's brains out. Aren't you afraid he'll cheat on you?"

"Alton?" I ask, shaking my head. "He's not like that. I don't think he'd ever do that."

"Right," she says, rolling her eyes. "They dogs…they all dogs. Give any man half a chance and he'll chase after the next bitch in heat."

I think about this for a second before dismissing the idea completely.

A little time goes by before she gets up from her chair, throws her towel over her shoulder, and says, "I gotta get back."

We walk back inside, and I toss the empty beer bottles in the trash. Back at the front door, she says, "I don't know, but you need to get laid. Go to his office in a tiny dress and let him see you ain't wearin' no panties. Screw him right there on his desk."

"He would never have sex in public," I say.

"Then screw him *behind* his desk," she laughs.

After she leaves, I walk outside and straighten up. I watch Trevor walking back and forth from the boathouse to the trash pile. On the way back in, he looks my way and gives me a smile. It's hard to pretend I wasn't just staring at him, so I smile back and keep cleaning up.

I sit on the edge of the dock with my legs dangling over the side splashing a little in the water. Everything Trish just said plays in my head.

Then I turn around when I hear Trevor's cowboy books clink against the wood dock as he walks closer. "Mind if I join you?" he asks.

Caught by surprise, I say, "Sure."

When he sits down, I ask, "How's it coming?"

He wipes his forehead with a towel and says, "It's taking a little longer than I hoped, but we're getting there."

Sitting almost shoulder-to-shoulder, he leans towards me, touching the side of his arm to mine. "You and your husband must love coming out here in the evenings."

I take a deep breath of the evening air and say, "It is nice." Then I look at him and say, "You finished for the day?"

"Yeah, I'm calling it quits."

"Want a beer?"

"Sure," he says with a nod.

I come back with two cold beers and hand one to him.

He's very attractive, with this rugged look and blue eyes. He reminds me of Paul Newman when he was young. I look down and see he doesn't have a ring on his finger or even a tan line. Sounding nonchalant, I ask, "So, you're not married?"

"Never been married," he says, shaking his head. "Couple close calls, but it didn't pan out."

He takes a big gulp of his beer and says, "What about you? What's your story?"

"Me? I got married right out of college."

He takes another sip and says, "The last thing I wanted to do when I graduated from college was get married. I had too many oats to sow before I was ready to settle down."

Sounding stoic, I say, "I was way too young. I don't know what happened. I was having a great time being a single college girl. I should have done the same thing… maybe traveled some…but I got married."

He looks around at our gorgeous house and says, "Looks like you did okay for yourself."

I lean over, kick the water a little, and say, "I guess so."

He sets his beer on the dock, looks at me squinting his eyes from the evening sun, and asks, "You alright?"

"Yeah," I say looking down.

"What is it?" he asks. "Maybe talking about it might help."

Still looking out, I say, "You know, sometimes I feel trapped here. I used to be a teacher, and I loved it. After we had kids, my husband wanted me to stay at home and eventually I agreed. I thought I'd go back one day, but it doesn't look like that's going to happen." I pick up a leaf laying on the deck beside me and toss it in the water. I shake my head and say, "I know I'm being silly. There are women who'd love to stay at home with their kids but sometimes I don't really know who I am anymore."

He turns so he's facing me while I'm still looking out at the lake. He leans over on his left arm and says, "I don't think that's silly at all. I know I couldn't stay home all day. I'm sure a lot of women feel like you."

I lean back on my arms and accidentally put my hand on his. I pull my hand back and say, "Sorry about that."

He shakes his head and asks, "Your husband won't let you go back to work?"

I shake my head and say, "I don't know. It's been so long since I've asked. It's never the right time. I eventually stopped asking."

"Then ask," he says.

"Maybe I will."

Sitting out here, I didn't realize the kids were already home from school. Jacob comes out the back door, and I scoot a little to my left. He sits beside me and asks, "What ya' doing out here?"

"Hey sweetie," I say, ruffling his hear. "How was school today?"

He looks at both of us sitting here and says, "Uh…fine."

"Trevor was just about to leave," I say, standing up. Trevor follows suit. He gives us both a smile and says, "I better be going. Thanks for the beer."

I walk inside with my hand on Jacob's shoulder and start dinner so it's ready by six-thirty. I put some lasagna in the oven and pull out the lettuce for a salad. Then I stop for a moment and think more about my conversation with Trish. She's right. This is not the way a marriage is supposed to be. Whatever the reason—however it started—somewhere along the way I quit being the woman a husband needs. It's pretty clear that Alton's not going to do anything about it, so I have to do it myself.

When Alton comes home at 6:10, I meet him at the door and give him a kiss. It's not the kind of kiss I had planned, because he pulls back after a quick second and asks, "What's for dinner?"

"Lasagna," I say.

"Wonderful," he says before walking over to the entry table and thumbing through today's mail.

One of the problems with my new plan is that Alton always goes to bed at nine-thirty. I'm usually up until eleven or twelve. Tonight, I follow him into the bedroom and climb into the bed right after him.

"Hey," he says, with a smile. "Why are you in bed so early?"

A little embarrassed, and not wanting to be too obvious. I give him a subtle smile and say, "I don't know. I'm a little tired tonight."

"You feeling okay?" he asks.

"I'm okay," I say, pulling back the covers. "I just thought I'd go to bed early."

I watch as he goes through his same nightly routine—slow and easy, he takes off his shoes, socks, and slacks. He puts his shoes on the shoe rack in the closet and folds his slacks at the crease before putting them on a hanger. He throws his shirt and socks in the hamper. Then he puts on his pajama bottoms. Once in bed, he removes his glasses and shuts them inside the case on his nightstand before clicking off the light.

When he lays back in bed, I put my hand on him and start caressing his chest. When he doesn't respond, I move my hand down his stomach and ask, "Do you want to—"

He pats my shoulder and says, "It's okay. I know you're tired."

He reaches over, clicks off the lamp on his nightstand, kisses my forehead, and turns to the wall.

– CHAPTER 10 –

The next day is laundry day. I'm not sure how I became the kind of woman who says things like *laundry day*, but that's what I do on Tuesdays. Before I got married, I'd do laundry every few weeks because I'd hang my clothes back up after wearing them. Sure, I'd wash my panties and socks after wearing them once, but as for the rest of my clothes, I'd give them a quick once-over and see if they passed the sniff test. If so, I'd hang them up or return them to my dresser.

Alton never wears anything more than once except for his slacks that he hangs up every night. He doesn't even wear his jeans twice. A year after I started staying at home, he was searching through his closet for his favorite collared shirt and found it still in the hamper. As nice and polite as any husband can ask his wife, he asked if I wouldn't mind doing laundry once a week. So, now every Tuesday is laundry day and his shirts are always pressed with starch—but only one spray and no more. His pants are ironed right along the front crease. His socks are laid out in the drawer like a row of soldiers instead of rolling each pair together into a ball. His underwear are folded along each side and then down the middle; just like his maid used to do.

Don't sweat the small stuff…right? So now, the thermostat is set on 65 degrees until he leaves for the day and I turn it up to 72. I vacuum all the carpets so it leaves these triangle imprints in a straight row. I wash and iron the sheets and pillowcases once a week—that was another discussion. All the cans and boxes in the pantry are in a perfect line with the labels facing forward. He makes a friendly comment every time I leave a drawer open, even a hint, so I find myself walking by and pushing in drawers that are already closed. Before I even get out of the shower, I have to squeegee the glass so it won't leave water-mark spots from the minerals contained in the water itself. He has this uncanny ability of noticing even the smallest of details—including every sliver of dust that collects in the corners of the windows.

I have to admit, he's never rude or demanding. No, he calmly explains how these things are really important. It's not that important to me, but not worth an argument. So, I usually go along to get along. When I don't or forget, I sometimes catch him cleaning up behind me. A time or two I got out of the shower while he was in the bathroom and he walked into the shower after me, squeegee in hand, with me standing right there.

"Sorry," I said. "I forgot."

"No problem," he answered, wiping down the glass himself.

Alton always overthinks things and explains why everything has to be a certain way. Dinner is always on the table at six-thirty, just like it was the whole time he was growing up. Our kids have to be in bed at eight-thirty because "studies show kids do better in school if they have plenty of rest." I had no bedtime when I was growing up, so I stayed up past midnight sometimes. I would have probably ran away from home if I had to go to bed that early. Alton goes to bed at exactly nine-thirty every night. I usually stay up and watch television but keep the sound down so I don't wake anyone up.

I start thinking about my conversation with Trish while I'm folding clothes. *A few times a week? Once or twice a day?* It's hard for me to believe how seldom Alton and I have sex nowadays. Sometimes I feel like we're just resetting the clock. It's not like I don't do anything between our bi-monthly time together. I'm probably on a similar schedule as Trish and her husband, but without the husband part. Something about it makes me feel guilty, but I assume he's doing the same thing.

If things are going to change, I know it won't happen by talking, because we don't talk about sex…ever. I know I'm part of the reason our marriage has lost all its passion, and I need to do something about it.

"Go to his office in a tiny dress, and let him see you ain't wearin' no panties, and screw him right there on his desk."

"What the hell?" I say to myself. "I got nothing to lose."

I leave the laundry in the basket without putting anything away and walk back into my closet. I slide my clothes from right to left until I find the dress that I know will do the trick. I turn to the mirror on my side of the closet and hold the dress in front of me, just below my chin. It's red, stops above my knees, and shows way too much cleavage for most occasions. I take it off the hanger, grab my matching red heels, and lay them on the bed.

I jump in the shower and wash my hair, shave my legs, armpits, and everywhere else, and scrub any trace of old makeup off my face. I quickly dry off and spend fifteen minutes blow-drying my hair, thirty minutes styling it, and another thirty minutes on my makeup.

Back in the bedroom, I go to my dresser and pull out the sexiest bra I own. Just as I close the front clasp, I stop for a second and consider my mission. I unclasp my bra, glance at my bare breasts in the mirror, and toss my red bra back in my drawer.

Standing beside my bed, I slip my dress over my head and adjust it on my shoulders so my breasts are barely hidden underneath. It's been eight years, another child, and eighteen pounds since I bought that dress for a cruise we were going on for our anniversary. Back then, it earned me a couple of compliments when I wore it, but not a whole lot more.

Looking in the mirror, I swing to my left, then over to my right, to make sure it doesn't look too tight from the side. Some of the weight I've gained has gone to my boobs, so the dress still looks pretty good. I'm determined not to let our anniversary thing happen again.

Before heading out the door, I grab my best perfume and spray a little on my neck, cleavage, and wrists. Then, I pause for a second. *I'm going to do it.* I reach under my dress, step out of my panties, and spray my perfume one last time.

I lean a little closer to the dresser mirror, tease my hair one last time with my fingers, and brush the tiny spot of lipstick off my teeth with my fingers. I haven't looked like this in a long time. I stand up straight, take a step back, and with a smile whisper, "Hello Paige…it's been a while."

After finding a parking spot in front of Alton's office, I pull down the sun visor and look at myself one last time to make sure everything is perfect. I apply one last layer of red lipstick and rub my lips together.

Once inside his building, I can feel the eyes of several men follow me to the elevator. *That's been a while, too.* Once inside, I push the button to the ninth floor and wait as people get off on the way up. One man who looks dressed for success gives me a little, almost flirtatious, nod before stepping off on the eighth floor.

Now on the ninth floor, I walk down the hall to Alton's corner office on the right. It has a nice view of downtown. It's been a while since I was here last. I walk in and notice, for the first time, that at some point he changed the furniture in the waiting room.

I walk in and greet Lauren, his secretary of eight years. I never want to be one of those wives who come in and everyone hates her, and *Mrs. Warren* made me uncomfortable from someone about the same age as me, so I told her to call me Paige.

"Paige!" she says. "Long time, no see."

"Hi Lauren. Nice to see you. Is Alton available?"

"He's in a session," Lauren answers, looking down at her watch. "He'll be out soon. You want me to message him you're here?"

"No, no," I say, and walk to the waiting room. I take the first chair and grab one of the five psychology magazines off of the coffee table. I thumb through the magazine until I find an article about love versus lust. I look up at the ceiling and smile a little in amusement.

I barely get started on the article before a woman comes in and sits on the couch to my left. Five minutes later, a man arrives. Even though there's room on the couch for two, he takes the chair across the room, sits down, and crosses his arms. I catch a glimpse of the ring on his finger and assume they're married.

I return to my magazine and read this article explaining how love is actually stronger than lust—a force that draws couples together and can lead to a fulfilling relationship—while lust is a temporary sexual desire that may or may not lead to love. I smile, and almost laugh, given the reason I've come here today. Very discreetly, I glance up over my magazine a time or two and catch the woman draw a tissue out of the box on the side table and dab the tears in her eyes. The man, looking like he'd rather be anywhere but here, looks over at her, closes his eyes, and subtly shakes his head.

Just as I go back to my magazine, the door to Alton's office opens and a woman who looks about thirty years old steps out and turns back around to him. I can't see Alton, but I can tell by their conversation that he's right inside the door.

She has bleach blonde hair, the figure I had before three kids, and she looks a little more like a woman about to go out on a date than into a therapy session. "Thank you for *squeezing* me in," she says, with a sexy tilt of her head and what looks like a flirtatious smile. There's something about the way she says *squeezing me in* that catches my attention.

My husband reaches out and says, "Don't forget the things we talked about today."

She takes his hand still smiling and says, "You've been a big help, Mr. Warren."

Alton lets go of her hand and moves his hand to her upper arm. "See you next week?" he asks.

"Of course," she says, staring up at him with a smile as I sit here watching.

When she turns to leave, we make eye contact for only a second. I give her a smile, but she quickly looks down as all expression leaves her face. I watch as she walks out the door until, sounding surprised, Alton comes up and says, "Paige? What brings you here?"

Feeling the enthusiasm I had back in my bedroom sucked out of me just a little, I stand up and say, "Just thought I'd come by and say, hi."

When I walk forward, he turns to the couple still sitting in the waiting room, and says, "I'll be right with you."

I know better than to kiss him hello at his office. I tried that once several years back, and he spent fifteen minutes explaining how it wasn't professional for a therapist to be kissing in the office.

He puts his hand on my back (which is the closest we get to public affection) and walks with me into his office.

"You look nice," he says, sitting in his chair behind his desk. He gestures for me to take the chair on the other side of his desk and asks, "Where have you been today?"

Ignoring his invitation to sit across from him, I come around and sit on the edge of his desk to the right of him. When I cross my legs, my dress raises halfway up my thighs. Despite my effort, I don't think it's high enough for him to see the panties I'm not wearing. Showcasing the sexy smile that I mastered in high school, I reach forward, straighten his tie just a little, and ask, "Can't a girl come visit her husband once in a while?"

"Of course," he says, looking down at my freshly shaved and oiled leg brushing against his inner thigh. "I just wish you would have called first. Maybe we could have gone to lunch."

Scooting over so I'm right in front of him, I take his hand and place it on my right breast, covered only by my red, silk dress. I never go out of the house without a bra, because I have the kind of nipples that cause stares if I do. He may not know just yet that my panties are laying on the floor back home, but surely he knows from the touch of my firm nipples, that I'm not wearing a bra.

"What's this all about?" he asks.

"Damn," I say. "I must have forgotten to put on a bra today." I open my legs enough for him to see how forgetful I've been, take his hand off my breast, and lower it to my inner thigh, allowing him to slide his hand up a little.

Neither moving his hand any higher or lower, he says, "Paige, where's this coming from?"

This is the same question the kids and I hear all the time. I'm sure he asks his patients the same thing. Not getting the response I imagined, I think about calling this whole thing off. Instead, I press forward. I reach down and put my hand between his legs and rub just a little. I'm aware there's a difference between a college boyfriend with too much testosterone bouncing around and a forty-five-year-old married man with a wife of fourteen years, three kids, and a full-time job, but there's absolutely nothing here to show my efforts are paying off.

I slide down in front of him, undo his belt, and try to unbutton his slacks. He reaches down, takes hold of my wrists, and whispers like we're two teenagers afraid our parents might hear us. "My next appointment is here. It was at four and it's four now."

I let go of his belt, look into his eyes, and do my best to ask the question that's been bouncing around in my head since yesterday. Given how easily we talk about normal things, I don't know why it's so hard talking about sex, but we never do it. Stammering to get it out, I say, "Alton, do you…"

This is harder than I imagined. I'm not sure if I can say it.

"What?" he asks.

I take a deep breath, and try again, "Do you ever want me to give you…"

He sits there waiting for the rest of my question, though I'm quite sure he already knows what I'm trying to ask.

"To give you a—"

Before I can get the words out, his phone buzzes. He pushes a button and his secretary says, "Dr. Warren, don't forget the Campbells are waiting for you. Mr. Campbell says he has to get back to work."

"Paige," he says, pushing me back a little.

Exhaling with a roll of my eyes, I stand up, straighten my dress, and say, "Better take care of the Campbells."

He might think I'm a little sexually frustrated, but the truth is, this whole, embarrassing display did about as much for me as it did for him. I walk out the door without saying goodbye. I stop for a second when his secretary says, "Nice to see you again, Mrs..." she catches herself and says, "...Paige."

"It was really nice to see you, too."

"Have a good day," she says with a smile.

I smile back and say, "You, too."

By the time Alton gets home at six-thirty, my dress is hanging back in the closet, my breasts are covered by my white cotton bra, and my cotton panties are back where they belong.

It doesn't really surprise me when he walks into the house like I was never at his office two hours ago looking like a high-priced escort. I don't bring the whole thing up and neither does he. I'm not sure if I should feel more angry or humiliated.

When you're a kid it only takes one time to know you don't put your finger in an electric socket. Never again do I ask him that embarrassing question. It took all my courage to bring it up the first time, and I'll never humiliate myself like that again. And I never give him another blowjob. Needless to say, he never goes down on me, either.

That night, with so many questions and no answers swirling through my head, I go into the bedroom at eleven o'clock and sit on his side of the bed with him sound asleep behind me. I turn towards him, put my hand on his shoulder, and give him a little shake. "Alton," I whisper.

With disheveled hair, he stirs awake, looks up in a haze, and mumbles, "Is everything okay?"

I stand up, turn around and look out the bedroom window, bite my lower lip, and without turning back, ask, "Alton...do you love me?"

He sits up, fumbles to get his glasses out of the case, slides them over each ear, and asks, "Why would you ask that?"

So many times he does this—answers a question with another question. I turn back to him and say, "Please don't treat me like I'm one of your patients. You know why I ask it."

He shakes his head and says, "You've lost me."

"Why would I ask that? I just made a fool out of myself today."

He rubs his eyes and says, "I had a client."

How do you argue with that? I sit back down on the bed for a second in silence. Finally, I say "Come on. Let's be honest with one another."

"I am being honest," he says.

Getting a little emotional, I ask, "Do you know how hard that was for me?"

He looks down and whispers, "I'm sorry. If you would have called."

I bite my lower lip, shake my head, and whisper, "That would have defeated the purpose."

He puts his hand on my back and says, "I'm sorry."

"Then why didn't you do anything when you got home?"

"It was time to eat."

Tired of playing this game of skirting around the subject, I close my eyes and say, "It was *your* time to eat. One day…just once…couldn't we eat later?"

"I don't know," he says. "We always eat at six-thirty."

"And whose idea was that?"

With a shrug, he says, "I've always eaten at six-thirty, and I'm usually tired when I get home."

"Fine," I say, not ready to let this go for a change. "Then why didn't you do something tonight?"

He pauses for a second, and says, "Honestly, I didn't think about it. I know you don't like to go to bed early. If you wanted to have sex, why didn't you say something?"

Done pretending, I get up and say, "Jesus, Alton, I did…I did my part. I spent two and a half hours getting ready today. I put on my sexiest dress. Do you know what I had on under that dress?"

"I know you didn't have on a bra." he says.

"Nothing! I threw myself on you. You could at least meet me halfway."

"I'm sorry," he says, "You want to have sex? We can have sex right now."

I look down, and a tear falls down my left cheek. I turn back to the window and subtly wipe it away, so he doesn't see it. Still looking out the window, I put both my hands over my face, shake my head, and say, "I shouldn't have to ask. We shouldn't have to have this conversation."

Now sounding more awake, he says, "It never hurts to talk things out. Isn't that what we're doing…talking things out?"

I turn back towards him, and ask, "Who was that girl at your office today?"

Looking confused, or pretending to look confused, he gives me a slight scowl. "What girl?"

I roll my eyes and say, "Come on…you know who. That blonde girl who left when you opened the door."

"She's a patient," he says.

"What's her name?"

"What?"

"Her name…what's her name?"

He squints like this whole thing is so confusing and asks, "Why are you asking these ques—?"

"Because I want to know. What's her name?"

"Traci," he says, raising his hand and shaking his head like it's no big deal.

"The same Traci who's been calling you?"

"Where are you going with this?" he asks.

"How old is she?"

"I don't know. Thirty-one, I think."

I take a deep breath, put my hand over my mouth, and pause to make sure I want to go here. I lower my hand and say, "I saw."

"Saw what?"

"I saw the way she looked at you."

He pulls himself up and leans back against the headboard. After staring at each other in silence, he lets out a big sigh, and says, "I'm her therapist. It's called transference. It happens. A patient sometimes unknowingly transfers feelings about someone else onto their therapist. I've explained this to you."

"Hmmm," I say, nodding my head. "I remember. I remember all about transference. What was *that* girl's name, Denise?"

"Oh my God," he says. "I thought we got over this. For the hundredth time, she…was… a… patient. That's it!"

"I know…I know…transference. And what about the girl before her?"

He brushes his hair back, takes in a deep breath, starts to say something, but I put up my hand to stop him. "Okay…okay," I say. "Maybe, I'm just being paranoid. What am I supposed to think? You don't kiss me, or even touch me. We never—"

"Let's be honest," he interrupts. "It's not all me."

I bite my lip and barely above a whisper, I nod my head, and say, "You're right. You're right."

Looking down, he says, "I guess over time I've learned to follow your lead. You know I don't believe in pushing sex on a woman."

"I'm not *a woman,* " I say. "I'm your wife. Maybe you should push now and then."

"The same is true for you," he says. "I think we both stopped trying."

I know everything he says is true. I sit back down and say, "I never feel like you want…or need…sex. I don't even feel sexy anymore." I look at him and ask, "Can I be honest with you? The truth is, I think on some level I've resented you."

"Resented me…why?"

My chin and lower lip quiver as I try not to cry again. "I never wanted to be a stay-at-home mom. You made me quit my job that gave me so much purpose."

"Then why'd you do it," he asks.

"I don't know. Part of me knew you were right. Lord knows, your mom and dad brought it up every time we got together. I knew it was my fault I got pregnant, so I felt like I deserved it. So, I gave up my job. But it's been eight years now."

"Do you want to go back to teaching?" he asks.

I breathe in deep, look right at him, and say, "Absolutely."

"Then why don't you?"

"Really?" I answer with a smile and wide eyes.

He nods his head and says, "Really."

I think about it for a second and say, "We're four months into the new school year. I'll apply for next year."

"Sounds good," he says.

I lean in, kiss him on the lips, and say. "I love you."

"Love you too," he says.

I pull back and ask, "Maybe we can work on the sex thing?"

"Sure."

"Maybe we can start tonight?"

I climb in bed and we make love for the first time in months.

– CHAPTER 11 –

Everything changed for me that day. *I'm actually going back to work!* For the first time in years, I feel like my life has purpose again. I go back to the old school where I used to teach at and talk to the same principal who was there when I left. She was thrilled to hear I wanted to come back. Next, I go to the store and buy some of the latest kindergarten books they're teaching from now. It's nine months until I'm back in the classroom, but I start making lesson plans and prepare worksheets for each lesson.

Ready to start over, Alton and I make love two times the first week—and once again the following week. Then things go right back to the way they were before. I go to bed early a couple of times but he's either too tired or doesn't get the hint. It's more than a month before we have sex again.

We don't eat out often—mostly when we're already out and about. We're coming back from Bekah and Beth's gymnastics and stop by a restaurant on our way home. In the middle of eating dinner, his phone—that's sitting on the table—rings. He looks down to see who's calling, gets up from the table, holds up one finger, and mouths, "I'll be right back."

I watch out the window as he paces back and forth while talking on the phone. I get a bad feeling in my gut from the expressions on his face and the way he keeps glancing back at the restaurant. He's out there fifteen minutes before coming back to the table. He doesn't say a word about his call which makes me even more curious about the person he was talking to. He picks up the check sitting on the table, takes out a credit card, and sets it on the edge of the table. The longer we sit here, the more irritated I get at the whole thing. This isn't something I want to talk about with the kids, so I wait until we get home.

It's eight-fifteen by the time we get back home. Walking in, I tell the kids, "Y'all need to get ready for bed."

Once they head upstairs, I turn to Alton, and say, "We need to talk…in the bedroom."

We walk into our room and close the door. He sits down on the bed, and I ask, "Was that her?"

With this puzzled look and asks, "Who?"

"Don't treat me like I'm stupid!" I say, raising my voice. "You know exactly who I'm talking about. Was…that…Traci?"

"I told you," he says, sounding exhausted. "She's a patient. She needed someone to talk to."

"Then why'd you go outside?"

"It's confidential."

"Bullshit," I snap back. "I'm not stupid. I saw you outside. There's something more to it."

"What are you suggesting?" he asks.

"I don't like it," I continue, "and I don't trust her."

"I understand why it might affect you like this," he says sounding like my therapist rather than my husband. "You were cheated on by someone you loved. Naturally, those feelings are going to affect how you process my professional relationship with a female patient."

"Stop it!" I demand. "That's a bunch of shit. I've seen you with female patients for years. I saw the way she looked at you. I saw the way she talked to you. I saw the way you talked to her."

"What are you talking about?" he asks.

"Oh, please," I say, crossing my arms. "Thank you for *squeezing* me in," I mimic, exaggerating her pathetically sweet voice.

"It wasn't like that," he says, with a huff.

"You think I didn't see the way you put your hand on her arm?"

Calm and tempered, he says, "You're making way too much out of this."

"Really?" I ask, now getting pretty angry. "She sure knew who I was. The second she saw me, she practically froze like she just saw a ghost."

"Honey…honey," he says, trying to calm me down. "You're getting upset over nothing."

I shake my head, dismissing this same lame argument men use to make women feel like it's all in our heads. I squeeze my arms that are still crossed, and say, "I don't know what's going on, but I don't like it. I want you to stop seeing her."

"I'm not *seeing her,*" he says. "I'm her therapist."

I clench my fists in front of him, and say, "Then I want you to stop being her therapist."

Alton looks at me in disbelief. I've never been this demanding—even the last time some girl started calling our house. As I stand here not backing down, he shakes his head and says, "I can't do that."

Now fuming, I lift up my hand between us, look away, and say "Alton!" like he's seconds away from making the biggest mistake of his life.

"I can't," he repeats. "She's in a very fragile state."

"I don't give a damn," I shout.

He comes to me, puts his hands on my arms, and says, "I understand, given your background, why you're upset. But she's suicidal and I'm the only one here for her. If I tell her I'm letting her go, it will push her over the edge. You just have to trust me."

"Well, I don't trust you!" I say, pushing away, much louder and edgy. "I don't trust her and I don't trust you."

He sits here staring at me like he can't believe what I'm asking—or demanding. After I continue to stare right back at him, he says, "I don't know what to say. I can't just release her…not now."

I'm so tempted to give him an ultimatum—it's either her or me—but I resist the urge to go there. "Then when?" I ask.

"I don't know. When she's a little stronger…more stable."

With my hands on my hips, I shake my head, and say, "She better get stronger soon…and I don't want her calling you anymore."

He holds up his hands and says, 'Okay…I'll talk to her."

I storm out and slam the door. The *bang* is much louder than I intended. It's the first time an argument between us has gone this far.

– CHAPTER 12 –

He must have thought things would return to normal, but they don't. Over the next three weeks, I don't interact with him when he comes home, and I don't talk to him at dinner. I spend the weekends away from the house, running errands and going places with the kids.

I cannot stop this feeling inside me that something's not right. I know the date and time we were at the restaurant, so I log into our cell phone accounts and search for the number that came in while we were eating at the restaurant. I find the number and search through his other calls. He's been talking to her regularly for the last six months. Not every day, but a couple of times a week. Some calls are quite long. Next, I scan through his texts. I can't see what they're typing, but the texts have been going back and forth, beginning at the same time.

The truth is, I don't know what the hell to think. This isn't the first time he's given his cell phone number out to those patients who need it—both men and women. When I think about the way this woman looked at him, and how he touched her arm, I can't help but think the worst. But Alton is right. This *is* his job—I knew it when I married him. I know he forms a bond with his patients…it's part of the profession. He's never given me any reason to doubt him before. Then again, maybe I've been too trusting. Maybe I've been blind because I'm not the jealous type—-at least not with him.

I want to know the truth. I want to know what's going on.

– CHAPTER 13 –

Two weeks later, I'm cleaning up the kitchen around noon, when I look out the window and see Trevor waist deep in water beside a tractor that's digging holes for the posts. I know he works hard out in the hot Texas sun so I sometimes bring him lunch, a pitcher of water, or a cold beer. As quick as I can, I make two plates, each with a sandwich cut in half and a side of chips. It's not the kind of sandwich I typically make the kids. The toasted bun is piled high with turkey, a slice of avocado, lettuce, tomatoes, oil and vinegar, paprika, salt, and pepper. I walk outside holding each plate and ask, "Want some lunch?"

"Sounds great," he says, pulling himself out of the water in one quick jump. He walks over to the patio table, peeks inside the sandwich, and says, "You need to open a sandwich shop."

"Hold on," I say, and run back inside, grab two cold beers, and come back out.

We sit at the patio table, and he eats his sandwich like he hasn't eaten in days. He takes a big drink of his beer and says, "Thank you…that hits the spot."

I take a sip of my beer, put it down, and ask, "I don't know how you work out here in this heat?"

"Ah, I don't mind," he says, with a smile. "I like it outside. It felt a lot hotter when I was working for someone else."

We sit here as a Jimmy Buffett song plays from his radio outside the boathouse. I start to sing along, stop and ask, "You like country music?"

"Does the music bother you?" he asks. "I can turn it down."

"I love country music," I say with a smile. "I used to go dancing all the time."

"You country dance?" he asks with a look of surprise. "I wouldn't have thought."

"Why not?"

"I don't know," he says with a shrug. "I guess I just see you around here. You got boots?"

"Boots, jeans…even a western belt with a big belt buckle."

"A regular cowgirl, huh?"

With a smile, I say, "I used to dance every Saturday night…but I haven't country danced since I got married."

He leans back in his chair and asks, "Why not?"

"I don't know. My husband isn't really into dancing…or country music."

We sit in the afternoon sun, relaxing for a bit. Then I say, "Before I got married, my boyfriend and I went dancing every weekend. We had this move we made up. We called it *our move.*"

Taking one last drink, he sets his empty beer bottle on the table and says, "Show me."

"Show you?" I laugh like he must be kidding. "You country dance?"

"Every chance I get," he says. "Show me."

"I can't," I protest, saying "no" but sounding more like I want to say, "Hell yes."

"Come on," he says, standing up and reaching out with both hands for me to grab hold.

I believe in being faithful—not because of some ink stains written on a book thousands of years ago, but because of my own moral code that I've always carried inside me. I think it came from listening to all the screaming when my mom came home late or didn't come home at all. Even when I knew my boyfriend was cheating, I could never do the same thing back—even if it was only to get back at him. Cheating just isn't in me.

But thinking about this Traci girl's face when she batted her pretty little eyes at my husband makes me feel like a fool sitting here at home day after day, never so much as looking at another guy. *"Thank you for 'squeezing' me in."* The way he reached out and slid his hand down the side of her arm. I think about those calls and text messages during our family time together and all the other calls when I'm not around. *I asked him. I asked him to stop seeing her, but he chose. I might not have said it's her or me, but that's exactly the choice he made.*

"I just want to see it for myself," Trevor continues, as he reaches down and slips on his boots. "Maybe I'll get some stares out on the dance floor."

"Oh gosh," I laugh, taking hold of his hands. I let him pull me up from my chair and onto our make-shift dance floor.

Standing in front of me, he keeps his left hand in mine and puts his right arm around my waist. His strong hand looks large around my tiny fingers. I put my other hand on his shoulder and feel the muscles in his back.

With Toby Keith playing in the background, we start sliding across the patio. *He has done this before.* He's smooth and his boots never leave the ground as we glide forward. *God how I've missed this.* After a few more steps, I gaze up into his eyes but quickly look down when he looks back into mine. "I'm not sure if I can teach it," I say, trying to remember all the steps. "He did everything. I mostly followed his lead."

"It's okay," he smiles. "Do the best you can."

When I agreed to do this, I didn't consider just how sexual this actually is. *"You two need to get a room. You looked like you were making love out there."* It starts from the very beginning. In a flash, I think about calling the whole thing off but I don't.

I take his hand and place it just above my left breast, his palm about an inch above my nipple. As soon as he touches me, I move his hand to my shoulder and say, "I forgot how intimate this is."

He moves a little closer and says, "Just show me."

I throw my head back, take a deep breath, and put his hand back on my chest. I'm wondering if he can feel my heart pounding, knowing my nipple is only one slight graze away. I take a deep breath and say, "Okay, his hand on my chest was my cue. It'd tell me we're about to do this."

We take two more steps before I stop. I release my left hand from his and put it on top of his hand that's on my breast. "Now with your hand here, you give me an easy push back."

When his hand pressed against my breast, something stirs inside me. I move back on his cue and say, "Now I move slowly to your right and then you turn me quickly to the left for a spin."

We go through the steps in slow motion. When my back is turned to him, I say, "Now here you spin me two times back to the right."

On the second turn, I say, "Now keep your arm extended like this…I'm gonna duck down and go under it. Give me your hand when I come back to you."

After I duck under his arm, I put my hand back in his and we're standing face-to-face.

"That's it?" he asks.

"Well, not yet," I say, trying to let go of his hand. "The rest gets a little more sexual."

He holds my hand a little firmer and says, "We've come this far…show me the rest."

Still standing in front of him, I say, "We kinda got this next part from *Dirty Dancing*. You lift me up until my chest…well, let's just say my shoulders…are eye level to your eyes. Then slowly lower me back down to the floor in front of you."

He puts his hands on my waist and lifts me off my feet with no effort at all. There's something so sexy about a man sweeping you off your feet right in front of him. Obviously deciding against the shoulder suggestion, he stops when my breasts are right in front of his face. My boyfriend would usually reach in and kiss my cleavage, but I leave that part out. He pauses for just a second like he's seen *Dirty Dancing* before. As he slowly lowers me back down in front of him, we're so close my breasts graze against his chest. As our faces pass by each other, we're only inches apart.

He's biting his lower lip with a smile and his bright blue eyes mesmerizing me. As he lowers me back to my feet, I'm breathing heavily, and say, 'Now turn me once to the right and stop when we're side by side, both facing the same way."

After I spin once, I let go of his hand for a second to wipe away the beads of sweat that have formed above my lips from a combination of the Texas sun and the adrenalin surging through my body. "Now I fall back into your right arm for a couple seconds and you put your left hand back where it started."

He cradles his arm, and I fall back. Just as he brings his hand closer to my chest, I shake my head and say, "I can't. It's too…"

"Too what?"

"Too close."

Laying back with him holding me in his arms, I feel my heart racing in my chest, so I exhale loudly with my lips puckered like I'm trying to whistle. I look down, breaking his gaze, and say, "I think you get the idea."

The smile on his face reminds me of this gorgeous man I once saw on a poster hanging in an Abercrombie and Fitch store window, wearing jeans and nothing else. I let go of his hand and return to the patio table. I pick up the plates and beer bottles and say, "I've got to get some things done." I point behind him and say, "And you need to finish our boathouse."

– CHAPTER 14 –

Something stirred in me that day. I felt a fire inside me that I thought had long burned out. I start listening to country love songs again and I open the window when Trevor's working outside to listen to whatever he's listening to. Now I put it on in the car, which catches the kids off guard.

"When did you start listening to country music?" Bekah asks.

"I've always liked country music," I say, turning the volume up a bit. "Don't you like it?"

"Uhh…no!" they all say, at about the same time.

So, I'm a little more selective when they're in the car. After a couple days of Kacey Musgraves, the Dixie Chicks, and Taylor Swift for good measure, they're soon singing along.

I turn to our son who's now seven years old and say, "You need to learn how to country dance."

"Mom…no!" the girls pipe in.

I look at him in the rearview mirror and say, "You'll see one day. There's nothing sexier than a man who can dance."

Bekah looks up from her phone and says, "Gross."

Nothing really changes between Alton and me. I've pretty much determined that I'm not going to budge until this girl gets stronger—or whatever. We're pretty cool to each other as we go about our evenings and weekends. To the kids and any outside observers, they'd never know anything is wrong. Then all hell breaks loose.

I usually vacate the bedroom by nine-fifteen and come back about two hours later. But tonight I decide to take a late bath with all the extras—the door locked, lights off, a lemon and honey bath balm, two candles flickering on each side of me, a glass of red wine…well you get the idea.

While drying my hair with a towel, I open the door when I hear Alton's phone buzzing from the nightstand at nine twenty-five. Not aware that I'm watching, he leans over to read the text and smiles a little. He clicks his phone closed and leaves it face down on the nightstand.

Ten minutes later, standing in my bathrobe with a towel around my wet hair, I walk by and ask, "Who's texting you at this hour?"

"What?" he asks, in a lethargic state like he was already asleep.

"I heard your text. Who was it?"

He sits up a little, takes a deep breath, and closes his eyes.

"It was her?" I ask, like I can't believe what I'm hearing…or not hearing.

He rubs his eyes and says, "We had a session today. She wasn't doing well. She just texted me to tell me she's okay."

"Jesus!" I snap. "I told you to tell her not to call you outside of work."

"I did…I told her."

I think about demanding his phone, but quite frankly, in that moment I don't really care.

"She called at exactly nine twenty-five. How did she know?"

"Know what?"

I spell it out like I'd talk to my kindergarteners, "How…did… she…know…you…go…to…bed...at…nine…thirty?"

"She doesn't know," he insists. "It's just a text."

I close my eyes, and ask, "How's her therapy going?"

"She's doing—"

"You know what?" I interrupt. "I don't give a damn. She can text or call you all she wants. Hell, she can move into the guestroom and you can have a *consultation* whenever you want. Better yet, I'll move into the guestroom."

I walk over to the bed, grab my pillow, and walk out, slamming the door for real this time. It *booms* through the house like someone fired a gun. I grab a blanket from the closet and take my place in front of the television.

He startles me when he comes up from behind about twenty minutes later in his stupid pajama bottoms and a t-shirt. He stands beside me and says, "I know you're angry. I think we should talk about it."

I hit mute on the remote control. Still looking at the television, I say, "That's just it…I'm not angry at all."

"You're not angry?" he asks.

"Nope," I answer, still staring forward. "The truth is…I don't really care."

He comes from behind the couch, stands beside me with his hands on his waist, and repeats, "You don't care?"

I look right at him, fake a smile, and say, "Nope…I don't care at all."

"A little more time, that's all I—"

I stop him with a little laugh and say, "Maybe I wasn't clear. I…don't… care. We wouldn't want to hurt her precious little feelings, or her self-esteem, or whatever the hell we'd hurt. I'm so past this now."

He puts down his head and says, "I wish you'd trust me here."

I grab my pillow and blanket and pop up from the couch. "Oh my God," I shout. "Are you listening? I don't care!"

Trying to catch me as I walk by, he asks, "You don't care about her calling me, or you don't care about me?"

I shake my head with a huff, walk up the stairs, and go into the guest bedroom. I know more than Alton thinks I know. I've never known Alton to lie to me, but lying and affairs go hand in hand like salt and pepper shakers. It's the one thing I'm sure he'd never tell me the truth about.

– CHAPTER 15 –

The next day, I see the kids off to school and take my cup of coffee into the bathroom. I wash my face and look up at the mirror. Then I lean in a little closer to see myself up close for the first time in a long time. I have faint lines under my eyes, a hint of purple from staying up late at night, and my skin isn't as radiant as it was ten years ago. My hair looks full and as good as ever as long as I pluck out the straggling grey strands that pop up every now and then. I may not look like a twenty-something, but in some ways I look better than ever.

I strip off my nightgown and look at myself in the mirror—turning from one side to the other. My breasts actually look better now that they're a little bigger after having three children. The rest of me is a different story. I'm about fifteen or twenty pounds heavier than I was in college. My stomach still has a post-pregnancy pooch, my arms could be firmer, and most of the weight I gained went straight to my butt where it found a home. But the best part of me is still my legs. Yeah, they need to be toned, but they're still here.

I pull out some shorts, a t-shirt, and my running shoes from the closet and head out the front door for a run. The minute I get to the sidewalk, I cut right and head out on my first jog since I was in college.

Two weeks later Trevor is busy out back. Coming in from my daily jog, I jump in the shower, wash off, and put on a little makeup. I put on my white shorts and my old bathing suit top that accentuates my breasts.

It's eleven fifteen when I go into the kitchen to search for the fastest way to a man's heart. Gone are the simple turkey sandwiches. Thirty minutes later, I walk out the back door with oven baked chicken, fried rice with olive oil, soy sauce, and veggies. Two slices of garlic bread rest on each side of the plate. Now the cold beer is in a chilled beer mug.

I walk out, sit on one of the patio chairs facing the boathouse, and wait for him to come out. He finally walks by, wiping the sweat off his forehead, and wearing jeans and a grey t-shirt.

"Lunch?" I ask.

He walks up to the table, and says, "What's all this?"

"Thought you might be tired of sandwiches."

He sits down cautiously and gives me a *what's going on* look.

For the past two weeks, I've gone jogging every day and eaten salads, which is working wonders, so I mostly pick at my food and watch him devour his. He finishes his chicken, wipes his mouth, and says, "This chicken was delicious!"

I repay his compliment with a welcoming smile.

He scoops up some rice and veggies onto his fork, takes another bite, and says, "This is the best rice I've ever eaten."

"I'm glad you like it."

I look over at the boathouse and say, "It's really coming along. How much longer will it be?"

"I hope to have it done in the next two weeks."

Shit, I think, but don't dare say. Two more weeks and I'm right back here all alone with my dishwasher, vacuum cleaner, and Tuesday laundry days.

"Two weeks?" I ask.

"Yep, two more weeks and I'll be out of your hair.

"Won't you have some touchups or something?"

"I don't think so," he says, drinking his beer. "But if you see something, I'll come back and take care of it."

"Great," I say, "I'm really excited. Can I see it?"

He finishes up the last of his rice, downs his beer, and stands up from his chair. I reach up for him to take my hand and help me out of my chair.

We walk to the boathouse and he asks, "You haven't been in here?"

"I was waiting for the steps," I answer.

As we get closer, he says, "Yeah, they're going in tomorrow."

Instead of climbing up like a toddler trying to get out of his crib, I move in front of him and ask, "Can you give me a hand?"

He puts his hands on my bare waist and lifts me up. I turn around and offer him my hand, even though I know he doesn't need it. Once inside, I look around and say, "Wow! I had no idea you were doing all this. It looks really nice."

We walk over to the sink and he says, "There's a sink and a mini-fridge." We walk to a door in the back. He opens it and says, "And a full bathroom to rinse off when you and the kiddos come back in."

He points up and says, "Look up. There's plenty of storage for all your boat equipment and toys. There are stairs over here to walk up."

I take two steps up while he puts his hands on my waist for support. I catch him looking at my legs. I peek into the storage and say, "There's a lot of room up here."

When I'm done, I turn around for him to lower me to the floor. He points over to a box on a shelf in the back and says, "This is what I'm working on today. It's a security system in case anyone breaks in here. There are cameras, both inside and outside. You can adjust them or toggle them on and off right here."

I can't believe the detail. He's obviously proud of his work. "This is absolutely amazing," I beam. "I was expecting a boathouse—you know, a garage for the boat. I could live out here."

"If you like camping," he laughs.

I smile again, and say, "I love camping."

We walk out of the boathouse, but this time he goes first and helps me down. As he lowers me down in front of him, he says, "A little camper *and* a country dancer."

I delay my response to give us time to walk over to the dock and sit down. I hope he follow me…and he does. As soon as he sits down, I ask, "Want another beer?"

He gives me a smile and says, "Why not?"

I jog inside and come back with two beers. I hand him one and sit in the chair beside him. I take a drink and say, "I love camping. I used to work at this restaurant off the lake in New Braunfels. I'd go kayaking, paddle boarding, or tubing all the time. I love to sit out by a fire and sleep in a tent."

Sounding surprised, he says, "You are full of surprises."

"Do you camp?"

"Of course," he smiles. "Camp, hunt, fish, jet ski, go boating, just about anything outdoors."

"Oh!" I say, reaching out and patting his hand resting on the arm of his chair. "One of my old buddies had a jet ski and would take me with him. I love to jet ski."

My hand stays on his for more than a second, so he looks at me trying to figure out what's going on.

When I finish telling him about the jet ski, I release his hand, grab my beer, and take a drink. He looks over at me and asks, "Not to get too personal, but what's a girl like you doing here?"

I lean back in my chair, take another sip of beer, and close my eyes, taking in the sun. Then I say, "I ask myself that question all the time. I used to love camping on the river." Making air quotes, I say, "'But sleeping outside with snakes, and insects, and a bunch of partying college kids' doesn't appeal to him. He talked about renting an RV once, but to me that isn't camping."

He nods a little and says, "I know what you mean."

I open my eyes, look over at him, and say, "You know I used to play volleyball in high school?"

"Really?"

"All-district."

"That's impressive."

I set my beer in my lap and continue. "I like—or used to like—playing volleyball, ultimate frisbee, going camping, hiking, rock climbing… everything. I always wanted to get certified to scuba dive one day."

"I love scuba diving," he interrupts. "It scares most women."

"Not me," I say. "I love to snorkel. I can hold my breath when everyone else swims up. Every time I see scuba divers on television, it makes me want to get certified."

He looks over and says, "So, no country dancing, camping, hiking… nothing?"

"Nope," I answer. "He won't even go bowling."

"Sounds like a match made in heaven."

I press my lips and huff through my nose. "Don't get me wrong, Alton is a good man. His life is perfect if that's what you're wanting. We're just very different. My ideal vacation is going to Hawaii, laying on a beach in Barcelona, or hiking up Machu Picchu. We've gone to some really nice places, but we spend most our time in every museum in town. I like museums…I do…but two weeks of it gets old."

He gives me a nod and says, "Why don't you do it, anyway? Take the kids and do whatever you want to do?"

"I don't know," I say with a shrug. "It's different when you're the woman. The man kind of sets the tone for things. If the man likes to fish…there's fish on the walls. They like to hunt…deer heads are on the walls. They like museums…fine art is on the walls. I've thought about taking the kids, but it's pretty hard doing it by myself. Plus, I think they've gotten used to this way of living. It's all they've known. If I took them camping, they'd probably sit on their phones complaining the whole time. It would have been different if I had married someone else and they were raised that way."

"Makes sense," he says.

I lean over my chair and start picking the label off the bottle. Talking quieter, slower, and with more emotion, I say, "I hear a lot of women complain that their husbands control them. Alton would never do that. Still, I feel like I'm slowly losing myself. I guess we all grow up, get married, and lose ourself along the way to some extent, but I feel like I'm not the person I want to be. I didn't dream about big houses and fancy cars. All I wanted to do was teach school. I really, really loved it. But after the kids were born, I agreed to stay home."

"Why?"

"Alton wanted me to stay home after our first child was born. By the third child, it was a losing battle. Alton was home schooled by a nanny and butlers or something. His whole family pressured me. His mom's a pediatrician and cited all these statistics. They made me feel selfish…and maybe I was. I eventually gave in."

"So you don't like it here?" he asks.

I look down, shake my head, and say, "I don't like it here…not really. It wasn't so bad when we lived in town, but way out here I feel kind of trapped. These people around here are so fake. They wave when they drive by and then pull down their garage door, lock themselves inside, and I never see them again. I think I'm supposed to join some coffee club, or this bingo dice game they play on Wednesdays, but that's not my thing. You know my friend who comes over?"

"In the tiny bathing suit?"

"Yeah…that's her. I think she's in love with you, by the way." He laughs and I say, "She's the only real person around here. If it weren't for her, I think I'd go insane."

"Jesus," he says.

I look at my watch and say, "Shit, my kids will be home in a while. I've got to get some things done." I pause a second to build up the courage to ask what I came out here for. I turn to him, point to the radio where The Zach Brown Band is playing, and ask, "Will you take me dancing?"

He tilts his head in disbelief and asks, "Are you sure?"

"It's just dancing, right?"

"Sure," he shrugs.

"Harmless."

"I guess," he says with a smile.

"Then will you take me?"

"Sure…when?"

"Every week or two Alton speaks at a conference somewhere. He wrote this book, *When Therapy Fails. E*ver read it?"

"I think I missed that one," he says with a smile.

I shake my head and say, "Me neither, but everyone in the psychology world has a copy. Anyway, he'll be gone this Thursday and will return on Saturday. How about Friday night?"

"The Broken Spoke?" he asks.

I've been there a couple of times years and years ago. I give him a full-teeth smile, and say, "Sounds great. The kids go to bed at eighty-thirty. How about we meet there at nine-thirty?"

"Sounds good," he says, and goes back to the boathouse.

Over the week, things stay the same between Alton and me. Although it was never said, I think he knows it was her or me. I make sure dinner's on the table at six-thirty, clean up the table and the kitchen, watch a little television without talking, and he heads to our…his bedroom at nine-thirty. As soon as he leaves, I flip the channel to the kind of shows I enjoy and head up to the guest bedroom a few hours later.

Except for us sleeping in different rooms, nothing has really changed. The kids don't even know we're sleeping in separate rooms. They never see us kiss, but they never saw us kiss, before. They never hear us making love…but that falls under the same umbrella. Nope, our home still looks perfect.

– CHAPTER 16 –

Trish comes over on Friday and we lay out back. This time I come out in my new, tiny, two-piece. The second I walk out the back door, she takes one look and says, "Holy shit! Look at you."

"You like it?"

"It's not the bathing suit I'm talking about. You look hotter than a two-dollar pistol. What you been doing?"

"I started jogging every day and I went on a diet. I've lost fifteen pounds."

"Lay your fine-ass down here," she says, patting the dock beside her.

We lay there listening to Trevor's country music and all I can think is, *I'm going dancing tonight!* I slide my bathing suit top down so it's right above my nipple, open my legs a bit to allow the sun to shine on my thighs, and prop one leg up so I can tap to the beat of the song on the radio. Then I hear cowboy boots tap across the dock. Shading my eyes, I see him standing about ten feet away, staring down at us. He has electrical wire hanging on his shoulder. I give him a smile and he smiles back.

After he walks into the boathouse, Trish looks at me, then over at him, and asks, "What is going on?"

I give her a smile, roll my eyes, and say, "Oh, nothing."

She sits up and says, "Any fool can see that smile wadn't nothin,' and you might as well strip your bathing suit top right off. You obviously lost all that weight for someone…so tell me what's going on."

"Nothing really," I say. "We've spent some time talking…that's it."

"By the look you just gave each other, that must be some talk."

"Okay," I begin, and stop to gather my thoughts.

"I knew there was an ok," she laughs. "You got to spill your guts now."

I lean closer and whisper so Trevor can't hear me talking. "Okay…we danced *one* dance up there on the patio."

"You're shittin' me?"

I shake my head and say, "I'm not shittin' you."

"To this?" she asks.

"I love it."

"Oh, I get it," she nods. "Country dancin,' rubbin' all up on each other… very sexy."

"Kind of sexy," I agree. I take a deep breath and say, "If I tell you something, do you promise not to tell anyone?"

"I promise...I promise."

"Not even your husband."

"Cross my heart."

'Okay…we're going dancing tonight."

She sits up and screams, "Holy shit!"

I glance at the boathouse and say, "Shhhh."

She leans forward and whispers, "What about Alston?"

"Alton," I correct her. "He's gone. He went to speak at some conference."

She raises her sunglasses and says, "Paige, you know I love you. Do you know what you're doing?"

I sit cross-legged in front of her and say, "I guess we haven't talked in a while. I took your suggestion. I went to his office in my sexiest dress—"

"And no panties?"

"And no panties. I showed up, and this woman was leaving. They didn't know I was there, and she smiled at him with this look…you just had to see it. He reached out and stroked her arm. This is the guy who won't even kiss his own wife in public. Then, she turned and saw me. The look on her face told it all."

"Wait…wait," she says, waving her hand. "You think Alston is screwin' this girl?"

"I don't know. I looked at our cell phone bills and they've been calling and texting each other for six months."

"I told you," she says shaking her head, "They dogs…they *all* dogs."

"I told him weeks ago to stop seeing her. He denied it…said it's transference. You ever heard of it?"

She shakes her head.

"It's when a patient develops feelings for their therapist."

She shakes her head again and says, "I don't give a shit what they call it. You can put lipstick on a pig, but it's still a pig."

"What?"

"They can call it some fancy word, but it's still the same thing." Then she stops and asks, "Wait a minute…wait a minute. What about the sexy dress with no panties on?"

"I spent two and a half hours getting ready. I sat on the edge of his desk and put his hand on my breast. I pretty much put his hand between my open legs. It did nothing. I got down and tried to open his pants to—"

"Blow him?"

"Yeah," I whisper, looking towards the boathouse so Trevor can't hear. "I tried to blow him."

"And?"

"Nothing. He stopped me. He said he had an appointment."

"Bullshit!"

With a shrug, I say, "He did have an appointment."

She laughs out loud and says, "If I showed up at Cliff's work in a tiny dress, no panties, and wanting to give him a blowjob, he'd quit his damn job so fast it'd make your head spin."

I look over, squinting from the sun in my eyes, and ask, "You think he's seeing this girl?"

"Hell yes, he's screwin' that girl. I told you."

I put up my hand and say, "You know, I don't even care. If I was in love with him, maybe I would, but I'm not. We're just too different. I really wish love was something I could simply will into existence. If so, I would have been in love by now. But love doesn't work like that. Lord knows I've tried."

"So you don't love him?" she asks.

I lean back and say, "That's a different question. I do love him—or care about him—but it's like the way you love your dad or your brother. But I'm not *in love* with him. I've never been *in love* with him."

"You wadn't pregnant," she says. "Why'd you marry him?"

"I don't know. I just broke up with my boyfriend who I loved so much. Look where that got me—heartbroken. I think I was determined to find someone who wouldn't cheat on me. Then Alton came along. He was so sweet and sensible. We were like best friends, but I knew he wasn't the one for me. I tried to slow things down. I even tried to break up with him once, but he wouldn't let it go. Next thing, he's back, and I'm standing in a big church about to get married. I wasn't as assertive back then. I knew I shouldn't do it, but things had gone too far. I didn't know how to stop the whole thing."

Trish gives me this serious look and says, "Paige, I know how you feel. You know that boyfriend who can't talk right no mo'?"

I nod.

"Well, he's my second baby daddy. I was twenty-one. He was good to me, but…I don't know…I was young and not ready to settle down. I started messin' around with this other guy. Well, he found out and went ballistic. He took off to his parents with our baby. I went over there and was bangin' on the door like some rabid dog, so they called the cops. The cops said it wasn't kidnapping because it was his baby too. I didn't have no money for an attorney, so I knew I couldn't win. When he went to court I wasn't even there. He got full custody of our baby. The papers gave me one hour a week visitation. Can you believe that shit? *One* hour and it was *supervised*! I think they were afraid I'd run off with her…which I would have. I also had to do drug testing, which I failed. I had to take these stupid anger classes I couldn't afford." Tearing up a little, she says, "I've never seen my baby again. She's sixteen now."

I don't really believe in all this hoodoo stuff, but I have to ask. "I thought your mom put a hoodoo curse on him. Did you get your daughter back?"

She puckers her lips and says, "Nope…I guess that wadn't justice."

I lean in and take her in my arms. She sits back up and says, "Anyway Paige, that was the biggest mistake of my life. They always find out…just like you did with your boyfriend. They always find out, and when they do, it never turns out good."

I nod my head to acknowledge everything she's saying. Then I say, "It's not like that. We're not having an affair. We're just going dancing. Do you know how many times I've asked Alton to go dancing, or camping, or hiking…or just have fun? Before we got married, I kept doing the things *I* enjoyed. Then I was raising kids and my old friends either got married or moved away. Next thing, I stopped doing these things. It was okay when I was teaching, because it fulfilled me, but then I had to quit my job." I look down and say, "I don't know the answer right now, but I can't keep going like this. I know you have to change when you get married, but I don't know who I am anymore. I get up, make breakfast, get the kids off to school, clean the house, cook dinner at five-thirty, and watch television until I fall asleep. I don't know who this person is who I've become…but it's not me. She looks like me; she talks like me; but she's not me. But the person I am is still here, deep inside me, waiting to get out. If I don't do something soon, I really believe I'm going to regret it for the rest of my life."

She puts her hand on my shoulder and says, "I understand what you're saying."

"I really believe this is all going to come to a head. Alton isn't being smart. I know he's getting together with this girl—maybe when he goes out of town, and I'm going back to work in six months. I'll stay until school starts. Then I'm out."

It's five-thirty and I need to start dinner. We walk inside, then stand outside the front door so we have some privacy. I barely close the door when Bekah opens the door and says, "Mom, I need a new sports bra and got to get some glitter for my project."

"Okay…just give me a second."

Jacob walks by and says, "Mom, I'm hungry."

"Dinner will be ready in an hour. Grab a snack out of the pantry to hold you over."

"What snack?"

"Whatever you want…just give me a second."

"Can I have some chips?"

"YES!"

"Geez," I say shutting the door and turning to Trish "The fact is, I'm not having an affair. I'm not looking for sex. I think he's a nice guy—that's all. All I want is to have *one* night doing what I love. Is that so bad?"

She reaches in and gives me one last hug. "I love you," she says. "I'm here no matter what you do."

Beth opens the door and asks, "Mom, can I go to Shelly's house tomorrow night? She wants to go—"

"Give me *one* second," I say, and push the door closed.

I turn to Trish, roll my eyes, and say, "Gotta' go."

"Be…..careful," she says, and we hug goodbye.

– CHAPTER 17 –

As soon as we finish dinner, we go to Target to get a sports bra for Bekah, glitter and two spiral notebooks for Beth, socks for Jacob, a pack of pens, the list of things Alton needs, toiletries, some groceries, and all the other stuff that fills our basket. It becomes a two hour ordeal.

By the time we get back home, I take a long shower and start getting ready. I do everything except for my makeup and I wait to change into my dancing clothes. At eight-thirty, I come out to kiss the kids goodnight.

I tried to keep things pretty low-key until they go to bed, but the second Bekah sees me, she says, "Mom, you look beautiful. Are you going somewhere?"

"Yeah, mom," Beth joins in. "You're really skinny."

I skip the whole question about where I'm going, and say, "Okay, okay, kids, upstairs to bed."

Back in the bathroom, I put on my makeup and spray my hair. I pull out the same jeans I wore to the Fort Worth Stockyards…what…fifteen years ago. After these past weeks of salads and running, they slip on, button up, and fit like they did when I was in college. I put on the silk shirt I just bought at Target. I slip on my boots and spray perfume on all my erogenous zones. I stand in front of the mirror and turn around to check out how I'm looking from behind. *Not bad.*

I hurry downtown and pull into The Broken Spoke parking lot in the middle of Austin. If you want to find a real Texas honkey-tonk, this is the place. From the outside, you might think you're entering a saloon or something in Tombstone in the 1800s. I walk inside to find the place hasn't changed a bit since I was here back in college.

The second I walk in the door, Trevor is standing inside waiting for me. I've never seen him cleaned up like this. He is absolutely gorgeous. He has on light blue jeans, a collared light blue shirt that's rolled up at the sleeves, and maroon Ostrich skin boots. Not that he needs any help, but the boots make him an inch or two taller.

"Paige," he says, leaning forward for a hug with a welcoming smile. When I give him a hug, he kisses my cheek. He puts his hands on my shoulder, looks me up and down, and says, "Aren't you something."

Repaying him with my best smile, I say, "You look pretty nice yourself."

We walk past the pool tables in the front, through the hallway full of 8X10 photos of famous singers and politicians hanging on the wall, and go to the cashier to pay the entry fee. The place has a hardwood dance floor, an eerily low ceiling, and large fans people stand in front of from time to time to cool off. At the back of the large dance floor is a live cover band playing old and new country music.

"Here we are," he says, looking around.

"Here we are!"

A shock of adrenalin fills me as I hear the band singing *Wave on Wave*, by Pat Green and watch people spinning around as they dance by. I reach in my pocket and pull out a ten-dollar bill, but before I can hand it to the cashier, Trevor hands him a twenty.

"I can get mine," I protest.

"No problem," he says. "This is your night. Enjoy it while it lasts."

We walk in and go straight to the bar for something to drink. "What are you having?" he asks.

The music is a little loud now, so I shout, "A beer—no, I'll take a Jack and Coke." I hand him the same ten-dollar bill.

He waves it away and says, "Put that away." He turns to the bartender, holds up two fingers, and says, "Two Jack and Cokes and two tequila shots."

We find a table and sit side by side. It's been a while since I've had a tequila shot, but some things you don't forget. I lick the spot between my thumb and pointer finger and sprinkle plenty of salt on my wet hand. We tap our shot glasses on the table, I lick the salt off my hand, down the tequila shot in one gulp, and follow it up with the lime.

"Whoa," I say, shaking my head and taking a sip of my Jack and coke.

He smiles, watching me down the entire shot. He leans over until I feel his lips touching my ear and says. "You really are a cowgirl."

"It's been a while," I smile.

We sit here tapping our feet to the beat of the music. When the next song starts, he says, "Well, you ready?"

The song is slow and has an easy beat—perfect for a warm up after a long time away. He takes my hand in his and we head out. On the edge of the dance floor, he turns to face me and puts his hand behind my back. Anyone who's danced regularly knows you dance pretty close. I wrap my left hand around the back of his neck and we start moving across the dance floor to the flow of traffic.

After one time around the room, he leans forward and says, "Damn, you're a good dancer."

"I had a good teacher. You're a good dancer too."

When the song ends, it's obvious we're both ready to pick things up. Halfway through the next song, we're turning, spinning, and moving in perfect rhythm. Anyone looking on would think we've been dancing for years. After two more songs, we return to our chairs and finish the rest of our drinks.

"Ready for another?" he asks.

Alton and I never drink more than a glass of wine and never drink Jack and Coke. "Absolutely," I smile.

He stands up and heads back to the bartender. He fills out his jeans nicely and his fitted shirt shows off his broad shoulders and trim waist. He walks with this natural confidence that's very attractive. A woman just a table away watches as he walks by; then another while he's standing at the bar. I smile, watching them watching him.

He comes back with two more drinks and two more shots of tequila. *Tap…lick…salt…tequila…lime.* "Damn," I say, shaking my head.

Back on the dance floor, I'm more relaxed and at ease. We catch the end of a fast song, but then they slow things down with *The Dance,* by Garth Brooks. He lets go of my hand and puts his left arm around my waist and his right hand on the back of my neck. I slide my fingers in his belt loops and rest my left hand on his shoulder.

As we move slowly forward to the music, he puts his head against mine. I close my eyes and lay my head on his chest. Our bodies move as one until we stop and simply sway to the music. While I'm melting in his arms, he gently kisses my neck right below my ear. A wave of excitement ripples down my neck. I continue dancing like I didn't feel what he just did.

Two more drinks, one more shot, and about ten songs later, we're out on the dance floor and he places his right hand on my breast. When I look into his eyes, he says, "You ready?"

I give him a nod and he pushes us apart. I move to his right and he turns me to the left. A couple spins and I duck under his arm. Next thing, he picks me off my feet above his head. Something about this part must cause guys to think the same thing. Before lowering me down, he leans in and presses his lips very lightly against my shirt. When the move is over, I fall back into his arms, but this time he puts his hand back where we started, just a little bit lower on my chest. The thought of his hand on my nipple causes me to smile.

Unlike most bars, The Broken Spoke closes at midnight. Before I know it, it's eleven forty-five and they just announced last call. Back at the table, I take a napkin and wipe the sweat off my face. He does the same.

"Another drink?" he asks.

"I can't. I've had too much. Maybe some water?"

I watch as he walks away and his same fan club gives him the same stares. The lady at the end smiles, but he doesn't respond at all. When the line moves forward, a redhead in jeans and a low cut top walks up beside him, gives him a big smile, and I can tell she says, "Hey, handsome." Something is said back-and-forth before he turns around with two water glasses, points them towards me, and says, "I'm with someone."

I smile.

A guy comes up and says, "Is there any way you can show my wife and I what you just did out there?"

I want to spend every minute I have with Trevor. With a smile, I say, "Maybe next time."

Watching this beautiful man in tight jeans and cowboy boots standing at the bar, I put my head down in my arms and wonder, *How did I end up where I am?*

Then I feel his hand on my shoulder. "You okay?" he asks.

I look up, dab my face again, and say, "I'm great."

He sits beside me and turns his chair so it's facing me. He takes my hand in his and asks, "What's wrong?"

Starting to tear up, I look up at him and say, "I feel like Cinderella. I'm at this wonderful ball, but I know the clock is about to strike midnight."

He kisses the back of my hand and says, "Paige…do you know I've only seen you smile…really smile…twice. Once when we danced at your house and again tonight."

I put my head back down and wipe my eyes.

He puts his hand on my back and asks, "Doesn't Cinderella get her prince in the end?"

I look up, dab my eyes and my face, and say, "It's a fairy tale."

"You can dream," he says.

I look into his eyes, put my arms around his neck, and pull him to me. I kiss his cheek, pull back so our faces are inches apart, and whisper, "Thank you. Thank you so much for this."

We walk to the bar to clear our tab and I ask, "You sure you don't want me to get some of that?"

He hands the bartender his credit card. Shaking his head, he says, "This night's on me."

After signing his credit card bill, he takes my hand and we walk out together. "Where'd you park?" he asks.

"This way," I say, with his hand still in mine as we walk to my car.

Halfway there, I ask, "Where did you park?"

He points to a gold Infinity. "Right there."

"You have an Infinity?"

"You don't think I drive my work truck all the time, do you?"

"I didn't know."

When we reach my car, I lean back against the trunk and ask, "Do you know the last time I've danced? Twelve years ago—and that was at a friend's wedding."

He steps closer and says, "You're a great dancer—one of the best I've ever danced with, and I go dancing a lot."

With a smile, I say, "A good leader makes it easy."

He gives my hand a little squeeze and says, "I hope you got what you were looking for. I'll be through with your boathouse soon but we can still be friends if you want."

"My husband is seeing another woman," I interrupt.

"What?"

"It's true. My husband is seeing another woman. I've asked him to stop, but he won't."

He looks up, laughs, and says, "You've got to be kidding me. Is he crazy?"

I shrug.

"How do you know?" he asks.

"Oh, I know."

He looks back down and stares into my eyes. With our eyes locked on each other, we move closer for a more than friendly kiss right here in public with people walking right by us to their cars. I put my hand on the back of his neck and pull him in tighter. I open my mouth and we kiss, really kiss, for the first time. Fire surges through my body. As we continue kissing, I open my legs and pull him into me. Feeling him press against me, my heart pounds in my chest as blood surges between my legs.

We kiss, and kiss, and I feel his hand under my armpit holding the side of my breast. I don't try to stop him…he's already had his hand on my breast out on the dance floor.

With my hormones raging, and not wanting things to get out of hand, I pull back, lay my head on his chest, and whisper, "Hold me."

He puts his arms around my waist, holds me tight, and I stay in his embrace.

Alton comes home the next day, thumbs through the mail as he always does, goes into the bedroom, and unpacks his suitcase. I grab a beer from the kitchen, go outside, and sit in a lounge chair out on the dock. He comes out a little later, sits down across from me, and asks, "Drinking beer in the middle of the day?"

I take a drink and nod back at him.

"Yeah," he says, "I've seen the beer in the refrigerator lately."

"I like beer," I say, looking out on the water.

We both sit here in an uncomfortable silence until he asks, "Do you want to talk?"

For the past few weeks, I've been walking around here feeling indifferent to him. The more I've thought things through, indifference has been replaced by anger. I'm angry that somehow *our life* slowly became *his life.* I'm angry that everything I enjoyed, and the things I wanted out of life, somehow faded away in the background. It all happened so gradually—like the frog you put in cold water and slowly turn up the heat until it's too late for him to get out. Several times I asked him to go dancing. When I turned on country music, he nonchalantly changed the station. Usually when I want to do something outdoors he avoids it. Now my job is to clean the house, and I do it the way he wants. Mostly, I wanted to teach, but I lost that argument too.

But thinking about these things, I realize that Alton never *demanded* anything. He'd always ask pretty nicely. No, I did it all. I moved in with him when I was pretty happy being independent. I broke up with him, but kept taking his calls and went to dinner with him as friends when I knew he wanted more. I married him knowing I was looking for someone else. I missed those pills knowing how he felt about keeping his kids in daycare.

Like the mob who makes people dig their own graves, I dug this hole for myself, one shovel of dirt at a time. I was so afraid of becoming my mom and now I've become someone I like even less. No, I can't be angry at Alton—he is who he is. I'm angry at myself. I dug this hole, and now I have to stop digging.

Picking at the label on my beer, I shake my head, and barely above a whisper, say, "No, I don't want to talk."

"You don't want to talk?" he repeats.

I shake my head no.

He gets up, and in his usual Alton way, says, "I know you need some time…and that's okay. We can talk later."

– CHAPTER 18 –

Monday morning, Trevor comes over to work on our boathouse. The closer he gets to finishing the job, the more I know I'm going to miss him after he's gone. I come out at noon with lunch and we take our places at the outside table.

For the most part, we eat without talking. Then he looks over at me and says, "Paige, I know what happened the other night can never happen again. I just want you to know that I had a really good time. I hope, in some small way, it helped you with whatever you're going through."

A little emotional, I give him a slow nod and say, "You know, I used to smile a lot."

Without saying a word, his eyes get shiny as he stares at me.

"You didn't know me back then. I worked at this little restaurant and everyone…just about everyone…commented on my smile. One guy said I had the most beautiful smile he'd ever seen."

He gives a nod, showing his kindness and empathy. Then he reaches over and puts his hand on mine.

"I had so much going on. I loved my job, would hang out with friends on the water, I played volleyball, and did some volunteer work. I didn't want to be some tycoon, but I did want to make a difference in the world somehow. Then I did it. I taught kindergarten and saw the effect I had on so many impressionable children. Each year, I watched as they took the things I taught them and moved on. They'd often come back and thank me. I know it's silly, but I felt like I was making a difference."

A smile spreads across his face.

"You know, I was nominated teacher of the year at my school."

Another smile.

I take a big drink and say, "Those babies are going to high school soon."

He squeezes my hand and says, "I hate to see you like this."

Feeling so empty, I reach forward, kiss his lips, and with my mouth only inches from his, I say, "Then take me away for a while."

He nods his head and asks, "Where?"

"I don't care. You like to fish…let's go fishing. Better yet, let's go camping."

With a smile, he says, "We can do that."

"Okay," I say, now smiling. "This Friday, I'll let Beth and Bekah spend the night with their friends. I'll take Jacob to his grandparents."

"What about your husband?" he asks.

"I'll figure it out."

For the rest of the day, I stay outside with him while he builds the stairs to the boathouse. I bring him boards and nails, and hold the tape measure while he cuts each board. Then I hold each board while he screws them in place.

At one point, he's squatting down and I come up behind him and drape myself over his back. He reaches back and runs his fingers through my hair. With a giant smile, I kiss his cheek.

He turns around, looks right into my eyes, and says, "You have the most beautiful smile I have ever seen."

That evening after dinner, I ask Alton if we can talk. When the kids get up from the table, I pick up the plates, set them in the sink, and sit back down across from him. I take a deep breath and say, "I wanted to let you know that I'm going away for a couple days."

His eyes dart down at the table, then up at me again. "Where are you going?"

Wanting to stay as close to the truth as possible, I say, "I need to get away to think about things."

He gives me an understanding nod and says, "Are you taking the kids?"

"No. I'm leaving Friday morning after they leave for school and I'll be back Sunday. The girls can spend the weekend with their friends, and your mom has agreed to take Jacob."

He leans forward and reaches for my hand, but I pull back a little. Concerned, he says, "I know you're upset about patients calling me. I'd probably be ups—"

I shake my head and say, "I don't want to talk about that."

He looks up at the light fixture and says, "I just wish you could somehow under—"

I don't want to spend this time debating this back and forth again. He doesn't know I've seen all the calls and texts and now I know everything. Cutting him off, I say, "Please stop. I know what you have to say and you know how I feel about it. It doesn't really matter anymore."

"Okay...okay," he says. "Can I ask where you're going?"

I wasn't really expecting this. "You know how I like being outdoors… well maybe you don't know anymore. Anyway, I'm going to find some place outdoors, sit by a lake somewhere, and gather my thoughts."

Friday morning, before walking out the door for work, he says, "I hope you enjoy your weekend. I'm sure a little time alone will do you some good."

– CHAPTER 19 –

I drive to a Wal-Mart parking lot where Trevor is waiting in his pickup truck. The bed of his truck is packed with a kayak, a tent, sleeping bags, lanterns, a camping stove, and all kinds of camping gear.

I jump in and joke, "Where's the RV?"

"It's in the back," he laughs.

Once we're outside of Austin, I ask, "Where we going?"

"Huntsville State Park…ever been there?" I shake my head, and he says, "It's one of my favorite places to go camping."

He thumbs through his phone and picks some music for the ride. "A little country music?" he asks.

I smile and say, "Maybe just a little."

The whole ride to Huntsville, we talk and laugh while listening to country music playing in the background.

Four hours later, we check in at the front office and drive through the park looking for our spot. This place is beautiful with tall pine trees, a big lake for fishing and boating, playgrounds, a little stage for the snake and baby alligator shows, and men and women's restrooms with showers. We catch sight of a white-tailed deer running across the road and a couple racoons and squirrels. We were warned at the office to keep an eye out for alligators.

Trevor backs into our spot and we unload the back of his truck. He grabs the tent out of a grey plastic tub and we have it set up in about twenty minutes. After putting our clothes and stuff inside the tent, he hangs a lantern on a limb and we stand there with our hands on our hips, admiring our work.

"Good job," he says.

"You did most of it," I reply.

By now it's after three o'clock and he asks, "What do you feel like doing?"

"Did you see the guys playing volleyball when we drove in? You want to go check it out?"

"Sure," he says. "I want to see what you got."

When we walk up, there's a game that's in full swing. It's not families out there with little kids. No, it's two guys and a girl on one side and three guys on the other. When one of the guys hits the ball wide, and another guy chases after it, the guy closest to us asks, "Hey guys, y'all want to jump in?"

"You sure?" Trevor answers.

At 6'3", I'm sure Trevor is welcome at any volleyball game. They probably let me in to be nice.

"Yeah," the guy says waving us in. "We can use two more. Let's put one girl on each team."

After some brief introductions, Trevor ducks under the net and heads to the opposite side of the court. I take my place in the front right. The guy on the other team delivers a fast, overhand serve to the guy in the back. He sets up the guy next to me, who spikes it down the line. We all exchange high fives. Trevor rolls the ball back under the net and we all rotate. I switch to the back.

Everyone's casually standing around on the other side, waiting to see if *the girl* can get it over the net.

"You okay serving?" Chris, the guy next to me asks. "You can serve underhand if you want."

It's been a while since I've played, but I've done this a thousand times. I might be even more rusty, except all through college I played with friends on the weekends and joined a few intermural leagues. "I'll figure it out," I answer.

"No pressure…no pressure," Trevor yells from the other side of the net.

I throw the ball two or three feet above my head and send it across the net. It hits the right back corner, just inside the line….*ace.*

"Wow!" a couple of guys shout. The guy in front of me turns around and we fist bump. Everyone on the other team takes two steps back and spreads out to cover the lines.

My next serve flies across the middle and drops in a gap between two guys on the back row…*another ace.*

"I thought you had it," one of the guys says to the other.

"It was on your side," the other guy answers.

Now that I'm warmed up, I toss the ball high above me, jump up as it comes down, and with a loud *POP,* it screams barely an inch above the net. A guy dives, gets a hand on it, but it flies off towards the water.

With the ball back in my hands, Trevor and everyone on his team, squat down with their legs spread wide in ready position.

"Cover the line," one guy yells, pointing to the very spot I have my eye on. The girl moves one big step right into position.

Wanting to show off a little for Trevor, I start three steps further back, throw the ball about four feet high in front of me, jump up on my way forward, and *BOOM!* The ball fires right at Trevor's feet. Ready and waiting, he drops down on one knee, pops the ball up with his wrists, and the guy next to him gets it back over the net. Back and forth it goes. When the ball floats down in front of me, I jump high and everyone backs up. I lightly tap the ball over the net and it falls to the ground for the point.

"Ohhhhh," the guy next to me yells and we high five.

Next, I toss the ball high, blast it over the net, but one of their guys returns it. He sets up Trevor, who crashes it over the net. I dive, get a hand on it, and keep it in play. Now Trevor gets another chance, and he doesn't let this one get away. He jumps high, smashes it straight down at the ground, and my turn serving is over.

It's pretty obvious the game has picked up a notch. For two hours, the points go back and forth. *Bamm…Pop…I got it…and set me up,* echoes across the park. We win one; they win one; and then comes the tie-breaker. I've developed a rapport with Chris, the tall guy next to me, and set him up again and again. *Point…point…point.* We give each other a double high five after each point. On game point, I put it high over his head right in front of the net. He smashes the game winner down the line.

"Yes!" he shouts, wrapping his arms around me, and lifting me off my feet. We all meet under the net and exchange handshakes.

Trevor comes over, puts his arm around my shoulder, and says, "What was that?"

"Where you guys from?" Chris asks.

"Austin," Trevor answers.

"You guys come here often?"

I look up at Trevor with a smile and say, "Not often enough."

The guy on the other side of me says, "Next time, your wife is on *our* team."

Your wife. I roll my eyes and Trevor pulls me in.

One of the guys points at a group of tents along the water and says, "We're right over there. You guys want to come over for some cold beer and a warm campfire?"

Trevor looks down at me for my thoughts. I press my hands together in front of my mouth, and give him my best *please,* puppy dog face.

"Sounds great," Trevor answers.

Walking back to our tent with his arm across my shoulder, Trevor looks down and says, "All-District, huh?"

"Yeah," I answer. "I actually got a couple scholarships out of state, but I could never afford out of state tuition even with the scholarships. Plus, I didn't want to be that far away from my boyfriend."

"I see why you miss it," he says.

Trevor walks into the tent, grabs a clean shirt, and comes back out. He pulls his sweaty t-shirt over his head, displaying the build Trish and I have ogled over in my backyard these past months.

Jesus Christ! I say inside, but keep those thoughts to myself. I grab my own fresh shirt but do all my changing inside the tent.

When I come back out, he asks, "You want to eat something first?"

We stopped at a restaurant on the way here, so I say, "I'm fine…unless you want something."

"I'm good," he says.

By the time we make it over to the guys from the volleyball court, the sun is down and they have a raging campfire going.

"There's my partner," Chris says motioning us in. "Grab a beer!"

Trevor pulls two beers out of an icy cooler and tosses one my way. We sit beside each other on a log. Four women, who must have stayed back during the volleyball game, come closer and introduce themselves.

"I heard you schooled these guys on the volleyball court," one of the girls says.

I smile and say, "I had a good time."

"There's some brisket on the table," another woman says.

This is Texas hospitality. Plus, there's something about camping out that brings folks together.

"Want some?" Trevor asks.

"A little," I say, starting to stand up.

He waves me back down and says, "I'll get it."

He comes back with a small plate for me and a bigger plate for him—brisket, potato salad, and coleslaw. Barbeque and Texas go hand in hand.

Next thing, a guy pulls out a guitar and starts playing. Soon we're singing, laughing, and drinking beer together. After about an hour, Trevor reaches out and puts his hand on my inner thigh. I look over and watch him staring into the campfire, singing, "Country roads…take me home…to the place…" I smile, lift his hand off my leg, and lace it into mine. He looks at me with a big smile and together we all shout, "West Virginia… mountain mama…take me home….country roads."

It's eleven-thirty and we've gone through about every sing-along song there is—Sweet Caroline, Margaritaville, Stand by Me, Hallelujah, Let it Be, Sweet Home Alabama, and Brown-Eyed Girl. Then one of the guys and his wife stand up and he says, "We're going to call it a night."

"Yeah, we're going kayaking in the morning," Chris says. "Y'all want to join us?"

I look at Trevor. He shrugs his shoulders, and says, "Sure!"

Walking back to our tent, Trevor catches my arm swinging back and forth and puts his hand in mine.

"I like that," I say.

He pulls me against him, holding my hand in his behind my back. He reaches down and gives me a kiss right in the middle of all these tents where God and anyone else around can see.

Back inside the tent, I spread out one of the sleeping bags and put the other right beside it. He takes off his shirt and climbs inside his sleeping bag wearing his shorts. I leave my shirt and shorts on and climb inside the other sleeping bag. Laying here on the ground with crickets, owls, and katydids, creating a melody all around us, I take a deep breath of the fresh campfire air, and say, "I love it here."

I'm exhausted from the long drive, volleyball, singing by the campfire, and all those beers. I start to doze off pretty quickly, until he whispers, "You sure are a long way away."

We both laugh, which echoes through the tent. "You have room in there?" I ask.

"I have an idea," he says.

He gets up, unzips his sleeping bag, and lays it on the floor of the tent. He lays in the middle, as I unzip mine, lay beside him, and throw my sleeping bag over both of us. We lay spooning with his arm around my waist. He kisses the back of my head and rubs his hand up and down my leg. I reach down, grab his hand in mine, and lay in his arms with our hands pressed against me. We fall asleep and wake up in the same position.

It's hard to sleep late when you're camping. With the morning sun shining in, Trevor gets up and asks, "You want some breakfast?"

I sit up, wondering just how bad I must look. My hair is probably in tangles. I grab a brush and start running it through my hair. Putting on his shirt, he says, "Don't worry, sunshine. You look beautiful."

After I get up, get dressed, and do my best to look halfway decent, I walk out of the tent and find a fire going and him fixing pancakes and bacon.

"Need any help?" I ask.

He hands me a cup of coffee and says, "Do you know how many times you've fixed me lunch? Sit down…relax…I've got this."

We finish our pancakes, bacon, and coffee and drive down to the pier with his kayak.

"You made it!" Chris says. He looks at me and says, "Let me guess…you're a world champion kayaker."

Trevor looks at me and says, "State champ."

We paddle out and follow the others as they head out. We continue across the lake and watch as a flock of birds soar across the water. An hour later, Trevor and I paddle inside a cove, stop in the middle, and drift around. I'm in the front and he's behind me when he points to the left and whispers, "Look….look right there."

"What?" I ask, not seeing anything.

"The alligator—right there on the bank."

It's so well camouflaged I almost missed it. It's big and beautiful, just sitting there so still. "Wow," I say with a smile.

He scoots down a little and lays against the back of the kayak. We exchange a smile, then he pulls me towards him so I'm lying back on his stomach with my head just below his chin. We're both looking up at the sky as he strokes my cheek with his thumb. As I feel the ripple of the water beneath us, I take a deep breath, close my eyes, and whisper, "This shouldn't feel this good."

"Why not?" he asks.

"I barely know you, but I'm so comfortable being with you."

"It's not like we just met," he says. "We've seen each other almost every day for three months."

"Still," I say, "I've been married fifteen years and don't feel this comfortable lying next to my husband. He'd never lie here like this. He'd probably be afraid some bird somewhere might see us touching in public."

We laugh as I lie on him wrapped in his arms. We slowly drift with the current in the bright sunshine. Just when I feel like I might fall asleep, I feel his hands move up my sides and rest on my stomach underneath my shirt. I look down and see the palms of his hands on my belly button and the tips of his fingers tucked just inside my shorts right above my bathing suit. Seeing his hands—feeling his hands— just inside my shorts causes something to stir inside me that I haven't felt in years. I can feel my heart beating faster until it's pounding as all the blood in my body rushes to the same spot just under his fingertips.

I catch myself breathing deeper, and faster, as I watch his hand rise and fall on my stomach to the rhythm of each breath. I cover my mouth with my hand in an effort to muffle my heavy breathing. I suck in my stomach and watch as the gap between his hand and my shorts widens. His fingertips are now touching my bathing suit bottoms.

Honestly, I'm not sure what he's doing. *Is he trying to tease me?* If he's trying to turn me on, it's working. I wonder if he knows what he's doing to me. *He has to know.*

Other than my uncontrollable breathing, I don't make a sound. On the outside, I'm doing my best to pretend I'm half-asleep. On the inside, my heart, my whole body, is racing. Seeing his hands inside my shorts so close, I feel like I'm back in high school again. I don't think I've ever been this turned on by a man's hands on my body. He, on the other hand, seems to be lying here under me like this whole thing is no big deal—the most natural thing in the world. It's driving me crazy.

Then he stirs, like he might have been asleep this whole time. He pulls his hands off my stomach and he says, "You ready to go?"

I want to say, *Hell no, I'm not ready to go! I want to stay here forever with your hands on my body.* Instead, I sit up, move back to my seat at the front of the kayak, and with a frustrating deep breath, say, "Sure, let's go."

We return to our new friends and paddle around the lake before returning to his truck.

"Ready for more volleyball?" Chris asks.

Trevor looks at me for guidance, so I say, "I don't think so. We're going fishing."

Sitting on the bank, I smile as Trevor puts a worm on his hook and another on mine. We stand up and he asks, "You want me to cast it out for you?"

I put my finger up to my lips, rock side to side, and in a childish voice say, "I know I'm just a wittle girl, but can I pweese twy?"

"Okay…okay," he says, with a laugh before taking a step back so I don't hook him in the neck.

I cock the rod back, click the release, and sling it over my shoulder. The line flies thirty feet high and soars across the lake.

"What the hell!" he laughs with wide eyes. "So I guess you've done this before?"

I press my lips together with a mischievous smile and say, "Maybe once or twice."

"When?"

"That guy I told you I dated in high school—well he loved to hunt, fish, camp… all that stuff. I picked up a thing or two along the way."

With our lines out in the water, Trevor lays back on the grass with his hands locked behind his head for a pillow. When I don't get a bite, or even a nibble, I prop my pole up on a log and join him on the grass, using his stomach for my pillow. Feeling the sun on our faces, he runs his fingers through my hair again and again.

I don't understand why so many husbands and wives can't talk about sex. They sleep in the same bed, have sex, and kiss all over each other; but don't really talk about it. They can talk about everything else, but for most couples, sex is too uncomfortable a subject. Brad and I used to talk about sex all the time—sometimes it seemed like that was all we ever talked about. Alton and I never talk about sex. If we did, it'd probably wind up in some discussion about the psychology of the human psyche.

Maybe it was partly my fault, but now I swear…swear…this will never happen to me again. I might as well start now. Looking up at the sky, I ask, "Did you know when we were lying in the kayak that your…that your—"

"Hands were in your shorts?"

I twist around, look up at him, and say, "Yeah, did you know your hands were in my shorts?"

"I did know."

"Why did you put them down there?"

"I don't know," he answers. "Something felt right. Your stomach is so soft and beautiful. I'm not sure what I was doing, but I didn't want to go too far. I'm sorry if it made you uncomfortable."

"Do you know what you were doing to me?"

"Yeah…I figured it out."

I reach back and take his hand that's been brushing my hair. I breathe deep, and say, "You were driving me crazy. I don't think I've ever felt like that before."

"What if I had gone further?"

I look back at him with a smile and say, "Oh, I think you would have felt for yourself what it was doing to me."

"Maybe I'll find out sometime."

I kiss his hand and say, "Maybe."

After two hours of mostly resting in the grass, we get two bites and no fish. I don't really care. I'm happy just reeling my rod in every now and then and casting it back out again.

Back at the campsite, Trevor starts a fire and we sit there drinking beer. After about an hour of talking, he says, "Okay, it's your choice. We can throw on some cheap steaks or cook hot dogs over the fire."

"Hot dogs! Definitely hot dogs!"

He pulls a pack of hot dogs, buns, ketchup, and mustard out of the cooler and some metal sticks out of one of the plastic bins. After eating a couple hot dogs, we melt some chocolate and marshmallows and make smores.

Wiping the marshmallow off my lips, I say, "This is the best meal I've ever had."

"Really…at this fancy restaurant?"

I grin, move my lips close to his, and say, "I'd rather eat out here any day."

He closes the distance between us and kisses me.

I pull back and say, "Do you like kissing in public?"

"Kissing you in public?" he asks. "I'm not sure I could keep my hands off of you. Do you like kissing in public?"

I give him a full face smile, kiss him again, and say, "I love it! I love your hands on me, no matter where we are."

He gives me a wink and says, "I'll have to remember that." He stops cold and says, "Hey! I think you got your smile back."

The smile on my face slowly fades, as I think about this. I slowly nod and say, "I don't ever want to lose it again."

My eyes fill with tears. One drops down my cheek. He moves my head against his chest and wipes it away. I wipe the next tear that just fell down my other cheek and say, "I'm leaving him."

He pulls back so I'm looking right at him, and asks, "You're what?"

"I'm leaving him."

"You're leaving him?"

"I have to," I continue. "If I stay, I'll lose myself forever."

"But I thought you're going back to teaching?"

"I am," I say, wiping my eyes. "But it goes way beyond teaching again. This is who I am, and I can never be who I am with him. Do you know how much fun I had playing volleyball yesterday?"

"Oh, yeah."

"I haven't had that much fun since I got married. But it's not just about dancing, or volleyball, or fishing, or sitting by a campfire. I want to laugh again. I want to be silly sometimes. I want to kiss in public. I want to be alive again."

"When?" he asks.

"I can't right now. I don't have a job. I'm going to wait until the school year starts and I'm working again. I won't be able to afford our house on the lake, but I don't want that house, anyway. I'll get the kind of place I want. Maybe I'll move back to San Marcos."

"What about the kids?" he asks.

"That's the difficult part. I really thought when we had kids that they'd be more like me—easy and carefree. But how could that happen when I'm not even like me anymore. I've raised those kids single-handedly. I do everything—cook, wash their clothes, take them everywhere, and make sure they're taken care of. I'm at all their school events and know the names of all their teachers. Alton doesn't even know their friends. He's there when it works for him. But even with this, they're more like him than they are like me. They love their life out at the lake. I hope everything I've done is enough, but if it isn't, I still have to do this."

He takes my hand and says, "If you can't wait; if you need somewhere to go; you can stay at my house."

I shake my head and say, "I can't do that—-ever again. That's how I ended up in the situation I'm in today. I don't want anyone else to prop me up again. I have to do it for myself."

"Well, I'm here. I'm here if you need me—even if it's just to talk."

While we keep talking, the fire slowly burns out. "You want me to put on a few more logs?" he asks.

I look at my watch and say, "I'm kind of tired. Are you okay if we lay down?"

With a nod, he says, "I was thinking the same thing."

Inside the tent, I kick off my shoes and socks and lay down on top of the sleeping bags. Then I hear, *Thanks for squeezing me in,* and remember the look on her face and all those phone calls. I sit up, close my eyes and shake my head. For the first time I see the life I want to live and it's not as Alton's wife. That vision changes everything.

I hadn't really planned for this moment. I unbutton my shorts and take them off. I slide down my panties and hunt though my suitcase for the best pair of panties I brought with me. I didn't pack anything to brag about. The ones I find are white, cotton, and not real sexy. I put them on and take off my t-shirt, unclip my bra, and toss them aside. I put on a clean t-shirt and lay back down between the two sleeping bags.

"Can I come in?" Trevor asks from outside the tent.

"Come on in," I answer.

He comes in, takes off his shirt, and lays down in his shorts.

Just like last night, I spoon in front of him, but this time, when he puts his hand on my leg and slides it up to my hip, his fingers find nothing but my cotton panties. He slides his hand up and down my leg a second time. Then he puts it on my stomach slides it down, and stops with his hand resting on my panties.

I turn onto my back, pull him down to me, and open my mouth to a kiss that's both intense and beautiful. For the first time in years, I feel wanted…really wanted. He slides his hand under my shirt and caresses my bare breast. I pull him down for another kiss. Then he bends down, lifts my shirt, and takes my nipple in his mouth. From the time I first needed a bra, I was always embarrassed by my nipples that would stiffen through my shirt for any reason—or no reason at all. I was the butt of quite a few jokes. Then I discovered how much this turns guys on. Well, Trevor is turned on. He sucks on my nipple and a wave of pleasure shoots through my body.

"Do you want?" He asks.

I close my eyes and give him a subtle nod.

He slowly moves on top of me, bumping knees on the way. Then he kisses me through my panties and slides them off. He starts at my left knee, and one slow kiss at a time, works his way up my leg until he reaches his destination. It's been so long, and I'm so turned on, that the moment his mouth touches me, I grab a handful of his hair and scream, "Oh, my God!"

With a big smile, he puts his hand over my mouth and whispers, "Shhh, someone's gonna call the Park Ranger."

I'm not sure how long he plans on doing this, but it only takes a minute before I orgasm for the first time in years. I hold his face in my hands, pull him back up, and whisper, "I want you. I want you inside me."

I unbutton his shorts and force them down with my foot. As soon as he starts moving inside me, I try to keep it down, but I release a pretty loud moan and call his name again and again. In this moment, I feel all the love, and lust, and desire, that I traded away so many years ago for a life of security, build up inside me. I'm right on the edge when he gives me this beautiful smile, thrusts one last time, and together we collapse in the tent.

We stay right where we are with him still lying on top of me and both of us breathing heavily. I caress the middle of his back with my hands and lightly rake my fingernails up and down his back until he falls asleep.

The next morning, we tear down the tent and pack all our stuff back in his truck. He plays Kenny Rogers on the drive home. I turn up the volume, kiss his cheek, and say, "This was the best weekend ever."

Back in Austin, he takes me back to my car. I get in, roll down the window, and he leans in for a goodbye kiss. I pick up Jacob from Alton's parents and both the girls from their friends. When I walk into the house, Alton greets us at the door.

I go upstairs, put away my stuff, and sit on the bed thinking about this weekend and my life here. At 6:15, Alton taps on my door and peeks inside. "Hey, are you going to fix something to eat or do you want to go eat somewhere?"

I shake my head and say, "I got the kids something on the way home."

He stands there baffled, like he's trying to figure out what's going on. "Can we talk?" he asks

I shake my head.

He throws his hand up and says, "We have to talk sometime."

I look down, not wanting to make eye contact, and say, "I tried that. It didn't work."

He sits down on the end of the bed and says, "About that. On Friday, I released Traci as a patient. She'll be seeing someone else from now on. No more phone calls."

This takes me by surprise. "How did she take it?" I ask.

"Mmm…she was okay. She'll be okay."

I look at him and say, "This doesn't really change anything."

With a confusing scowl, he says, "This doesn't change anything?"

I close my eyes and say, "Alton, our problems go way beyond this one girl. We're different…we're very different people."

"How are we different?" he asks.

I'm stunned by his response. I can't help but laugh. "Really? You don't know how we're different? That just shows how lost I am. I've morphed into this person…this person I'm not. I've changed so much that you don't even recognize your own wife anymore sitting right here in front of you."

He takes this better than I expected he would. With a nod, he says, "I know you gave up your job and I'm sorry."

"Are you?"

"I am sorry, but it was best at the time. It was best for the kids. Now it's time for you to go back to work."

I look right at him and ask, "Do you know I like to play volleyball?"

"Volleyball?" he says all confused. "I remember you *used to* play volleyball. Is this what you want? You want to play volleyball?"

I'm afraid where this might go if we continue. I'm afraid of the things I might say. Right now, all I want is peace…peace until school starts again. "It's okay," I say. "I'm not a teenager anymore. I probably couldn't play volleyball again if I tried."

He puts his hand on my leg and says, "Paige, I want you to be happy."

"I want me to be happy, too. I need some time to figure things out. Can you give me that?"

"Sure," he says, and walks to the door.

He turns around when I say, "Alton," rubbing the line of goosebumps on my arm. "It's really cold in here."

Looking a little confused, he says, "Hmm, I didn't turn it down. It should be on sixty-three. I'll check to make sure."

– CHAPTER 20 –

Monday morning, Trevor's truck pulls back into the drive. He walks around the side, and I meet him in back. I'm not sure how he feels after our weekend together. Maybe this was a one-time thing for him.

"Hey," I say, with a smile.

He gives me this look that says it all. I throw my arms around his neck and kiss him again.

He's supposed to finish the boathouse on Friday. Then he'll be gone. Wanting to cherish every moment we have together, I spend all week out here with him—even on laundry day. I mostly watch as he does his thing, but I help him whenever I can. We don't have sex again—he doesn't even touch me that way—but we exchange kisses and hold hands during his breaks.

On Friday morning, I meet him outside with this dark gloom all over my whole body. I kiss him hello and say, "So this is it, huh?"

"What do you mean?" he asks. "It's not like I'm dying or something." He gives me a little smile and says, "I think we'll find a way to get together."

My face lights up and I say, "Really?"

"Plus, I imagine there's a few things I'll have to touch up. Sometimes my work is a little shabby." He walks over to the boathouse steps and bounces up and down a couple of times. "Like this board. I think it's coming loose."

A little confused, I say, "I don't get it. How did it come loose with all those screws we—"

He stops jumping and gives me a grin.

I smile from ear to ear.

We walk inside and he says, "Look at that plug on the left…it doesn't work for some reason."

I shake my head and say, "Oh, that damn plug."

"You see that sink back here," he says, walking towards it. "I hooked up the cold water but completely forgot to hook up the hot."

"You *are* forgetful," I say.

"And the security system still needs to be programmed. That might take all day."

I put my hands on my hips and say, "I bet that damn thing will never work right."

We both bust out laughing.

"Don't find them all at once," he suggests. "Give your husband a chance to find some of them."

Today, all that's left (besides those touchups later) is to clean the place up. All morning we haul trash, boards, boxes, and dirt out of the boathouse. Back and forth, we walk with full hands.

I don't have on a fancy dress, I'm wearing tennis shoes instead of high heels, I have on a sports bra and cotton panties, and my hair is covered in dirt. I haven't even showered today, so I imagine I look pretty bad. When we walk back inside the boathouse, I put my hands on his shoulders, push him against the back wall, lower myself to my knees, and unbutton his jeans.

He puts his hands on my face and moves me up so I'm looking into his eyes. He shakes his head and says, "You don't have to do that. Let's make love."

The smile on my face disappears, and I look at him as serious as I've ever been. Staring right at him, I say, "You don't understand. I want to do this. I have to do this. I've never wanted to do anything so badly in all my life."

I go back down and lower his jeans. He relaxes, leans back, and lets me do my thing.

Then I look up at him and say, "You can watch if you want."

Back at the campsite, when he did this same thing to me, I thought I had died and gone to heaven. But it doesn't come close to the thrill I feel right now. Hearing him moan makes me want him more. Having him…all of him…draws me so close it feels like we're one. With him watching the whole thing, I'm not sure who's enjoying this more.

When I'm finished, I stand up, press my lips to his, and bury my head against his chest. He brushes my hair back and says, "Thank you, babe."

A big smile overtakes me and I say, "I loved it."

One more trip to the truck, and we sit down side-by-side on the edge of the dock holding hands. "You're really amazing," he whispers.

Looking out, I lay my head on his shoulder. Suddenly, I jerk up when I hear someone behind me say, "Paige…you here?"

I jump to the left and spin my head around. Trish comes walking up in her bathing suit and says, "Hellooooo…I knocked on the front door and figured you must be back here." She looks at me, and then at Trevor, and asks, "What y'all up to?"

"Just taking a break," Trevor says.

"I see that," she remarks.

Trevor lifts himself up and says, "Well, I need to run to the dump." He smiles at Trish and says, "Nice to see you again."

"Nice to see you too," Trish says with this mischievous smile.

Once he drives off, Trish lays her towel on the dock, sits down, and looks at me with wide eyes. "Well," she says, "I take it the little camping trip went well?"

I close my eyes, nod my head, and say, "It was amazing?"

"Camping was amazing?"

I smile and say, "Camping was amazing."

She puts her hand over her mouth and says, "Did you?"

I start to deny it, but instead I close my eyes and nod my head.

She leans back, pulls her hair back, and says, "Wow!"

The way she said it, I can't tell if she's happy for me or not. I imagine it's both. I shake my head and say, "I know, I know."

"Well," she says, "I can't say you didn't try. If your husband's so stupid to see his own wife in front of him, half-naked trying to save their marriage, then he don't deserve that wife." I sit down in front of her and listen while she talks. "He's an idiot. You're hot. If that didn't work I don't know what else you can do." Then, she gives a little laugh and says, "Okay, you had your fun. So what about your marriage?"

I take both of her hands and say, "I can't. I just can't do it anymore. We are just too different. Love to him is a partnership—a house, a wife at home, a good job, and our kids. All you have to do is look at his parents. It's the way he was raised and he can no more change who he is than a lion can become a lamb. Well, I can't change who I am either. Lord knows I've tried. I hate the person I've become. I feel so empty and alone. The truth is, I knew it when I married him. I knew it, but I did it anyway. I did this and now I have to fix it. I don't want to be one of these women who wakes up one day with regret. I don't want to feel like I've wasted my whole life. I don't want to hate Alton and if I stay any longer, I will."

"Damn!" she says.

"Trevor has awakened something inside me. I have no idea where it might go—maybe it won't go anywhere. Maybe he's just a moment in my life, but I never want to go back again. If I do, it will kill me."

A tear rolls down my cheek. Trish squeezes my hand and says, "I'm just afraid for you."

"What can he do?" I ask. "Divorce me? That's going to happen, anyway. Take my home? I don't want it. Take my kids? Well, then I'll see them as much as I can and make the most of it. He's already taken everything else. He's taken my spirit. He's taken my personality. He's taken my love for life."

"Just be careful," she says.

"I will. I'll stay until I have a job teaching again. Until then, I'll keep cooking dinner at six-thirty. I'll wash clothes every Tuesday. I'll make sure the cabinets are closed, and I'll freeze my ass off every night I go to sleep." We both laugh together. "I'll just keep doing the same things I've always done. I'll focus on my kids and prepare myself to lead a classroom again. No one will even know anything has changed."

I lean forward, kiss her on the lips for the first time, and wrap my arms around her.

– CHAPTER 21 –

The next day is a beautiful, sunny Saturday. A truck and large trailer stop on the street in front of our house. Sitting on the trailer is a brand new, twenty-six foot, center console, Key West boat. Alton walks out as proud as a mother hen and the kids and I follow behind him.

"Our boat…our boat," Jacob screams, running to the boat.

Alton turns to me and says, "Isn't it a beauty?"

Feigning interest, I say, "Very pretty."

"Where do you want to put this in?" the guy in the truck asks.

"There's a boat ramp a quarter mile down." He walks around the truck, opens the front door, and says, "Here, I'll show you."

The kids jump in the back of the boat and ride along.

Thirty minutes later, Alton comes puttering up in our brand new boat. The kids are all smiling and waving like crazy as they get closer.

"Come on, mom," Jacob yells.

You'd think I'd be thrilled—a boat to go out fishing on—but I know that's not the reason Alton bought it. I wave back and yell, "It's okay. I have things to do today."

Alton comes in with the kids a couple hours later and says, "The boathouse doesn't have hot water."

"Really?" I ask.

"Can you call that guy to come back out?"

"No problem," I say. "I'll call him tomorrow."

– CHAPTER 22 –

Over the next two months, Trevor and I get together when we can. He comes over once in a while during the day and we sometimes meet for lunch. Yes, we manage to have sex two more times and each time we get more and more comfortable with each other.

He's between jobs, and we agree to go hiking through the Barton Creek greenbelt. I always did my hiking around San Marcos, and the one time I tried to get Alton here, he suggested I go alone.

We park right off MoPac Expressway and head into Austin's rolling hills. We walk down a rocky trail for about half a mile through some of the most gorgeous natural scenery in Texas. As we walk through giant shade trees, Trevor reaches out and pulls me up some rocky points. We cross paths with mountain bikers, rock climbers, and people coming and going in bathing suits. Halfway there, he points to the left and says, "I just love bluebonnets."

I nod my head and say, "Me too."

Then we come to our first stop—Twin Falls. It's a beautiful place with two waterfalls pouring into a swimming area. Children, young couples, families, and teenagers are lying out, splashing around and diving off rocks. After thirty minutes of resting on a nearby rock, we jump in and swim around. I swim up to him, wrap my arms and legs around him, give him an open mouth kiss in front of all these people, and say, "Thank you. I can't believe how much everything has changed for me. This is the life I always wanted."

With a smile, he says, "You know, babe, it's like you were made for this stuff. It's hard for me to see you anywhere else."

Babe! It sounds so wonderful. I kiss him again and say, "I'm sooo happy."

We lie out for another forty-five minutes and then head back down the trail. About a mile further, we reach Sculpture Falls. It's another secluded swimming area that's a part of the Edwards Aquifer. It keeps the temperature at seventy degrees in the summer. The water is clear and beautiful and most people are hanging out above and below the falls.

Again, we lay out our blanket, but this time when he sits down, I sit on his lap facing him and wrap my legs around him. He takes his finger, moves my hair aside, and asks, "Do you know how beautiful you are?"

I kiss him, pull back, and with a smile say, "Do you know how handsome you are?"

He takes the back of his hand and softly rubs it up and down my bare stomach. Then he reaches down and pops open the button on my shorts. I look to my left and right and say, "You are too much."

He slides down the zipper on my shorts and moves his hand inside my bathing suit. Breathing heavy, with a slight moan, I say, "You…you…are so bad."

When he drops me off back at my car, I lean against the door and say, "You know what day this is?"

"What day?"

"Four months ago today, we went dancing at The Broken Spoke. It was our first real date. It was the day I was born again."

"You got your smile back."

"I got my smile back."

I put my hands on his hips, shake him a little, and ask, "When does your new job start?"

"Tomorrow."

I look at him, showing my disappointment, and say, "I will hate not seeing you for so long."

Weekends are never an option because the kids and Alton are home, so he says, "Maybe we can grab lunch one day."

"Just *one* day?" I ask.

"You're pretty far from my job. You'd have to come my way."

I pause for a second and say, "I'd drive to the ends of the earth to see you."

"It's not *that* far," he says with a smile.

"Sooooo,"I continue. "I'd like to spend the night with you."

He gives me a puzzled look.

"Well, Alton is leaving in two weeks for another conference. He leaves Thursday and will be back Friday night. I can't do the *I need to get away* thing again, but maybe…maybe you can come over after they go to sleep. I can see if the girls want to spend the night at a friend's house."

He looks up and says, "I don't know, Paige. Are you sure?"

With a confident nod, I say, "We haven't been together in weeks. I want to be with you. I want to lay next to you."

He gives it some thought and says, "Let me know."

– CHAPTER 23 –

Early Thursday morning, Alton gets up, goes through the same routine he goes through every time he goes out of town, and places his packed suitcase beside the front door. I'm cleaning up the breakfast we all just ate when he comes into the kitchen.

"I'm heading to my conference," he says.

"Where is it at?"

"Denver."

"So when will you be back?"

"My flight lands Friday night at five. I should be back by six…six thirty."

"Right in time for dinner." I say. As I load the dishwasher and fake a smile, I say, "Have fun."

He stands there for a second like he wants to say something as I load the dishwasher. Then he turns around, picks up his luggage, and walks out.

I pick up my phone and text Trevor.

Today: 8:47 a.m.

> Hey, sweetie. Hope your job is going well. The girls are going to their friends after school. Jacob is here. Come over at 10:30. Come around back and don't knock. Just text me when you're here.

Today: 8:50 a.m.

Will do. See you soon.

At 10:30, I get a text that Trevor is outside the back door. I open the door as quiet as possible and whisper, "Shhhh, come on in."

We walk through the living room and tiptoe up the stairs holding hands.

He gives me a friendly pat on the butt on the way up and says, "Nice ass."

I turn around, lift my finger in front of my lips, and whisper, "Quiet…silly boy."

Once we close the door to my room—the guestroom—he looks around and says, "So, this is it."

"Home sweet home."

I take off my robe and reveal my white nightie that shows the dark circles of my nipples. "Damn, you're beautiful," he says.

"We need to get you out of these," I say, unbuttoning his jeans.

We make love and lie in bed face-to-face with his hand on my breast. My eyes stay fixed on him and watch as he slowly falls asleep. I start rubbing his face with my thumb until he opens his eyes. Looking all sleepy-eyed, he asks, "You're not tired?"

"Mm-hmm," I say, still stroking his face. "I don't want to sleep. I don't want this night to end."

He gives me a sleepy smile and slowly closes his eyes again.

I know how hard he works. I kiss his nose and whisper, "It's okay. I'm happy watching you sleep."

Then it happened. In the middle of the night, the doorknob twists and the door opens. Jacob is standing there rubbing his eyes. 'Mom, I had a bad dream."

I throw the covers over Trevor and say, "Oh. honey…it's okay. It was just a dream."

"Can I sleep in your bed?"

Trevor puts his hand between my legs and gives me a squeeze.

I turn to Jacob, and say, "No baby. You should stay in your room. It was only a dream. You'll be okay."

Trevor falls back asleep. I'm determined to stay up all night long. I lay here, just watching him breathing. He gives a brief smile, and I wonder if he's dreaming about me. I lean down and kiss his chest. As much as I try to make this moment last forever, sometime in the middle of the night I close my eyes and doze off. I lay with my face inches from his until morning.

Wanting to make sure he's gone way before Jacob wakes up, I had set my alarm for seven o'clock. The next morning, I give him a little shake and whisper, "Sweetie…. sweetie, you've got to go."

He stirs awake, gathers his boots, and walks down the stairs and out the door barefoot. I open the door and look around for his truck. He obviously parked it down the street. As I watch him walk away, I whisper, "God, I love him."

I close the door so softly that it barely clicks.

– CHAPTER 24 –

Because Brad lied to me so many times, I swore I would never be with a liar again. I also swore I'd never lie—no matter what. It's easy to be truthful when you never do anything you have to lie about. But the reality is, an affair is a lie. There's no way to sugarcoat it. You can't carry on with someone else without lying again and again to cover it up. I'd feel worse about it, but I know from all those phone calls that Alton has been lying to me for months.

Three weeks later, Trevor comes over to fix the security system, *again*! He explains what he's doing, then asks, "You want to get away again?"

"Camping?" I smile with wide eyes.

He presses one eye shut and says, "I was thinking Miami—hang out on the beach and do a little surfing?"

I've never been to Florida, and I've never even tried to surf. The idea is exciting. "When?" I ask.

"When do you want?"

"Not this weekend, but the next."

"Sounds good."

Two weeks later, I tell Alton I'm going to visit my mom and Kristi back home. There's no conference, no sleepovers, and no grandparents to rescue him. The kids are home and Alton will have to do a little parenting for a change.

So, today I'm loading my suitcase into my car and heading to my mom's house…well kinda.

We arrive at this cute hotel on Ocean Drive right on South Beach. The second we open the door to our room we can see the incredible view of the ocean from our balcony. I jump into Trevor's arms and kiss him again and again all over his face and say, "You are the sweetest man ever!"

He twirls me around, sets me on the ground and asks, "Are you tired? Do you want to rest a bit?"

"Do you want to rest a bit?" I ask.

"Not really. You?"

"Hell no…let's go!"

We go right out on Ocean Drive and walk down the street in our bathing suits and flip-flops. "Wait," I say. "I *have* been here before."

"You have?" he asks.

"Well, kind of. I used to watch Miami Vice and this is the place. This is where it was all filmed."

He laughs, grabs my hand, and we walk further down the street.

This place is so beautiful—white buildings with colorful, beachie trim. The sun shines bright…just like I like it. We walk past restaurants, sidewalk cafés, and bars everywhere selling overpriced drinks.

I look down the street and say, "I can't wait to see this tonight."

"Oh, you will," he laughs.

We walk further down to this little shop on the corner of the street with t-shirts hanging on a rack outside. "Want to look around?" I ask, nudging him inside.

While Trevor's trying on sunglasses and looking at himself in a little mirror, I thumb through the rack of bathing suits and covers, t-shirts with prints of sunny beaches on the front, and I look through a bunch of gold bracelets and necklaces hanging on a spinner rack. I spot this charm bracelet with a little gold heart.

Trevor walks up from behind, kisses my neck, and says, "What you got there?"

I reach over my shoulder and put my hand on the back of his neck. "Just a little bracelet. I thought it was pretty."

"You want it?" he asks.

I shake my head and put it back on the rack. "Nah, I just thought it was nice."

We walk around, eat some nachos, and drink two pina coladas. We get up to leave and he asks, "How about we relax on the beach for a while?"

"Absolutely," I say.

He gives me a smile and says, "I've never seen anyone look so cute simply saying absolutely."

I put my hands around his neck, look deep into his eyes, and say, "I've never seen anyone look so cute just sitting here doing nothing."

We head down to the beach, grab some beach chairs, and lay side-by-side with our hands locked together.

"Oh my God, this was a good idea," I sigh.

He looks over at me and smiles. Then he says, "Three more months."

"Three more months?"

"Three more months and we can go wherever we want, whenever we want. Well, at least on the weekends. You're gonna be busy with a bunch of kids learning how to take a nap and break crackers on the line."

I laugh, squeeze his hand, and say, "There's a little more to it than that. It's not like when we were kids. These kids learn so much in one year."

He pulls me in for a kiss and says, "I know, I'm just teasing."

He puts suntan lotion all over my body and rubs it in—focusing plenty of attention on those trouble spots on my breasts and upper legs. Then he lays back in his chair and asks, "You want to go surfing tomorrow?"

"Absolutely."

"Are you excited?"

"I can't wait."

"You'll be great," he laughs.

That night we're back on the street, but this time the place is alive and kicking. Music blasts from the clubs and out on the street. We hit one club after another, drinking all the specialty drinks until we find a Cuban club jamming with Cuban music. People are dancing on the floor, on the tables, and on the bar.

"Wanna dance?" he screams.

"Hell, yeah!"

We combine country, rock, and a few jitterbug moves to create our own kind of Cuban dance. We're swaying, spinning, twirling, and swinging back and forth to the music. I scream in his ear, "I don't know what they're saying, but this music is awesome!"

We're not driving, so four hours later, and a boatload of rum runners, frozen margaritas, and hurricanes, I'm as drunk as I've ever been. Next thing, we're dancing in a big circle with a bunch of people we don't even know. I'm sweating, exhausted, and drunk as hell; but not ready to go anywhere. He looks like he's just getting his second wind.

Then, the music slows down. He wraps his arms around me, and I put my arms around his neck and hold him tight. He makes me feel so safe just holding me. He places his hands on my butt and the feeling of him, rubbing against me, makes me so hot I want to strip his clothes off right here. I reach up, pull his ear to my mouth, and yell, "I'm in love with your body."

In a move that brings tears to my eyes, for the first time he says, "I'm in love with *you*."

I kiss his face again…and again…and again. Each time I say, "I love you…I love you…I love you."

Dancing the night away, I stop, look right at him and yell, "This is what it's all about!"

"Absolutely," he says.

"Hey, that's my word," I tease. I pull him to me and shout in his ear above the music, "Take me back to the hotel. I want you!"

We pay our three hundred dollar tab and walk out onto the street. I'm wibbly, wobbly, and stumbly as I wrap my arm around his shoulder and lean on him for support. We take a few steps and I turn to him with a smile and say, "Yours so mush fun."

He gives me a kiss and says, "We're so much fun. I couldn't do it without you."

Drunk and half out of my mind, I throw my arms around his neck and say, "Wills you marry me?"

The surprise on his face is bigger than Texas. "You're drunk," he laughs.

"I'm sooooooo shrunk," I shout.

He takes my face in his hand, looking all serious, and says, "I meant what I said in there. I love you." He takes a box out of his pocket and says, "Here, this is for you."

I open the box and take out the charm bracelet we were looking at earlier. He takes it out of my hand and clips it on my wrist. I put my head on his chest and melt in his arms. I look up and say, "I loves you so mush, too."

After staying like that for a moment, he asks, "Do you like this place?"

I let go of him, take a deep breath of the ocean air, throw my hands up high, and scream to everyone within a hundred miles, "I LOVES SIS PLACE!"

So happy to be alive, I run across the street to our hotel. But I'm so drunk that I get halfway cross the street before I see a red convertible Mustang full of a bunch of teenagers speeding from my right.

"Paige!" Trevor screams.

I try to stop but fall forward in the street.

"Baaaaaaaam" the horn blares.

All I see is the Mustang barreling down on me. It feels like everything slows down as the car's headlights blind me. I can tell he doesn't have time to stop. In that second, I realize this is the end for me.

The driver of the car slams on his brakes and his tires scream against the road. But it's too late. I close my eyes and cover my face with my arm, knowing what's about to happen.

Then, at the speed of light, Trevor grabs my arm and yanks me out of the road.

The car skids to a stop three or four feet past the spot where I was just lying. The guy in the passenger seat jumps up, looks over the windshield, and shouts, "Fuck lady…get the hell out of the road."

Trevor throws me over his shoulder, holds up one hand, and yells, "Sorry…sorry…sorry."

Half of Miami just witnessed the whole thing unfold. When the car drives on, Trevor carries me to the other side of the street, sits me on one of the restaurant chairs, and brushes my hair out of my face. Breathing heavily, he asks "Are you okay?"

I nod my head and say, "I din't sees zat cars."

He drops his head on my lap and says, "Oh my God…Oh my God…I thought I lost you."

Still drunk, and barely able to talk, I kiss the back of his head on my lap and say, "You shave me. You shave my lives."

The next morning, I wake up with a hangover and a big bruise on my left side. I don't remember everything, but I sure know how close I came to being killed. Trevor is sound asleep beside me. I put my hand on his back and whisper, "God I love you. I want to spend the rest of my life with you."

He stirs awake and says, "Good morning, Babe," like it was just another night on the town. "How you feeling?"

I lean over, kiss his back, and say, "Like the luckiest woman in the world."

We eat breakfast and go to the South Point of South Beach, and he rents a surfboard. We walk down to the water, and I watch as he paddles out, waits for the right wave, starts paddling in, and pops up on the board like he's done this a thousand times. Back and forth he swerves with the wave, and at one point his surfboard flies up and comes back down under him.

As the wave brings him in, I run out and meet him half-way. "Oh my God," I scream. "Show me…you have to show me how to do it."

He lays the board down on the sand and tells me to lie down on it.

"You keep your weight on the back of the board," he says. I scoot back so my torso is on the board and my legs are dragging behind in the sand. "When the wave hits you," he explains, "brace for the impact. As soon as you feel it pulling you forward, paddle a little, and when you feel steady, lift up and arch your back like you're doing a pushup. Then pop up on your knees and immediately jump to your feet—all in one motion. Spread your arms and gain your balance. It's kind of like riding a bike. Look where you want to go, lean a little, and point your hands that way."

We go through each step three times, then he asks, "Are you ready to try it?"

"Let's go!" I say.

On the sand, I looked pretty good. I was ready to get out here and show off for him. But out on the water with the waves rocking the board up and down, it's a whole different game. He holds the board steady and tells me to get on. When I'm lying beside him, he says, "You have a sexy butt."

I laugh.

"Okay," he says. "I'll find your wave. When I yell, *GO,* I'll push you with the wave. Just do the same thing you did on the sand."

I know I can do this. "Go," he says, pushing me forward. As soon as he lets go I fall off the board.

Back up again, he pushes me forward. I go about six feet and fall off again. Over and over, he yells, "Go," pushes me forward, and I fall off the board, but go a little further each time.

Each time, I swim back and yell, "Again."

This goes on again and again until he pushes me forward, I steady myself, jump up on my knees, and crash off the board. I tumble round and round, pop back up and yell, "I almost did it!"

Back again, determined not to give up, I push forward, pop up on my knees, and crash down. "One more time!" I yell.

Go…push…knees…*crash.* Go…push…knees…*crash.*

Then, after I don't know how many tries, I'm up on my feet and go forward a foot or two before I crash.

"YES!" Trevor shouts.

With a few more tries, one second becomes ten, and then fifteen, and then thirty. "You're surfing," he laughs, throwing me up in the water.

We stay out in the water until dark, taking turns--him surfing and then me surfing.

Exhausted and sunburnt, we head back in and sit at a sidewalk café. He looks at me with a smile and says, "You are amazing!" When the waiter comes, he says, "This is your big day. We have to celebrate. Do you like lobster or crab legs?"

"Crab legs…for sure."

He looks up at the waiter and says, "Two frozen margaritas…keep them coming…and two of the king crab leg boils."

Waiting for our food, a lady comes by with a basket of roses and asks, "A rose for the pretty lady?"

I start to say no, but he asks, "How much?"

"Five dollars," she says, pulling one rose out and handing it to Trevor.

"I'll take the whole basket," he says, with a smile.

My eyes open wide as I sit here holding thirty-eight roses.

Sitting at the table, eating crab legs, shrimp, crawfish, sausage, and potatoes with our hands, I look over at Trevor and ask, "How many times do you wear your jeans before you wash them?"

Not understanding the question, he gives me a puzzled look and says, "My jeans? I don't know. It depends if they're dirty or not."

I drop my crab legs on my plate, lean over the table, and kiss him with a giant grin. I pull back, look into his eyes, and say, "I love you so much."

Back home, sitting at the kitchen table eating the dinner that I didn't even start cooking until a quarter to seven, Alton is visibly irritated. He takes one bite and asks, "How was your mom?"

Unsure how to answer, I say, "Oh, you know my mom."

– CHAPTER 25 –

Trevor starts another job that's three hours out of town and will last six weeks. No more lunches, no more stopping by during the day, and no more meeting him at his worksite. For three weeks, we don't see each other and it's driving me crazy.

The following Tuesday, Alton lets me know he's going out-of-town Thursday and Friday. I'm ecstatic. I text Trevor:

Today: 11:33 a.m.

> Alton's leaving next
> Thursday morning. Come
> over?

Today: 11: 35 a.m.

> 11:00?

Today: 11:36 a.m.

> Absolutely! Doors
> unlocked. Come on in but
> be QUIET! You know
> where I'll be. First door on
> right. BIG SURPRISE

At 11:05, he creeps up the stairs and opens the door. He peeks inside and asks "So, what's the big sur—"

I'm lying naked on my bed, with my right leg bent at the knee. Using a red marker, I drew a heart on my inner thigh with an arrow through it. "I'm yours," is written under it.

"Oh my God," he says, looking down at me, not with a smile, but like he's staring at the Mona Lisa.

I give him a seductive smile and ask, "What took you so long?"

I expect him to come forward and take me. Instead, he stands at the end of the bed, looks at my naked body, and says, "I don't know what I did to deserve you."

I sit up, crawl to the end of the bed on all fours, kiss him, and say, "Everything. You saved my life. I owe you my soul."

"Your soul?" he grins. "I'll be happy with your body."

"It's already yours," I smile. "Do whatever you want with it."

– CHAPTER 26 –

Every week that goes by is the countdown to the start of school, and the start of my new life. Now the kids are home for the summer, so I can't see Trevor at my house and it's very difficult to get away for a quick lunch or meetup. I keep hoping Alton will go out of town, but he doesn't. Two weeks turn into three, and then four, and then two months—still no conference.

Then, on his way out the door for work on Thursday, he stops and says, "I have a conference tomorrow in Phoenix."

"Oh," I say. "When will you be back?"

"I'm the last speaker. I'm going to stay the night and head back Saturday afternoon. Probably be back by one or two."

"Why didn't you let me know sooner?"

A little snippy, he says, "We don't really talk anymore, do we? What does it matter?"

"It doesn't," I say, returning my attention to the sink.

Part of me knows this isn't smart. If Alton finds out about my plan, it will ruin everything. Our divorce will be ugly. But the truth is, I don't really care. In one more month, I'm telling him I want a divorce anyway, and right now a month feels like an eternity. It's been seven weeks since I last saw Trevor, so I text him:

Today: 9:36 a.m.

> Alton's leaving tomorrow.
> He'll be back Saturday. I
> have to see u. Even if it's
> for a few hours

Today: 9: 38 a.m.

> I'll be there around 11:30.
> Can't wait to see you.

Today: 9:41 a.m.

> Absolutely! Come around
> back. Keep quiet. Kids are
> here.

Alton leaves at eight for Phoenix. I'm so excited. I put on some country music, turn it up loud, and dance in the kitchen like I'm holding him in my arms. Round and round I spin. Beth comes in, catches me singing and dancing, and yells above the music, "Mom! What are you doing?"

"I'm dancing."

All day long, I'm glowing with anticipation. A little later, Beth walks in the room and asks, "What's gotten into you?"

"I'm happy," I answer with a full-teeth smile. "Can't I be happy?"

"I guess," she answers.

Giving her a hard time, I say, "Doesn't dad dance around the house when I'm gone?"

"Yeah, right," she says on her way out of the room.

Then, at six o'clock, with the country music blaring, one of the kids hits the power button on the stereo. I come out of the kitchen, go around the corner, and say, "Hey!" Then, stunned and frozen in place, I say, "Shit."

It's Alton in front of the stereo.

"It's a little loud," he says, looking over at me.

"Alton….what…what happened?"

He goes over, picks up the mail, and says, "Oh, I got the day wrong. The conference is next week."

I turn away and almost cry. I walk upstairs, sit on the bed, and text Trevor.

Today: 6:32 p.m.

> He's back. Won't be able to see you. Sorry. Talk soon.

A few minutes later, Alton knocks on the door, and asks, "You in here?"

I put down my phone and pull myself together. From inside the closed door, I say, "Yeah…just straightening up in here."

Sounding a little annoyed, he says, "It's six thirty. Were you going to fix dinner or not?"

"I don't feel good," I say. "Can we order some pizza or something?"

"Pizza? Why don't you call in some Chinese food?"

"I don't care," I say. "That sounds fine. I'll call right now."

I'm so upset that my stomach is in knots. The last thing I want to do is sit at the table for an hour with Alton. I scoop some cashew chicken and rice (Alton's favorite) on each plate, but don't eat anything myself. I walk up to each kid, kiss them goodnight, and say, "I'm still not feeling well. I think I'm going to go upstairs and lay down for a while."

I go upstairs with a bottle of wine, run a hot bath, and soak in the tub. Upset, sexually frustrated, and sleepy from the two glasses of wine I drank in the bathtub, I click off the light and lay down in bed. Then I hear the television playing downstairs. I figure the kids left it on.

I walk downstairs, see Alton watching television, and say, "Oh," a little startled. "I thought the kids left the television on. It's nine-fifty. What are you still doing up?"

"I don't know," he answers. "I have a lot on my mind. I thought you were asleep."

"Okay," I say. "Have a good night."

I walk back upstairs and fall asleep.

– CHAPTER 27 –

Sound asleep, I'm in the middle of a dream when I hear a faint, "Paige," in the background. I stir a little and close my eyes to go back to sleep. Then I sit up when Alton opens the door, sounding frantic, talking low, and out of breath. I turn his way, and he whispers, "Paige…Paige… get up. Someone's trying to break in the house. Get the kids. Get the kids and lock them in your room."

"What?" I mumble, trying to gain my bearings. I rub my eyes and ask, "Somebody's what?" I look at the clock that shows 11:18 PM.

"Get the kids!" he orders.

I sit on the side of the bed, doing my best to figure out what's going on. Then, I jump up, and say, "Oh shit!" *Did he miss my text?*

I grab my robe, run down the hall, turn around the corner, and head down the stairs. I get three steps down and hear a deafening, *BAMMM,* echo through the house. One more step and I hear another loud, *BAMMM.*

The sound stops me cold. Bekah and Beth open their doors at the same time, so I scream, "Get back in your rooms! Close your doors."

I'm so sick with fear I can barely move further. I inch down three more steps until I see Alton with a gun in his hand and smoke billowing up from the muzzle. Trevor's on the other side of him, right inside the back door, wide-eyed, and stumbling backwards in shock. Clutching the gaping hole in his neck, he falls back and slams against our marble floor.

"NO!" I scream at the top of my lungs, flying down the stairs. "WHAT HAVE YOU DONE?"

"It's him," Alton says, stunned. "It's…it's the guy who built our boathouse. He was breaking into our home."

Running across the room, I fly past Alton, and drop to my knees beside Trevor. I clench his neck, trying to apply enough pressure to stop the blood that's spewing out everywhere. It soaks his shirt and pools around both of us as I lie here crying, "GOD NO…NO…NO…NO…NO."

Both my hands are soaked in blood. In what will haunt me forever, he looks right at me with a blank face. He tries to talk, but blood gurgles out of his mouth and down his cheek.

"Stay with me," I beg, still keeping pressure on his neck. I lay my head on his chest and cry, "NO…no…no…no!"

Not letting go of his neck, I turn to Alton and scream, "WHAT THE HELL HAVE YOU DONE?"

Alton takes a tiny step forward, looks down at the gun in his hand, and drops it beside us. Then he mumbles, "He was breaking in."

"NOOOO," I scream again. Shaking my head with tears falling down my nose and onto Trevor's face, I cry, "Stay with me, baby. You're going to be alright. Everything's going to be alright."

Trevor opens and closes his mouth one last time, gasping for breath. Blood gurgles down the side of his face when he mouths, "Love you." Then he takes one last breath. His face goes still, and his body goes limp.

Sobbing and struggling to breathe, I keep repeating, "Don't do that. Please don't do that."

Slumped over him, hopeless and panicking, I have no idea what to do next. I open my mouth, press it against his bloody lips, and breathe into his lifeless body. He doesn't move. I put my hands on his chest and start frantically pumping again and again. Seeing him fade away, I cry, "Don't…don't leave me…please, please, please don't leave me." I stop and breathe into his mouth again. Then I go back to pumping his chest and breathe into him a third time. When I start pumping again, and take another deep breath, Alton puts his hand on my arm and whispers, "Paige, he's gone."

Ignoring him, I cover Trevor's mouth with mine and try to breathe into his lifeless body again. This time, my gasping cry is all I get out.

"He's gone," Alton repeats a little louder.

I lean over him, pick up his head, and rock him back and forth in my arms. "Oh, baby…oh my baby," I sob, as his blood pours all over me. I look up and cry, "I can't go on without you." I know he's gone and it's all my fault. Still looking up, I pray, "Oh God, bring him back. Please bring him back and I swear I'll never see him again…just bring him back."

Then the whole world stops and the only sound is the ticking of our grandfather clock in the hallway. *Tick..tick..tick..tick.* I stare back down at his bloody face, then lean against the back door with his head now on my lap. After a few minutes, I look down at my nightgown that's completely red. I stare at my hands that are also covered in blood.

I look up at Alton, who's standing there watching me cry, like he's in a trance. He slowly shakes his head and repeats, "He was breaking into the house."

With the back of my head against the door, I'm gasping for air. The pain feels like a fire burning me from the inside out. This man, this beautiful man, is lying here lifeless on my lap and there's blood everywhere.

"What's going on?" Alton whispers.

Wiping my eyes, I stare at him with a blank face and don't respond.

"Paige," he repeats a little louder, "What's going on?"

With tears running down my face, I close my eyes and slowly shake my head. When I'm able to talk, I open my eyes, and say, "I…I love him."

He takes a step back and asks, "You love him?"

I nod my head.

We stay here with me on the floor, my dead lover's head on my lap, and Alton standing over us. He stumbles back, sits down on the second step of the stairs, and asks, "You were seeing him?"

Without answering, I glare right at him—my face filled with hate.

He bends down, takes hold of the hair on both sides of his head, and shakes his head. He looks up with red eyes and asks, "Do you know what you've done?"

Did I hear him right? "What *I've* done?" I ask.

He looks at the blast of blood splattered all over the back door, the blood still slowing oozing across the white tile, and this lifeless man on my lap. He stands up from the stairs, comes forward, and kneels down beside me. He puts his hand on my shoulder and says, "It was an accident."

I can't stop crying.

He sits down on the floor next to me and says, "You two were having an affair? What will the police think?" He touches my face that's covered in blood and looks at his own fingers. Again he touches my cheek and turns my face to him so he has my attention. "I've spent years dealing with courts and the criminal justice system. You were having an affair with the man I shot. They'll think I killed him on purpose because I was jealous. It will ruin me."

Defeated and still crying, I pull my face away, shake my head, and whisper, "I don't give a shit."

"But you know it's not true."

Full of nothing but contempt, I stare at him another sharp glare.

A few minutes pass by with me still holding Trevor and crying. Alton is sitting beside me like he's trying to figure this out. Then he says, "Paige, you're covered in blood. Go upstairs. Go upstairs and take a shower."

"What," I whisper.

"The kids don't need to see you like this. Go upstairs and clean up a little."

I look down and softly stroke Trevor's face. His eyes are open and his hair is caked in blood. I take his head off my lap and gently place it on the bloody tiles. Still in a daze, I walk up the stairs crying, one slow step at a time. When I'm at the top, Beth starts to open her door and asks, "Is everything okay?"

Covered in blood, I quickly slam the door shut, and say, "Just go back to sleep."

I get in the shower, rest my head against the wall, close my eyes, and cry. *How the hell could this happen?* I think of Trish's words when we were out on the dock, *It never ends good.*

I shake my head and whisper, "Nooo…nooo…nooo." I slide down the wall as the water rains down on me. I want to wake up again and discover this is all a horrible dream. When I open my eyes, and follow the red, bloody, water as it runs over my body and circles down the drain. It's not just blood…it's *his* blood. I take a washcloth, scrub *his* blood off my legs where I was just holding him, and kiss the bloody rag. I sit here crying and scrubbing until the water running off of me is clear again.

I get out of the shower, look at my face while wiping off the foggy mirror, and see there's still blood on my cheek and forehead. I grab the washcloth and scrub it off. Holding on to the sink for support, I ease myself down to the floor, lower my head, and start crying again.

I stumble into my room and put on some clean clothes. Then I head down the stairs but stop halfway down.

"ALTON NO!" I shout.

Stunned, I ball my hands up into fists with my eyes open wide. Alton has Trevor wrapped in the rug from his office, and he's on his knees, putting the fourth line of duct tape around the rug. The end of the carpet is seeping blood.

I run down the stairs, try to push him aside, and scream, "What the hell are you doing? We have to call the police!"

He pushes me back and says, "And what? Tell them I just killed your lover and my wife just got out of the shower from washing all his blood off of her? They'll arrest both of us."

"Stop!" I scream.

"Paige," he says, holding me back with one arm. "We don't have a choice. We have to do this."

"Do what?"

"We have to get him out of here."

Not sure what he's talking about, I repeat, "Get him out of here? Have you lost your mind?"

He puts his hands on my shoulders and gives me a shake like it might snap me out of this. "Paige…Paige," he says. "Think about it. Think about our kids. What will this do to them? Think about your job. How will you ever teach again?"

Not able to think about anything right now, I ask, "What are you saying?"

"We can make this go away—like it never happened."

Confused, I ask, "What?"

"We have to make this go away."

"How?" I shout, looking down at the floor. "Look at this place. How do we possibly make this go away?"

"It's our only choice," he says.

I put my hand over my mouth, start crying, and ask, "What are you going to do with him?"

"We'll go out on the boat."

My eyes open wide and I say, "No! I'm not going to do this! If you want to do it, you're going to have to do it by yourself."

"Fine," he says, "Go to the boathouse. There's a cinder block right inside to the right and some tie-downs hanging on the wall. Throw them in the boat."

I go out, grab the tie-downs, and toss them inside the boat. There's a cinder block, just like he said. I bend down, and with a little effort I pick it up and drop it inside the boat. When I come out of the boathouse, the back door to our house is now open. Alton is trying to pull one end of the rug out.

"I can't pick him up," he says. "You have to help me."

"No!" I shout. "I won't do it."

"I'm going to get blood all over this patio. We have to go through the grass. Bring the boat around to the right."

I ease the boat out of the boathouse and come towards the side of the house. Now he's dragged the rug to the side, and he's struggling to drag it closer. I stand there with tears streaming down my face. The boat is a little higher than the side of our lawn. When he gets Trevor next to it, I get out and watch as he leans Trevor's body against the side of the boat Then he picks up the other end of the carpet, and drops Trevor inside the boat with a *thud.*

I put both my hands over my face, and cry, "Oh my baby. I'm so sorry."

Alton climbs onto the boat, grabs a jacket and cap, and starts the motors. "Go inside," he says. "Clean everything up with bleach before the kids get up." He backs the boat up a little more, turns it hard to the right, and slowly putters down the inlet that leads to the middle of the lake.

Back inside, I look at the bloody disaster that was once our home. *Call the police,* I think to myself, but realize it's too late. He's right. At this point, who will believe me? We'll both be arrested.

I grab a cleaning bucket, a stack of cleaning rags, a brush, and a jug of bleach from the laundry room. Returning to the back entry, I don't know where to start. There's so much blood everywhere. It's all over the back door and splattered on each wall. There's a giant pool of blood right in front of the back door and spots twenty feet wide on both sides. There are blood spots on the couch and bloody footprints going across the floor and up the stairs that lighten with each step until they disappear.

It will take forever to clean this up. I get down on my hands and knees and begin with the pool of blood in the middle. I reach down and drag the rag across the blood. Immediately, it's soaked in blood. I dunk the rag in the bucket, and the water turns red when I wring it out. I repeat this again, and again, and again. *Wipe…dunk…wring,*

I look down at my hands that are again stained red with Trevor's blood, and cry. For three hours, I clean and cry; clean and cry; and clean and cry; until the tiles sparkle, the back door is bright white again, and the wall is tan with only a shadow of the blood that I just cleaned up. One step at a time, I scrub the blood out of the couch and each step going upstairs.

Alton returns at three-thirty with rollers and the spare paint from the garage. He sits everything down in front of the back door and says,

"Gather all your clothes, put them in a trash bag, and bring them back down."

I close my eyes, trying to shut him out.

"Paige!" he barks. "Put your clothes in a trash bag."

Within two hours, you'd never know what just happened. Alton sits at the kitchen table like he's thinking things over. Then he says, "We have to get rid of his car."

"What?" I ask, walking around like a zombie.

"His car…we have to get rid of it."

"He probably parked down the street."

"You have to drive behind me so I have a way back."

We walk down the street and his Infinity is parked three houses down. "The keys!" Alton says. "What about his keys?"

"I don't know. Did you check his pockets?"

Looking frazzled, he says, "I didn't even think about it."

I turn to him and say, "Alton! We can't do this. We're going to get caught. People always get caught. This is simple…his keys…and you didn't even think of it? What else didn't you think of? We have to stop all this and call the police. Just tell them the truth."

"It's too late," he says. "I just dumped his body in the middle of the lake. They'll never believe us."

"I don't care," I say.

"Hold on, hold on," he says, lifting the handle on Trevor's car door. The door pops open. He sits inside and finds the keys in the ignition. "Do you want to drive this or follow behind?"

"I'm not going to drive his car," I insist.

"Then go get your car and follow me."

We drive four miles down the road and Alton parks the car in a self-storage parking lot. He gets in my car and says, "I'll get a storage place tomorrow until I can figure out what to do with it."

By the time we get back home I'm exhausted. I head upstairs and Alton goes to his bedroom. I sit back on my bed, hugging my pillow, and cry. I think about our time together playing volleyball, fishing, and singing by the campfire. I remember our time hiking in Austin and surfing in Miami. *"This is all my fault," I cry. "You saved my life, and now I took yours."*

The next morning, Beth is the first one up. She comes downstairs, and says, "It smells like bleach down here."

"It's okay," Alton says, "I spilled something on the floor and your mom cleaned it up."

Each kid comes down, says the same thing, and Alton gives the same answer. I sit on the couch not saying a word and not cooking breakfast. I'm dying inside, looking out at the boathouse with my eyes filled with tears. I can see him walking in and out of the boathouse in his blue jeans carrying wood or wires; that day when he winked at me as he walked by; how we put down each board and he screwed them in place; how I wrapped my arms around him while he was kneeling down and he turned around and kissed me. I look over at the patio table where we shared breakfast—and our first dance. I close my eyes and the tears spill down my cheeks.

Alton comes over and says, "I've got to go. I'll be back in a little while." I wipe my eyes and give him a nod.

– CHAPTER 28 –

I walk back upstairs and lie in my bed. *How do I go on?* I'm so lost now that my whole world just fell all around me. The hurt is so deep––like a fire that's destroying everything in its path. I feel this pain in my stomach that doubles me over. I lie in a ball and cry.

As the hours slowly tick by, my body is weak and feels like it's shutting down on me. I can't sleep, have no energy, no appetite, don't want to shower, and I have no will to live—much less to move out of this bed. I'm struggling just to breathe in…and breathe out. I want to die. If it weren't that my three kids could find their mother dead in her room, I'd slit my own wrists.

Unable to move, I lay here staring at the wall. My eyes glaze over and all I see is the light from the sun slowly creep down the wall in front of me until it finally disappears. Then the room is as dark as my soul. It's like a dark cloud, or fog, that's all over me. I lie here all night long, bawling with the constant image of Trevor, covered in blood and dead in my arms.

I lie in this cold dark room, as hour after hour slowly passes by. Eventually, the sun beams back into the room and climbs up the wall. I can hear the kids outside the door getting up and around. My world has stopped turning but they're acting like it's just another day. I'm too sick and too heartbroken to get up. Then I hear Alton and the kids walk out the front door. Hour after hour passes until the sun slowly slips back down the wall and disappears again, leaving me back in the dark. Exhausted, I slowly fall asleep and dream.

I'm walking down the stairs and hear those two blasts that now sound more like two explosions. Here Alton is, still standing in front of me with that gun in his hand. And here's Trevor, right behind him clenching his neck, looking at me as if to say, what's happening? Then he crashes to the floor— except this time it all happens so slowly. I stand over him crying while his blood is pouring out everywhere—not just in the room, but throughout the entire house until Alton and I are standing in blood up to our knees. I'm kneeling down in this sea of blood and Trevor has this look...this look that says, I'm in trouble, aren't I? "Help me," he mumbles as blood gurgles out of his mouth and onto the floor. I try with every fiber of my being to save him—breathing and pushing, breathing and pushing, breathing and pushing. We're both covered in blood when he looks right at me and mumbles, "Why? Why did you do this to me?"

I jerk awake, lean over my bed, and throw up on the floor. I'm too terrified to go back to sleep. I know I'll relive the whole shooting over and over again and it feels too real. I can never go back to sleep again.

The sunlight on the wall rises and falls two more times, until Alton slowly opens the door and asks, "Are you okay?"

With four days of tears stained on my face, I glare at him. I feel as much hate as any person has ever felt for another person. He turns around and walks back out of the room.

I stay in bed and the darkness turns into light and then crawls down the wall again. Bekah and Beth open the door and walk over to my bed. Beth puts her hand on my shoulder, and says, "Mom."

Lying away from them, now facing the window, I don't have the energy to answer, nor do I want them to see me like this.

Bekah asks, "Mom, can we get you something to eat?"

Without looking at them, I shake my head and cry. A moment later, I hear the door click closed after they walk back out of the room.

Every ounce of strength I have to get out of this bed has abandoned me. The next day, when the house is quiet, I build up enough courage to slowly lift myself up. I stumble into the bathroom and look at myself in the mirror.

I see this person I don't even recognize staring back at me. She looks like someone ready to die. I open the medicine cabinet and there they are staring at me from the top shelf—the pain pills from the prescription I filled two years ago. I take the bottle down, remove the cap, and pour the pills into my hand. There are only six pills and that won't be enough. I grab the bottle of Tylenol and dump them all into my hand. I look down at six pain pills and about twenty Tylenol capsules. I think about writing a letter to my children but what would I say?

Your mom was heartbroken. I'm sorry, but I'm a coward. I took the easy way out, and now you'll never see me again.

I see no way forward. I just want out. I stare at all the pills in my hand and stuff them into my mouth. Then, I drink enough water to get them all down. I walk over to the window, shut the blinds, close the drapes, and return to my bed and cry.

I don't remember anything that happens after that. I lie in bed not thinking, or dreaming, of anything. The world has simply disappeared.

I don't know if I've been here five hours or five days. Laying here barely alive, I hear Alton screaming in the distance. I force my eyes open and see him washing my face with a cold rag in one hand and the empty prescription bottle in his other hand. My head is hanging back in his arms and my arms are dangling at my side. I open my eyes just a bit more because he's slapping my face and yelling, "Paige…Paige …Paige!" He's the last person I want to see. I pull away and lie back down on the bed. "You have to get up," he says.

What has he done? Did he pump my stomach or something? I ball over and mumble, "Leave me alone."

"Please get up, Paige."

I close my eyes and whisper, "Get out."

"You need to go to the hospital."

I shake my head and scream, "Get out!"

With the curtains now closed, I no longer know the difference between night and day. After what feels like an eternity, I awaken to a warm body pressed against the warmth of my stomach. Using all my strength to open my eyes, I see Jacob sound asleep in front of me. I stroke the hair and kiss the head of my little baby boy. He stirs awake and looks up at me with the face of an angel. Seeing me practically comatose, he starts to cry. He wipes his eyes, and says, "Mommy, wake up." When I don't respond, he shakes my arm and with trembling lips, he says a little louder, "Mom, please get up."

My one way out of this mess is gone. I pick myself up and sit on the edge of the bed, put him on my lap, and rock back and forth. With tears in his eyes, Jacob asks, "What's wrong, mamma?"

I kiss his cheek and say, "Mommie's sad."

"You're sad?"

I nod my head.

Somewhere along the way, I lost all sense of time. I pick up my phone that's still charging on my nightstand and push the side button. It's Saturday. I've been in bed for eight days.

I take Jacob in my arms, give him one last kiss, and lower him to the floor. I look on the other side of the bed and the vomit is gone. Maybe it was just a dream. I lift myself to my feet and slowly walk down the stairs, holding myself up by the handrail. When I get to the bottom step, Bekah and Beth come up and say, "We'll fix you something to eat."

Alton stands a few feet away, watching as I walk to the couch.

Bekah sits on one side of me, Beth sits on the other, and Jacob is on my lap.

Bekah gets up, goes into the kitchen, and puts some soup in the microwave. She comes back holding a bowl and spoon. She looks at me and says, "Here's some soup for you."

I look at her, try to smile with my eyes full of tears, and say, "Thank you, sweetie. Put the bowl on the coffee table and I'll try to eat it in a minute."

Beth lays her head against my shoulder and says, "I love you, Mom."

I grab a tissue, wipe my nose, reach forward, and take the soup off the table. I take a sip, then another, turn to Bekah, and say, "Thank you. I love you very much."

When I finish the soup, I want to go back upstairs and back to my bed…but I can't. I know this is a wound that will never heal. I fear if I return to the dark side, I may never come back again. I don't care about me, but now I'm thinking a little clearer, and I don't want to do that to my kids.

Eventually, Bekah and Beth get up from the couch. When Jacob gets off my lap, I get up and walk into the kitchen. The place is a disaster. For the first time, I realize how helpless Alton really is. The sink is full of dishes. Pots with food baked inside are sitting on the stove. A cereal box is open on the table with bowls and spoons scattered around. The trash is overflowing. There's a pizza box open on the coffee table along with paper plates that still have pizza crusts on them.

I go to the sink, turn on the water, and add some dishwashing soap. Alton walks up beside me and says, "I was just about to hire a maid to clean all this stuff up."

I turn, glare at him, and say, "I can't stand to look at you. Go to work."

"It was a mista—"

"GO TO WORK!" I scream, with the kids looking on.

PART THREE

A TANGLED WEB

"She must feel like Lucifer's frigid breath is running down the back of her delicate neck."

— Gabriel F.W. Koch

"Killing is not nearly as easy as the innocent believe."

—J. K. Rowling

"Those who plot the destruction of others often perish in the attempt."

—Thomas Moore

– CHAPTER 29 –

By the time Alton comes home at 6:20, the kitchen is clean, the trash is empty, and dinner is on the table. We eat without saying a word. After the kids go to bed, Alton comes into my room, stands near the door, and says, "Paige, a detective came by yesterday. I told them we couldn't talk, so he left his card. He's going to come back."

"Good," I say. "I'll tell them what you did."

Looking down, he says, "Paige…you did it too. You put the stuff in the boat and cleaned it all up."

I look right at him and say, "Then I'll tell them what *we* did."

"And what then?" he asks. "Our kids will grow up without a mother or a father. Who will raise them? Your mother? Do you really want my parents raising your children?"

I throw up my hands and ask, "What do you want from me?"

"I don't know," he says. "Eventually, they're going to come asking questions. I'll do all the talking. Just sit there acting surprised. Yes, he built our boathouse, but the job was over months ago. He came back a couple times to fix some things, but that's it."

I scowl at him in disgust.

"I had a man come over and replace the back door. The walls are repainted. We should be okay." He goes on and on about this and that— all the things we need to say.

"We never saw Trevor Friday night."

"We were at home all night with the kids."

"Our marriage is good—we have troubles like anyone else, but things are good."

I mostly shut him out. This all sounds so stupid and he doesn't know what I know. Trevor was here many times over the last seven months. We called and texted each other and ate together at restaurants. Surely they'll trace our phones. We went to Huntsville and to Miami, for God's sake.

But I don't want to go through this anymore. I want to tell the police everything. It was Alton who shot him. I was up in my room. Let him explain how he thought he was shooting an intruder. He dumped the body. I might have helped clean up, but I didn't do it. If I have to go to prison for that, then I will.

After listening to him talk without even acknowledging what he's saying, I look at him and say, "Alton, I don't love you."

He nods his head and says, "After everything that's just happened, those feelings are pretty understandable."

I shake my head and say, "Stop with all the psychology bullshit. I haven't loved you since I came to your office that day and you humiliated me."

"Is it about her—Traci? I told you, I dropped her."

I look at him and say, "I saw. I went online and saw all the phone calls and texts between you two."

He sits down on the end of the bed. Stammering a little, he says, "It's true. I downplayed it. I knew it wouldn't look good if I told you the truth, but I swear nothing ever happened. I was her therapist. You have to believe me."

I look right at him with contempt and say, "I don't have to do anything. I don't have to cook dinner when you demand, wash your clothes once a week, vacuum the floor with some ridiculous lines, close the cabinets every time I walk by, and I don't have to listen to your bullshit."

With a scowl, he says, "Listen to you. Listen to the way you talk now."

"This is me," I say. "I cuss sometimes. I like beer and hate wine. I enjoy camping, and fishing, and dancing, and surfing."

"Surfing?"

I tear up a little and say, "Yeah, I like to surf." I stop for a second before continuing. "You probably weren't sleeping with this girl—you don't even sleep with your own wife. What do you think drove me to him? But if you were, or if you weren't, I don't really give a damn."

For years, he's been the one calling all the shots. But those days are over, and I'm sure he doesn't like my new rules. He takes my hand, but I pull away.

"Just stay," he begs. "We have to show a united front. What will it look like if you leave now? Just stay until this blows over—three months tops. Just go on like nothing happened. Do what you want…start teaching. Then I'll give you the divorce. You can have the kids and I'll take care of you. You can have this house."

I give him an indignant look and say, "I got news for you. I hate this house. I don't know how I can live here for another three months."

"Fine…fine…we have plenty of money. I'll give you money to get your own house." He looks down and says, "I wish I would have gone to that conference, but I didn't. I can't take back what's done. I understand if you don't want to be with me. Start over. Start over with the kids anywhere you like. I won't stop you."

He's right. Nothing will bring Trevor back to me. I nod my head, wipe my nose, and say, "Three months?"

"Three months."

I look right at him and say, "Just stay away from me. Do you understand? Stay…away…from…me. I start school in three weeks. I'll leave in three months and I'm taking the kids with me."

"Fine," he says.

"When the police come, you do all the talking."

– CHAPTER 30 –

Well, two weeks later, the police come knocking at the door. I don't answer it. That evening they come back, and thank God Alton is home when they do. I figure they came in the evening knowing we'd both be here.

"There's two police at the door," Jacob yells across the house.

Alton opens the door and looks surprised to see a couple of cops standing in front of him. "Mr. Warren?" the first officer asks.

"I'm Dr. Warren," he says with a firm handshake. He always pulls the "Dr. Warren," crap to make himself sound important.

"I'm detective Robert Cummings."

"And I'm Detective Larry Anderson," his partner says, also accepting a handshake.

I stay on the couch not making a move to invite them in. I'm hoping Alton will handle this whole thing by himself. "Is there something we can do for you?" Alton asks.

"Can we come in?"

"Oh, sure...sure," Alton says, walking him to the couch. "How can we help you, Detective?"

I sit on the couch beside Alton, wanting to tell them the truth. When they start talking, I nod every now and then, but add nothing to the conversation.

"Mr. Warren—"

Alton corrects him again. "It's Dr. Warren."

"Dr. Warren, we're here investigating the disappearance of Trevor Evans."

"Trevor Evans?"

I understand he did some work for you?"

"Evans…oh yes! He built our boathouse out back. Would you like to see it?"

"No, I don't think that's necessary."

"Yeah, he finished a few months ago."

"Well, his sister had us do a welfare-check after he didn't return her calls. He hasn't been seen by anyone in the last three weeks."

Ready to give an academy award-winning performance, Alton looks shocked and says, "Oh, no. I hope he's okay."

"I hope so, too. When was the last time you saw him?"

Alton looks up in thought and says, "I think he's been back a few times since he finished. One of the plugs didn't work, and the sink was leaking or something, but that was months ago."

Cummings writes something on his tablet and says, "So, you haven't seen him since then?"

"No," Alton answers. "I sure hope he's okay."

The detective looks at me and asks, "And you?"

"What about me?" I ask.

"Have you seen him lately?"

Expressionless, I shake my head.

The two detectives glance at each other. "So, that was the last time you saw him?"

Trevor's truck has been here a number of times since then. I think about it for a second, and say, "Oh, he came back to fix the security cameras in the boathouse a few weeks back."

"Yes," Alton says, snapping his fingers. "He was over…what…about three weeks ago for the security system."

Cummings writes this down on his tablet, looks right into my eyes, and says, "Three weeks ago, huh?"

I just sit here.

Anderson leans forward with his hands on his knees looking more at me than at Alton. "Do you have any information that might help us locate Mr. Evans?"

I shake my head and say, "I'm sorry."

Anderson fixes his gaze on me a little too long. Then they both get up, give a smile, and shake our hands. "Okay," Cummings says. "We're just following up leads. Obviously, you don't know anything." He hands us each a card and says, "If either of you hear from him or remember anything, please give me a call. Better yet, come down and talk to us."

The second they walk out the door, I put my hand on my forehead, pace back and forth, and say, "Shit…shit…shit!"

"What," Alton asks.

"What? Were you listening? They know. They know we're not telling the truth."

He comes up, puts his hands on my shoulders to stop me from pacing, and says, "You're being paranoid. They're just asking questions. It's their job."

"Don't touch me," I say, pulling away. I close my eyes and say, "Did you see the way that Anderson guy looked at me? The way he questioned me about the last time I saw Trevor?"

"Of course," Alton says. "That's why they came. Don't worry, you handled it well."

"Alton!" I shout. "He was here. His car was parked out front, you idiot. That's why I said he was here for the security system."

"Good…you did good."

"But he was here more than that. He came here many times during the day."

He stops me and asks, "He came to our house?"

"Of course he came to our house. That's how we met."

"Did you…did you have sex in our house?"

I fold my arms and say, "I'm not going to discuss anything about us."

Raising his voice a little, he says, "I want to know."

I step back and say, "Oh, there *is* blood flowing through those veins of yours. Well, I don't give a damn what you want to know."

With rage on his face, like I've never seen before, he screams, "TELL ME!"

"I LOVED HIM!" I shout. "IS THAT WHAT YOU WANT TO KNOW? I LOVED HIM AND YOU KILLED HIM. I TOLD YOU NOT TO BUY THAT FUCKING GUN, BUT LIKE EVERYTHING ELSE, YOU DID WHAT YOU WANT." Now crying, I slam my fists against his chest and say, "I HATE YOU. I HATE YOU. I HATE YOU."

I fall down on the floor in front of him and cry on my hands and knees.

Alton turns around and walks off.

Two weeks later, I go to the introduction for new teachers at the school and check out my new classroom. I've dreamed of this day for almost a year. I bought everything to make my classroom the most amazing room in the school, but now my world has been turned upside down. I have no joy and nothing to be joyful about. All I feel is a pain so deep and nothing will change that. I actually thought about telling the principal that I've changed my mind, but I must have a job when I move out in two months. Plus, I hope teaching again will take my mind off of Trevor.

I can't think about anything but that horrible night. We had so many great times—so many moments when I looked into his beautiful face and kissed his beautiful lips—but the only image I have of him now is him dead in my lap, his skin practically white, with blood gurgling from his mouth and his blank eyes staring up at me as if directing me to save him.

I still dream about Trevor dead in my arms. But every now and then, I have another dream, and this one tears my heart out. I dream I'm in the backyard and Trevor comes from around the boathouse.

"Oh, my God. Oh my God," I scream. I run up, throw my arms around his neck, and kiss him all over his face. "Where have you been?" I ask.

He brushes the hair from my eyes and says, "I had to go away for a little while, but now I'm back."

"So you didn't…you didn't—"

He kisses my lips and says, "I'm fine. Everything's fine."

"Why did you leave me?" I ask. "I was worried sick."

He takes my face in his hands and says, "I'm sorry, babe. I didn't mean to worry you."

He takes my hand, and we walk upstairs to my room. Halfway up the stairs, he says, "Nice butt." I turn and say, "God, I've missed you,"

I'm lying in bed with the same red heart on my inner thigh. He reaches down, gently kisses the heart, and says, "Do you know how beautiful you are?"

I pull him to me, close my eyes, and say, "Promise me you'll never go away again."

When I open my eyes, he's gone.

My dream feels as real as the day I last held him in my arms. For a brief moment, I feel that same incredible love again, and I want to hold onto it forever. But it always ends the same way. I wake up and he's always gone. I'm left back in my bed wanting to die. I claw my pillow and cry so hard, saying, "Baby…oh my baby. I love you."

Then I pray for that dream again so I can hold him once more.

– CHAPTER 31 –

Three weeks into the school year, I'm actually beginning to enjoy my job again. These kids are at the age that I love so much. They love their school, their teacher, and their mommy and daddy. Every day, they come in and show me their new jacket, or the ribbon their mom put in their hair that morning, the button on their coat, or the dollar they got from the tooth fairy last night. It's such a magical age.

No one will ever say I got my smile back again, but I do manage to smile every now and then. When I do, I immediately think of Trevor and stop myself. I feel sad…or guilty. I have no business smiling. I have no right to ever be happy again.

Several teachers ask if everything is okay. I just nod my head. Usually when a loved one dies, you have support from those around you. But I have no one to support me. I'm all alone in this.

A week later, walking to my car, I notice a black sedan parked in front of the school. Detective Cummings steps out and says, "Mrs. Warren, we'd like to have another word with you, if you don't mind."

"What would you like to know?" I ask.

Sounding like he's my friend, he says, "I think it's best that we talk down at the station."

I start to tremble and ask, "Do I have to go?"

"Why wouldn't you want to go?" he asks with a puzzled look. "We're just trying to find Trevor Evans. Maybe you can help us. You want to help us don't you?"

I stand here looking at him and his black car, trying to decide what to do. "Can I take my car?" I ask.

He opens the back door and with a smile, he says, "No need. We'll bring you right back. It won't take long…I promise."

I move forward, climb inside, and he closes the door. Detective Anderson is in the front passenger seat. He looks back with a smile and says, "Hello, Mrs. Warren. Nice to see you again."

Terrified, I nod my head.

Down at the police station, we all walk into a small, white room with a desk, three chairs, and a camera in the far corner hanging near the ceiling blinking on and off.

"Want a cup of coffee…or some water?"

"Some wa—" I say, with my mouth so dry I can't talk. I clear my throat and say, "Some water would be fine."

He gives me a smile and looks over at Anderson who walks out and comes back with a glass of water.

"Thank you," I say, taking a sip. "How can I help you?"

He looks down at his tablet and says, "We were just going over our notes from our visit a few weeks back. We were wondering if you wanted to add anything."

I sit here and my eyes dart back and forth between them. Then I look down and whisper, "Add something?" I shake my head and say, "No."

Anderson and Cummings look over at each other.

"Well," Cummings says, tapping his tablet with his pen. "You said the last time you saw Mr. Evans was three weeks before he disappeared. Is that right?"

I look around, and say, "Do I get some rights or something?"

Cummings smiles at me and says, "You're not a suspect." He looks at Anderson and asks, "She's not a suspect is she?"

"Not at all," he says, shaking his head.

"Yes," I say nervously. I take a sip of my water, shaking so badly you can see the water ripple in the cup as I bring it to my lips. I clear my throat and say, "That's right."

"Hmm," he says, pressing his lips together. "Well, when was the last time you talked to him?"

"Talked to him?" I repeat. "I don't know. He was working on the boathouse and I was his main contact. We'd talk quite a bit."

"The boathouse that he finished four months before he disappeared?"

"Yes," I say. "But he had to come back to fix things."

"How many times?"

"I don't know, maybe ten or fifteen times?"

He writes this on his pad and says, "That's a lot of things to fix."

I nod my head and say, "I guess so."

"Did you see him any other times?"

"Why would I see him other times?"

"I don't know," he says. "I'm just asking." When I don't answer, he says, "Did you?"

Doing my best to provide cover for myself, I say, "We might have gone to lunch a couple of times."

He raises an eyebrow and asks, "Lunch? Why did you go to lunch?"

I can already see how difficult this is going to be. I shrug my shoulders and say, "I don't know. Sometimes he was working and was hungry, so he'd ask if I wanted to join him."

"For lunch?"

"Yes, for lunch. We might have gone to dinner."

He sits back in his chair and says, "There's no reason to be so nervous here. We're simply trying to get answers. We hope you can help us."

"I've just never talked to the police before. I've never been at a police station."

"I understand," he nods. "This might be a little uncomfortable, but we have to ask. So, all you did was go to lunch a few times?"

I nod my head.

"How are things with you and Dr. Warren?"

"Okay, I guess. We have problems like anyone else."

"Were you in a relationship with Mr. Evans?"

"In a relationship?"

"Were you having a romantic relationship with him?"

"Romantic relationship? No…why would you ask?"

He rubs his chin and says, "Mrs. Warren, we know you were in a personal relationship with Mr. Evans…Trevor. We talked to his sister and found your cards at his home."

Here we go. I sit here, not responding. Then my eyes turn red and fill with tears. I lower my head and nod a little. He hands me a tissue to wipe my eyes. Talking so low that I'm surprised they can even hear me, I say, "I couldn't say that in front of my husband."

"We understand," he says, handing me another tissue. "When did it end?"

I shake my head and say, "It didn't end."

"So this must be really hard for you."

I nod again, wiping my nose with the tissue.

"When was the last time you talked to him?"

Still looking down, I whisper, "I did text him."

"And when was that?"

"I don't know, maybe three weeks before you came to our house."

"On the twenty-third?"

"What day is that?"

He looks at his tablet and says, "It's Friday."

"I guess so."

"Because that was the day he was last seen. His sister talked to him on the twenty-third. She never heard from him again."

Wiping my nose again, I nod my head.

"Did he come over to your house on that Friday?"

Without looking up, I slowly shake my head.

"Did you meet him anywhere?"

I continue to shake my head.

"Have you talked to him since?"

"No," I whisper.

"What did you last talk to him about?"

Tears fall down my cheek. I wipe my eyes and say, "My husband was supposed to go out of town. I texted him to come over. Then my husband came back home so I texted him not to come."

"So your husband was home?"

I nod my head.

"All night."

Another nod.

"Do you think your husband might have been involved with his disappearance?"

I shake my head and say, "He didn't know I was seeing him."

"When did your relationship begin?"

Still crying and speaking softly, I struggle to get the words out. "I don't know. He was working at our house. It started pretty innocent. We kinda became friends. I guess it turned into a relationship about seven months ago."

He writes on his pad and asks, "Was he wanting to break up with you?"

Surprised by his question, I look up, look back down, and say, "No."

"Were you trying to break up with him?"

I shake my head and say, "I loved him."

"Loved him?"

I start to cry more and say, "I still love him."

He reaches out, puts his hands on my arm, and says, "Mrs. Warren, we're trying to find him…or find out what happened to him. Can you tell us anything to help?"

"I wish I could," I say, "but I haven't heard from him either."

"Nothing?" he asks.

I shake my head.

He leans closer and asks, "So, you texted him not to come over and that's it."

I nod.

"Nothing more."

I look up and mumble, "No."

He stands up and says, "Okay then, I think we're done here. I thank you for coming down and talking with us."

I get up, hand him back the water cup, and ask, "Are you taking me back to my car?"

"Of course," he says with a smile.

We step outside the room and he says, "Oh, one more thing. Would you mind if we come over to your house and look around?"

"Look around?"

"It's nothing, really….pretty standard. We just want to check you off our list and move on. It's a formality, really. Maybe we can find something there that will help us find Trevor for you."

Not sure what the hell to do, I stand here doing nothing.

He puts up his hands and says, "Unless you don't want us to look for some reason."

"I guess so," I say.

"Very well then," he says. "Give me just a second and I'll drive you back."

They both walk off and leave me here all alone. I sit back down in the chair until they come back about thirty minutes later. "Ready to go?" Cummings asks.

I nod, get up, and follow him to his car. He drives unusually slowly until we're back at the school. They drop me off and drive away. I get in my car and call Alton.

"Hello."

"Alton, they came to my work."

"The police?"

"Yes, the same detectives."

"What did you tell them?"

"They wanted me to go down to the station with them."

"And?"

"They drove me down there."

"What? Why did you go?"

"I don't know," I say. "I thought they would arrest me if I didn't."

"What'd you tell them?"

"Nothing….really."

"Nothing really?"

"I told them we were seeing each other."

"What? Why'd you tell them that?"

"They already knew. They talked to his sister and found my cards at his home."

"Okay…okay," he says. "No big deal. What else?"

"I told them I texted Trevor the day he disappeared. I first told him to come over, but when you came back home, I texted him not to come."

He pauses a moment, then asks, "Is that true?"

"That's true," I say.

"Okay…okay. Anything else?"

"That's it. Except they asked if they can look around the house."

"What?" he shouts. "What'd you say?"

"I didn't know what to say. I thought if I said no they'd be suspicious."

"So you agreed?"

"Yes."

"Jesus, Paige," he yells, "Why'd you do that?"

"Don't yell at me," I say. "I didn't know what else to do."

"I'm on my way home," he says, and hangs up the phone.

What have I done? I drive to the house to make sure everything looks okay before they arrive. When I drive up, there are four police cars parked out front and a Suburban with its back doors open. Our front door is open and men are coming in and out holding cases and stuff.

When I walk inside, Cummings comes up and says, "The back door was open. I hope you don't mind that we got started. It shouldn't take too long."

I sit down on the couch and watch as five guys spread out around our house. They briefly look through the cupboards, the shelves, and all over the kitchen. Then two guys go into our bedroom. I can see them walking back and forth and hear them opening drawers. Two more guys go up the stairs and start searching through each bedroom.

Then a guy comes in with a bottle and starts spraying everywhere. They start at the front door and spray the door, the walls, and the floor. Then they walk around spraying here and there until they come to the back door. The guy sprays the floor, stops, and directs another man with a camera to come over. The guy takes five or six pictures of the tiles. He sprays the walls and they take more pictures. Then he sprays the back door, opens it, and takes pictures of the inside, the outside, and the side of the door.

Cummings comes up to me and says, "If you don't mind, we need this area."

I get up from the couch—more spray and more pictures.

Right then, Alton comes in the front door. Cummings walks up and says, "We're almost finished and we'll be out of your way."

"Do you have a warrant?" Alton asks.

"We had consent for the search," Cummings answers.

Alton stands there watching as they spray the stairs and snap pictures of every step. He closes his eyes and slowly shakes his head.

Then the guys come down from my room carrying boxes of stuff. They carry them out to the suburban. The guys outside come through the house with more stuff in boxes.

Three hours after they started, the last guy leaves our house. Cummings comes up to me and says, "Thank you for your cooperation, Mrs. Warren." He walks by Alton, gives him a friendly nod, and with a smile, he says, "That's it. I told you it wouldn't take long."

Alton stands by the door, peeking out the window until the last car drives away. I'm sitting on the couch with my head down.

Alton turns around and says, "Why? Why the hell did you tell them they could come in the house?"

I shake my head and say, "Oh my God. Oh my God."

Alton, who's remained calm throughout all of this, starts pacing back and forth, pinching his lower lip. Now sounding shaky, he says, "Let me think. Just let me think a minute."

I look up and ask, "What was that stuff they were spraying everywhere?"

"Luminol," he says. "It's used to detect blood."

"But we cleaned up all the blood."

"It doesn't matter," he says, shaking his head. "It can detect blood that has been diluted."

"Why were they taking pictures of the back door?"

"I don't know," he says. He walks over, looks at the door, and says, "Jesus…the sticker is still on it."

"Oh, no…oh no…oh no," I say, rocking back and forth.

He walks out the back door, comes back a few minutes later, and says, "They took the security system."

I put my head back down and say, "This can't be happening."

Raising his voice, he says, "We were fine. They wouldn't have been here if you didn't give them consent."

I jump up from the couch and scream, "I TOLD YOU! I TOLD YOU NOT TO DO IT." Beginning to cry, I say, "We were going to be okay. It was an accident…a big mistake. Now you dumped him in the fucking lake and they'll never believe us."

He leans against the back of the couch and says, "Just let me think a minute."

"You can't!" I scream. "You can't think this away. We're all over that security video. What about the neighbors…and his car? How do you know someone doesn't have a security camera that caught it parked here all night?" I stop, put up my hand, and say. "It doesn't even matter. They know. They didn't take pictures of the front. They took pictures of the back tiles, and the wall, the couch, and the stairs!"

"I saw!" he snarls. "You don't think I saw?"

I put my head down and say, "Why did I listen to you? Why do I *ever* listen to you? Now we're going to prison for murder."

"Wait," he says firmly. "As long as we stick together...as long as we stick together we'll be okay."

I get up from the couch and say, "I'm not listening to you anymore. You've ruined my life. Do you hear me? You've ruined my life."

He puts his hands out and says, "Calm down."

"Calm down?" Then I scream, "CALM DOWN! HOW CAN I CALM DOWN? I'M GOING TO PRISON AND YOU EXPECT ME TO CALM DOWN?"

He sits down, and in a tempered voice, says, "We'll just tell them the blood was there from a few days ago. You were cooking and cut—"

"Stop it," I scream. "Just stop it."

"Do you have a better plan?"

I nod my head and say, "Yeah, I've got a better plan. I want the money you promised me. You're going to go to your office and get your checkbook. You said you'll give me seven hundred thousand—then we must have a lot more from all those stupid books you wrote. Write me a check for a million. We'll sort the rest out later."

"And then what?" he asks.

"Go get your checkbook," I demand.

He goes into his office and returns with his checkbook in a beautiful leather cover with a W in the middle. He puts my name on the payee line then writes, "One million—" He stops, looks up at me and says, "I have to move some money around."

When he hands me the check, I yank it out of his hand and say, "I'm depositing this check into my own checking account in the morning. If it bounces, I'll tell the police everything."

I get up, go into the closet, and pull out four suitcases—one for me and one for each of our kids. Then I head upstairs to my room.

"You're leaving?" Alton asks.

I turn around and say, "I cannot stay here another minute with you. Once I get a place, I'll meet you somewhere so you can see the kids."

"Paige," he pleads, "we can figure this out. If we just stick together, we'll be okay."

I shake my head and say, "We can't figure this out. What you did is insane. Tell them the truth. If you're lucky, they'll believe you."

"They won't," he says.

"Then maybe a jury will believe you."

"What about you?" he asks. "You're in this just like I am."

I shake my head and say, "You were the one who got rid of his body. I just cleaned things up. I might go to prison for a little while…if I do then I do."

"What will you say?" he asks.

"Nothing. I've said too much already. I'm going to shut my mouth and hire an attorney."

"Paige," he says. "You're going to stand by me…right?"

"You're our kids' father. I don't want you to go to prison, but what you did was stupid. If it comes down to it, I'll tell the truth."

"I panicked," he says.

"And you'll have to pay for it. But you don't deserve to go to prison for murder."

I turn around and head back upstairs to pack my stuff. My bedroom is a mess. I gather up what I can and go into each of the kids' rooms and pack what I think they'll want. What I don't get I'll buy.

Two at a time, I carry the suitcases out to my SUV. When I'm at the door with the last suitcase, Alton walks over and says, "Paige…no matter what happens, I do love you. I'll always love you."

Without stopping, I shake my head, and walk out the door.

I pick up the kids and head to a hotel until I can figure out where to go next. I call my school and tell the principal I'm sorry, but I won't be coming in. I'm sure she'll soon know the reason why.

A mile down the road, Jacob looks in the back and says, "What are all the suitcases for?"

I look at him in the rearview mirror and say, "We're going to stay at a hotel for a few days?"

"Are you guys getting a divorce?" Bekah asks.

"Right now, we're taking a break."

Jacob starts to cry and says, "I don't want to stay at a hotel. I want to stay with Dad."

Bekah puts her phone down and asks, "Does this have something to do with the guy who was working on our house?"

"What?" I ask. "Why would you say that?"

"Duh," she huffs. "We're not stupid."

Not sure how to respond, I say, "You're just a kid. You have no idea all the things that go on in a marriage."

"Like screwing the guy working on our house?" she mumbles under her breath just loud enough for me to hear.

I'm so shocked she'd actually say something so hateful. Without thinking, I hit the brakes hard enough that everyone is thrown forward just a bit. Looking at her through the rearview mirror, I ask, "What did you say?"

She looks back at me with this fake smile and says, "Nothing."

After everyone is settled back in and we drive a little further down the road, with Jacob still crying, Bekah looks up from her phone and says, "Well, I'm not leaving my school. All my friends are there."

– CHAPTER 32 –

After a long, sleepless night, with Jacob in my bed and the two girls in the other, I wake up the next morning and get busy looking for a house to buy. I've got to find a place where the kids can stay in the same school district. My search for homes in Austin turns up way too many houses. I narrow my search to the school district I need and find eight that I want to go look at.

The next day, I meet with a realtor and spend the entire day going from one house to another until I'm exhausted. This day was supposed to be the happiest day of my life. Instead, I'm heartbroken, scared to death, and rushing from one house to another—not looking for my dream house but a house my kids will accept.

Walking inside our fifth house, my phone rings. I figure it's Alton calling me, but when I look down, I see Trish's name on my screen. Mentally and physically exhausted, I say, "Hello."

"Paige…where are you?"

"I'm staying at a hotel."

"Paige, the police just left here. They were asking about Trevor."

"What?" I say, stepping outside so we can talk in private. "What did they want to know?"

"Everything! They asked if you were seeing him."

"What'd you say?"

"I said, not as far as I know. They wanted to know the last time I saw him at your house. They asked if I saw his truck at your house on Friday the 23rd, a couple weeks ago."

"What'd you tell them?"

"Hell, I don't know what I ate for dinner yesterday. I told them I have no idea. They kept asking me questions, but I said, 'All I know is he worked on their house.' What's going on?" she asks.

"I can't talk about it right now. I'll come over to your house after I drop off the kids tomorrow."

"Paige, they went up and down the street talking to everyone. I hope you're okay."

"We'll talk tomorrow. I'll tell you everything."

"Okay," she says, "Be careful."

– CHAPTER 33 –

The next morning, when I'm leaving the high school heading to visit Trish, a police car drives up behind me and turns on his lights.

"Shit," I say to myself, looking down at my speed. I'm only a couple miles over the limit, so I have a good idea why they're stopping me. I'm nervous, scared, and start shaking and sweating. I pull to the side of the road, and an Austin police officer walks up to my passenger window. This seems strange until I turn to my left and see Detective Cummings outside my door. *Is he going to arrest me?*

I roll down my window, stuttering and stammering, and get out, "Hell…hello, Detective Cummings. How can I help you?"

With a friendly nod, he says, "Good morning Mrs. Warren. We've had some developments in the Trevor Evans case. We'd like to have a chat with you down at the station. Maybe you can fill in the details."

"Details? I told you everything I know."

He nods again and says, "Yes, ma'am. What we found might help jog your memory."

"Do I have to go?" I ask.

"Well, we'd like to keep this friendly. Cooperating will make things a lot easier on you."

I sit here trying to figure out what to do.

"Or we can get an arrest warrant, if you want to go that route."

I definitely don't want to go that route. "I guess you want me to ride with you again?"

"Yes, ma'am, if you don't mind." He points down the road to the right and says, "Why don't you pull into that parking lot."

Once at the police station, we head to the same room as the last time. Again, we're joined by Detective Anderson. I watch as he opens his folder, look up at the blinking camera, and ask, "How can I help you, detective?"

He flips through his notebook pad until he finds a clean page, then he asks, "We just need to get a few formalities out of the way."

"Formalities?"

He goes through all this legal stuff about my right to stay silent, hiring an attorney, and something else that goes in one ear and out the other. I'm too shaken to hear what he's actually saying until he asks, "Do you understand these rights as I've explained them to you?"

I nod my head and mumble, "Yes, sir."

His tone and mannerism gets real serious—very different from the last time we were here. He folds his arms and says, "When we last spoke, you said you hadn't seen Mr. Evans in the few weeks before he disappeared. Is that correct?"

"That's right," I say.

"Never saw him on that Friday evening?"

"No, sir."

"And were you home all night?"

"Yes, sir."

"And your husband was home all night?"

I'm starting to wonder if we're going to go through the same questions over and over again. "Like I told you, he came in around five-thirty or six. He was home after that."

"And you know nothing about Mr. Evans's disappearance."

"No sir."

He looks at Anderson, back at me, and says, "Mrs. Warren, be straight with us. Did you have anything to do with Trevor Evans's disappearance?"

"No, sir!" I insist. "I love him."

"Was he breaking up with you?"

"No."

Did he strike you? Maybe you were defending yourself. A woman has the right to defend herself against an attacker. That's not a crime…it's self-defense. Just tell us what happened so we can help you."

My hands start to shake a little. "He never struck me. We were in love."

"Maybe you got into an argument. It's easy to lose your temper when you're upset. I know I sometimes lose my temper with my wife. It happens."

"We never even talked that day."

"Was there an accident? Tell me about it. Did he slip and hit his head? Maybe you just panicked. If it was an accident…it was an accident. Tell me about it."

I shake my head and say, "There wasn't any accident."

He drops his pen and says, "Mrs. Warren, let's stop the bullshit, okay? We already know from his cell phone that he left work and went to your house that night. We have a witness who saw his car parked on your street after midnight. It's pretty clear he was killed in your home. The place smells of bleach, the bottle of bleach in the laundry room is almost empty. From the stamp on it we know you recently purchased it. There's traces of blood everywhere. We got a good blood sample off the baseboard of the back door and underneath the couch. I'm betting it's going to come back as Mr. Evans's blood. When it does, it's too late for talking. You are going to be arrested. Are you listening? You're going to be arrested. Do you want that?"

I look down and shake my head.

"I've been doing this a long time. I know just by talking to you that you know more than you're letting on. I can either tell the prosecutor you cooperated and things will go well for you, or I tell him you refused to talk. Then you're going to prison for a long time. What's it gonna' be? If it was an accident, or he was hurting you, just let me know now. I want to help you, but you have to tell me the truth."

I look down and say, "I am telling the truth."

"Think about your children. Do you want them to see you being arrested?"

I tear up and wipe my eyes.

He takes a deep breath and says, "So, are you going to tell me what happened?"

Still looking down, I say, "I told you what happened."

In an about face, he stands up, looks over at Anderson, and says, "Mrs. Warren, please stand up." Confused, I look up at him.

"Please stand up," he repeats. I stand in front of him. "Please turn around," he orders.

With tears streaming down my face, I say, "So, I'm going to jail?"

He clicks one handcuff on my wrist and says, "Mrs. Warren, you're under arrest for the murder of Trevor Evans. Please put your hands behind your back."

Oh my God! Panicking, I turn back to look at him and say, "Wait... wait...I'll tell you. I'll tell you everything."

He looks back at Anderson, removes the handcuff, and we sit back down. "Now don't bullshit me," he says, with an angry tone. "I don't have time for it."

Rubbing my wrist, I say, "You're right...you're right. I'll tell you everything. He did come over that night."

Cummings settles back down in his chair and says, "Okay then."

"I texted Trevor and told him to come over Friday night. Alton *did* come back home, so I texted Trevor not to come over. I was upset I couldn't see him, so I went to bed early. Alton woke me up in the middle of the night and told me to get the kids...someone was breaking in the back door. When I realized what he was saying, I was afraid it might be Trevor at the door. I ran down the stairs and heard two gunshots. Alton was standing there holding a gun and Trevor was dead in front of him."

I still can't tell this story without tearing up. He hands me a tissue as I continue. "Alton told me to go upstairs and take a shower, because I had blood all over me from holding Trevor. When I came back down, he had Trevor." Now I start really bawling . "He…Trevor was…rolled…he had Trevor rolled up in a rug. He…he…he… started saying we need to make it all go away." I look down, wiping my nose, and whisper, "I tried to stop him. I swear to God, I tried to stop him."

When I slump over, he puts his hand on my back, hands me another tissue, and asks, "So, what happened to his body?"

I'm afraid to even say it. It sounds too horrible. I pause, and pause, and pause, until he repeats, "Mrs. Warren, what happened to the body?"

Still crying, he hands me a third tissue. Struggling to breathe, much less talk, I say, "Alton…Alton put…he put…he put him in our boat and dropped him somewhere in the lake."

I lower my head and cry. He lets me finish before he asks, "So, y'all dumped the body?"

"Alton did," I say, shaking my head. "I didn't want anything to do with it. I refused to even help him pick Trevor up. I damn sure wasn't going to go with him. He told me to clean up the blood before the kids woke up. I stayed back and cleaned everything up."

I expect them to start congratulating each other since they just cracked the case, but he looks at Anderson, turns back to me, and starts tapping his tablet with his pen. "So, your husband shot him?"

I nod my head, and say, "He did…but he didn't know he was shooting Trevor. He thought someone was breaking into our house."

He looks at me and asks, "Do you know how to drive your boat?"

"I've driven it before."

"But on this night you never drove it?"

I shake my head and say, "No, sir."

They glance at each other again.

"And Alton was there all night long?"

"Yes sir…well, except when he left on the boat."

He taps his pen twice more and says, "Mrs. Warren, do you want to spend the rest of your life in prison?"

Looking down, tearing the tissue apart, I shake my head.

"Then stop lying to us."

I nod my head and say, "I know I lied to you before. I was scared, but I'm telling you the truth now."

He leans forward and says, "Mrs. Warren, try again."

I look up, dab my eyes, and say, "What?"

"We interviewed your husband. He was in San Antonio speaking at a conference that weekend."

"San Antonio?" I ask.

"Yes, he spoke at a conference in San Antonio."

My mind goes back to the day Trevor was killed. I don't know what to think. *Did I hear him wrong?* I rub my forehead and say, "I thought he was going to Phoenix."

"Nope," Detective Cumming says, "he spoke at a conference in San Antonio."

Shaking my head, I ask, "He told you that?"

He gives me a nod.

I shake my head and say, "Well, he's lying."

Cummings looks at his pad and says, "I spoke with the lady, Ms. Bowerly, who arranged the speakers that day. She confirmed that he spoke there Friday morning. She's sending the video of him there."

I can't even process what he just said. I tilt my head and ask, "Who?"

"The lady from the conference confirmed he spoke that day. She's sending the video."

Now, I'm not sure what to think. I raise my hand and say, "Well, he must have come back home after he finished speaking."

"He came back home?" Detective Cummings asks.

"That's right. Like I said, he came back home around five or six."

With a look of confusion, Cummings says, "He says he was in San Antonio until Saturday morning."

"He's lying," I insist. "He came back Friday evening."

He nods his head and writes on his pad.

I think about it for a second and ask, "So, he's saying he was gone?"

"That's right. He said he left in the morning and wasn't there at all that night."

I stare at Cummings and say, "Well, he's a liar." Then it hits me. "Is he saying that *I* killed Trevor?"

"Nope. He said he doesn't know what happened, but doesn't believe for a second that you killed him. He insists it must have been an accident, because you'd never do anything like that. Said he came home, and it smelled like bleach. You said you spilled something."

I can't believe what I'm hearing. *He's putting this off on me? I've spent all this time covering for him, and now he's turning on me?* Now the gloves are off. I'm no longer looking down and barely talking. I point at his tablet and say, "He did this. He did the whole thing. I'm not saying he killed Trevor on purpose—I'm sure he didn't. But he damn sure wrapped him in a rug, took him out on the lake, and dumped him. He says he left San Antonio on Saturday? He's a damn liar. Call the hotel. Find out when he checked out."

"We did," Cummings continues. "They show he checked out of the hotel Saturday morning. He says he was eating at a restaurant in San Antonio Saturday night until ten-thirty."

"What?" I ask. "That's bullshit. We ordered Chinese food and ate at home. He was watching television until at least nine-thirty when I went to bed."

"You ate Chinese food? Who ordered it?"

"I did."

"Who paid for it?"

"I did."

"So, we have proof that he was in San Antonio, and it was you who ordered and paid for the food in Austin?"

I nod my head and say, "I know it sounds bad, but I'm telling you the truth."

Cummings nods and says, "We'll check. We'll get his credit card charges. We'll check every toll from San Antonio to Austin. We'll check every city on the way to see if he was pulled over. We'll even check every gas station along the highway and get their security video from that night. We're going to figure this out. If he's lying, we'll find out."

I sit here rubbing my temples and whisper, "He said I did it?" I look up and repeat, "He's lying. I'll cooperate with you however I can."

I can feel a change in the room. Cummings is more relaxed, now talking like he's on my side again. Then he asks, "You just saw the man you loved shot and killed. Why didn't you call the police?"

"I wanted to," I say. "I kept telling him to. He said it would ruin him, ruin our kids, and I'd never teach again. I don't know. I was devastated and not thinking straight. I went upstairs and washed all the blood off me, thinking we're about to call the police. When I came down, he had Trevor wrapped in the rug. It felt like the wheels were in motion and it was too late to stop."

As soon as I get the words out, I realize this is the story of my life. Again and again, I've gone along because it was easier to listen to Alton than call it off and go my own way. It's never worked out for me before and now look where I am.

"Do you have any proof that your husband was there that night? A text message or anything?"

"We didn't text. How do you prove someone was at home?"

He shakes his head, leans closer like he's trying to console me, and says, "Until today, we knew he was killed but didn't know how. We knew it had to be violent. Do you know where the gun is?"

"It's in his nightstand. I didn't even know he had a gun. He asked a couple of years ago and I told him not to buy it. I'll take you to it."

"We looked in the nightstand. We looked all over the house, but it wasn't there."

"Then he got rid of it. He probably threw it in the lake."

Suddenly, like a flash of light, it comes to me. All I can think is, *I got you...you son of a bitch! You're going to prison.* I stand up, spread my arms, and say, "I got it! Trevor's car—Alton drove it to a storage facility that night. The next day, he rented a space and put Trevor's car in it. I wasn't even there. His name and signature will be on the paperwork. Find the storage facility and it will prove he killed Trevor."

"Great," Cummings says, standing up. "Let's go."

We drive to the storage facility and walk inside. "Do you know the unit number?" Cummings asks.

"I have no idea."

He walks up to the clerk, flashes his badge, and says, "I'm investigating a murder. This is Mrs. Warren. Do you have a storage facility rented to Alton Warren?"

She looks on her computer and says, "We do."

"And who signed for it?"

She pushes some keys and says, "Alton Warren."

After hearing everything else, I was afraid he might have put it in my name. I smile, step forward, and ask, "And who's been paying for it?"

She looks down and says, "Alton Warren.

I turn to Cummings and say, "I told you!"

"What unit number is it?" Cummings asks.

With a frown, she asks, "Do you have a warrant?"

Looking at me, he says, "This is his wife. Anything in there is community property." He turns to me and asks, "Do I have your permission to open it?"

"Absolutely," I say.

"Do you have a lock cutter?" he asks the lady.

She goes into a closet in the back and comes out with a lock cutter. She rides us in a golf cart to the far end of the facility and says, "These are our larger units."

Cummings goes up and snaps the end of the lock in two. I'm standing here with a hint of a smile. With wide eyes, I watch as he bends down, grabs the handle, and pulls the door up.

My smile morphs into a stunned, open mouth. The storage facility is full of stacks and stacks of boxes. I walk inside, throw off one of the lids, and see it's all his old patient files.

Soft and slow, I say, "It was here…I swear it was here?"

Cummings drives me back to my car and says, "You cooperated with us, and I appreciate that. Honestly, I don't know who to believe. One thing for sure, we're going to get to the bottom of this. For now, you're free, but don't go anywhere. Oh, I would hire a good attorney."

– CHAPTER 34 –

I return to my hotel, get back on the internet, and Google, "austin criminal attorneys." A long list of lawyers pops up. It goes on for many pages. I have no idea how to pick a lawyer, but I know I'm in big trouble. I click on each page and everyone looks like he or she is a great lawyer. Something inside tells me I should hire a man. Some ads state how long the attorney has practiced law. Some are board certified—whatever that means—but it seems important. Surely they get better the longer they're an attorney. After I go through eight or nine pages, I go back and look at them again. Then, I stop on one guy who has a couple of great testimonials on his page. His clients like him—that's as good as anything. I call his office and schedule an appointment for the following afternoon to discuss my case.

The kids won't last long at this hotel before I have a mutiny on my hands. The next day, I take them to the house I put an offer on yesterday. Jacob is thrilled. He runs around like an airplane soaring through each room. Beth picks the room she likes best. Bekah looks down at her phone and under her breath says, "No way."

We stop for an early lunch before returning to the hotel. I'm trying to digest what Cummings said when Trish calls. *Shit, I never made it to her house.*

"Hello?" I say.

"Paige, I thought you were coming over yesterday."

"I know. I had to go talk to the police."

"Are you okay?" she asks.

I start sobbing uncontrollably. I step outside in the hall and say, "No."

"What happened?" she asks.

"Trish, I need your help. It's horrible. Come down here, and I'll tell you everything."

"Did Trevor hurt you?"

"I can't talk over the phone."

"Where are you?"

I give her the address to the hotel and she says, "I'm hauling ass right now. See you in a few. Oh…what room are you in?"

"Just text me when you're here, and I'll come down."

Twenty-five minutes later, I get her text. I tell the kids to stay in the room and walk down to the lobby. The second I see her, she runs up and throws her arms around me.

"Oh, Trish," I cry. "Thank you for coming."

"What's going on?" she asks.

We find a place to talk, and I start at the beginning. "Trish, Alton was going out of town, so I texted Trevor to come over."

"Oh shit," she says, "Did you get caught?"

I shake my head and continue. "Then Alton came back home. I texted Trevor and told him not to come over."

"Okaay."

Then I break down and can't talk.

"What happened? Tell me what happened."

Still looking down, I say, "I…I…don…don't know. I guess he didn't get my text."

"Holy shit," she says.

"Alton woke me up in the middle of the night and said someone was trying to break in the house."

Trish's eyes open wide.

I put my hands over my face, and say, "He shot him. He shot and killed him."

"What the fuck!" she screams. She leans forward, takes me in her arms, and says, "I'm so sorry."

I don't even know how to tell her the rest of the story. I grab her shoulders, move her back a bit, and say, "We did something horrible."

"What!"

"It was Alton's idea. He said we had to do it."

"Do what?"

"He said we had to get rid of the body."

"Get rid of the body? What the fuck!"

"He rolled him up in the carpet from his office, put him in the boat, and dumped him in the middle of the lake."

"Oh my God!" she says, covering her mouth.

"I didn't do it," I say. "I told him to call the police. He did it all. I wouldn't even go with him."

"Okay," she says. "That's why they're asking about Trevor. It sounds like you did nothing wrong."

"I don't know what I was thinking. I put this cinder block and some tie-downs in the boat. I cleaned up the house while he was gone."

She looks at me and says, "Paige, you got to get a lawyer. Do you need some money? I'll give you all I have."

I shake my head and say, "I have money. I called an attorney and made an appointment for later today."

"Good...good," she says, "Who'd you hire?"

"Some guy from the internet. He had some good testimonials."

"NO!" she shouts. "You can't pick some guy off the internet. My brother did that. He was dating this girl who accused him of assault. This bitch was crazy. My brother had already caught a felony for theft, so he refused to plead guilty to something he didn't do. It wasn't until the middle of the trial that my bother realized his lawyer didn't know his ass from his elbow. He was convicted and sentenced to five years in prison."

"I hope it's not the guy I called," I say. "I don't have any idea who to hire."

"Wait a minute," she says. "There's this guy…Richard Brunick. He represented Cliff when he caught a case. They had his ass. He was caught red-handed, but this Brunick guy went to trial and he was found not guilty. He's freakin' awesome."

I take my phone, look online, and the only Brunick we find is a law firm named *Brunick and Brunick*. I call the number.

"Uhm…can I talk to Richard Brunick?"

"Ryan Brunick?" the lady asks.

I cover the phone and ask, "Ryan Brunick."

"That's him," Trish says.

I tell the lady, "Yes, I need to talk to Ryan Brunick right away."

"What kind of case do you have?"

"I don't know…criminal…murder."

Like I didn't just drop a bomb on her, she casually says, "Why don't we schedule you an appointment. When can you come in?"

"Right now?"

"Hold on," she says, and puts me on hold. She comes back on the line and says, "Come on in."

"Do you want me to go with you?" Trish asks.

I shake my head and say, "I got myself into this. I have to do this on my own."

I walk into the most gorgeous office I've ever seen. I've never been in a law office before, but this place is incredible. I walk up to the receptionist and say, "I just called. I have an appointment to see Ryan Brunick."

She hands me a clipboard and pen and directs me to complete a two-page client information sheet. I fill it out, hand it back, and wait in an expensive leather chair. There's a large portrait of a handsome man hanging on the wall with a gold plate at the bottom that reads, "Ryan Brunick." Something tells me I've come to the right place.

A few minutes later, a woman walks up with dark hair and beautiful green eyes, wearing a dark blue business suit. With a smile, she extends her hand and says, "Hello, I'm Hope Brunick. Come on back."

We walk down a long hallway with hardwood floors until we get to a giant corner office. She has beautiful furniture and a giant desk full of papers. Behind her desk is a view of the Capital that fills the entire window. Hanging on the wall is one award after another.

Best of the Best;

Top Ten Trial Lawyers;

Austin's Best Lawyers;

Winner–Austin Journal Reader's Poll;

Texas Trial Lawyers Association List of Outstanding Lawyers;

American Trial Lawyers Association;

She sits down and asks, "How can I help you, Mrs. Warren?"

I look around and say, "I'm sorry. I have an appointment with Ryan Brunick. My friend recommended him to me."

Her smile fades, and with a tinge of sadness, she says, "Ryan Brunick was my father. Unfortunately, he passed away six years ago. Maybe I can help you?"

"I don't know," I say. "I'm in a lot of trouble. I need the best. Are you the best?"

She laughs a little and says, "I understand. I get that all the time. I can assure you, he taught me everything he knew."

"How long have you been an attorney?"

"Sixteen years."

"Do you handle murder cases?"

"All the time."

"Mr. Brunick represented my friend's brother in court and won. Do you go to court?"

"All the time."

"Do you win?"

She smiles and says, "I do pretty good."

"Okay," I say.

She starts by saying. "What you tell me is confidential. You need to tell me everything. I can't help you if you're not honest. Why don't you tell me what happened?"

I sit down and tell her the whole story—crying when I talk about Trevor's death. I start explaining how he built our boathouse and end with the police spraying that stuff and taking pictures. I expect her to freak out, but she sits here like this happens all the time. She writes notes on one page after another on her pad and says, "Uh-huh" over and over. She asks questions every now and then; things that I never thought of.

When I'm done, she asks, "So, it was all his idea."

"Yes Ma'am."

"You never discussed it ahead of time?"

"We didn't know it was going to happen."

"You didn't carry Trevor to the boat?"

"No, Ma'am."

"You didn't go on the boat when he disposed of the body?"

"No, Ma'am"

"All you did was clean up afterwards?"

"Yes, Ma'am." Then I stop and say, "Oh, except I drove behind him to the storage facility where he parked Trevor's car."

She puts her pad on her desk and says, "If what you say is true, I don't see you being charged with murder. You might be charged with participating in the disposal of a corpse and that's pretty serious."

"Can I go to prison?"

"Can you go to prison? It's a felony in Texas, but with your limited involvement, and if you cooperate, you'll probably avoid any prison time."

"Cooperate?" I ask.

"If you testify in the case."

"I can't do that," I say. "I can't testify against my husband."

She folds her hands and says, "Let me explain how this works. There's no way you can clean your place up enough to erase all the evidence. That stuff they sprayed, it's Luminol. It's a water-based solution that can detect blood that has been diluted up to ten thousand times. When it comes in contact with blood, it turns a pale blue color. That's what they were taking pictures of. I'm quite sure they know he was killed in your home. Your husband's idea that you cut yourself in the kitchen will never fly."

I shake my head and say, "I didn't think it would."

"You were seeing this guy. How's things with you and your husband?"

"We haven't really talked in months. I don't love him—I never loved him. We weren't okay before this, but now I can't stand to look at him."

"Are you planning on filing for divorce?"

"As soon as possible."

"Okay...I can work out a plea deal in exchange for you testifying against him."

"I already told them," I say.

"Told the police? You talked to them?"

"They were going to arrest me. This guy put handcuffs on me and said I was being arrested for Trevor's murder."

"Damn," she says. "Did you tell them what you told me?"

"Word-for-word."

She nods her head and says, "I assume you don't have cameras in your house?"

"No ma'am...only outside." I lean in and say, "There's this one thing. Evidently, Alton told the detectives he was at a conference all weekend."

With a little laugh, she says, "He's not all that bright, is he? That's pretty easy to disprove. All it takes is one call."

"They did call. Someone told him he did speak at the conference. They're sending the video."

With a scowl, she says, "Okay."

"But it was in San Antonio. He could have made it home in plenty of time."

"So he's saying you did it and you're saying he did it?" She writes this down and says, "Shit, that's the worst."

"Why is it the worst?"

"Well, they might not know how it happened or why it happened, but they'll fill in the details. Your boyfriend was leaving you, so you killed him; your husband was jealous, and he killed him; you both hatched a plan and carried it out together. They'll come up with their own theory of how it happened. I doubt they'll ever say he was killed by mistake."

"I swear," I say sternly. "What I told you is the truth."

"The fact is, they don't have to prove exactly what happened. They'll try you both together and let you fight it out."

"So I'm going to prison?"

"Well, they have a big problem. The jury has to believe beyond any reasonable doubt. They will know one or both of you were involved, but may not be able to agree on who killed him or if it was a mistake. It can be a hung jury or they could find you both not guilty. The prosecutor will be real eager to make a deal in exchange for your testimony."

"He's the father of my children. They will hate me if I testify against him."

"Think about it. You're really not testifying *against* him. All you're doing is telling the truth; and your truth, if accepted, should exonerate him—at least for murder. If you don't cooperate, the prosecutor's not going to say, 'We don't know what happened,' and go away. They'll try you both together, as co-conspirators. Under the law in Texas, if you were carrying out a felony, it doesn't matter who did what. You'll both get the same conviction if you had any involvement."

"I can go to prison for murder even though I didn't kill him?"

"It happens all the time. If the jury doesn't know how it happened, but knows it was in your home and you were both there, then it's a real possibility."

"I don't know," I say. "I need some time to think about it."

"Here's the problem," she continues. "You told your husband you're going to hire an attorney. I'm sure he's talking to an attorney right now. It's not fair, but the first one to cooperate gets the deal. If he offers to testify, and it sounds like he will, he'll be the witness and you'll be on trial for murder."

"So, I need to decide right now?"

"I would," she says. "You might want to protect your husband, but you're looking at life in prison for something you didn't do. Think about your kids. What if you both go to prison?"

"I told him not to buy that damn gun. I didn't even know he had it. When I look at him, all I see is Trevor's dead body in my arms. I have no love left for him. If it weren't for our kids, I'd never see him again."

"This is extremely serious," she says.

"I know."

"The fact is, you didn't kill him. If you don't do this, you're playing with fire."

"Can't we go to trial and be found not guilty?"

"Sure," she says with a nod. "But innocent people get convicted all the time. Are you willing to gamble with your life for something you didn't do?"

"If I testify, will I have to go to prison?"

"Given your limited involvement, it's my hope we can work out a reduced charge and avoid any jail time."

I think about it for a minute and say, "Okay…I'll do it."

"Very well," she says. "Let me do some work, make some calls to the detective and the District Attorney, and I'll get back with you. One last thing, don't talk to anyone about your case. Until this is over, the only person you discuss this with is me. That's very important."

"Yes, ma'am." I stand up and ask, "How much do I owe you?"

"I'm going to assume at this point that we're going to work out a plea. I'll need a $20,000.00 retainer. If not, it will be a lot more expensive."

I give her a check and tell her to wait until tomorrow to deposit it.

She puts the check on her desk and says, "I'll call you when I know more."

A week later, she calls me back into her office.

"Did you work things out?" I ask.

"Not yet. They have an idea what you both are saying. They want to gather some more evidence before they're ready to take one side or the other. In the meantime, I want to try something."

"What's that?"

"I hope to make this go away now. I want you to call your husband from my office. We'll use your cell phone and record the call. Don't be too forward. Tell him you're scared. Then say something like, "You thought you were shooting an intruder. Just tell them it was a mistake." She looks at me and asks, "Can you do that?"

"I think so."

She reaches behind her desk, pulls out a recording device, hooks it to my cell phone and gives me a nod."

"Hello?" he says.

"Alton?"

"How you holding out?"

Sounding down, I say, "Not so good."

"How are the kids?"

"You know, they don't like all this. Maybe you can take them for dinner or something soon."

"I'd love that," he says.

When he doesn't say more, I say, "Alton, I'm scared."

"I understand," he says. "After all you've been through, that's very normal."

I roll my eyes and say, "It's just that…we should have just called the police. I know you thought you were shooting an intruder. I think we should just explain to them what happened. It was a mistake...you know?"

He doesn't say anything. Hope rolls her finger round and round for me to keep the conversation going. "You there?" I ask.

"Yeah, I'm here."

"They're suspecting that I killed Trevor. I think we should just tell them the truth about what happened."

Just when I think he's not going to respond again, he says, "I think you should, Paige. Honesty is the best option."

He's obviously being evasive. I'm not sure what to say to get what we need, so I ask, "Alton, did you tell the detective that you were in San Antonio at a conference?"

"I *was* in San Antonio at a conference."

This beating around the bush isn't working, so I get right to it. "When I talked to the detective, he made it sound like you're saying I did this."

"I didn't say that," he answers. "I told them you would never do something like that."

I look at Hope and say, "Alton, we both know you—"

"Hey Paige," he interrupts. "I have a patient coming in. I've got to go."

"Hold on, Alton. All I'm saying is I don't think you meant—"

"Hey Paige. I've got to go. Why don't we talk when I pick up the kids?" *Click.*

About ready to throw my phone against the wall, I scream, "I hate you, you son of a bitch!"

"Jesus, Paige," Hope says, "He's out to get you."

"You think so?"

"Of course he is. He's trying to pin this whole thing on you."

"But he shot someone he thought was breaking into our home. Sure, he might be guilty of getting rid of the body. He would have me convicted of murder to avoid that?"

"It's a felony. He could get up to twenty years."

"Does that mean I can get twenty years too?" I ask.

She shakes her head and says, "This guy's out for you. It sounds like he's willing for you to take the fall for everything. We're talking about murder here."

"Can he do that?"

She thinks for a second and says, "It doesn't seem possible. We just have to prove that he came back. When we prove he's lying—that he was at the house that night—his whole story falls apart. They'll have to believe you. I have a good investigator. Text me his license plate number. If he came home after that conference, we'll find out."

Suddenly, I realize we have all the evidence we need. I look at her and ask, "If we can prove he was there the night Trevor was shot, you think you can get me off?"

"Look, the two of you are pointing fingers at each other. I seriously doubt the prosecutor will try to prove you two were working together. Now this whole case will come down to who the jury believes. We prove he was there, and his whole story will look like a lie."

I look forward, and confidently say, "Then we got it!"

"What?" she asks.

"The outside security camera. Trevor installed a security camera inside and outside the boathouse in case anyone tries to break in and steal the boat. I can't believe this, Trevor will be the one to save me."

She sits back in her chair and says, "We may have one problem. What if your husband erased the video?"

I shake my head and say, "I was there when Trevor hooked it up. He showed me everything. He said a backup is stored in the cloud in case a thief takes the computer or tries to erase it. The police took the whole thing when they raided our house. They have the evidence we need."

"Wow, Paige!" she says. "This is incredible. I'll call the prosecutor and request all the evidence in the case. If you agree to testify against your husband, they'll strike a deal. I'm sure of it."

I stand up and say, "You know, I'm really glad I came to you."

She shakes my hand, and I walk out. For the first time since this started, a smile spreads across my face. *He thinks he's so smart? He tried to get me? Now this whole case is about to come crumbling down on him.*

Hope schedules a meeting with the prosecutor for Monday morning. That's four days away. I go to her office every day and go over everything again and again. She explains how I'm just there to tell them what I know. The prosecutor won't be interrogating me, although she might want to clear up some confusion.

It all seemed pretty simple to me—I was asleep; woke up; heard two blasts; saw Trevor falling to the floor; Alton dumped the body; and I cleaned up the house before the kids woke up. It's not hard to say when you're telling the truth.

But Hope wants to make sure we cover all the details. I soon realize nothing is simple. The law is really tricky. It twists the truth into a pretzel, manipulates and confuses, and soon you're questioning your own memory. One thing for sure, I should have told Alton to shut the hell up and just called the police that night. There was no way we were ever going to dump a body and get away with it. There are way too many things you have to keep straight and it only takes one thing to trip you up. Alton was stupid to think this would ever work, and he's just as stupid to believe he'll get away with it now. There's got to be a driver who passed him on the highway between Austin and San Antonio; a neighbor who heard the shots and stuck their busy-body nose out the window to see what was going on; or maybe another boater was out on the lake at three in the morning (well, scratch that last one.) I'm sure I wouldn't have been able to get away with it and I have to believe Alton won't get away with it either.

- -
- -
- -
- -

– CHAPTER 35 –

Monday morning, we're down at the courthouse to meet with the prosecutor and tell my story…all the sordid details. In the lobby, Hope says, "They have the evidence ready for us to review. Again, they just want to hear what you have to say. They won't question you. They're here to listen. Tell them what you know. Nothing you say can be used against you later. I'll ask if you're willing to sign a statement and testify in court. Don't hesitate for a second when you answer. I'll work out a plea deal to put this all behind you."

"So, I have to testify, right?"

"If it comes down to it…yes."

I take a deep breath, feeling like I'm about to have a heart attack. "Well, great," I say with a big sigh.

"You ready to go in?"

I nod my head.

We walk in like a mother hen with her baby chick following close behind. The female prosecutor, Detective Cummings, and Detective Anderson meet us at the front. The prosecutor shakes Hope's hand and says, "Nice to see you again, Ms. Brunick. I heard about your trial last month. I don't know how you do it. He was a bad actor."

"He was innocent," Hope says.

"Yeah, right. All your clients are innocent."

Hope gestures to me and says, "This is Paige Warren."

The prosecutor shakes my hand with a smile. Cummings looks a little angry, or maybe he's just in a bad mood for some reason. Without so much as a handshake, he gives me a simple nod, and says, "Mrs. Warren."

We walk down the hall and into a conference room where there are two boxes waiting for us on the table. Hope walks over to the boxes and asks, "Is this the evidence I requested?"

"It's all there."

She takes off one of the lids and says, "Is the video from the security system in there?"

"It sure is. I watched it last week."

"Very good," Hope says. "I want to let you know that I filed Mrs. Warren's petition for divorce last week. She is willing to be a cooperating witness. She will testify against him."

The prosecutor tilts her head and says, "I don't think that's going to happen. I kept our appointment today so I could personally hand over all the evidence to you. I should tell you that last Thursday, your client was indicted for first-degree murder and disposing of a corpse."

"Indicted," Hope says. "What the hell are you saying? You've ambushed us."

Raising her hand, the prosecutor says, "This isn't an ambush." She hands my lawyer a document and says, "Look, you're going to get this, anyway. This is an affidavit signed by Dr. Warren. He says he was in San Antonio Friday night. We verified that. He didn't return home until Saturday afternoon. We verified that, too. He swears, under oath, that when he got home Mrs. Warren had already cleaned the house where the investigators found the blood evidence. The whole place smelled like bleach. He asked her what happened and she said she spilled something. Later, he went out to the boat and found the keys in the ignition. He always hangs the keys up, so he knew she took the boat out. After the police left their house, your client admitted that she was having an affair. Dr. Warren asked her if she killed Mr. Evans and she denied it. He doesn't believe she'd ever do something like this, but now he's not sure what to believe. He's agreed to cooperate with our office."

Hope reads the affidavit, tosses it on the table in disgust, and says, "Oh, this is all a bunch of bullshit, and you know it. You just took the first deal you could get. Now you're getting in bed with this lying snake?"

"His statement checks out," the prosecutor continues. "We have a video of him speaking at the conference. It's also in there."

Beginning to tremble a little, I say, "He came back from San Antonio Friday night—I swear."

The prosecutor pulls out a different file and hands over another disc along with a photocopy of a hotel receipt. Pointing at the receipt, she says, "He checked out of the hotel on Saturday at noon. This is the video of him at the front desk."

Hope reads over the receipt.

"He says he has proof that he ate at a restaurant in San Antonio on Friday night."

With a huff, I say, "But he hasn't brought it in, huh? That's because he's lying. He was at our house Friday night watching television."

Hope holds up her hand to keep me from saying more. She looks at the prosecutor and asks, "So, you're going to partner up with this…this slime? Nothing in this evidence contradicts what my client is saying. We all know he was in San Antonio that morning."

"And checked out the next day?" Detective Cummings interrupts.

"So what?" Hope says, scowling at Detective Cummings. "He could have gone right back the next day and checked out of his hotel to cover for himself. He had plenty of time to dump the body and return to San Antonio." Shaking her head, she asks, "Have you actually watched the surveillance video from their house?"

"I did," the prosecutor answers. She goes back to the box, shows us another disc, and says, "Here it is." She puts the disc into the television DVR. It powers up and we all watch when she pushes play. The camera doesn't show the whole backyard as I thought. There are two videos side-by-side. One view is from the inside of the boathouse and the other shows only the back half of the backyard and the water. We all stand here watching as the video plays.

The video is silent until the clock on the video reads 11:18 PM. You can hear two loud blasts in the background. At 11:56 PM, I come walking across the backyard and into the boathouse. Once inside the boathouse, I take the tie-downs off the side wall and throw them in the boat. Then I walk over to the cement block, struggle to pick it up, and throw it in the boat. I climb onto the boat, start it, back it out of the boathouse, and park beside the dock for twelve minutes. Then I back the boat up until it's out of the view of the camera. You can't tell what happened after that. Eleven minutes later, you can hear the boat drive away.

Hope looks at me and I say, "He told me to put those things in the boat. He was having trouble carrying Trevor out, so he told me to pull the boat around to the side."

Detective Cummings isn't buying it. Looking right at me, he asks, "I thought you told me you never drove the boat that night?"

"I didn't," I say. "Well, I backed it out, because he told—"

Hope holds up her hand and says, "Paige, it's better that you don't say anything else right now."

Detective Cummings turns back to my attorney and says, "We're still investigating and he's gathering evidence to support his claims, but right now, everything he said has checked out. Mrs. Warren has lied to us at every turn. Hell, she denied she was even having an affair or that she saw him that night. There's only one person on that surveillance video, and that's your client."

My attorney turns to the prosecutor and asks, "So, we came all the way here for you to charge *my* client?"

I look around and ask, "Am I getting arrested?"

The prosecutor folds her arms across her chest and says, "She could have been arrested at her school in front of her children. Would you want that?"

I want to scream, but I shut my mouth and say nothing. My lawyer picks up one box and I pick up the other. Detective Cummings says, "Mrs. Warren, I'm going to have to take you into custody."

"Please don't do this,' I sob. "It's not like he's saying."

My lawyer takes a step back when Detective Cummings says, "Please turn around and put your hands behind your back."

Detective Anderson comes forward and stands beside me like I might run or something. I put down my purse, turn around, lower my head while crying, and put my hands behind my back. The first handcuff clicks several times and then the second.

Hope stacks one box on top of the other and says, "I'll come down first thing in the morning to see you."

They march me into the hall with everyone around watching. Inside the elevator, I'm standing in embarrassment while several people who get on and off look right at me. We walk down the sidewalk and into the jail facilities for booking.

As soon as we arrive, Detective Cummings looks at one of the officers there and says, "Paige Marie Warren—first degree premeditated murder and disposing of a corpse." The officer takes my arm and sits me down on a chair with my hands still handcuffed behind my back. A woman comes up maybe fifteen minutes later and uncuffs me. She hands me a baggie, and tells me to put all my personal belongings inside. She hands me a piece of paper and pen to write down any phone numbers I need from my phone. Then she gives me an embarrassing black and grey striped top and bottom and a pair of rubber slip-on shoes. We go in a room and she instructs me to strip down, bend over for an inspection, and change into my new inmate clothes.

When I walk out looking like a criminal, a man confirms all my personal information, asking me one question after another. Then he fingerprints me and instructs me to stand in front of a camera for my mug shot. I'm sure this photo will be all over the news and on the internet. I don't know if I'm supposed to smile, look stunned, have no expression, or cry. I stand up tall and stare straight ahead with my eyes full of tears. I do my best to hold them in.

Then they allow me to make two calls. I once had so many friends, but over the last ten years, I don't even know where they all went. It seems like Trish and Kristi are the only friends I have left, and Kristi is back in Fort Worth. My first call is to my mom.

A recording comes on that says, "Hello, you have a collect call from Paige Warren at the Travis County Corrections facility. Do you accept the charges?"

"Yes," she answers.

"Hello, mom," I say.

"Paige, what are you doing in jail?"

"I was arrested today."

"For what? I hope you don't need me to bail you out."

I start to cry and say, "No, mom, there's not any bail. I was arrested for murder."

"Murder! What the hell did you do? Did you kill Alton?"

"No mom, I didn't kill Alton. I didn't kill anyone. It's a long story. I just wanted you to know in case you wanted to come visit."

She pauses for a minute and says, "I told you, Paige. Way back in high school, I told you to settle down when you were running around with that boyfriend of yours. Now murder? Good grief!"

"Mom," I interrupt, "can you come visit?"

"I'll come visit, but I can't today. I'll try to make it Wednesday after Kevin goes to work. Will you be out before then?"

"I don't think so."

"Well, tell me what happened."

"I can't," I say. "I can't talk to anyone about the case. I just need to see you. Can you please come?"

"Okay, okay," she says, a little testy. "I told you I'll be there Wednesday…or maybe Friday."

I start to cry and say, "Please come, mama. I love you."

"What?" she asks.

"I said, I'll see you on Wednesday."

Next I call Trish.

"Hello, you have a collect call from Paige Warren at the Travis County Corrections facility. Do you accept the charges?"

"Yes!"

"Paige?" she says. "What happened?"

"I was arrested today. I went with my lawyer to talk to the District Attorney's office and I was arrested."

"Sweet Jesus," she says. "Are you in Travis County?"

"Yeah."

"Can I come see you?"

I turn to the officer and say, "Can someone come visit me?"

"Give us about two hours to finish the booking process. Visiting hours end at eight-thirty."

"You have to wait two hours. Visiting hours end at eight-thirty."

She exhales and says, "Geeze Paige, I'll be there in two hours."

I turn to the officer and ask, "Can I make one more call?"

She gives me a nod.

"Hello, you have a collect call from Paige Warren at the Travis County Corrections facility. Do you accept the charges?"

"I do," he says.

"Dean…it's Paige."

"Paige, are you in jail?"

"Yes."

"Oh, no." he says. "Are you okay? Do you need me to bail you out?"

"No…there's no bail."

"What are you charged with?"

I start crying and say, "Murder."

"Murder! What happened?"

"I can't talk about it. I just wanted you to know."

"Definitely," he says. "You're in Travis County?"

"Uh-huh."

"I'll be there in the morning," he says. "Don't worry. I'm sure it's a big mistake. We'll get this figured out."

Crying again, I say, "Thank you Dean."

"Of course," he says. "I love you. I'll see you in the morning."

Once I'm through with my calls, they walk me to an empty jail cell. I walk inside, sit on the bed, and they slam the door closed. When I first saw this room, I was glad I wouldn't be with other inmates, but the longer I sit here, the more I wish I was with other people. I'm sitting here with nothing…absolutely nothing…other than the thoughts of the meeting we just had with the prosecutor. *How? How is this happening?*

Three hours go by before an officer comes in and announces, "Paige Warren, you have a visitor."

I walk to the visiting area in my striped uniform looking like one of those chain gang members on the side of the road. Trish is already sitting on the other side of this plexiglass when I walk up and pick up the phone.

"What the hell, Paige? What happened?"

"I don't know."

"I'm sorry. I came here an hour ago, but I had to register and go through this clearance. So they arrested *you*?"

"That asshole is now a cooperating witness. He's going to testify against me. He's making it seem like I was the one who shot Trevor. He's saying he wasn't even there that night."

"How can he do that? How can they arrest you? They have to have proof."

"They have proof. They have me on video. I'm the one in the boathouse loading the tie-downs and the cement block into the boat."

"What?"

"The video doesn't show the whole backyard. It only shows the area around the boathouse. He told me to get the boat, load that stuff in, and drive it closer. It doesn't show who put Trevor in the boat and drove off, but you'd sure think it was me."

"That's just great," she says. "Did you hire that Brunick lawyer?"

I shake my head and say, "He died, so I hired his daughter. She has all these awards and stuff on the wall of her office. She says he taught her everything she knows."

"I don't know," Trish says. "This is just starting and you're already in jail."

I raise my hand and say, "I think she knows what she's doing. I have to trust that she does. She's my lawyer."

Trish rolls her eyes and says, "I hope so." Then she says, "There's no way he can pretend he wasn't at your house. Someone had to see his car there." Speaking lower, she says, "Do you want me to say that I saw it?"

"Don't, Trish," I insist. "All I have is the truth on my side. Either it will free me or it won't, but I have to stick with the truth…no matter what. My lawyer has an investigator. Alton thinks he's so smart, but he can't think of everything. I have to believe something will trip him up."

"Are you okay in here?" she asks.

"What can I say? It sucks. I'm all alone in a little cell. The boredom drives you crazy. It sure gives me time to think."

We talk for another fifteen minutes. Before she leaves, I say, "I feel so alone here. I don't even have my mom for support. Please keep visiting me."

With a sympathetic look, she says, "I'll come here every day."

Then I remember the house I'm buying. "I just signed a contract for a new house. This ruins that. I may need to sign something to allow you to handle these things for me." I pause a second and ask, "Can you do me another favor. Alton has the kids. Check in on them now and then. Let me know how they're doing."

"No problem," she says.
Before hanging up the phone, I say, "I love you."
"Love you too, sweetie. I'll be back tomorrow."

-245-

– CHAPTER 36 –

After a long night in jail, it all sets in. *I'm in jail for murder. First he kills the only man I've truly loved, and now he's making it look like I did it.* After staying up most of the night, the corrections officer opens my cell door and says, "Your lawyer is here."

They take me to a different room this time. A buzzer activates the door and the officer escorts me in. We don't have to talk through a window or use phones. There's a round table in the middle of the room with four chairs. My lawyer is sitting at the table with a legal pad and one of the boxes sit open in front of her.

We shake hands and she says, "Listen Paige, I'm your lawyer. You have to be straight with me. If there's something you're not telling me, then I can't help you."

"Ms. Brunick—" I begin.

"Call me Hope."

"Okay, Hope. I'm telling you the truth. Yes, I put those things in the boat because he told me to do it while he was taping up the rug. I pulled the boat around and he put Trevor in the boat. I wouldn't even help him and I refused to go on the boat with him. I stayed home the rest of the night."

"Look," she says. "I spent all night going over these documents. I'm not concerned about him checking out of the hotel the next day…that can be explained. But now he's saying he has proof that he ate in San Antonio that night."

"He doesn't," I say. "He can't. I went to bed at nine-thirty and he was sitting on the couch watching television. He turned it off and went to bed. He didn't have time to go back to San Antonio and eat dinner. It didn't happen."

"Then great," she nods. "He'll look like a fool. These people are betting their whole case on his credibility. When his credibility crumbles, so does their case."

"It will," I promise. "I know it looks bad that I'm the one who went in the boathouse, but that's all I did. He's the one who shot him. He's the one who took him out on the boat."

"If you say he killed him…then I believe you. A person can't kill someone and pretend to be a hundred miles away. It might be easy to say, but eventually the cold, hard, evidence will trip you up. We just have to prove he's lying."

"How?"

She looks at me like it's as simple as one plus one. "His cell phone," she says. "People today don't seem to realize that your movements are being tracked all the time. The prosecutor told me they've issued a subpoena to your cell phone provider. It will show he was in your house that night and not in San Antonio."

"Yes!" I shout. "I never thought about that. But will it really prove it? Will it show that he never left?"

"Well," she says cautiously, "it can…as long as he didn't turn off his phone. Then it stops sending a signal to the cell towers."

"Shit," I say, covering my head with my hands. "He used to do psychological evaluations on criminals waiting to be sentenced. He's testified many times. That's why he thinks he can pull this off. I'm sure he knew to shut off his phone."

Hope shakes her head and says, "He's not as smart as he thinks he is. What's it going to look like if his cell phone mysteriously shuts off right before the murder and then comes back on the very next day? It may not trace him back to San Antonio but it's the next best thing."

"Has your investigator found anything?" I ask.

"I haven't heard from him, but I'm sure he's working on it."

I can't believe what has happened. I lean back in my stool and say, "Everything looks like it's against me. Can you win my case?"

Hope sits back and says, "My dad told me this story many years ago. I go back to it every time a case looks hopeless. There was this kid who wanted a bike for Christmas, but his dad couldn't afford it. So, his dad took the newspaper he was reading and found a long, boring financial article that his son could never understand. His son could barely read. He tore it into a bunch of small pieces and told his son he'd give him the bike if he could put it back together in less than fifteen minutes."

I sit here listening

"This boy picked up the pieces, grabbed some tape, and set them on the kitchen table. Ten minutes later, he came back and the whole article was taped together in perfect order."

"How?" I ask.

"Exactly! His dad looked at the article and asked, 'How'd you ever do this?'"

"'It was easy,' his son said with a big smile. He flipped the paper over and said, 'There was this picture on the other side. I put the picture together so you could read your story.'"

I smile a little and say, "Very smart."

Hope nods her head and says, "My investigator is amazing. My dad used him for years. We just have to look under every rock and flip things over. If it's out there, he'll find it."

"So, what's next?"

"You have your first appearance on Tuesday. I've filed a motion for the court to set bail, but it will probably be denied. The evidence against you is too strong. Other than your children, you have no reason to return for trial. You're just too big a flight risk. I expect the judge to deny it."

"How long will I have to stay in jail?"

"My dad was never one to allow cases to drag on. We have a better investigator than they do—he works faster and smarter. I'm filing a motion for a speedy trial under the Constitution. Since you're in jail, your case will take priority. I expect to go to trial in four or five months."

"Will we be ready by then?"

"That's the plan."

"Now what?"

"Well, I'm going to go over every shred of evidence in these boxes. When they receive my motion for a speedy trial, they'll know I mean it. They'll expedite subpoenas and get ready for trial too. I expect to get the majority of their evidence within a month or so."

"So, what do you think about the case?"

"I watched the video again last night. Their case has a number of problems. They have to get every one of the jurors to vote guilty. I only have to get one. It's called a hung jury."

"And I get to go home?"

"It doesn't work like that. They can try your case again. We have to put on a strong enough case that I'm able to convince the prosecutor that another trial will result in another hung jury."

"And they let me go?"

"Well, they have plenty of evidence on their side. Maybe we can work out a deal you can live with—something that allows you to see your kids before they're grown."

"I'll have to go to prison?"

She reaches over and shakes my arm. "Paige, it's way too early to start thinking about that. We're at the beginning. We'll know a lot more when my investigator finishes doing his thing. Let's take this one step at a time."

For the first time, I consider the idea of actually going to prison for a long time. *How can I go to prison for something I didn't do?* Hope stands up and says, "Let me get back to my office. I have a lot of work to do."

– CHAPTER 37 –

My hearing on Tuesday goes exactly like Hope said. The courtroom is packed with reporters and spectators. Trevor's whole family is sitting on the front row looking like they'd throw the switch on the electric chair themselves if they were given half a chance.

After my case is called, I stand in front of the judge and confirm that I understand the charges against me. Then, looking at the judge, I say, "Not guilty," loud and clear.

Hope argues the motion to set bail so brilliantly I actually thought the judge would grant it; but he considers it for about two seconds and says, "Bail is denied."

Then Hope hands the court and the prosecutor the Motion for Speedy Trial. "Big surprise," the prosecutor says.

The judge looks at his calendar and says, "I'm setting this case for September 8th. That's four months away."

"We'd like a priority setting," Hope announces.

"Very well," the judge says, granting the request. He looks at the prosecutor and says, "You better be ready."

"We will be," she responds.

Outside the courthouse, the reporters flock around Hope like a bunch of ants after their hill has been poked.

"Ms. Brunick...Ms. Brunick, are you actually planning to try this case?"

"You bet," she answers.

"Will your client accept a plea?"

"She's innocent. Why would she plead guilty to something she didn't do?"

"Rumor is, there's a video showing Mrs. Warren loading the victim onto her boat and taking him out on the lake. Any comment?"

"Where would that rumor come from? Only the police and the prosecutor have the evidence in this case."

"Is it true?"

"I won't comment on the evidence in this case."

"Ms. Brunick, you've won all eight of your murder trials. The evidence against your client is pretty damning. Do you really think you can win this one too?"

"Other cases don't matter, do they? I assure you, we plan on a vigorous defense of an innocent woman. We expect her to be found not guilty."

"Ms. Brunick, are you—"

"That's all I have right now," Hope says, cutting them off. "Thank you for your questions." She walks down the street to her office.

– CHAPTER 38 –

Jesus! When I thought about going to jail, I had these terrible images of women, who are as big as men, beating me up if I didn't give them money or cigarettes; being raped by guards or other inmates while I'm in the shower after everyone quietly slips out when my eyes are full of soap; working ten-hour days in this hot Texas sun picking up trash along the highway; and eating food that has no flavor and almost makes you want to throw up.

Okay, the food thing might be true, but the people here are pretty nice. I was moved from the city jail to the facility out to Del Valle where you stay until trial. At least now I'm in a pod with other inmates, so I don't feel like I'm in solitary confinement. That can drive a person insane. I make friends pretty quickly as my old self slowly returns.

After the story broke on my case, it was all over the news, the internet, the papers, our neighborhood, the grocery store where I shopped, and the school where I taught. I'm the woman who cheated on her husband and killed her lover. I shot him six times, stabbed him, or shot him and stabbed him, depending on who's telling the story. We're all watching television in here when Nancy Grace screams into the camera, "What kind of monster kills her lover, dumps his body, and then tries to blame her husband? An evil person…that's who."

Everyone turns to me, not like I'm a monster, but like I'm a hero around here.

"Girl, he must have really done you wrong!"

"He messed with the wrong bitch!"

"Did he cheat on you? Serves him right. I would have cut his dick off."

I follow my lawyer's advice and just stay quiet. It's not easy to do when everyone's talking about me killing the person who I loved so much.

Trish deposited eighty dollars into my account—it's all the money she had, bless her heart. Luckily, I got my check from Alton that I deposited before he turned on me. I paid Hope another $130,000.00. I gave Trish my bank card and pin number so she can put money into my account. I told her to take some money out for her troubles, but she's never taken a penny. I lost my $5,000 escrow money on the house I wanted to buy, but that's for the best. Oh…and my mother never showed up on that Wednesday, Friday, or any other day. Dean showed up the next morning just like he promised.

I do get out of here for all my court appearances, and Hope schedules a lot of them. Trish is there in the front row every time. She asked Alton if she could bring the kids to see me, but no dice. Maybe it's for the best. For all they know, I killed the man who built our boathouse after cheating on their poor dad.

A month after I was indicted, the prosecutor turns over two more boxes of stuff. Hope (she's definitely "hope" to me now) went over everything before coming to the jail with one full box and a lot to say.

I walk in, looking like a zebra at the zoo, and sit down to get an update.

"This doesn't look good," she starts.

"What do you mean?"

She pulls out a document. It's the hotel bill with a credit card receipt attached proving Alton checked out of the hotel on Saturday at 1:22 PM. She holds up a disc and says, "It's a video of him, larger than life, standing at the counter handing over his credit card."

"So what?" I say. "He had plenty of time to go back and do that."

She hands me a photocopy of a receipt from a Mexican food restaurant in San Antonio. Alton signed it at nine forty-five on Friday night.

I look at it, look at it a second time, and say, "What the hell? I promise you he was sitting on the couch in our living room at nine-thirty."

Then she hands me another document that's a computer printout from the hotel parking garage. "This documents every time his gate card shows him going in and out of the gate," Hope says, pointing at one of the lines. "Look here, he arrived on Friday at 10:09. He left on Friday night at 7:20 PM. He returned at 10:01 and never left again until Saturday afternoon."

Then she delivers another blow. She hands me the records from the cell phone towers. "Alton never turned his cell phone off. His cell never left San Antonio. It was at the hotel until he left at 7:20 PM. It shows him going downtown and returning to the hotel at 10:08 PM. The next time it pings is Saturday at 1:48 PM when he drives back to Austin."

I start to say something, but she says, "Oh, there's more." She shows me the final nail in my soon-to-be coffin—my cell phone records. She points at the page and says, "It shows your cell phone leave the house on Saturday morning at 12:15 AM, travel through the inlet, and out to the lake. It heads back to the house and stops at a nearby dock for about thirty minutes. There's a hose at the dock to wash your boat. Then the phone returns to your house at 3:30 AM."

I can't believe what she's saying or the documents she's showing me. Sounding confused, or exhausted, or both, I slowly shake my head and say, "I don't understand this. I don't understand what's happening."

I take the records from the garage and look at each entry: *Arrived at 10:09; left at 7:20; returned at 10:01.*

Feeling lightheaded, I point to the corner of the table and say, "Can I see the receipt? Maybe it's the wrong day, or the wrong place, or it's not his signature." She hands me the receipt and I look at it closely. *Friday, July 23rd*. Alton practically scribbles his signature. I've seen it many times. "That's it," I mumble. "That's his signature."

Hope crosses her arms and leans back with this puzzled look, like she's trying to process what's going on in my head.

Now talking like I'm in a daze with my eyes glassed over, I say, "Maybe he forged this. Maybe he made it on the internet or something."

Hope looks at me for a second, then reaches out, puts her hand on my arm, and talks to me as tenderly as a mother would talk to her own daughter. "Paige, he didn't create these. He didn't even produce them. These records came straight from the restaurant. There's an affidavit from the owner. They also have the receipt from your credit card company."

I close my eyes and ask, "And the cell phone records?"

She puts her hand on the documents and says, "These are the business records from your cell phone company. They show the data, or ping, recorded by each cell phone tower as your cell phones traveled from one location to the next."

Sounding half out of my mind, I look up at her, cover half my face with my hand, and ask, "Am I going crazy?"

She gives me this sideways look and asks, "Are you okay?"

Looking pale, like I might throw up or pass out, I shake my head, and mumble, "Something isn't right."

With her hand still on my arm, she says, "Tell me about it."

Looking forward, with my mind far away trying to remember that terrible night, I say, "I was there; Alton came home; he woke me up; I heard two gunshots." Now talking like I'm in a trance, I describe things just like I remember them. "Alton is standing in front of Trevor with that gun; I'm holding Trevor in my arms crying; I'm in the shower washing blood off of me…there's so much blood. I'm walking down the stairs and Trevor is wrapped in that rug…the rug from Alton's office. Alton leaves in the boat; I'm cleaning up all the blood…there's blood everywhere."

When I finish, tears are falling down my cheeks. I wipe them away and say, "I don't understand this. I don't understand what's going on."

Hope hands me a tissue and says, "Paige, I want you to see someone. He's a friend of mine. He can help you."

I wipe my face and say, "Help me?"

"He can help you remember what really happened that night."

– CHAPTER 39 –

Two days later, a psychiatrist comes to the prison. I wait in a private room so we can discuss my case. By now, I'm paranoid of everyone. Alton knows too many people. He knows lawyers, and judges, and every psychiatrist and psychologist in town—hell in the country. *Maybe he got to my lawyer?* I don't want to be here. When the doctor comes in and introduces himself, I'm afraid to shake his hand.

My psychiatrist comes in, extends his hand, and with a soft smile, he says, "Paige Warren, I'm Dr. Welby."

I'm slow to shake his hand. After the last few months, I'm pretty much paranoid of everyone. I glance nervously up at him.

He sits down on the chair across from me and asks, "So, how are you doing today?"

I hesitate for moment before I answer. Looking at the floor, I say, "Not so good."

"Well," he says with a sigh, "I'm sure this isn't easy for you. No one wants to be here. Most of my patients don't come here voluntarily, but I'm glad you agreed to see me."

I sit here without responding.

Maybe sensing my distrust, he asks, "Are you okay, Paige?"

I look up and ask, "Do you know my husband, Alton Warren?"

"I know him," he says.

"You know him?"

He sits back and says, "I know him…most people in my profession know him. But I've never worked with him. I saw him at a conference once, but I've never even talked to him."

I look up just a little and ask, "Can I trust you?"

He sounds very professional. Leaning forward, with his elbow on his knees, he explains, "You don't have to worry. Everything you tell me is strictly confidential. I'm here for you…and only you. You can trust me."

This doesn't really alleviate my concerns, but I have nowhere else to turn. I give him a half smile and look back down.

Then he asks, "Do you want to talk about things?"

I take a deep breath, nod my head, and say, "I guess that's why I'm here. I suppose you want to talk about that night?"

"That night?" he asks.

I struggle to get the words out. "Yeah, that night when everything happened."

With another smile, he says, "Why don't we take a step back. I'd like to get to know you first. Why don't you tell me about your family?"

Then he asks me different questions to get to know me better. Looking down the whole time, I tell him about myself, my family, and my hobbies and interests. I answer questions about my mom and growing up the way I did. I tell him about Dean and how he's the only dad I've ever known. I tell him about Trevor and me. Then he asks me about my favorite place to relax.

After I finish telling him all about my life with Alton, he says, "I want to talk with you about the night Trevor was killed. Can we do that?"

I nod my head.

"It's been a while and all the details might be a little foggy. I'd like to see if we can go back to that day. Is that okay?"

I nod again.

"I want you to take a minute and relax."

I take a couple of deep breaths and lean back in my chair.

"Do you feel relaxed?"

I slowly nod once more.

"As you sit here relaxed, you're no longer in jail. You're sitting by the lake in Huntsville. It's a beautiful, sunny day and you've been camping. The lake is so calm and relaxing. A little ripple floats towards you."

A smile spreads across my face.

"Sitting by the lake, you're connecting with your inner self. You can feel your heart beating, your pulses, and every breath you take in and out. All the negative energy is leaving your body. Now you're getting even more relaxed. Your arms are relaxed…your fingers are relaxed. Now you're so relaxed that it goes down to your legs. They feel so light and easy. Even your toes are relaxed."

For the first time ever, I feel almost weightless.

"As you sit by the lake, everything else melts away."

Now his voice gets fainter and fainter. I can barely hear him at all.

"Oh, it's so beautiful today. A cool breeze is blowing through your hair."

I look up with a smile, breathe in the fresh air, and turn from side to side.

His voice is almost gone. "Tell me about the la…"

With such a big smile, I say, "It's beautiful. Oh look…a bird just flew over me. It's red…it's a red cardinal. I love cardinals. I'm holding my fishing pole. I'm going to cast it out in the lake."

"That's wonderful isn't it. Cast it out."

I can actually feel the fishing pole in my hands. I throw my line out. "'Oh…I threw it so high…and so far. I've never thrown it this far before."

I sit down with my fishing pole, look to my left, and Trevor is sitting beside me. He's fishing too. I smile at him and he smiles back at me. Then, the cardinal lands in front of me. I reach down and it jumps into my hand.

"The red cardinal is on my hand," I say in amazement.

"That's wonderful. Can you feed it the seed in your pocket?"

I reach into my pocket and it's full of bird seed. I grab a handful with my free hand. I barely open my hand when the cardinal jumps on and starts eating the seed.

"Oh, oh…he's eating the seed. He likes it."

Sitting here with Trevor and watching the bird eat the seed, I hear, "Paige, can you leave the bird and go somewhere with me?"

"No, I want to stay right here."

"It's okay. We can come back."

"Where do you want to go?"

"Can we go to your house back on July 23rd?"

Frowning like I did when I was a little girl, I shake my head.

"Why don't you want to go with me?"

About to cry, I say, "I'm afraid. I'm afraid to go back there. I don't like it back there."

"It's okay. There's nothing to be afraid of."

"I'm afraid of him."

"Who are you afraid of?"

"Alton."

I remember nothing after that.

That afternoon, my psychiatrist calls Hope. She gets on the phone and says, "Dr. Welby?"

"Hi, Ms. Brunick. I wanted to let you know that I saw Paige Warren earlier. I just finished my report and I'll get it to you."

"How'd it go?"

"She's a very pleasant woman. I think a jury will like her."

"Was she able to go under hypnosis?"

"She was."

"And what happened?"

"Ms. Brunick, Paige has been through a lot. Not only the shooting of the man she loved, but her whole life. Has she talked to you about it?"

"Not really."

"It wasn't good. She was raised by an abusive and uncaring mother. Her mom brought many men into her life who physically abused her. One of her mom's husbands sexually abused her for three years, starting when she was ten. Her mom also had a boyfriend who sexually abused her when she was fifteen. She told her mom each time, but her mom sided with the men after they denied it. She pretty much raised herself. She was kicked out of the house at seventeen and had to live with a friend. The only constant person in her life, before her present family, was a step-father named Dean. She calls him her father."

"Jesus," Hope says.

"She should have gotten help long ago. She's a strong woman who has kept this bottled up inside her for many years. It's the only way she knows how to cope with it all. There was one boyfriend," he looks at his notes and says, "yes, a guy named Brad, who she confided in about most of this stuff. He used it against her which reinforced her need to never talk about it again. Ms. Brunick, she needed therapy and counseling—and lots of it."

"Obviously."

"After it didn't work out with her boyfriend, Paige was lost. She married her husband to find the stability she never had. Unfortunately, he wasn't able to give her the love she so desperately needed. She found that love in Trevor Evans. It wasn't just his love she was drawn to. He opened up a whole world to her that she longed for. He freed her sexually to love and be loved. Losing that love, and that world, would be devastating to her. I'm not sure she could mentally or emotionally survive having it taken away."

"I picked up on that."

"Was this Trevor Evans ending the relationship?"

"Not as far as I know. Paige acts like they were great."

"And maybe in her mind they were," Dr. Welby says. "I'm really concerned for her. There's no telling what she might do if he decided to end the relationship."

"Did she talk to you about that night?" Hope asks.

"It was very difficult. She didn't want to go back there again. She started talking like a little girl and went into a fetal position on the floor. She kept saying she was too scared to talk about it."

"So she didn't?"

"I told her there was nothing to be afraid of—I'm here and everything will be alright. I got her to a place where she was able to go there."

"And?"

"As painful as it was, she went through it…step by step…like she was reliving it all over again. She got extremely emotional. She told me the exact same story. She came down the stairs and her husband had shot Mr. Evans. She spent a lot of time talking about seeing him dead and holding him in her arms. It's what she remembers the most. Then, she said she took a shower and when she came back down Alton had him rolled up in a rug, took him out on the lake, and she stayed home cleaning everything up."

With a big sigh of relief, Hope asks, "So she didn't kill him?"

"When we talked the first time, you told me that all the evidence points to her, right?"

"It sure looks like it."

"And her husband has a solid alibi?"

"It looks iron-clad."

"Ms. Brunick, the idea of her killing the man she loved and so desperately needed, is so unacceptable that her mind may have blocked the whole thing out and created this alternative reality where she stood back and her husband did it all. How many times has she told this story?"

"Well, she told me, my investigator, and the prosecutor. She had three interviews with the police. I think she told her close friend."

"So, she's told it many times. The mind can play tricks on us. We can repeat the same story so many times that we actually begin to believe it."

"Oh, God," Hope says.

"One thing for sure, *she* now believes Alton killed Mr. Evans. I'm afraid what might happen to her if she comes to the reality that she was the one who actually killed him. When she does, she needs to be stronger emotionally. It will take months, if not years, of therapy to prepare her mind to accept it."

Hope lets out another sigh and says, "What a mess."

"Ms. Brunick, Paige does not belong in prison. She needs professional help."

"You're talking about an insanity defense?"

"I am. I can explain to the jury the effect that her mom and all the men in her life had on her. The sexual abuse she suffered, and having no one believe her, caused irreparable damage. Her boyfriend caused her to retreat deeper and deeper inside herself, and her marriage only exacerbated the issues she was already dealing with."

"Dr. Welby, have you testified in an insanity case before?"

"A few times."

"And how many of those times did the jury find the defendant not guilty due to reason of insanity?"

"Well….none."

"That's because Texas wants to make sure no one is found insane. It has one of the nation's highest bars for a successful insanity defense. It's almost impossible. It's not enough to prove the defendant was suffering from a severe mental illness. You also have to prove the defendant didn't know his conduct was wrong. This is where they get you. Especially, like in Paige's case, where she was fully functional and had never sought treatment for mental illness. For fifteen years, Paige was married to one of the best psychologists in the state. I'm sure he'll be their star witness. Pleading insanity would be a sure conviction."

"What are you going to do?" Dr. Welby asks.

"I don't know. I don't know what the hell to do. I was hoping you could figure all this out. Now, I have more questions than I started with. One thing for sure, I have a trial to deal with and we're at the start of our investigation."

With an audible sigh, Dr. Welby says, "Ms. Brunick, I fear what a trial might do to Paige. I fear what she might do in the middle of trial if she's confronted with all the evidence against her. I don't think she's mentally or emotionally able to handle it."

Hope sits back in her chair, looks up, and says, "Well, thanks again for everything."

"Well, let me know if I can help in any way." Then, before he hangs up, Dr. Welby says, "Oh, Ms. Brunick."

"Yeah?"

"Paige needs to find a good therapist—someone she can trust. I'm not sure if she completely trusts you or me. She needs to find someone who has nothing to do with this case."

"I'll see what I can do."

PART FOUR

JUDGMENT DAY

"There is no client as scary as an innocent man."
> J. Michael Haller, Attorney at Law

"Justice? You get justice in the next world, in this world you have the law."
> — William Gaddis

– CHAPTER 40 –

The months pass by slowly. Then, Monday morning, I'm taken to the courthouse in a van that has to stop for the crowd that's surrounding the entire courthouse. There are people shouting into the darkened windows of the van and others holding signs like:

"GUILTY!"

"Burn in hell Murderer"

"Death, Death, Death"

"Justice for Evans"

One sign has a needle and syringe.

A woman comes up to the window and runs her finger across her neck, mimicking the slicing of her own throat. As far as I know, I'm not even subject to the death penalty. Reporters are snapping shots through the window, pointing a microphone at the van, and shouting,

"Why'd you do it? Are you sorry?"

Another crowd is waiting for Hope. She pushes her way into the courthouse shouting, "No comment…no comment."

I'm led to a room where I'm able to make myself presentable. The courtroom is jam-packed. When I walk in, everything stops. Some guy with a pad and colored pencils starts sketching feverishly. The prosecutor has two attorneys at her side. Hope is already at our table all by herself.

I'm brought to the table, my handcuffs are taken off, and I sit down. Hope puts her hand on my back, leans closer, and says, "You look wonderful. You ready?"

I'm not sure what she's asking. "Am I supposed to do something?"

She gives me a smile and says, "Just sit there and look innocent. The jury will be watching you."

I turn around and see Dean and his wife sitting on the front row behind me. We exchange a smile. Trish is right beside them. She's been to the jail every day since this started. I move closer and say, "Thank y'all for being here."

Dean leans closer and gives me a hug.

The prosecutor looks over at Hope and says, "Can we talk?"

They go into another room and the prosecutor says, "Ms. Brunick, the family wants the body for a proper burial. Lake Travis is one of the biggest lakes in the state. Divers have been looking for months and can't find it. If your client will finally tell the truth and take us to the body, we'll agree to forty years."

"She is telling the truth. How can she take you to the body if she doesn't know where it is?"

"Oh, come on," the prosecutor laughs. "You can't seriously believe that."

Hope presses her lips together and shrugs her shoulders.

"Think of your client. With this deal, she'll be able to see her kids again one day."

"If she lives that long. They won't even know her by then."

Trying to reason with her, the prosecutor says, "Forget your ego for a minute. You're going to lose this one. What will that do to your perfect record?"

"I'm not worried about my record," Hope assures her. "If we lose, we lose, but Paige can never bring you to that body."

Right after they return, the judge comes into the courtroom and everyone stands up. With a smile, he introduces himself, and gives instructions to everyone in attendance—mostly about how he'll send out anyone who causes a disruption.

"Let me talk to the attorneys at the bench," he says.

All three lawyers walk forward and the judge asks, "How long are we looking at here?"

The prosecutor says, "We don't have a body, so that cuts a lot of the medical and forensic testimony. I would say four days."

"Then we should finish this week or early next week," Hope says.

"Another quick trial?" the judge asks .

"I like to keep it simple," Hope says. "We don't want to bore the jury."

"All right," the judge says. "You can return to your tables."

Then the judge says, "Bring in the jury."

Soon, the courtroom is full of potential jurors. The judge introduces himself, both attorneys, and then me. I stand up and smile. After giving some instructions, he says, "The prosecutor has the burden of proof here, so they get to go first."

Eight hours later, we have our jury.

– CHAPTER 41 –

The next morning, the prosecutor calls Detective Cummings. He introduces himself, explains how Trevor's sister didn't hear from him for two days and called the police. He went out to the house he was working on and the couple there said he left Friday and never came back. He searched Trevor's house and found three of the cards I gave him sitting on his dresser. The prosecutor puts one of the cards up on the screen. It shows a man and woman walking on the beach hand-in-hand. He reads for the jury what it says inside.

> My love,
>
> These past months have been the best of my life. I don't have the words to explain just how much fun I've had with you camping, fishing, hiking, and surfing (definitely surfing!) Oh, and lying in bed with you. I can't get enough of your hands on my body and mine on yours. You are so sexy!
>
> What I love the most is simply sitting with you talking. You're everything I always wanted in a man.

I start to cry as he continues to read the card. I take a tissue from the box on the table and wipe my eyes.

I want you to know that you saved me--and I'm not just talking about saving me in Miami. You have made me soooooo happy. I'll spend the rest of my life making you happy too.

Love you,

Paige

The prosecutor asks, "After you found the card, what did you do?"

"We went to talk to the defendant at her home. Her husband was there at the time."

"What did the defendant say when you asked her about Trevor?"

"Well, the defendant didn't say a whole lot. She seemed evasive, like she was afraid to talk. They both admitted that he worked on their boathouse. Her husband said he finished months ago."

Hope jumps up and says, "Objection, hearsay."

"Sustained," the judge says.

The prosecutor asks, "What did the defendant say regarding Mr. Evans?"

I turn to Hope and ask, "Why is he testifying to what I said? Isn't it hearsay?"

Hope shakes her head and whispers, "It's an exception. What the defendant says is not hearsay."

Cummings continues. "The defendant said she saw him last approximately three weeks before Mr. Evans disappeared when he came back to fix something on the boathouse."

"Did you ask if she was in a relationship with Trevor Evans?"

"Not in front of her husband. I asked her about that when she came down to the police station."

"And what did she say?"

"She denied any relationship."

"What went through your mind when you heard this?"

"Well, we knew she wasn't telling the truth from the cards and from talking to his sister. We were well aware they were having an affair."

"Is this the only time she was dishonest?"

"Well, she wasn't truthful at her house when she said she hadn't seen or talked to him in three weeks. We had her come to the station for a little sit-down. We hoped she'd be a little more honest if her husband wasn't around."

"And was she?"

"Oh, no. Like I said, she first said they weren't in a relationship. After we told her about the cards we found on his dresser, she admitted she had lied to us. She said they were in a relationship. She said she invited him over that night, but then texted him not to come."

Several jurors glance over at me.

"Anything else?"

"She said Alton was home Friday evening."

The prosecutor asks. "Tell the jury, after she left, did you execute a search warrant?"

"We didn't have to. Mrs. Warren…I mean the defendant…gave us consent to search her home."

"And what did you find?"

"Well, as soon as I walked into her home, I could smell bleach. Our team went through the house and used luminol—it's a water based substance that can detect blood. We found evidence of blood on the floor near the back door, on the walls, on the couch, and on the stairs leading up to the defendant's bedroom. It was obvious that someone had tried to clean the blood up with bleach."

"And did you recover evidence from the house?"

"We found cards under her mattress given to her by Mr. Evans. We seized a laptop belonging to the defendant. We also found traces of blood under the couch and on the back door seal. We sent the blood off to the lab to be tested."

"Anything else?"

"We recovered a surveillance video system from the boathouse."

"What'd you do next?"

"We had Dr. Warren come in for an interview."

"I don't want you to tell me what he said…that's hearsay. He will be here to testify for himself. Can you tell the jury about his demeanor when you interviewed him?"

"He was very cooperative. He seemed calm and forthright—sounded very honest."

"Objection," Hope says. "This witness is not qualified to determine whether Mr. Warren was honest or not."

"Sustained."

I'm not sure what sustained means. Did we win or did they?

The prosecutor asks, "What did you learn from that interview?"

"We learned he wasn't even in Austin on the night of the murder. He was in San Antonio at a conference where he spoke. He didn't come back until Saturday."

"That was another lie told by the defendant?"

"Yes, ma'am."

Louder than I intended, I turn to Hope and say, "It's not a lie. He was right there."

The prosecutor stops and looks over at me. The judge, and all jurors, do the same. Hope holds up one finger and whispers, "Shhh."

The prosecutor looks back at the jury and asks, "One more thing about your interview with Dr. Warren. Did he try to blame the murder on the defendant?"

"Not at all. He was actually very defensive of her. He said she couldn't have been involved in Trevor Evans' murder. She would never do something like that. Something must have happened. He said it must have been an accident."

"After interviewing Dr. Warren, what did you do next?"

"I called the woman who organized the conference in San Antonio." He scans through his papers and says, "Yes…Mrs. Bowerly. She confirmed he spoke at the conference and sent us the video."

"And then what did you do?"

"We asked the defendant to come back in."

"And did she?"

"Yes, she agreed to come back in."

"And what did she say?"

"Nothing at first. She denied everything and said she hadn't seen Trevor Evans for weeks. Then we placed her under arrest. Once we handcuffed her, she started crying and said she wanted to tell us the truth…or at least her version of the truth."

"And what was that?"

"She told us she texted Mr. Evans to come over that Friday because her husband was going out of town. Then her husband came home—"

"Which we know is not true."

"Yes ma'am. He had proof he was in San Antonio all weekend."

"And what'd she say about texting him again?"

"She said she texted him to come over but after her husband returned, she texted him not to come."

"Did you later recover those texts?"

"Yes, I did."

"How?"

"Our forensic team was able to pulled them off her computer. We found the texts there."

The prosecutor puts the texts up on the big screen and asks, "Is this the text from that day."

"Yes, ma'am."

She hands a copy of the texts to each of the jurors.

Thursday: 9:36 a.m.

Alton's leaving tomorrow.
He'll be back Saturday. I
have to see u. Even if it's
for a few hours

Thursday: 9: 38 a.m.

> I'll be there around 11:30.
> Can't wait to see you.

Thursday: 9:41 a.m.

> Absolutely! Come around
> back. Keep quiet. Kids are
> here.

Friday: 6:32 p.m.

> He's back. Won't be able to
> see you. Sorry. Talk soon.

Friday: 9:36 a.m.

> He's gone. Come on over.

I haven't seen these texts since that horrible day. I'm stunned. I turn to Hope and whisper, "I never wrote that last text. Alton must have taken my phone when I was asleep."

Not showing a lot of concern, Hope nods her head.

I turn to the jury, point at the screen, and say, "I never wrote that. I never wrote that last text."

The whole courtroom stops. The judge looks at Hope and says, "Counselor, talk to your client. We're not going to have these outbursts."

Hope leans over and whispers, "It's okay. Let me handle this."

The prosecutor continues. "So, when the defendant said she texted him not to come over, was this the truth?"

"That part is true."

"Is it the whole truth?"

"No. Obviously, she texted him later to come to the house."

"She lured him to his death?"

"Obviously, she did."

Almost all the jurors look over at me. Trevor's sister shakes her head in disgust.

"What happened next?"

"She started telling me this whole story about how her husband came home. He woke her—"

"Detective Cummings," the prosecutor interrupts. "Why don't we just show the jury what she said."

She pushes play on the video that shows me talking at the police station:

"You're right...you're right. I'll tell you everything. He did come over that night. I texted Trevor and told him to come over Friday night. Alton did come back home, so I texted him not to come over. I was upset I couldn't see him, so I went to bed early. Alton woke me up in the middle of the night and told me to get the kids...someone was breaking in the back door. When I realized what he was saying, I was afraid it might be Trevor. I ran down the stairs and heard two gunshots. Alton was standing there holding a gun and Trevor was dead in front of him."

"Then what happened to his body?"

"Alton...Alton started...he told me to go up and take a shower, because I had blood all over me from holding Trevor. When I came down, he had Trevor...Trevor was...rolled...rolled up in a rug. He started saying we had to make it all go away. He...he...he...put him in our boat and dropped him somewhere in the lake. I tried to stop him. I swear to God, I tried to stop him."

"So, y'all dumped the body?"

"Alton did. I didn't want anything to do with it. I refused to even pick Trevor up. I damn sure wasn't going to go with him. He told me to clean up the blood before the kids woke up. I stayed back and cleaned everything up."

"So, your husband shot him?"

"He did...but he didn't know he was shooting Trevor. He thought someone was breaking into our house."

After the prosecutor stops the video, she asks, "How did you respond?"

"We told her that her husband told us he was in San Antonio at a conference on Friday."

"What was her response?"

"She said he was lying. First, she said he was supposed to go to Phoenix and he never spoke at the conference."

The prosecutor admits into evidence the video of Alton speaking at the conference for fifty minutes and plays it for the jury. When Alton walks away from the podium, the prosecutor clicks stop on the player. Then she asks, "You told the defendant you had proof he spoke at the conference on Friday?"

"We did."

"What did she say?"

"She seemed confused. Then she changed her whole story. She said he returned to Austin after speaking in San Antonio. She said there was plenty of time."

"Detective Cummings, did you tell the defendant that her husband said he had proof that he was at a restaurant in San Antonio on Friday night?

"Yes ma'am."

"And what did she say?"

"Again, she said he was lying—that there's no way he'll have any proof."

Moving on, the prosecutor asks, "Mr. Cummings, when you executed that search, you testified you were able to get blood samples from the house?"

"Yes, we found blood under the couch and on the back door sill."

"Was it tested for DNA?"

"It was."

"And did you get the DNA results?"

"Yes ma'am. It took about six weeks to get the results back. The test showed it was 99.999%. genetic match to Trevor Evans"

"Did you find any other evidence?"

"We found a trash bag in the garage near the entry. There were women's clothes inside. The clothes were covered in blood."

The prosecutor shows Cummings my clothes soaked in Trevor's blood. I start crying in front of the jury.

"Did you have this blood tested?" the prosecutor asks.

"Yes. Again, it was a genetic match to Trevor Evans."

People in the courtroom gasp. Someone shouts. The judge bangs his gavel. "Order! Order!"

Things settle down and she asks, "Was she untruthful about anything else?"

"Yes, ma'am. We asked her if she drove the boat that night."

The prosecutor plays the video.

"Do you know how to drive your boat?"
"I've driven it before."
"But on this night you never drove it?"
"No, sir."

Then the prosecutor ends with a bombshell. She stops the video and asks, "Detective Cummings, you said you recovered a surveillance video from the boathouse. Did you watch the video from that night?"

"Yes, I did."

"Let's play it for the jury."

The bailiff turns the lights down a little and everyone in the courtroom stares at the screen waiting for it to play. It's a split-screen, showing inside and outside the boathouse. It's dark outside, and completely silent, until you hear two loud gunshots coming from the house. Several of the jurors jump in their seats. Some people in the courtroom gasp.

Forty minutes later, I'm picked up on the video halfway across the backyard. I walk across the lawn and go inside the boathouse, throw the tie-downs and cinderblock in the boat, back the boat out of the boathouse, move it out of the view of the camera, and a few minutes later you hear the boat drive off.

The lights turn back on and the prosecutor lets the image sink in. I feel the mood in the courtroom change. The jurors look at me like I'm a murderer. Trevor's parents cry, and his sister has this look like she's about to jump over the rail and strangle me.

The prosecutor stands up and says, "No more questions."

When we recess for lunch, Trish walks up to the railing. I walk closer and say, "Thanks again for coming."

She leans in and whispers, "Is your lawyer going to object or something?"

I shake my head and say, "I think it makes the judge mad."

Trish rolls her eyes and says, "I hope she knows what she's doing."

"It's too late now," I respond. "I have to trust her."

After lunch, my attorney asks the questions.

"Detective Cummings, Paige was very cooperative wasn't she."

"Well, she came down to the station."

"She came down three times, correct."

"I believe so."

"Don't you find that remarkable that a woman, who you allege just killed her lover, would come for an interview not once, but three times?"

Cummings gives a little shrug. "Not really. It's not uncommon for a person who's accused of a crime to try to talk their way out of it."

"But she was cooperative, right?"

Cummings thinks about it for a second and says, "I would say no. She gave us no helpful information until after she was arrested."

"You said my client lied about being in a relationship with Trevor Evans, correct?"

"Correct."

"She was married. It's not really surprising that someone would lie about something like that, right?"

"Yes, ma'am. I would agree with that."

"About the conference in San Antonio, you were aware that Mr. Warren stayed at the hotel where the conference was held?"

"Correct."

"Were you able to find one single witness who saw him at the hotel after he spoke?"

"We didn't really look."

"You didn't look?"

"We had sufficient evidence that he was there."

"And that evidence is the video of him speaking and him checking out of the hotel?"

"Not just that. We also have the records from the garage confirming he was there all day except when he left to eat."

"Did you check the video from the hotel lobby?"

"I did."

"And was he in the lobby any time that evening?"

"No, we didn't see him in the lobby."

"The prosecutor here talked to the jury about circumstantial and direct evidence. An actual witness who saw him would be direct evidence, correct?"

"Correct."

"And you don't have that."

"No…no witness."

"So you relied entirely on circumstantial evidence, right?"

Cummings shakes his head and says, "We have the video of him at the conference, his car in the garage, proof he ate at the restaurant, the location of his phone the entire day, and him checking out the next day. I would say that's stronger than any direct evidence."

"Of course you do," Hope says.

"Now Detective Cummings, you watched the same video we watched today showing Paige getting into the boat and backing it out, correct?

"Correct."

"Let me ask you, did you watch any of the video footage from the weeks and months prior?"

"Prior to Friday the twenty-third? No, ma'am."

"Well, let's take a look."

Hope turns on the monitor, backs it up two months, and plays the video showing the back yard. She moves forward, pushes play, and repeats this again and again. Then she asks, "Do you find anything different about the earlier videos compared to the video from Friday the twenty-third?"

"Not really, except it seems to have a different angle."

"That's right," Hope says. "From the time the security camera was installed until three days prior to Trevor being killed, the camera showed the entire backyard. On the night of the murder, it only shows the back part of the yard."

"That's what it looks like."

"Do you know who changed the camera angle?"

"I do not."

"Don't you find it odd that three days before Trevor was murdered, someone changed the angle of the camera to cut off the view of the house?"

"Not really. I don't know why that happened or who did it."

"And the video never actually shows who carried Trevor Evans out of the house and put him in the boat."

"Well, it's pretty clear it was the defendant. She was the only one out there that night."

"But it doesn't show on the video, does it?"

"No, it doesn't show on the video….oh, except it does show the defendant go out to the boathouse, load a cinderblock and tie-downs, and back the boat out."

"Again, circumstantial evidence."

Cummings looks at the jury and says, "If you say so."

"Don't you find it strange that she just killed her lover and walks right in front of the surveillance camera?"

"No. Maybe she forgot about the camera."

"I guess that's possible," Hope says. "Oh…one more thing. Did you check if the Mexican food restaurant where Alton ate that Friday night had security cameras inside or outside of the restaurant?"

Ready for every question, he says, "We did. The owner said there were no cameras."

"Thank you. Pass the witness."

Next, the prosecutor calls the general manager for the hotel where Alton stayed. He brought all the records with him. He testifies when Alton checked in and when he checked out. He then plays the video of Alton checking out of the hotel on Saturday at 1:22 PM.

Then the prosecutor hands him some documents and asks, "What are these records?"

"This is from the garage entry and exit gate. It shows each time a guest goes in or out of the garage."

"And when does it show Dr. Warren entered or exited the garage?"

"If you look here, he entered the garage on Friday at 10:09 AM. He left again Friday night at 7:30 PM. He drove back inside the garage two hours later at 10:01 PM and left again on Saturday afternoon at 1:39 PM."

"And did Dr. Warren enter or leave at any other times?"

"No, he did not."

"So, was Dr. Warren's car in the garage all night long?"

"Yes, it was."

"Are you sure?"

"Definitely. If he left, it would have shown up on this report."

"And did Dr. Warren have any contact with anyone at the hotel that evening?"

"Well, not directly," he says, "but at 10:20 PM he requested a wake-up call for nine a.m."

"Pass the witness."

Hope gets up and asks, "Can you tell this jury, are you aware of any witnesses who saw Mr. Warren at the hotel at any time after speaking at the conference until he checked out the next morning?"

"No, ma'am."

"Not the wait staff."

"No, ma'am."

"Security?"

"No, ma'am."

"Anyone at the front desk?"

"No, ma'am."

"And that wake-up call, do you have to personally call the front desk?"

"No, you can request a wake-up call from the phone in your room. All we know is that it was placed at exactly 10:20 PM."

Hope stands up and says, "No further questions."

"You may step down," the judge says. He looks at both attorneys and says, "Why don't we adjourn for the day. We'll reconvene tomorrow morning at nine a.m."

As Hope gathers her things, Trish, Dean, and his wife come over and we visit before I'm taken back to my cell. Hope turns around with some boxes and asks, "You ready to go? I have some work to do before tomorrow."

After she walks off, I turn back and ask, "What do you think?"

Dean lets out a big sigh and says, "I don't know. I don't know what to think."

Trish puts her hand on her forehead and says, "Jesus, Paige! That Cummings asshole was their biggest witness, and she barely asked him anything."

"What's she supposed to ask?"

"Hell, I don't know…something."

I look down and say, "I don't know, she must know what she's doing."

When I look back up, just about everyone has cleared out of the courtroom. Then, with wide eyes, I whisper, "Oh my God."

Trish gives me a puzzled look and asks, "What is it?"

Looking back at Trish, I whisper, "That's him…that's Brad, the guy I dated in college."

Brad is standing at the back of the courtroom staring right at me. When he gives me a smile, I'm not sure what to do. I smile back, and with a nod I mouth, "Hi."

The next morning, the courtroom is packed again. I glance back and Brad is sitting on the back row. The prosecutor calls an expert from the cell phone company. He explains how a cell phone sends a signal to each cell phone tower as it moves from one zone to the next. Through triangulation, you can track a phone as it travels by each tower.

"Did you research Alton Warren's cell phone on Friday and Saturday?"

"I did. Mr. Warren's cell phone left the tower near his home on Friday morning at 8:09 AM. It moved down IH-35 until it reached downtown San Antonio."

"The tower where the Omni hotel is located?"

"That's correct."

"What time was that?"

"10:09 AM."

"When is the next time it moved?"

It stayed at that same location until Friday at 7:30 PM where it traveled further downtown."

"What time did it arrive?"

"7:52 PM. And it left that location at 9:52 PM and returned to the previous tower."

"Back at the hotel?"

"That's correct."

"What time?"

"10:10 PM."

"And did his phone leave that location at any other time?"

"Not until Saturday at 1:38 PM. It traveled back up IH-35 to Austin and then to his home."

What time did it arrive back at his home?"

"Saturday at 3:22 PM."

Next, the prosecutor shocks everyone with my phone records. She puts the document on the screen and asks, "And did you run a report on the defendant's cell phone on Friday?"

"I did."

At this point, most jurors lean a little closer, eager to hear this testimony.

Using the cell records and a map, she asks, "Did it leave her home at any time on Friday?"

"No ma'am. It was there all day and night."

"Did it ever leave the home?"

"Not until early Saturday morning. It leaves her home on Saturday at 12:14 AM. It pinged off one tower and then the next as it moved away from her home and towards the middle of the lake. It stays at that location for fifteen minutes and returns back to her home."

A huge gasp comes from the courtroom gallery. People start talking out loud. The judge bangs his gavel and says, "Order….order."

"Oh," the witness continues. "Early Saturday morning it travels to a location about five miles away. It stopped at a storage facility and returned home."

"No more questions," the prosecutor says.

Hope stands up and says, "No questions."

I look back at Trish who's sitting there with wide eyes.

I can't believe the things they're saying. *I never went out on that lake. I have to do something.* I stand up in front of the jury and say, "Your Honor, can I say something?"

The judge turns to the jury and says, "Let's break for lunch. It's 11:42. Why don't we meet back here at 1:00."

As soon as the jury walks out, the judge turns to me and says, "Mrs. Warren, I've warned you. This is your last warning. If you want to say something then you have to testify…under oath. I will not tolerate another outburst in my courtroom. Do you understand?"

I nod my head.

"Do you understand?" he repeats.

I look down and say, "Yes, sir."

I turn around and Trish is standing at the rail behind me. She looks at me exasperated, and says, "Paige…what the fuck?"

I shake my head and say, "It's not what it seems."

With raised eyebrows, she says. "Well, it seems pretty bad."

With my hands trembling, I nod my head and say, "I know."

She looks at Hope, back at me, and whispers, "I feel like I'm watching my brother's trial all over again. Your lawyer isn't doing shit. She got nowhere with that detective and she didn't even ask this guy a single question."

Dean stands there without saying anything.

"I don't know," I say, shaking my head. "She has a plan."

"Jesus, Paige."

I look down and repeat, "I know."

After lunch, the prosecutor does the unthinkable. She calls Beth to the stand. Hope said they probably wouldn't call her because she's young and my daughter, but here she is sitting down in the witness stand in front of me, lowering the microphone to her lips. Hope's investigator tried to talk to her but Alton refused. We have a pretty good idea what she's here to say.

Sitting in front of everyone, she looks even younger than she actually is. She looks up at me and starts crying. I cover my face and start crying too.

The judge hands her a tissue and says, "It's okay. Take as much time as you need."

Once she calms back down, the prosecutor begins. "Please introduce yourself to the jury."

With her lips trembling, she says, "I'm Elizabeth Warren."

"Are you nervous?"

She nods her head.

"Do your friends call you Beth?"

She nods again.

"Can I call you Beth?"

She wipes her eyes and nods again.

Looking sympathetic, the prosecutor says, "There's a court reporter taking down everything that's said in here today. It's important that you answer verbally. Can you do that?"

She nods, and then catches herself and says, "Yes, ma'am."

"Beth, do you know the difference between right and wrong…the truth and a lie?"

She nods her head and says, "Yes."

"If I said that your mom is wearing a blue dress today would that be the truth?"

She looks at me, nods her head, and says, "Yes, ma'am."

"If I said you were in tenth grade, would that be true?"

She shakes her head and says, "No, ma'am."

"Okay, I know this is hard for you, Beth, so I won't keep you long. How do you know Paige Warren?"

She looks at me and a tear drops down her cheek when she answers, "She's my mom."

"Beth, I need you to tell me about that Friday night when Trevor Evans was killed."

Sounding like a little girl, she asks, "When I heard gunshots?"

"Yes…the night you heard gunshots."

"Well, I was asleep in my bed. Then I heard two loud bangs that woke me up."

"What did they sound like?"

"I don't know….kind of like a gun…I guess."

"What were you thinking?"

"I was scared, I guess. Maybe someone was breaking in and killed my mom."

"What did you do?"

"I don't know...nothing really. I stayed in bed and hid under my covers."

"Did you go downstairs?"

She shakes her head and says, "I was too afraid."

"Can you tell us what happened next?"

She starts to cry without answering.

"I'm sorry, Beth, but we have to know."

"I could hear my mom crying downstairs."

"And did you also hear your dad crying?"

"No, ma'am."

"Was your mom screaming?"

"I don't know. Maybe a little."

"And did you hear your dad screaming a little?"

She shakes her head.

"I'm sorry Beth, but you have to answer."

She looks down and says, "No, only my mom."

"Did you ever see or hear your dad downstairs?"

Still looking down, she shakes her head and whispers, "No, ma'am."

"Then what happened?"

"Well, I heard my mom coming up the stairs. She was crying, so I opened my door to...like...see what was going on."

"And what happened?"

"I don't know. My mom...like...slammed my door and told me to go back to sleep."

"So what did you do?"

"I got back in my bed."

"Beth, did you see your mom before she slammed the door shut?"

She pauses for a moment, looks right at me, and says, "Maybe for a second."

"And what did you see?" Her lips start shaking and tears fall down her face. Then she starts gasping for air. The prosecutor isn't deterred a bit. "What did you see?" she presses.

Beth wipes her eyes with the tissue and says, "Like….blood."

"You saw blood?" the prosecutor repeats.

Beth nods her head and says, "Yes ma'am."

"And where was the blood?"

In a flat whisper, she says, "All over my mom."

Surely some of the jurors couldn't hear her. The prosecutor waits a second and asks, "It was all over your mom?"

She nods her head and says, "Yes, ma'am."

"Nothing further," the prosecutor says, "Pass the witness."

Hope gets up and says, "Beth, I'm your mom's lawyer. I'm sorry you had to come here today. I only have a few questions."

She nods her head.

"After you heard the gunshots, did you stay in bed until you heard your mom coming up the stairs.?"

"Yes, ma'am," she nods.

"You never opened your door before you heard your mom upstairs?"

"No, I was…like…afraid."

"So, you never came downstairs?"

"No, ma'am."

"So, your dad could have been downstairs but you didn't see him, right?"

Obviously confused, she looks at me and says, "I don't know."

"Beth, one last thing. Do you remember eating dinner that night?"

She shakes her head and says, "No, ma'am."

"Do you remember eating Chinese food?"

"No, ma'am."

"Do you remember if your dad was home and eating dinner with you that night?"

She shrugs and says, "It was a long time ago. I don't remember."

"Okay...okay…that's all I have."

Beth slowly steps down and walks between our table and the prosecutor's table. We share a sympathetic smile as she passes by. Several of the jurors are wiping their eyes as she walks out.

The judge looks at the jurors and says, "Let's take a fifteen minute break."

Next, the prosecutor calls Alton to testify. He gets on the stand with a cheery smile and introduces himself. He gives all his background about being this hotshot psychologist who writes books that are taught all over the country. He explains how we've been married for fifteen years, I've been a great wife and mother, and he's still very much in love with me. I want to slap him.

After rambling on and on about how important he is, he finally gets to the point. He explains how he often speaks at conferences around the country. On Friday, July 23rd, he spoke at a conference in San Antonio."

"And that was you on the video we saw yesterday speaking in San Antonio?" the prosecutor asks.

"Yes, it was."

"What time did you finish speaking?"

"About three thirty on Friday afternoon."

"Then what did you do?"

"I took a nap afterwards. Then I woke up and worked on my computer dictating medical reports. That night, I left to eat at a Mexican food restaurant. I was gone about two hours."

"Have you heard the defendant's position in this case—that you were at the house the night Trevor was killed?"

"I was told that by the detective."

"What did you think when you heard this?"

He looks at me and says, "I don't know why she would say that. I'm not sure if she simply forgot or is just mistaken, because I was in San Antonio until Saturday afternoon."

As I listen to him testify, this anger starts building up inside me. I turn to Hope and say, "He's a liar."

She leans closer and motions with her hand for me to talk lower.

"And that you were the one who killed Trevor Evans?"

He looks down, looking all sad, and says, "Yes, I heard that."

The prosecutor hands him a document and says, "Do you recognize this document?"

He takes a look and says, "Sure. It's my credit card receipt from the restaurant I ate at that night."

"What time did you sign your credit card bill?"

"It looks like 9:45 PM."

She hands it to the juror on the end. He holds it, looks at both sides, and passes it on to the next juror.

"And did you leave the hotel for any reason other than to eat for two hours?"

He looks right at the jury and says, "I did not. I was at the hotel the whole time."

"And when did you check out again?"

"It was Saturday afternoon."

She hands him another document. "Do you recognize this document?"

"Yes," Alton says. "That's my credit card receipt from the hotel. It shows I checked out on Saturday at 1:22 PM."

She hands it to the jury and again they pass it down the row. Then the juror at the end hands it to the back row, and they do the same thing.

She hands him another document and asks, "And do you recognize this document?"

"It's my credit card receipt from the gas station I stopped at on my way home. I filled up my car with gas and got some coffee at 2:01 PM."

Once more, each juror looks at the receipt.

I don't know much about the law, but on television the lawyer objects or something. Hope's just watching the show and writing on her pad every now and then.

"Dr. Warren, were you aware that the defendant was having a sexual relationship with Mr. Evans?"

The smile fades from his face. He looks down, showing more emotion than I've ever seen. Looking like he might start crying, he says, "She told me after the detectives left our house."

"Did this surprise you?"

He pauses, like this is way too emotional for him. "Yes ma'am. I love her. I was shocked…and hurt."

"Dr. Warren, what happened when you got back to Austin on Saturday?"

"Well, I walked in and the house had a very strong smell of bleach. I asked about it, and Paige told me she spilled something and cleaned it up. I just blew it off. Then I went out to the boat a little later and noticed the keys were in the ignition."

"And why was that important?"

"Well, I never leave the keys in the ignition, so I knew she had taken the boat out. This surprised me because she's never taken it out without me. I clicked the boat on and saw that the gas was pretty low, so I knew she went quite a ways."

"Did you notice anything else?"

"Yes, the tie-downs that are always hanging on the wall were missing."

"What did you do next?"

"I went back inside and asked my wife if she'd gone out on the boat."

"And what did she say?"

"She said she hadn't."

I cannot just sit here while they tell one lie about me after another. If Hope won't do anything, I will. "He's lying!" I shout. "He's sitting up there lying!"

The judge bangs his gavel and say, "Mrs. Warren, we talked about this!" He turns to the jury and says, "You will disregard the defendant's statement." He throws his glasses on the bench and says, "Let's take a fifteen minute break."

We all watch as all the jurors walk out of the room. Before the judge can say anything, I look up and say, "I'm sorry judge, but—"

He's fuming and his face has turned a shade of red I've never seen before. He points right at me and practically shouts, "Mrs. Warren, I warned you! One more outburst and I'll find you in contempt of court and you'll watch the rest of this trial by video. Do you understand?"

My heart is beating a mile-a-minute. I look up and say, "Yes, sir."

"You better!" he demands.

When the jury returns, the prosecutor pauses for a second and asks, "Dr. Warren, when the boathouse was built, did Mr. Evans install a new security system?"

"He did."

"Have you ever operated the camera on the system?"

Alton shakes his head and says, "I don't even know how. I would have to ask my wife."

"One last thing," the prosecutor says, picking up the bag with my bloody clothes. "Can you identify who these clothes belong to?"

He sits there with his head down.

"Dr. Warren?"

"Yes," he says, slowly. "Those are my wife's clothes."

The prosecutor stands up, glances at our table barely able to hide her joy, and says, "Pass the witness."

Hope stands up, and the first question she asks shocks me, the prosecutor, Alton, and everyone else in the courtroom. "Mr. Warren, did you kill Trevor Evans?"

The prosecutor jumps up and practically screams, "Objection, Your Honor! Dr. Warren is a well-respected doctor around the country. He is not the one on trial here."

The judge nods his head and says, "Sustained."

I'm not sure if *sustained* means the judge liked the question or didn't like the questions. The prosecutor's tone sounded bad—like Hope did something wrong, but Hope goes on like it doesn't bother her a bit.

"Mr. Warren," she continues. "You testified yesterday that you were aware that Paige told the detectives that you came back to your house on Friday night around six, correct?"

"I was made aware of that, counselor."

"So you knew it was important that you prove you were in San Antonio Friday night, correct?"

With a nod, he says, "I'd say that's correct. That's why I presented my receipt from the restaurant I ate at."

All his answers are well thought out—like he's afraid of being tricked or tripped up. His tone is measured and he pauses each time to think about the question. Now I'm glad I don't have to testify. I'd probably start out this way and end up a mess. I'd probably blurt out the first thing that pops into my head; sit there with my head down looking guilty; or both.

"Yes, we saw the receipt," Hope acknowledges. "And you do a lot of talking around the state don't you."

"That's right, counselor."

"What's that book you wrote again?"

"I've written seven books, counselor."

"I know, but the big one. The one they teach in colleges."

He looks at the jury with a proud smile and says, "You're talking about *When Therapy Fails.* I have a copy in my car if you'd like me to bring it in."

"I'm sure you do," Hope says with a smile before asking, "You know a lot of the people in your profession, don't you?"

"I'd say that's true, counselor."

"How many people attended that conference in San Antonio?"

"I don't know…maybe two hundred."

I wonder if he's making the number bigger so he sounds more important.

"And how many of those people did you know?"

"I can't give you a number, counselor."

"How about an estimate?"

"Maybe one hundred or so."

"One hundred!" Hope says with wide-eyes like she's impressed. "Out of one hundred people, do you have a single witness who can come in here today and tell this jury that they saw you any time Friday after you spoke?"

"Not really. Like I said, I took a nap and did some work in my room."

"Yeah, but you came down to the reception desk to tell them the time you needed to wake up the next day, right?"

"No, no, counselor. I did that from the phone in my room."

"I'm sure it'd be an honor to have dinner with you. With all those friends and colleagues you know, not one of them joined you for dinner that night?"

He shakes his head and says, "That night I ate alone."

Hope rubs her forehead in a way that I can't tell if she's frustrated or just thinking of her next question. Then she asks, "Did you have an affair during your marriage?"

This comes out of left field and catches him by surprise. Sounding angry and indignant, he says, "I did not, counselor!"

Hope pulls out a photo of that same bleach blonde Traci girl that I saw in his office. I have no idea where she got it. "Can you identify this woman?" she asks.

"That is one of my patients."

"What's her name?"

He looks at the judge and asks, "Do I have to answer that?"

The judge nods his head and says, "Yes, sir."

"Traci Franklin."

"Isn't it true you had an affair with this woman during the marriage?"

The prosecutor jumps up and says, "Objection! This is irrelevant. She's just badgering this witness."

Hope also stands up and says, "Oh, it's very relevant, Your Honor. Just give me a little latitude here, and I'll show the relevance."

"Overruled," the judge says.

So did we win that one or lose?

Again showing his indignance, Alton says, "I know what you're trying to get at, counselor. No, I did *not* have an affair. She was a patient. My wife *accused* me of having an affair with her, but that would be unethical on my part. Our relationship was strictly professional."

Not learning her lesson, Hope presses on. "She accused you, because she came to your office and saw you two together, didn't she?"

"Counselor, it's not like you're saying. Ms. Franklin was coming out of therapy."

"And she smiled at you, didn't she?"

"I don't know, counselor. She may have."

"And you reached out and stroked her arm, didn't you?"

"What?" he answers, quite surprised. "Stroked her arm? I never did that. It's ludicrous."

I know the truth. It takes all the self-control I have left to sit here and listen to this crap. I almost yell out again but look up at the judge and bite my lip.

Hope doesn't let it go. "Whatever happened there, this is the day when Mrs. Warren got concerned about your relationship, right?"

"I think she already said something because this patient was ca…well my wife was already concerned."

"What were you about to say?" Hope asks.

Alton doesn't respond.

"Because this girl was calling and texting you, right?"

"Yes counselor," he says, getting a little more irritated with every question. "She called my cell, but she's not the only patient I've given my cell number to in case of an emergency—both men and women. She was prescribed medication by her primary doctor, and she was having some depression issues. Then later she was…she was actually suicidal. She may have called me a few times."

"A few times," Hope says, standing up with a stack of documents. "Look at these cell phone records. These records show there were over six hundred and fifty calls and texts in the seven months before Trevor Evans was killed."

Shifting in his chair, but not rattled at all, he says, "Yes, there may have been a period that we were in contact quite a bit."

"Purely professional?"

"Purely professional," he answers.

"But then all your calls suddenly end one month before Trevor was killed, correct?"

"That's true. I knew my wife was upset about her calling me. I tried to explain how this patient was having problems with her medications, so I gave her my number to call me if it persisted. No matter how hard I tried to help my wife understand, she was still upset and accusing me of an affair. It was causing problems in our marriage. You know, I loved my wife, so I transferred this patient to another therapist to ease my wife's concerns. That's why our calls stopped."

He has an answer for everything.

"You *loved* your wife?" Hope asks.

"I love her. I meant to say I love her."

"And you've never seen this Traci Franklin again?" Hope continues.

"I have not."

"And your relationship was always professional?"

"Of course, counselor."

"And you haven't seen her since you released her as a patient?"

"No, counselor."

"Mr. Warren, when we watched the video yesterday showing the backyard, it doesn't show who actually carried Trevor's body out to the boat does it?"

"I guess not."

"Or who put Trevor's body into the boat, does it?

"No, it doesn't show that."

"Or who actually drove the boat out on the lake?"

"Well, I have to disagree with you there, counselor. It shows my wife in the boat and then she drives off."

"Actually," Hope says, "it shows her back the boat out of the boathouse. We don't know who was on the boat after that."

Most jurors look at Hope like this is getting ridiculous. One juror rolls her eyes, a couple shake their heads, two others just sit back with their arms crossed.

Alton shakes his head and says, "If you say so, counselor."

"Can you explain to this jury why, three days before Trevor was killed, the camera outside the boathouse was adjusted, so it only shows the back half of the yard?"

"I have no idea," he answers.

"Isn't it true that *you* adjusted the camera so it wouldn't show you carrying the body to the boat?

His eyes open wide again. Shocked she'd suggest such a thing, he says, "First, I didn't carry the body…Mr. Evans…to the boat. But to answer your question, I wouldn't even know how to adjust it."

I'm starting to panic. I'm now wondering if I hired the wrong lawyer. Her dad might be a brilliant trial lawyer, but she seems to crash and burn with every question.

Hope points at me and says, "Are you suggesting that this woman…this tiny woman…was able to pick up Trevor Evans, who was twice her size, and carry him to the boat?"

"I'm not suggesting anything. Like I told the detectives, it's hard for me to believe she did this…that anyone would do something like this."

Then Hope takes out a picture and puts it on the big screen. It's a photo of Alton and Traci. She turns to Alton and says, "Is this you lying on that beach towel?"

He looks closer and says, "It appears so."

"And who is that woman lying beside you?"

Unless she has a twin sister, we all know the answer. "Traci," he mumbles.

"Who?" Hope asks. "I couldn't hear you."

"Traci," he repeats. "Traci Franklin."

"And where are you?"

"I don't know," Alton says with a little smirk. "Why don't you tell me."

"How about Cabo San Lucas. Does that ring a bell?"

Just when I think Hope is getting somewhere, Alton shrugs like it's no big deal and says, "We went to Cabo…so what? This was *after* I was her therapist. It was after I found out my wife was cheating on me and was arrested for murder."

"But you just told this jury you hadn't seen her since—"

"I…I didn't think it was important since it was *after* all this stuff we're talking about."

"So, you lied to this jury."

"I misspoke," he says.

"What else have you lied about?"

"Nothing!" he belts out. Then much calmer, he says, "Nothing."

Hope pulls out another 8X10 photo and says, "Are you aware of the car Ms. Franklin drives?"

Alton thinks about it for a second and says, "I think it's a Ford Probe."

"A green Ford Probe?"

"I think that's true."

The prosecutor jumps up and objects again. "Relevance! We are getting way off track. What in the world does her car have anything to do with the murder of Trevor Evans in the defendant's home?"

Now sounding angry, the judge turns to Hope, and says, "Counselor, we *are* getting way off track here. He said he didn't start seeing her until *after* Mr. Evans was killed. I'm going to stop this—"

"I'm almost finished," Hope says. "Just a few more questions on this."

"Hurry, Counselor," the judge admonishes.

Hope hands Alton a clear photo of Traci about to get into her car and asks, "Is this your patient, Traci Franklin?"

The photo is so clear that her face can't be mistaken. "Uh," he says, "Yes, that's her."

She hands him another photo of the front of her car with her sitting inside and asks, "Driving a green Ford Probe?"

"It looks like it."

"And read to the jury what her license plate number is."

"Her license plate?" He reads the same numbers on her license plate that everyone's staring at on the big screen.

Hope hands him the same records from the parking garage that the prosecutor admitted earlier. She gives him a little nod and says, "Detective Cummings was searching for *your* vehicle on Friday and Saturday." She points to the document on the screen and says, "Look at the lines I've highlighted. These show every time Traci Franklin's vehicle entered and exited the parking garage. It shows your patient, who you never saw until after the marriage was over, enter the garage when?"

The prosecutor jumps up again and says, "Objection…Ms. Franklin's whereabouts are irrelevant to—"

"Overruled!" the judge barks, motioning her back down.

I definitely know we won this one.

He swallows hard, and says, "Uh…Friday morning at 10:33 AM."

And it leaves the garage when?"

Having a hard time answering, he says, "Friday at 6:02 PM."

"That's right. And it shows the car return to the garage when?"

Now talking sheepish, he says, "Friday the twenty-third at 11:40 PM."

The courtroom murmurs and stirs again. The jurors stare at Alton.

"And when does it leave the garage again?"

"Uh….Friday at 3:22 PM."

"And it returns one last time when?"

Alton just sits there.

The judge sits back and says, "Answer the question, Dr. Warren."

"At 1:06 PM."

"Mr. Warren, the whole time the police were searching for *your* car, you were driving Ms. Franklin's car, weren't you? This way you could claim your car never left that hotel."

"No…no, ma'am," Alton says. "I *was* in San Antonio all day. I ate at a restaurant on Friday night. You saw my credit card receipt."

"And you went to a restaurant that you knew wouldn't have cameras, didn't you?"

"That's not true," he scoffs. "I didn't know if they had cameras or not."

"That's really unfortunate for you, isn't it. It sure would prove your testimony if there were cameras there, wouldn't—."

"It absolutely would," he blasts back before she can even finish the question.

Hope hands him a photo of a Mexican food restaurant and asks, "Is this the restaurant you ate at that night?"

Alton sits there without answering.

"Mr. Warren?"

"Yes, I believe that's it."

"You *believe*. You don't sound too sure of yourself."

"Yes," he says. "I'm sure that's it."

Hope smiles and says, "Mr. Warren, this is a picture of a Mexican food restaurant right here in Austin."

The prosecutor gets up and says, "I object! Then this restaurant has no relevance to this case."

As soon as she gets her objection out, the judge says, "Overruled, sit down."

By now, I'm pretty sure overruled means we won.

Hope holds up the photo in one hand, the copy of the receipt in the other, and asks, "You don't know because you've never been to the restaurant that's on your receipt, have you?"

"I'm mistaken," he says. "It's been a while. I'm just mistaken."

"But they look nothing alike."

"I'm mistaken," he repeats.

I sit up in my seat. All jurors, and everyone in the courtroom, are now waiting for the next question.

Hope places a photo of another restaurant right next to his credit card receipt. The receipt has the same name that's written on the sign out front. Hope asks, "This is the same restaurant listed on your receipt, isn't it."

"Yes," he says. "That's the one."

"And look to the right," Hope says. "Is that your vehicle parked in front of the restaurant? The one with the license plate, "DR WARREN?"

The prosecutor jumps up and says, "I object. This video hasn't been authenticated."

Hope stands up and says, "I represent to the court that I have a witness waiting outside to testify as to its authenticity."

The judge nods his head and says, "Based on that representation to this court, and Ms. Brunick has been before this court many times, I'll admit the evidence conditioned on her providing the necessary testimony."

Looking confused, Alton takes a deep breath and asks, "How did you get this photo?"

Ignoring his question, Hope repeats, "Is that your vehicle?"

Alton looks at the prosecutor, back at Hope and says, "Yes, that's…that's my vehicle. Like I told you, I was at the restaurant."

"And you signed your check at exactly 9:45 PM, correct?"

"Correct."

Hope looks right at Alton and with a little smile, says, "Actually, this isn't a photo at all. It's a video from the ATM machine at the bank across the street."

She hits play and the clock on the video shows "Friday, July 23, 09:25 PM." The timer ticks forward. A man and woman walk out of the restaurant at 9:27 PM. Then there's nothing until 9:34 PM, when a woman with bleached blonde hair and the same height and build as Traci walks out of the restaurant, gets in Alton's car, and drives off.

The courtroom rumbles louder and the judge bangs his gavel. Over everyone else, Trevor's sister yells, "Oh my God!"

"Who is that woman getting in your car?" Hope asks.

When Alton doesn't answer, Hope puts another photo up on the screen, and says, "Well, maybe you're having a little trouble. We blew up this part of the video. You know her better than any of us. Tell the jury who just got in your car and drove off?"

The new image clearly shows Traci Franklin's face right as she leaves the restaurant. "Who is getting in your car?" Hope repeats.

The jurors glare at Alton, knowing the answer. Three are leaning forward waiting for him to explain this one. "It looks like Ms. Franklin."

"It sure does, doesn't it?"

The courtroom erupts, and the judge bangs his gavel again and again. I look over at Trish and she gives me a big smile. Dean follows with a quick wink.

The bailiff stands up, and Hope waits for the courtroom to calm down. Now leaning back in her chair, she asks, "Mr. Warren, are you aware that the video surveillance at your house sends all recordings to the cloud for storage?"

Now Alton looks like an entirely different person sitting up there. Long gone are the snarky "counselor" remarks. He's slumped over and hard to hear. He's no longer looking at the jury like he's there to school them. "I didn't know that," he answers.

"Even if you delete the video."

Alton looks around the courtroom, clears his throat, and says, "If you say so."

Hope walks forward with a disc in her hand and says, "I want to show you this video—not from the Friday when Mr. Evans was killed but from three days prior. From the saved tape we are able to find the thirty minutes that's somehow missing from the prosecutor's video."

Hope plays this video that shows Alton walk out of our house and go into the boathouse. Then the camera slowly moves from the back door of our house until it stops in the middle of the yard. Alton then walks out of the boathouse and back inside the house.

There are gasps in the courtroom. The judge bangs and bangs his gavel but everyone continues expressing their disbelief. Several people stand up. The bailiff goes into the gallery and says, "Quiet! Quiet or you'll be removed from the courtroom." The man with the pad and pencils starts frantically sketching Alton's face.

Finally, Hope hands Alton a credit card charge along with a receipt stapled behind it. "I want to show you this receipt for a new Persian rug. Do you recognize it?"

He nods his head.

She hands it to Alton and says, "Tell the jury when it was purchased."

He looks up and down the receipt, goes from the first page to the second a few times, and says, "July twenty-fourth."

"The day *after* Trevor Evans was killed?"

He doesn't respond.

"And whose signature is on the credit card receipt?"

He sits there without answering.

"Answer the question," the judge admonishes him.

Barely louder than a whisper, he says, "Mine."

Again, the courtroom erupts. Not waiting for things to quiet down, Hope stands up and shouts, "The truth is, *you* killed Trevor Evans, didn't you? You gave your little speech in San Antonio and headed back home in your girlfriend's car. She kept your cell phone in San Antonio and drove to that restaurant while you were in Austin. She made that wake-up call. You knew *exactly* where that camera was facing and stayed close to the house. You told Paige to put the tie-downs and cinder block in the boat so she would be seen on the video. You told her to pull the boat around so you wouldn't be seen dragging Mr. Evans across the yard and onto your boat. You loaded Trevor's body into that boat with Paige's cell phone in your pocket, didn't you?"

Shaking and barely able to talk, Alton says, "I have—"

"This was no accident. You planned this whole thing and murdered Trevor Evans."

"I have the right to remain—"

"You planned this, didn't you? You planned this whole thing and framed your wife!"

Alton looks at the judge and says, "Your Honor, I invoke my Fifth Amendment right."

Right then, the prosecutor stands up and says, "Can I have a moment to confer with Ms. Brunick?"

"Fifteen minutes," the judge says.

They both walk through the back door while the whole courtroom sits in silence—stunned and staring at Alton.

"Can I step down?" Alton asks.

The judge shakes his head and says, "No sir, stay right there."

I turn around and look at Trish on the front row. Wiping the tears from her eyes, she gives me a big smile and mouths, "Love you." Dean's teary-eyed too. He gives me a big thumbs-up.

Ten minutes later, Hope and the prosecutor walk back into the courtroom. Hope sits down beside me and whispers into my ear. Everyone, including the judge, is watching. We both nod several times before Hope looks over and nods at the prosecutor.

The prosecutor stands up and says, "In light of the evidence in this case, we're dismissing the murder charges against Mrs. Warren." She has to talk louder to be heard over the murmur in the courtroom. "The charges of disposing of a corpse will be reduced to tampering with evidence…a misdemeanor. She has agreed to plead to deferred adjudication with time served. In three months, all charges will be dismissed."

Trish starts clapping. Then Dean and his wife join in. Next thing, just about everyone in the courtroom is clapping with her. The judge doesn't bang his gavel and the bailiff sits here watching it all happen.

"So, can I leave?" Alton asks.

"You're not going anywhere," the judge says. "I suspect the prosecutor has more to say."

"Yes sir. I've called the Sheriff's Office. They're on their way to take Mr. Warren into custody."

People in the courtroom start cheering and whistling.

I don't want to stay here a second longer. I want out of here before they change their mind. I look up at the judge and ask, "I can go?"

"Yes, Mrs. Warren, you're free to go," the judge says.

I give Hope a big hug and start to cry. "Thank you. Thank you so much. Your dad would be so proud of you."

Her eyes well up with tears and she nods her head.

I turn around and Dean has his arms open wide and tears in his eyes. I throw my arms around his neck and he squeezes me so tight you'd think I might suffocate. I pull back, look at him about to cry, and say, "Thank you for being here to support me. You've always been my hero. You're the only father I've ever known."

Tears fall down his cheek. It's the second time I've seen him cry. The first was when the police took me away from him. He wipes his cheek and says, "You'll always be my girl."

I walk out of the courtroom hand-in-hand with the only other person who's been here for me. My mom couldn't make it, of course. We ignore the frenzy of reporters right outside the courtroom doors who want to know what just happened in there. With a big smile, I push through and say, "Talk to my lawyer."

It's a spring day and there's a cool breeze blowing in my face. As soon as we walk out the courthouse door, Trish hugs me and shouts, "You did it!"

I hug her with tears falling down my cheeks. "We did it. I love you."

She starts crying too and says, "I love you!"

I've been locked up for five months. I walk down the sidewalk and past a woman pushing a stroller. I give her a smile. A man and woman are eating at a sidewalk café. I stop and say, "Hello, have a wonderful day." I look up and scream, "WHAT A BEAUTIFUL DAY!"

Before getting in her car, I look across at Trish and say, "Thank you for sticking by me."

"Hell, yeah!" she says. "I knew you wouldn't lose." Then she gives a mischievous smile and asks, "Can I tell you something?"

The way she asked, I'm not sure I want to know what she has to say, but I give her a nod.

"Remember that day when you came back from camping with Trevor and you were talking about leaving Alton…and maybe losing your kids?"

I give her another curious nod.

"Those kids belong with you. I would never let that happen."

Her words puzzle me. I look across the car with a little scowl and ask, "What are you talking about?"

"Let's just say he got the justice he deserves."

This floors me and I think from the look on my face she knows it floors me. A little stunned, I look into her eyes and ask, "Did you do something?"

She looks down like she isn't going to answer. Then she looks up, gives me a little smile and says, "Of course not."

I stare right at her hoping she'll say more, but she doesn't. Then I get in the car and say, "Let's pick up my kids."

She drives me straight to each school where I check my kids out of class. I get stares from everyone at the school who are sure I'm guilty. I'm the parent who cheated on my husband and killed my lover. Soon they'll learn the news that I had nothing to do with Trevor's death.

I haven't seen my kids in almost five months. The second Jacob sees me, he runs forward and crashes into me, almost knocking me over. He wraps his arms around my neck, and starts kissing me. When I pick up Beth, she comes up, wipes a tear from her eyes, and says, "I'm really sorry, mom."

I kiss her face, and say, "It's okay, sweetie. You told the truth. Everything's okay."

Bekah walks up holding her bookbag and asks, "So, are you coming home?"

I give her a big smile and say, "Yeah, I'm coming home."

We go to Zilker park, sit by the water, and eat fried chicken, mashed potatoes, corn on the cob, and biscuits. And it damn sure ain't six-thirty. I will never eat dinner at six-thirty again.

– CHAPTER 42 –

Alton was arrested right there in the courtroom for first degree murder and disposing of a corpse. An arrest warrant was issued for Traci Franklin for first-degree murder. Two days later, she was picked up in Duval County on her way to Mexico, and now sits in the same jail I was just released from.

That evening, I turn on the television, and this is the big breaking news. Hope is standing in front of the cameras with her husband, Blake, at her side. He's showing a full-teeth smile, staring at her prouder than a mother hen. She can't answer the questions fast enough. She explains how her client was innocent and the evidence proved it. Her face is all over the country. I can't help but think she's about to be famous.

I turn the channel and watch the same news channels that were once ruthlessly declaring me guilty and questioning why I wasn't subject to the death penalty, now picking the prosecutor apart.

"How could they bring this case in front of a jury in the first place? Did they do a thorough investigation?"

Nancy Grace points her finger at the camera and practically yells, "This man…this man has no heart. The fact that he would murder someone and try to frame his poor wife and mother of his children is truly despicable. I have never seen anything like this in all my years covering trials. I'll tell you this…a lot of people owe this poor woman an apology."

– CHAPTER 43 –

Four days after he was taken into custody, Alton made his bed so there wasn't so much as a wrinkle. All his papers were in six stacks, looking like a new ream of paper that was just removed from the wrapper. Each stack was perfectly aligned with the other stacks in three rows. One might have thought he was an architect laying papers on a drafting board. All his clothes were folded neatly on his bed like they were ready for a military inspection.

Then, the great psychologist who wrote *When Therapy Fails* and spoke all over the country, wrapped his bed sheet around his neck and hung himself. Maybe, his way of life would never work in prison. You wear standard, unpressed, prison clothes; you have no control over the thermostat; there's no squeegee to clean the germs from the showers; and you eat dinner when they tell you to eat dinner. Perhaps, he was afraid of meeting some of those folks he's testified against throughout the years. Whatever the reason, I hope Trevor Evans was the last thing that went through his mind as he swung back and forth.

He left a note on his bed apologizing to Trevor's family for taking their son and brother and for all the pain he had caused them. At the bottom of the note was the GPS coordinates to the location of Trevor's body. He tossed Trevor's body off the boat tied to that cinderblock and continued for another thirty minutes across the lake to throw the police off.

Three days later, the news broke nationwide that divers just pulled Trevor's body, still wrapped in Alton's office rug, out of the lake. It brought me right back to that horrible night that's now my horrible nightmare.

After six months, the Evans' family is finally able to have an incredible memorial service, before giving Trevor a proper burial. The church is absolutely packed. Family, friends going all the way back to high school, colleagues, strangers who took an interest in the case, and reporters pour into the giant church. There are so many flowers that they fill the church and overflow along the sidewalk outside. I had no idea he was so loved.

Trish and I walk into the church and stop in front of a large portrait of Trevor with a big smile on his face. There are three smaller pictures of him—one when he was a baby; one as a teenager; and one of him in his twenties. I stand in front of the large portrait and can feel him smiling directly at me. Trish gives me a hug as tears stream down my face.

Not sure how I'll be received, we take a seat in the very back row near the end so I can leave if my presence causes a disturbance. I try to stay inconspicuous, but I can hear the whispers as people glance over at me as they pass by.

I have my head down and I'm dabbing the tears from my eyes, when Trevor's sister walks down the center aisle and stops in front of me. I look up and for a second I'm not sure if she wants me to leave. Then she reaches out for my hand, and says, "Trevor would want you to sit in the front row with us."

"Go," Trish says, waiving me forward. "Go up there where you belong."

Tears pour down my face and I can barely talk. I stand up and throw my arms around Trevor's sister's neck and cry on her shoulder while everyone watches. Finally, I pull back, look into her teary eyes, and say, "I…I loved…I loved him so much."

His sister nods her head, and with a tearful smile, says. "I know. He told me all about it. He loved you so much, too. He wanted to marry you."

I lay my head back on her shoulder and continue crying.

As people make their way up to the casket, I really don't think I have the strength to go forward. But I have to. I have to see him one last time to tell him goodbye.

I walk up slowly, until I catch the first glimpse of his face. To my surprise, they were able to make him look pretty normal. He's looking straight up at the ceiling like he's in a deep sleep. Crying, I collapse against the casket and fall to the floor. His sister leans over and rubs my back until I'm able to stand again.

I pick myself back up and look at the most beautiful man I've ever known. I see the face that melted my heart and the adventurous spirit that set me free. But, I can tell it's not him lying there. No, he's fishing by a crystal lake somewhere sipping his beer and tapping his cowboy boots to a good Willie Nelson song. He's eating hot dogs with a big smile on his face.

I unhook the clasp from the charm bracelet he bought me in Miami. There's a small gold heart hanging on it with a picture inside of Trevor and me sitting by the campfire in Huntsville. I lay the bracelet on his chest and whisper, "Good-bye, baby. I will love you forever. I'll be with you until we're together again."

I kiss my fingers and press them against the chain on his chest.

– CHAPTER 44 –

Alton and I never actually divorced, so after he died I got everything. Hope's investigator did a lot of digging because everything was well hidden. We had eleven million dollars in cash, stocks, bonds, and other various investments. He had one overseas account, an account in his father's name, and another account in his mother's name. I'll get all the revenues from that stupid book for the rest of my life. I direct that all proceeds be paid to a charity to help people struggling with depression. Alton had a life insurance policy that paid five million dollars. I put it into three separate accounts for each of our children.

I bought a cute house in San Marcos that sits right on the river so the kids can swim. Inside the garage is a kayak and tubes for floating down the river. The kids love it. There are four fishing poles leaning against the house and a volleyball net hanging in the backyard. Beth's really good. She just made the junior high volleyball team. The kids eventually adjust to the new temperature on the thermostat, eating dinner whenever we feel like it, and a house that looks lived in where people feel comfortable stopping in unannounced.

I also bought the lot to the left of our house and planted the bluebonnets all over the yard that Trevor and I love so much. I planted a beautiful redbud tree in the middle of the lot. Trevor once said he wanted to plant one in his own front yard. Leaning against the side of the tree is a surfboard where I painted, "In My Heart You Will Live Forever." During the spring, we tell people they've reached our house when they see the neon blue yard.

I know I still have a life to live, but what could have been always prevents me from living it. Finding love, or even dating again, will never happen. It feels like I'm alive, but my life has been suspended until I get over Trevor, which will take forever. My heart is still in the coffin there with him, and I don't think it will ever come back to me.

People tell me things will get better with time, but time stood still the night Trevor died in my arms. I read a couple of books about recovering after a loved one dies, but they didn't help. I also tried drinking enough tequila to drown away the hurt, but that didn't work either. So, I got into therapy with a woman who I love and trust. I see her twice a week. It's been a long road, and she says that we've only scratched the surface.

As she suggested, I'm trying to find as many things to do as possible so I don't sit around thinking about Trevor all the time. It helps a little. I'm not sure if I'm getting better or I've lived with this pain for so long that I've just gotten used to it. I hate the fact that as time passes by it gets harder and harder to remember the little things about Trevor like the way he talked and laughed, his facial expressions, and how he looked in his blue jeans and cowboy boots when we danced.

I once said I'd teach kindergarten even if I won the lottery. Well, I'm now at a new elementary school in San Marcos, doing my best to make a difference in the world. Shelly, a little girl in my class, came up to me this morning to show me her ears that got pierced yesterday. Pam got a new kitten they named Fluffy. Tearing up, Robbie told me that he couldn't sleep last night because his parents were arguing all night long. I held him close and told him he'll be okay.

Two months after I move into my new house, I throw a big party. The whole neighborhood and all our friends are here. Hope comes by with her husband, Blake, and their four year old little girl named Faith after her grandma. Blake seems like a really great guy. Hope brought along her sister, Grace, who brought her son, Wesley, her oldest daughter, Bonnie, and Bonnie's boyfriend of two years. Bonnie's about to start college and wants to be a lawyer and join the Brunick & Brunick law firm.

"Oh, Lord," I laugh. "I don't know if the world can handle another Brunick lawyer."

"Just always remember what grandpa taught us," Hope says.

"I know…I know," Bonnie laughs. "Keep it simple so a child can understand."

"Come around back," I say. "We're about to play volleyball." I turn to Bonnie and her boyfriend and say, "A group of kids are about to float down the river. Why don't you join them?"

The kids don't mind country music as much as they once did. We walk around back, and I put on some George Strait music. He's from San Marcos and got his start just down the road at an old dance hall called Gruene Hall.

I hand Grace a beer and say, "Nice to finally meet you. Your sister told me all about you. She's an incredible lawyer."

"I know she is," she agrees. "She learned from the best."

"Your husband couldn't come?" I ask.

She shakes her head and says, "My husband passed away. I don't think I'm real good at relationships."

I nod my head and say, "I know what you mean."

I walk them over to Dean who's sitting in a lawn chair beside his wife. As soon as he sees Hope, he stands up, shakes her hand, and says, "I don't know a lot about trials, but that was incredible. It sure looked hopeless. I thought my girl didn't stand a chance. Thank you for taking care of her."

Hope looks at me with a smile and says, "We just had to look under every stone."

Three months after the funeral, Detective Cummings calls me, but I don't answer the phone. He leaves a message wanting to talk again, but I ignore it. He calls two more times, but I don't answer those calls either.

Two weeks later, he pulls his car into the driveway, walks up to the front door, and rings the doorbell. All the kids run up and say, "Mom, that police officer is outside!"

I answer the door and ask, "May I help you, detective?"

"Well, Mrs. Warren, I first want to apologize to you. I think you deserve that."

I look at him and say, "You know, you were just doing your job. I don't hold anything against you. Would you like some coffee or anything?"

"A cup of coffee would be nice," he says.

We sit at the kitchen table drinking coffee and eating blueberry muffins when he says, "Nice place you got here."

"It's home," I say. "It's the kind of place I always wanted."

"Just one thing," he continues. "When Trevor Evans' body was pulled from the lake, there was a gun wrapped in the rug with him. We've tried to figure out why."

"It's like I told you. Alton had to get rid of his gun."

Cummings shakes his head and says, "No….it's not the gun he was shot with."

"Another gun?" I ask. "Yeah, he carried that gun for protection."

"Hmm?" he says. "His mother, father, and sister all said he had a shotgun for hunting but they never saw him carry a pistol before."

I shake my head and say, "I'm not sure what to tell you."

"There's just one more thing," he continues. "The gun wasn't loaded."

Making sure I heard him right, I ask, "Wasn't loaded?"

"Nope. There were no bullets in it. It was empty."

I look down at my coffee cup and try to understand what he just told me. He lowers his eyebrows and asks, "Is everything okay?"

"Okay," I mumble, still staring down. Then I look up and say, "Yeah, everything's okay." I walk him to the door and say, "I'm sorry I couldn't be more help."

After he leaves, I drive to the cemetery as I've done every day for the past seven months. This time Trish comes with me. She and Cliff sold their house in our old neighborhood and bought the house down the street from me. She fits in just fine.

I put fresh flowers in front of Trevor's headstone. Trish helps me rake up and bag the leaves. I clean the headstone with soap and water until it shines. We sit down cross-legged in the beautiful evening sun. A squirrel runs across the grass and shimmies halfway up a tree before stopping and looking over at us.

Looking at the headstone, Trish takes a deep breath, and says, "It's so peaceful here."

I give her a smile, close my eyes, and nod my head.

I usually spend this time talking to Trevor, but today I can't get Detective Cummings words out of my mind. *There's just one more thing. The gun he had wasn't loaded. It had no bullets.* It makes no sense. I don't even realize the scowl on my face until Trish looks over and asks, "You okay?"

I slowly nod a couple of times and return to my thoughts. Nothing more is said for five or ten minutes until, looking forward, I ask, "Do you really believe in all that hoodoo stuff?"

With this puzzled look, she says, "I don't know. My mom sure believes in it. It doesn't really work if you don't believe. Why do you ask?"

I pick a couple blades of grass out of the ground and say, "I don't know. I'm just curious. What is it? Have you ever seen your mom do it?"

"I saw it a couple times when I was growing up."

"How does it work?"

Shaking her head, she says, "You don't want to know."

I reach out, put my hand on her knee, and repeat, "Tell me…tell me how it works."

It looks like she's contemplating whether to tell me or not. Then she says, "A lot of people claim to be psychics or fortune tellers, but my mom is the real deal. She's a Roma. My whole family are Romanies."

"Roma?" I ask.

"That's our proper name. In America, and most of the world, we're called gypsies. We usually call ourselves gypsies now."

This is a little surprising. "You're a gypsy?" I ask.

With a nod, she says, "I don't go around telling everyone. My mom had these powers. She learned it all from my grandma."

When she stops for a moment, I ask, "What kind of powers?"

Slowly shaking her head, she says, "I don't like to talk about it. It's powerful. I saw things…things you wouldn't believe if I told you. She would meditate, but it was more than just mediating. She would conjure up these spirits and make potions that would bring blessings and curses."

I wait for more, but she leaves it at that. Then I ask, "What about this hoodoo?"

After a moment, she says, "You're the only person I've ever talked to about this. My mom told me this story so many times so I'd never forget it. My family come from Romania. They traveled to Russia and worked in the theater or something. One day, the Russian government came for them so my grandpa, my grandma, and my mom fled to Paris with the other gypsies. This was right before Hitler invaded France. To Hitler, the gypsies were no better than the Jews. My mom, my grandma, and my grandpa were rounded up one morning and sent to some giant arena in the middle of the city. She was a little girl at the time. Most people thought they were being sent there to register with the city and they'd be returning home, but they were held there for four days with no food, no water, and no toilets. When the doors opened, the French police officers marched them to a train station where a train was waiting to take them to Auschwitz. My grandfather had connections. He knew some guy who was smuggling Jews out of France. Somehow, my family managed to escape."

I listen in amazement.

"They traveled by foot across France and into Spain where they got on a boat headed for New York. But gypsies were wanted in New York about as much as they were wanted in Europe. My grandpa was killed during a robbery. After he died, my grandma couldn't find work. She heard about this place called Nawlins, where gypsies were welcomed. So, they moved there and my grandma opened a place one block off of Bourbon Street where she read palms and told fortunes. My grandma taught it all to my mom, and my mom took over after she died. They call my mom the queen of Nawlins. She's good. She doesn't have to steal people's money—she's made a fortune by telling the truth…even if you don't want to hear it. She has an herb, or a root, or a potion, for every illness. I saw people come to her for cancer. After a while, people came from all over because they were sick, or wanted to hear their fortunes, or wanted a blessing."

"Her place in Nawlins is kinda spooky, with lots of candles, this crystal ball on the table, and a black cat sleeping in the corner. I'd never go in there at night. But it was mostly for show. She didn't need any of that stuff. She learned about hoodoo from this old black woman who was blind. It was passed down to her from her mom who was an African slave."

As I hang on every word, Trish talks slow and easy as she tells me more about this hoodoo stuff. I see a side of her I've never seen before. The deeper she goes, the more her Louisiana accent comes out mixed with some kind of African slang.

"My momma tried to teach me hoodoo a couple times when I was just a girl. The first time, when there wasn't a soul around but me and her. There was this big ole' black cauldron with a fire burning bright under it. She throwed all kinds of stuff inside. You know…animal parts…like frogs, lizards, snakes, livers and hearts. She tored off some roots and throwed dem' on in there. When the pot was good and boilin,' she danced round and round in a circle repeating these strange words again and again. She had blood on her face and dead snakes hanging from her neck. The dance became frantic like she'd done lost her mind. It freak me out. I swear to God, she was possessed by some kind of African spirits."

The way she's talking starts to spook me. As the sun starts to set a cold breeze blows over us. I rub my arms to stay warm.

"Girl, dis here went on and on all tru da night until the words stuck deep in my head. I heard these sounds…sounds that scared me. Eventually, I fell sound asleep. When I woked up the next monin' the cauldron was gone and everyting had done been put away. My mamma was dead asleep and slept most da' next day."

I feel like I've gone to a place where I don't belong. I'm actually afraid to pry further, but I have to ask. "Did it work?"

"Bout a week later, some man in a fancy car come to our house bangin' on da' door like he done lost his mind. He was crying and begging my mamma to take off da' spell. His son come down sicker dan a dog and was about to drop dead. My mamma said she warned him—she warned him tree times—and now it was too late. What's done is done. He threatened to kill my mamma, but she told him to get out and if he laid a finger on her his whole family would be next. When he left our house, my mama sat me down and told me how he was evil and got the justice he deserved."

"Holy shit!" I whisper.

"Then my mamma warned me. She said you gotta' search your soul and make sure you're clean before you do this stuff. 'Don't pluck no splinter out of someone else's eye when your own eyes are full of wood.'"

For the first time, I realize Trish was right. I wish I'd never heard about this stuff. I look out in the distance thinking about my own soul. Then I turn back and ask, "Why haven't I ever heard of this hoodoo stuff before you?"

"It's powerful black magic," she says. "My mamma may be the last person who can do it."

Although she may have already answered my question, I give her an uncomfortable stare and ask, "Can *you* do it? Can you do hoodoo?"

She looks at me like I'm half-crazy. Then she looks down as if the question might just go away if she ignores it. After a little time passes, she says, "My mamma wanted me to take over her place one day. On my thirteenth birthday, she performed this ritual over me. She said my grandma speaks to her from the other side and one day she'll speak to me." Then Trish, looking down, asks, "Remember what I told you about my boyfriend?"

I give her a nod.

"Well, it wasn't my mom who done it."

"What?" I ask with wide eyes.

She takes a deep breath and shakes her head with this sad look as she continues. "You know that man I told you I was seeing? Lord how I loved him. I wanted to spend the rest of my life with him. Two weeks later, he was killed in a car accident."

I put my hand on her knee and ask, "You don't think?"

Looking out in the distance, she says, "Like I told you, it's black magic. That stuff scares me. It's about justice…you know, right and wrong.."

"Does Cliff know?" I ask.

She shakes her head and says, "I've never told a soul what I did…not even my mamma. As time went by, I convinced myself it wasn't me. That fan just fell…plain and simple. People die in car wrecks all the time. But it scared me so bad. I met Cliff and got the hell out of Nawlins. It broke my mamma's heart. We talk every now and then and sometimes, when I'm all alone, I feel her presence all around me and hear her voice. I've never dabbled in that stuff again. I want no part of it."

Then we sit here in silence until I squint my eyes and ask, "You never dabbled in it again until now?"

She looks right at me with this stare that gives me a chill. I look down and see goosebumps on my arms and legs. She never actually answers my question yes or no.

I look into her eyes and whisper, "So, it's all about justice, huh?"

"Yeah," she says with a nod, "rights and wrongs."

As I pull out one blade of grass after another, my mind goes back to that terrible night. She gently puts her hand on my leg, and it makes me jump. Then she asks, "Why you askin' these things?"

Without looking up, I ask, "You're my best friend, right?"

"Of course."

"I can tell you anything, right?"

Sounding concerned, she says, "Right."

"You can't tell a soul what I'm about to tell you. I didn't even tell my lawyer. I was too afraid what might happen to me if I did."

She stares at me with her mouth half open and asks, "What the hell happened?"

I tell her the story that no one else alive knows. I start at the beginning:

Sitting in Alton's waiting room, I watched as this beautiful, young woman smiled at my husband and said, "Thank you for squeezing me in."

I hear Alton's voice. "Don't forget the things we talked about."

She reached out and offered her hand to him. "You're incredible," she said, taking his hand in hers.

Alton reached out and caressed the side of her arm the same way he caressed my arm on our first date. "See you next week?" he asked.

"Of course," she answered gazing into his eyes.

When she turned to leave, we made eye contact for only a second. I smiled her way, but she quickly looked down as all expression left her face. I watched as she walked out the door.

I went inside his office and humiliated myself for the last time.

Over the next few weeks, she called and texted his phone several times. I didn't say a word at first and just tried to ignore it, but I finally confronted him and demanded he stop seeing her. When he refused, I searched through his phone records and found out he'd been talking to this woman regularly for hours and hours over the last six months.

I wanted to know what's going on. I wanted the truth. So, I opened my computer and googled, "Austin investigation equipment." The first page that popped up was "The Spy Shop." I drove straight there, walked in, and asked, "Do you have a device to record phone calls made at my home?"

I purchased the most expensive telephone recording device he sold. Back at my home, I connected it to my bedroom phone and hid the recorder behind my nightstand. It started recording any time someone in our home made or received a call—including the phone in his office.

For weeks, I listened as my husband and his girlfriend professed their undying love for one another. Yes, this same girl who he swore was only his patient—and nothing more. Honestly, I didn't know Alton had it in him. I guess there's a lid for every pot.

These calls were in my head that day over a year ago when Trevor and I drank a beer in my backyard, The Zach Brown Band was playing in the background, and I looked into Trevor's eyes and asked, "Will you please take me dancing?"

Time and time again, Alton would go into his office and they would discuss how much they wanted to be together, but Alton was afraid of losing his reputation and all his money in a divorce. The more they talked, the more I turned to Trevor. Somewhere along the way, I fell in love with him like I've never loved anyone.

Then, that day came when Trevor said, "I was thinking Miami—hang out on the beach and do a little surfing?" That was the weekend he taught me to surf, saved my life, and won my heart. I knew then I would marry him one day.

Exhausted after my weekend in paradise, I went up to my bedroom, sat on my bed, and pushed play on the recorder. It was more of the same stuff heard before until late Saturday night. Alton knew I was seeing Trevor. Then this woman asked Alton the same question I heard her ask before, "When are you filing for divorce?"

I sat there in shock when I heard his answer.

"I won't need a divorce. I'll wait until my next conference in San Antonio. I'll tell her I'm going to the conference to speak. It will be weeks since she's seen him, so she'll surely invite him to our house for the night. When he comes to the back door, I'll shoot him. We'll take the body out on the boat and dump him in the lake. By the time we're through, everyone will believe I was in San Antonio at the time, and she was the one on the boat. It's foolproof."

I played it again and again and listened as they discussed their devilish plan to kill the only man I've really loved and frame me for his murder. Then I sat there stunned in disbelief. Not knowing what to do, I drove to Trevor's house and explained the whole thing.

After I stopped the recording, he looked at me with wide eyes. Then he shook his head and says, "Take the recording...bring it to the police."

"I can't," I explained. "The guy at the pawn shop said it's illegal in Texas to record someone else's phone calls. The police can't use it, and I'll be the one charged with a crime."

Trevor looked down, rubbed his forehead, and asked, "Then what are we supposed to do?"

I handed him the tapes and said, "Keep these here with you. Hide them where no one will ever find them."

Staring into his eyes, all the anger inside me boiled over. The thought of it all infuriated me. "I can't believe he'd do this. He'd kill you over money? A divorce isn't enough for him? He wants to send me away so my kids grow up without their mother?"

I start to say more but stop. Seeing the look on my face, Trevor asked, "Paige...what are you thinking?"

I closed my eyes, shook my head, and said, "There's only one thing we can do."

With a look of confusion, he asked, "And what's that?"

That's when we devised our own plan. Alton deserved it. Trevor and I went to a pawn shop and bought a gun. When Alton comes at him with his gun, Trevor would kill him with the gun tucked behind his back. We could get any jury to believe it was justifiable self-defense.

We knew the day was coming, but didn't know when. I never thought it would be that weekend because Alton told me he was leaving for Phoenix. I guess he lied so I would believe he was far away and feel safe enough to invite Trevor over.

But Alton never went to Phoenix that day.

When I'm finished telling the story, I look over at Trish with my eyes full of tears and a heavy heart. I shake my head and say, "I told Alton to call the police. Then, when he started saying we'd both be arrested, I freaked out. What if they found out the whole story? I was scared and not thinking straight, and he already had Trevor wrapped in the rug. I didn't know what else to do."

When I'm finished telling the story, I look over at Trish with my eyes full of tears and a heavy heart. I shake my head and say, "I told Alton to call the police. Then, when he started saying we'd both be arrested, I freaked out. What if they found out the whole story? I was scared and not thinking straight, and he already had Trevor wrapped in the rug. I didn't know what else to do."

Trish slowly shakes her head. Then she looks up and asks, "What about his gun?"

I look down, cover my face with my hands for a second, slowly look up, and say, "That detective…Cummings…he came over today. He said they found his gun wrapped in the rug when they pulled Trevor out of the lake."

Trish gives me a sideways look.

"The thing is, he said the gun wasn't loaded. It had no bullets. But I'm sure. . .I'm absolutely sure there were bullets in that gun. The man at the pawn shop loaded it for us."

Trish is staring at me with wide eyes. Then she closes her eyes and says, "Oh my God….no!"

"That's why….that's why I asked about the hoodoo thing."

Trish doesn't respond.

We sit here staring at Trevor's headstone without saying anything more. As the sun disappears in the horizon, I look up and see a full moon in the distance. The sky turns dark, the wind picks up that gives me a chill. Then we get up, pick up the trash and the rake, and get back in my car.

We drive home without saying a word. I look over at Trish and she's staring out the window with this blank face.

I put my hand on her shoulder that causes her to jump a little. "What is it?" I ask.

With the same blank stare, she never answers me.

I simply let it go.

– EPILOGUE –

Trish and I never talked about this hoodoo stuff again. I've never heard anyone talk about hoodoo again. I never believed in all this witchcraft stuff before, but as soon as I got home, I went into Beth's room, found her Ouija board, and threw it in the garbage. Like Trish, I want no part of it.

What about Trevor? I have no doubt what Trish believes, but I don't know what to think. As time went by, I thought there must be a logical explanation. Maybe, I remember it wrong and that man never actually loaded the gun. Maybe Trevor took the bullets out and forgot to put them back in. Maybe he knew he couldn't live with himself if he actually killed Alton and arrived at the door knowing the gun wasn't loaded.

We had this foolproof plan…if there is such a thing. But Hope was right, there's no such thing as a foolproof plan. You can never think of everything. Something will always trip you up.

Now Alton is dead, Trevor is dead, and I lost the only person I ever loved. The truth is, we didn't really think this whole thing through. Now I realize, maybe there was more than one wrong that happened that day that had to be made right. Sometimes, justice is a two-way street. People always cry out for justice—but only when it comes to someone else. As for me, I choose mercy and forgiveness. I want no part of justice. Justice scares me.

SIGN UP FOR MY READER GROUP

Thanks for reading *The Intruder You Know – book one in my Hoodoo series*. I hope you enjoyed it. If so, please add your support by leaving a review on Amazon and by telling your friends and family.

Want more? Click the link below and join my reader group. You'll be notified when my next book is released. You'll get updates on the series, and I'll send you giveaways like free books from other authors!

https://readergroup.williamholms.com/

Notice any errors in the book? Email me and I'll email you the next book for free! You can also buy my books directly from my store for much less than the retail price and I'll send you a signed copy. Want me to speak at your event or book club, or just want to talk? Email me:

Email: author@williamholms.com

–ACKNOWLEDGEMENT –

I want to give my sincere thanks to all the readers who made *The Killing of Faith* series such a big success. I'm floored by all the emails I receive from my fans. Your encouragement keeps me writing. Thanks for continuing with *The Intruder You Know*.

Thanks to my incredible daughter, Kiersten Holms, for her help on my novel.

I have to give a big shout-out to my incredible Advance Reader Team who took the time to read this book, catch errors, and give some great suggestions. You get better and better with each book.

Thank you, Deborah Jesensek, Dee Wilson, Karen Silver, Ellen Aish, Susan Bartlay, Nora Wilkes, Ann Elliott, Jan Millen, Caroline Moreland, Theresa Collins, Diane Russo, Audrey Mayrent, Nancy Moser, and Elsie Hassell. My book is better because of you.